Wildewood *Revenge*

Part 1 of 'The Wildewood Chronicles'

by

B.A. Morton

ISBN   1480039217

EAN   978-1480039216

'Wildwood *Revenge*' is published by Taylor Street Publishing LLC, who can be contacted at:

http://www.taylorstreetbooks.com

http://ninwriters.ning.com

For

Holly Arden

'The Jewel of Ahlborett'

Acknowledgements

Many thanks to:

Jacoba Dorothy, Karen Charlton and Kristin Gleeson

Three accomplished writers and good friends, whose advice and generosity have helped make Wildewood shine.

The People of Upper Coquetdale

Who maintain the land and traditions and keep the rich history of this wonderful part of Northumberland alive.

Northumberland National Park Historic Village Atlas

A wealth of fabulous research.

Chapter One

Freezing fog enveloped the winter trees, while underfoot the forest floor was waterlogged after a winter of heavy snow had finally begun to melt. The trees shed their blanket of snow slowly, in steady drips and unsteady falls, shaking the canopy to reveal fresh green needles on evergreen giants and silvering bare branches on the deciduous ancient woodland. It was another world. A world far preferable to the one Grace had left behind in London.

The young woman exhaled, her breath misting in the chill air as she walked. Pulling her shabby sweater more closely around her slender frame, she ducked her head and continued. Far in the distance, beyond the forest boundary, the noise of artillery fire could be heard as the army bombarded their targets on the adjoining military range. The red warning flags were flying as she entered the forest, but Grace knew she was safe as long as she kept to the logging road. Red flags were red rags to the girl who thought risky was another word for dare.

She came here often, drawn to the stark beauty of the woods and surrounding crags. The woods were ancient and full of mystery. Sensible folk said she shouldn't walk alone, that strange things happened in the heart of the woods. But Grace, a girl who could never be described as sensible, merely smiled.

"Devoid of sound judgement and self-discipline," were the words used by the distinguished old gentleman in the wig less than a month before, and she had to admit on that particular occasion he'd been correct. She'd made one error, and her life and career were now in tatters. Now, she preferred the solitude where she could forget the past, ignore the present and invent a new life, although she wasn't quite alone; her dog trotted a little way ahead, nose to the ground, tail in the air. Little more than a pup, animated, energetic and lacking in discipline, rather like herself or so she'd been told.

On reaching the older part of the forest, Grace, who liked to think she was fearless, quickened her step. There was an eeriness here which did not marry well with an over-active imagination. Plantation trees gave way to ancient woodland. Gnarled trees clothed in lichen, and isolated stagnant pools reflecting images of winter's skeletal canopy. The many flooded gurgling culverts gave this area a sound and life of its own. The forest made its own music. In summer when the water flowed more gently it held a melancholy air, heavy and humid. Today there was mischief in the rushing brooks and Grace stopped, despite herself, to listen and take in the wonder of it.

She found her gaze drawn past the trees at the edge of the rough road and through into the gloom beyond. Weak sunlight fractured through to the forest floor casting uneven shadows, punctuating the deep darkness with unnatural light made otherworldly by the dancing fog. The dog, too, was distracted as he stood poised, wet nose tasting a myriad of scents from the damp air which swirled evermore thickly toward them. Slowly Grace turned to look over her shoulder but the way back lay shrouded in mist.

The dog growled once, a low uncertain rumble and the rough hair on the back of his neck bristled. With typical terrier curiosity and sheer bloody mindedness, he ignored his own sense of caution and with a bark of bravado he leapt the flooded ditch at the side of the road and disappeared into the gloom.

Grace yelled after him, her voice echoing in the stillness as it bounced from tree to tree, causing her to shudder at the strange acoustics. Damn the dog. She called again but with no real belief in his compliance, and this time her usually strong voice came out as little more than a whisper consumed by the thickness of the air. She hesitated, scuffing at the gravel with the toe of her boot. She would go after him, she knew that. She also knew despite her own bravado, there was an element of risk in the woods, not from mythical creatures, but from the very real threat of military manoeuvres.

As the troops weren't allowed to cross the forest boundary, she wasn't concerned she'd be flattened by a tank, blown up by a mine, or even spread-eagled by a strapping squaddie. In fact, she pondered slyly, a strapping squaddie might actually prove a much needed distraction. It had been some time since she'd been spread-eagled by anyone, but who knew about stray rounds from the ranges? Although Grace was game for most things, playing chicken with a bullet wasn't one of them.

She called the dog again, trying to inject an authoritative tone, and was rewarded by excited yapping some way off. She cursed again softly under her breath. The wood was awash with snow melt. If she went after him she would soon be up to her knees. There was no knowing the depth of the flooded culverts and they were icy cold. It wasn't a good idea to follow the dog. It wasn't a good idea at all. What was it the magistrate had said about poor judgement? She gave an involuntary shiver and pulled the cuffs of her sweater down over cold hands and the fleecy flaps of her hat over her ears. She shot a last glance back down the road then jumped the ditch and entered the wood.

The still, damp air clung to her clothes and beaded on the fibres of her sweater as she made her way carefully across the uneven and waterlogged ground. Her boots were quickly sodden and her wet combat trousers clung to her rapidly chilling legs. Why did a simple walk in the woods have to become so complicated? The story of her life, really. She didn't set out with the intention of creating difficulties, but she did seem to end up with more than her fair share.

How else could a simple favour for a friend result in the label 'forger' being attached to her name? Not discreetly either, but in big, glaring, angry font that shouted her shame to all who subscribed to the tabloid frenzy. It had been big news until something bigger came along and Grace was relieved she'd been side-lined by another more newsworthy crime.

There were probably many labels, other than forger which could have been more appropriately attributed, and more readily accepted by Grace: 'naive fool' perhaps or maybe 'reckless'. 'Forger', however, implied a degree of dishonesty and to her credit Grace was not dishonest, merely young and not fully attuned to the dishonesty of others. She was learning however, and the experience had left her with an overwhelming distrust of her fellow man.

Her progress through the winter forest, as she pondered on her ill luck, was laboured. Every step, involved a mammoth effort, to avoid slipping into deeper water. With each of those steps she imagined just what she'd do to the dog when she eventually caught up with him. His place in her heart was getting smaller by the minute.

The fog's strange disorientating properties meant she was forced to stop and get her bearings. She used the opportunity to catch her breath and call the dog again. There was no answering bark this time. In fact, she realised as she strained to hear him, there was no noise at all, no sounds of the forest, no birds and no artillery. Absolute and utter silence.

The abnormality of that did not occur to her as she let out a sigh of relief. If the firing had stopped then so had the risk of stray bullets. All the same the silence was unnerving, and the sound of her own ragged breathing seemed odd and out of place. She glanced around, peering through the trees in an effort to catch sight of him. She'd surely not come far enough to lose sight of the road, but like the dog, the road was nowhere to be seen and in truth she was hard-pressed to recall from which direction she'd come.

Grace began to feel uneasy. She felt the stirring of butterflies deep in her stomach, the prickle of raised hairs down her back and wished she'd left the dog to come home on his own. She debated doing exactly that and was about to give up and leave him to his rabbit, when her scrutiny was rewarded by a glimpse of movement ahead through the tangle of snowberry and briar.

"About bloody time," she grumbled. She pushed her damp fringe out of her eyes and clambered clumsily over the fallen tree blocking her path. The log was slick with moss and she paused momentarily to wipe the resulting slime from her hands, on the seat of her pants.

It was on straightening that she heard the noise, a strange hissing sound of something travelling at extreme speed, the sound, scarcely preceding, an extraordinary explosion of searing white hot pain. The missile collided with her thigh, the tremendous force of it knocking her clean off her feet. She went down like a felled creature. Fear, burning pain and confusion coursed through her body as she hit the waterlogged forest floor, but her overriding emotion was one of absolute astonishment as she realised she'd been shot.

Terrified, she floundered desperately in the melt water. Frantically she scanned the impenetrable barrier of trees. Someone was out there and for whatever reason she'd just become a target. She must move her position, hide, escape, anything but stay where she was, but none of these things were possible. Her leg would not respond.

The pain caused her to suck in air in frantic gasps as she tried to clear the confusion and make sense of her situation. Someone's aim was out. Someone's Intel was incorrect and whoever was responsible was in big trouble, just as soon as she sorted out the jumble in her head. She cursed the army, those blasted squaddies and their stray bullets. She cursed the dog and his disobedience, but mostly she cursed her own stupidity. When would she ever learn to take advice? Red flags meant danger for a very good reason.

"I'm here ..." she called out weakly. With a little more attitude she added, "You idiot, you've bloody well shot me!"

She hoped it was a mistake. The alternative didn't bear thinking about. She snapped her mouth shut when there was no reply. She should've taken notice of the red flag. She vowed in future to take notice of every warning and every piece of advice that came her way, and hoped the vow itself would bring about some miraculous turn in her fortunes.

When nothing miraculous transpired, she struggled to a sitting position, still bleeding, heavily. She needed to stop the flow quickly and pulled at the length of rope loosely hung around her neck. The dog's makeshift lead. If only the dratted mutt had been wearing it. Nevertheless, it would serve now as a tourniquet. The pain in her thigh increased as she tried to move to gain access to the rope. She stopped and glanced warily at her leg as it lay awkwardly just out of the water.

Normally the sight of a long slender arrow protruding from her flesh would have initiated a sudden and extreme reaction, but her response to the enormity of what had occurred was delayed by disbelief, her mind quite unable to comprehend. This was not right, like the incorrect piece forced into a jigsaw puzzle. She gazed as if somehow removed from the event, a voyeur at the scene of a terrible accident, as the blood flowed out of the wound, through the material of her trousers and leached into the water.

And then suddenly, as suddenly as the arrow itself, she came back with a rush and a hammering of heart beats and an overwhelming sense of panic. Her heart rate increased till it pounded like a mad thing in her chest and she tried in vain to calm herself. The quicker her heart beat the more blood she would lose. She'd read that somewhere, and was sure it was true. She glanced around wildly. Who could have done this? Not the soldiers surely, unless the British army had started recruiting archers? A madman living in the woods perhaps? Why would anyone do this?

She struggled to grasp the rope to stop the bleeding, but her hands were cold and she began to shake uncontrollably. She found no matter how hard she tried, she was unable to co-ordinate her actions. Sweat beaded on her brow despite the cold, and the pain's intensity increased. She would bleed to death here in the wood where no one would find her. She would slide beneath the icy melt water to lie on the bed of some stagnant pool, alone for ever. Lacking the energy or breath to scream, she began to whimper quietly with pain, fear and frustration, but mainly fear, and when the pain finally overcame her, she slipped just as quietly into unconsciousness.

Her last fragmented thought as her mind overloaded and cut out was that someone was out there, somewhere, very close by.

Chapter Two

The boy came silently. A wraithlike shadow slipping unseen between trees cloaked in frost. He stooped as hoary tendrils threatened to entwine him in their icy embrace, a slender bow held tightly in one hand while the other gripped a brindle terrier by the rough hair at its scruff. The dog remained alert. Ears pricked, its tail twitched with anticipation; the rasp of its breath the only sound to be heard in the silence of the winter forest.

The boy flicked a nervous glance around the tangle of waterlogged tree roots and eerie, stagnant pools. Afraid to proceed and unwilling to retreat, he rose slowly to his full height and peered at the body.

Slumped where it had fallen, it lay half submerged in the icy depth, one pale frozen hand outstretched, damp hair, obscuring the face. His heart lurched within its fragile casing at the reality of what had transpired. Summoning what little courage remained he made a hurried sign of the cross and backed carefully away.

Small and undernourished, with ragged, dark hair and clothes the colour of the forest, it was little wonder he'd remained unseen long enough to carry out such a heinous act. He paused, drawing on the strength of his natural camouflage and silently chanted the charms of protection he'd learned at the breast. The beat of his heart stilled and he stepped back through the thorny barrier of frozen bramble runners and drew close again.

He saw the blood first, staining the melt water as it seeped from the body, trapped within the confines of the frigid pool. He watched transfixed as the slickness spread and the body slid further beneath the blackness. He felt fear, an overwhelming sense of dread that welled unbidden from the centre of his being, despite the charms. Reaching out with a hesitant hand he paused midway and drew back quickly, as if scalded by some unseen source. The dog whined and the boy cocked his head, alert to whatever sound distracted it. Then he was up and running, back into the dense woods from whence he had come.

Light-footed, he covered the flooded ground easily. He dodged low branches and fallen trees with not a single snapped twig to shatter the silence, until, with relief as keen as a long held breath, he burst into the makeshift camp like a wild thing freed from a trap, and the phantoms he believed snapped at his heels were let loose. The horses strained at their tethers, whinnies of alarm accompanying the wild kicking at the anticipated threat. The roosting birds of the forest rose as one, a cacophony of alarmed pheasants and pigeons squawked and flapped for cover. Their noise reverberated around the small clearing and contributed to the overall commotion. The boy tripped, scattering embers from the smouldering fire, then recovered and steadied himself with an outstretched hand.

His stunned companion lurched backwards away from the shower of sparks, spilled the contents of his cup and muttered a curse beneath his breath as the hot liquid seared the back of his hand. He staggered awkwardly to his feet, dropped the cup in the dirt and stopped the lad's flight by grasping him firmly by the shoulders.

"For pity's sake, Edmund," he growled, flicking a wary glance around the camp. "What in God's name is wrong with you? You'll awaken the Devil himself with that racket."

"My lord, I've done a terrible thing," the boy gasped, glancing back over his shoulder fearfully. He took a ragged breath, his chest heaving with the effort. "I meant to take a deer, but I have taken a boy! I fear I've killed him."

The boy shuddered and the man felt the child's tremors through his own hands. The boy may be guilty of many things but he was not given to flights of fancy. Yet, there was no one in these woods. He would stake his life on it.

Miles of Wildewood - knight, mercenary and sometime scoundrel - possessed tracking skills that were second to none. He'd seen no signs when they'd made camp. He'd set up perimeter markers and traps, none of which had been tripped; he would have surely been alerted if they had. He chewed thoughtfully at his lower lip, narrowed his eyes and scanned the tree line. There was no movement, nothing amiss. Crossing to the tethered horses, he hushed them with a gentle hand and a soft mutter against velvet noses. Cocking his head, he paused and listened. The only sound to be heard was Edmund's frantic panting.

Turning back to the boy, he reached out a hand and shook him roughly. "Been at the ale again, eh, Edmund?" The boy was a devil for the drink.

"No, my lord, t'was a body, I swear it." There was no mistaking the terrified look on the boy's face. If there were any ale to be had, Miles reckoned the lad would have downed one there and then, just to quell the fear in his belly.

Miles cast an eye out to the gloom of the encroaching forest and sighed sourly. He had no urge to trample through water-logged mires. He was cold enough. He'd forgotten just how miserable a Northumbrian winter could be. His chest tightened with the effort of inhaling frigid air, but he couldn't afford to ignore the boy. If there was to be trouble then better he knew of it first-hand, rather than later at the hands of others. Pulling his knife from the leather sheath tied against his leg he turned back to the boy.

"Where, Edmund? Show me where this body lies."

Edmund led Miles swiftly back through the stillness of the forest, to the spot where his victim lay, allowing his master to see for the first time the limp and bedraggled body which had begun to slide of its own volition beneath the icy water of the woodland bog. The body was soaked and unnaturally still. Edmund's arrow expertly lodged in the thigh.

Miles paused to survey the scene, holding Edmund back with a raised palm. When he was satisfied that no one lurked in the shadows between the trees, he knelt on the sodden ground and with rough hands hauled the body clear of the water, noting with suspicion and mounting unease the rope tangled around the neck. He glanced up at the overhanging trees. He saw no limb that would have accommodated a makeshift gallows. What devilment had gone on here?

He removed the damp woollen hat and tossed it to the boy before smoothing the mud splattered hair back from the face and then leaning so close that his own warm breath would have tickled had the victim been conscious, he listened for sounds of breathing. He noted the pale smooth skin and fine bone structure, and was aware of a subtle fragrance, hovering just beneath the stink of rotting vegetation. He sat back on the damp ground pulling the body with him and assessed the situation.

"Edmund, you are indeed a fortunate miscreant. Despite your skill with the bow, your victim still lives." He grinned at the lad, who shook with relief. "But I see I need to further your education, for this is no boy. Don't you know a maiden when you see one?"

Although at a loss as to where this girl had come from, or how she'd breached his fail-safe systems, he had not the time to deliberate on the puzzle. He couldn't afford to linger, nor could he simply leave her to perish. In reality it would have been more convenient to pretend they'd not stumbled upon her and preferable for all concerned if Edmund had not skewered her with his suspect aim.

But as a knight, reluctant or not, he had a code of sorts to uphold. He accepted that lately he had been more scoundrel than valiant defender of the crown. Circumstances beyond his control had seen his honour tested. Perhaps in the guise of this strange bedraggled girl, the fates had sent him a reminder of how he should behave. Who was he to argue with fate?

He loosened the noose from around the girl's neck, noting the

14

redness of burnt skin, stripped off his belt and used it to stem the flow of blood. Then picking her up as if she weighed naught, he slung her across his shoulder as he would have carried the deer, had Edmund's aim had been true. With questionable care, and surprising speed he carried her back to the camp.

Dropping her limp body in an unceremonious heap by the fire, Miles pondered whether such a scrawny thing was worth his efforts at all. He had things to do. Plans that required set in motion, which he delayed at his own peril. There was no guarantee of her regaining her senses and, honour-be-damned, he'd no desire to be landed with a drooling halfwit. He crouched at her side and laid a palm against her cheek, felt her skin cold and clammy. He knew her leg required treatment and the arrow must come out, but it was not safe to linger here in the frozen wood.

Whoever she was, her kin would come looking and he doubted they would believe young Edmund had mistaken her for a deer. They would either be looking to rescue her or finish her off, and waiting around to find out was not an option.

"What did you see before you loosed your arrow?" he asked the boy, impatiently. He needed to understand the significance of what they'd inadvertently stumbled upon. It was not usual to come across young girls, alone in the deep woods, even more unusual to discover them near death with a rope around their neck. Despite his impatience at this unwelcome interlude, he was intrigued.

Edmund shrugged, bewildered. "A deer, I reckon I seen a deer."

"But obviously you did not. Did you merely see movement? Was the girl on the ground or in the air?" He pictured her suddenly, a fleeting image of a terrified face, as she swung, feet far from the ground. His hand strayed to his throat, where his own scars were barely visible, but engrained on his mind nonetheless. He dropped his hand and blinked the image away.

"In the air," Edmund pulled a face, suppressing his laughter. "How could she be in the air, she's not a bird?" He flapped his arms, hopping on one leg, a court jester in the making. Miles recognised fear edging toward hysteria as the boy attempted to rationalise his actions. He recalled his own first kill. Fear mingled with elation. It had left a bitter taste, but that was long ago and his palate had quickly grown accustomed.

Continuing his assessment of the girl's condition, Miles ignored the boy's antics and his interest grew, despite his initial reluctance. In his experience everything happened for a reason, good or bad. It was his task to determine how best to turn this misadventure to his own advantage. "Nor is she a deer, Edmund, but that did not stop you. Was she hanging? Or was she on the ground?"

"Does it matter, my lord?" shrugged the boy in confusion.

"It matters if we have come upon a hanging," replied Miles grimly. "The hangman may come looking for his corpse." He turned with a menacing grin that highlighted the scar tracing his jaw line. He couldn't help himself. Edmund was such an easy target. "Or indeed, he may be content to take the boy who loosed the arrow, in place of the corpse. Just think of it, Edmund, the world looks quite different from the end of a rope." And he should know.

Edmund paused, one foot hovering above the ground and allowed his arms to drop to his side.

"I think she be on the ground," he said quickly, He'd no wish to meet the hangman.

Miles shook his head impatiently. "You think? Maybe if you had thought before you released the arrow we wouldn't be in this predicament." He didn't need the additional aggravation. Not now so close to home, so close to completing his mission.

"Edmund make haste, prepare the horses, we need to leave now." He snapped the shaft of the arrow, to ensure it did not impede their progress but the girl lay unresponsive to any additional pain the action may have caused. She was either made of sterner stuff than he, or so far gone the pain had ceased to mean anything.

He checked her breathing again. Detected it; shallow but still there. He slid a rough palm beneath the neck of her woollen jerkin, ignored the swell of her breasts and concentrated his mind on the rhythm of her heart beating in her chest. The physicians he'd met on his travels, in lands far from this place, had held great store by the function of the heart in life and death. He was no physician, but it was true, he'd never felt the beat within the chest of a dead man and he'd seen and created many dead men.

"Edmund did you hear me?" He withdrew his hand and turned impatiently. The boy was a liability. "What have you there?"

Edmund grinned mischievously, fear now erased from his face. He lifted the small dog by its scruff for inspection. "He's mine, I found him in yonder forest. He'll bring us many rabbits." The dog wriggled in the boy's grasp, wagged its tail energetically and Miles allowed a reluctant smile.

"Rabbits yes, but no more deer, Edmund, or the king will have your head and mine." The boy dropped his gaze and Miles momentarily shared his unease at the strange turn of events. He turned away from the child, swept a quick glance around the campsite and added gruffly. "Keep him if you must, but make sure he doesn't stray. He has a wilful look about him. I fancy he would think naught of chasing my stock, supposing I have any left after all this time." The boy grinned again and nodded his agreement. "And, Edmund," added Miles, "make haste!"

Riding hard through the forest the horses picked their way sure-footedly through the bogs and beyond, where the moor rose above them, still snow covered. Here the land grew ever steeper and more rugged. The wind snapped cruelly across the vast empty terrain and the riders braced themselves against the biting weather.

All the while Miles held the girl against the warmth of his body. Her chilled dampness seeped through the cloak and into his clothes and skin. He fought the wheeze which tightened his chest as her cold impregnated him and he began to doubt his decision to bring her along. She would likely die and he would have received a soaking for naught.

Her head rested beneath his chin and he listened as she whimpered with pain. A good sign, she was regaining some of her faculties. He pondered on her identity, where she'd come from and how she'd gotten so close to them without being seen. He wondered about her strange clothes, and why she was dressed as a boy. Miles knew all about spies, had encountered more than a few on his travels. He knew how they worked, how devious they could be, but what would spies be doing this far north? Unless, word had got out of his return to these shores, and Sir Gerard had prepared a welcome.

He wondered a lot and in particular, he puzzled about why someone would want her dead. She was very young to warrant the noose, but who was he to question the law, or her, if indeed she had fallen foul of it. He had spent much of his time in questionable compliance with laws that changed as readily as the Monarch. It was not his place, nor his wish, to pass judgement on a scrap, who might yet succumb to her wounds.

His judgement was reserved for someone altogether more deserving.

Chapter Three

Cold, wet and hunched in the saddle, Miles was thankful for short winter days. Although keen to press on and reach his final destination, he was bone weary and grateful that the early loss of the sun brought an end to their frozen journey. As darkness closed in around them and the temperature continued to plummet, they came with immeasurable gratitude upon a low stone building, alone in the desolate landscape.

The boy, with little flesh on his bones, was frozen. He stamped his feet and blew onto his icy hands in an attempt to warm himself. Miles too had suffered the sting of the elements. His muscles ached with the strain of holding the girl. For the second time he doubted the wisdom of his decision to bring her along. He should have left her. Would have left her, he realised with a measure of self-loathing, but for the risk to the boy and himself if they were implicated in her death. He'd become corrupted by the life he'd led and perhaps it was time he considered how to make amends. With no energy or time to dig a grave in the frozen ground, he considered it prudent therefore, to ensure her good health. He lifted her from the horse's back and turned to assess their sanctuary.

The building had been a home, during the summer months when there was a living to be made up here in this high land of hardy hill sheep and buzzards. Now, still shrouded in thick snow it stood abandoned. Its sturdy walls had survived the worst weather. The adjoining outbuildings less successfully, however, they were sufficient to shelter the horses from the relentless wind which carried sleet and the promise of heavier snow to come.

Miles shouldered the door, thankful the roof was intact and the interior dry. He'd sheltered in far worse places, and there was something of comfort in the unassuming stone walls. He lowered the girl to the dirt floor, still scattered with last year's straw, and set about making a fire while Edmund attended to the horses.

"It's going to be a long cold night, Edmund," he said, when the boy returned. His voice was hoarse with the cold and lack of use. "If your petit cerf is to survive till morning we shall need to warm her." He held out an empty cooking pot and the boy nodded. Not keen to go back out into the cold, but resigned to his role as snow gatherer and general dogsbody, he paused at the door.

"Edmund, make haste," Miles added. "The sooner the arrow is removed and the humours restored the better for us all."

Edmund looked from the man to the girl, reluctant to leave. "D' yer believe someone was tryin' to kill her?"

Miles cocked his head. "You mean, other than you?"

"I didn't intend harm," the boy muttered, dropping his gaze to his feet.

"Indeed, Edmund, but now you see the result of using a weapon without clear sight."

"It will not happen again. Ye can be assured of that."

Miles shrugged; the boy had learnt his lesson. "No matter, Edmund, you made a mistake, and we will endeavour to put it to rights, now go."

He returned his attention to the girl who lay unmoving by the fire. He squatted alongside balancing on the balls of his feet and slowly drew back the cloak. He judged her taller than the boy, a little older, and slightly built, though the woollen tunic she wore hid most of her body from view. Her hair was fair or would be when clean, though oddly streaked with pink. It was short and unusually spiky apart from the fringe that fell across her eyes.

He ran his fingers roughly through the damp strands, checking for any wound that may have stained her hair. Why would a woman choose to wear her hair so short unless she was a spy and attempting to pass herself as a boy? Realistically, a female spy who made the most of her femininity and had a little more flesh on her bones would have stood more chance of infiltrating his defences than a scrawny boy. In fact, had she been more to his liking, he might well have enjoyed a little infiltrating of his own, and his nemesis Gerard would know that. He was therefore left uncertain and unconvinced at her purpose.

Perhaps the noose was the key, but who wanted her dead and for what reason? His gaze travelled to her leg and the arrow, part of which still protruded through the loose fabric of her leggings. What kind of a woman wore clothes such as these? She was odd there was no question about it, and oddness carried with it an air of mystery which made him suspicious. He had not survived the last ten years without developing a sense for such things.

He took his knife and slit the material from ankle to waist. She moaned softly as he unlaced and removed her boots. Good boots, he thought; lightweight and sturdy with soft padding at the ankle, they would be comfortable, though the fastening was unusual and they were certainly not footwear for a young lady. Then the trousers were off and that did cause her to struggle against him. He was surprised at her strength. Even in slumber she fought him and he smiled at her spirit. No doubt when awake she would realise the folly of her struggles, but for now he found it mildly entertaining.

"Hush, Mademoiselle," he muttered. "I mean you no harm; I'm trying to assist you, lie still." He stroked her hair, in the way he would to calm his horse, or a flighty hound, and then absently, he stroked her pale thigh for no other reason than the fact that he could. While his rough palm skimmed her soft skin, he considered the best way to remove the arrow, which ensured his mind did not stray to other matters of the flesh. Fortunately for her, the arrow did not appear to have hit bone. It would however, need to be removed and that was going to hurt. It was inevitable. Regardless of her undeniable fighting spirit, she would definitely need something to dull the pain.

He used the boiling water provided by Edmund to clean his knife, then took a small blue glass vial from his pack and took a moment to consider its use. The contents were precious, a concoction of opiates brought from the east and irreplaceable in this remote location. He was uncertain whether it might be needed again, or whether it would be wasted on a lost cause. Nevertheless, he propped the girl up against him, tipping her head back so she could be made to drink. He spoke softly against her ear and she roused slightly.

"Mademoiselle, you must drink this. It will make you sleep. When you awaken all will be done."

He took her incoherent muttering as acquiescence and poured half the contents into her mouth. She gagged and he held her mouth and nose closed with one hand to ensure she swallowed. Edmund looked away, reluctant to witness to her distress.

"Edmund, hold fast," Miles muttered. "You've seen worse on the battle field. I need your help here, hold her tight while I attend to the wound. It will cause her pain and she will fight you despite the tincture. You must hold her securely so the knife does not slip."

Edmund took Miles' place and did his job admirably for she did indeed howl and thrash when the arrow was removed and even more so when the wound was cauterised. He held her to him tightly, his small thin arms empowered suddenly with the necessary strength. He had never been as close to a girl before. When all was done, Miles was forced to prise him away he appeared so affected by the trauma of the operation and the nearness of the girl.

"Go and settle the horses, Edmund," said Miles gruffly, though his eyes betrayed his amusement. "I will attend to her now."

Edmund smiled weakly. He pulled on the girl's hat and wrapped a blanket around his shoulders before gratefully leaving the cottage.

Miles took the time to rinse his blood stained hands in the cooling water. He rolled his head slowly from side to side to free up his taut neck muscles. He badly needed to sleep, but wasn't quite finished.

Leaning forward he used his thumbs to gently rub away the muddy tears from the girls face. She was deathly pale and her clothes clung damply to her cold skin.

Lifting her arms, he pulled her woollen tunic over her head. Her clothes would dry overnight in front of the fire. He paused, distracted and undeniably interested when he saw how little she wore beneath; a short close fitting white sleeveless tunic that revealed her belly and the tiniest lace undergarments he had ever seen.

Tracing the outline of her right hip bone, a flurry of tiny butterflies tattooed in the deepest indigo blue, fluttered lifelike across her pale skin. If she wasn't a spy then she was some kind of temptress and his mind buzzed with possibilities, not all of them honourable. He smiled shrewdly and reassessed the situation. She was certainly not as young as he'd first thought. Maybe that explained the hanging; maybe she'd been the victim of a cuckold wife, or a guilty husband.

She shivered in the frigid air and he watched mesmerised as the butterflies twitched their wings tantalizingly. With a muttered curse he gave himself a shake and replaced the cloak. It amused him to know something about her, something she would no doubt prefer to keep hidden. She was indeed a puzzle, but there would be time enough to solve it later, when he had energy for the game. His priority now was to eat and sleep. He needed all his strength and wits for the days ahead.

Every day brought him closer to Wildewood and revenge.

Chapter Four

Grace woke in stages, each of her senses coming slowly and reluctantly back to life. She heard a boy's distorted voice, through muffled ears, as he discussed the food which she could smell cooking. The aroma, of stewed rabbit caused her stomach to recoil in response.

Struggling to open leaden lids, the room swam before her. When it slowed, she was able to make out the blurred figure of the boy as he squatted by the fire. A dog - her dog, sat by his side, tail wagging.

Damn that dog to hell, she thought.

She turned her head gingerly, and regretted the action when the room spun once more. Cold stone walls, rough earthen floor, a window small and unglazed - all spinning. She put out her hand, grasped desperately at the straw beneath her, applying the brake in the only way she knew how. She tried to slow the rotation further by keeping her head still and moving only her eyes. She realised there was someone else in the room, coolly observing her return to consciousness.

He sat relaxed against the wall, alongside the fire which hissed with its load of damp wood. His legs outstretched, booted feet crossed at the ankles, arms folded loosely across his chest. He studied her through the smoky interior from beneath half closed eyes.

Grace realised he was speaking to her, in the low raspy voice she recalled from her dreams. His rising intonation suggested a question, but she couldn't understand him. He wasn't speaking English and yet it sounded familiar. She stared at him blankly. Perhaps she was still dreaming. How else could this situation be explained? She had no memory of what had preceded this. No recollection of arriving, or indeed of leaving anywhere else. Merely a worrying blank void she desperately needed to fill.

She blinked slowly, dragged reluctant, sticky lids back open, trying to concentrate and focus. But her mind, incapable of normal cognition seemed reluctant to obey and determined to wander. She found herself drawn to his presence, fascinated by his appearance. Her pupils dilated, a witless rabbit caught in a hypnotic glare of light.

He appeared weary. A little unkempt, his collar length dark hair was pushed back roughly from his face, the moisture trapped in the damp strands glistening in the firelight. Here and there, small white lines betrayed the scars of old wounds. They dissected his eyebrow, highlighted the line of his jaw and marred the stubble that cloaked his chin. His eyes, which assessed her with lazy disinterest, were a striking blue, his lashes long and black.

He was not unattractive she decided as she studied him detachedly, though his appearance suggested he'd been living rough for some time, and an accumulation of sweat and grime had caught in the fine lines either side of his eyes. Laughter lines, her Grandmother would have called them, but there was no humour in his expression. Instead there was an aura of strangeness which initiated stirrings of unease within her.

He spoke again more insistently, his voice little more than a hoarse whisper but its tone demanding her attention. She shook herself, widened her eyes with difficulty and tried very hard to concentrate. It was French, she was almost sure of it, a kind of French anyway and she thought he was asking her name. How odd, she thought distractedly, a Frenchman in the middle of a Northumberland. Perhaps he was lost, it was easily done. She, herself had a terrible sense of direction. She tried to recall the French learned at school, but apart from the usual rude phrases that circumnavigated the school yard she was at a loss.

This wasn't getting them anywhere, she thought. Confusion clouded her usual directness. She could imagine all manner of things about him and who he might be, but that didn't explain where she was, how she'd got there and what on earth was going on. She swallowed with difficulty, took an unsteady breath and tried out her voice.

"Speak English, you're not in France now," she croaked. She dragged an insolent glare and a generous dollop of false bravado from the depths of her rapidly diminishing store of confidence.

Pulled out of his lazy reverie, he cocked his head and raised a scarred brow. "Pardon?" he responded. "I merely asked your name, Mademoiselle."

"My name?" She cast her eyes around the smoky room, with no idea how she'd ended up there. She had the worst hangover possible, and couldn't even remember the party. Maybe that was the answer. She'd obviously been to a party, done something stupid, which pretty much summed up her life so far and ended up here, with...him. She felt the flicker of self-doubt, spark into life and chose to ignore it. She'd left all that behind in London, the self-analysis of her own behaviour, the self-deprecation. She doused the flame before it could take hold and glanced back at him. She needed to get her life back on track.

"My name is Grace," she offered eventually with a shrug and a shield of indifference "Who the hell are you?" She watched as confusion swiftly flashed across his face. Perhaps he found as much difficulty with her accent as she did with his.

"Miles, Miles of Wildewood, my lady. The boy is Edmund."

"Miles who?" Bloody hell, whatever she'd had the night before; she

23

was making a sworn promise never to touch it again. She felt an unwelcome fluttering in the pit of her stomach and made a supreme effort to retain the contents.

"Okay, Miles, whoever, from wherever, how did I get here?" One pale hand strayed to her fringe and she wound the longer strands between finger and thumb. She glanced around bewildered, simply could not remember a thing, and felt a tiny ripple of alarm at the absurdity and recklessness of that.

Miles observed her through narrowed eyes. "Why, on the back of my horse, my lady."

In the boot of his car more like, thought Grace, with rapidly increasing unease, wrapped in a carpet and set for a shallow grave. Now that headline would definitely knock the forgery off the top spot. "My Lady...Oh for goodness sake...," she snorted. Did he think she was an idiot?

He leaned toward her, the curl in his lip betraying some undeclared intent. "Where are you from?"

She leaned back a fraction in response. "Tell me where I am and I'll tell you where I'm from."

Miles smiled slowly, settled back, lifted his cup and took a sip. He watched her and waited until the pause became almost unbearable, before speaking again. "You are currently sheltering atop Ahlborett Crag. Where are you from?"

"Why, here of course."

"Here?"

"Well, not exactly here. I mean I don't actually live in this..." she cast about looking for the right description "...cottage."

"What are you doing on my land?" he asked. He placed the cup on the beaten earth alongside him and wiped his mouth roughly with the back of his hand.

She followed the progress of his hand with her eyes, glancing away when she met the curl of his lip. "This is not your land," she muttered.

"I beg to differ." The curl turned into a smirk and ignited Grace's indignation.

"You can beg all you like," she snapped. "This land belongs to me."

He stared at her then, with new interest. "To you?"

"Yes."

"Perhaps you should tell me who you really are?"

"I've told you who I am."

He narrowed his eyes. "You try my patience, Mademoiselle. Tell me who you are and why you believe you hold title to the lands of Wildewood?"

"Oh please." She shook her head and stifled a smirk. "I try your patience. This is a joke right? The lands of Wildewood, I've never heard such twaddle, and I've never heard of Wildewood. I've lived here all my life. This land from the river to the crag and all the forest in between belongs to Kirk Knowe...and Kirk Knowe belongs to me." She stuck out her chin defiantly and foolishly ignored the red flag in his expression.

With surprising speed he whipped out his arm, caught her slender throat in his calloused hand and squeezed ever so gently. Leaning in close, he cocked his head, his raspy breath hot against her cheek. "You have appalling manners, Mademoiselle." Her eyes bulged with indignation, but she refused to let loose of the fear.

He drew out his dagger and placed the tip against the pale skin beneath her chin. She watched his eyes narrow as her skin depressed beneath the blade.

"How did you come to be in my woods? Who sent you alone into the grip of winter? Who seeks you with the rope? Or perhaps you are the seeker, petit espion."

And suddenly she was there, in the frozen forest. She remembered her walk in the woods, the chase after the dog, but what followed was hazy. She remembered fear, but could not recall the cause. She remained resolutely silent as he indented the blade a little more. She gasped as the pressure increased and as her softly exhaled breath whispered across his skin, she met his eye. Torture or entertainment, she had no idea what he intended and no intention of finding out.

"You will tell me," he said through gritted teeth.

"In your dreams," she whispered and she balled her fist, swung back her hand and connected as hard as she could with his groin.

His howl of pain ricocheted around the small room and was almost surpassed by the boy's spontaneous whoop of delight. He cursed wildly at the boy who ducked and beat a hasty retreat.

Throwing off the cloak, Grace leapt to her feet and stood momentarily triumphant in her underwear, her tormentor beaten at her feet. A sudden searing pain in her thigh and an alarming shift in her equilibrium robbed her of victory before she'd fully grasped it.

"Oh bugger," she cried and dropped to the floor like a stone.

Chapter Five

They glared at each other from opposite sides of the room. Miles counted back from ten and waited patiently until her expression eventually betrayed her discomfort and a sliver of fear. He picked himself up, resisted the urge to realign his equipment, and stood over her.

"Are you done, Mademoiselle?" he growled.

"My name is Grace," she muttered and this time Miles caught the hesitancy in her voice. As if she realised she'd gone too far and was concerned at the consequences of her actions. He'd succeeded in scaring her, but the knowledge didn't leave him with the air of victory he desired.

Stooping he picked up the cloak and offered it to her. "Cover yourself," he said quietly. "The night is cold, you must keep warm."

"What's happened to me?" she asked, as she drew the cloak around her.

He paused and considered his reply. He knew only that Edmund had mistaken her for a deer. What occurred prior to that, only she could tell and he realised there was far more to this girl than was immediately apparent. He consoled himself with the thought that her strange behaviour was obviously down to the tincture he'd dosed her with. Either that or she was possessed by demons, and the way her eyes darted back and forth, it was a distinct possibility. One he wished he hadn't thought of, but would also explain the noose. Witch hunting was becoming a popular sport, particularly among the devout and the ignorant. Regardless of the cause, he didn't care for the idea he'd been bested by a girl half his size. Nevertheless, tincture aside, he needed to know exactly who she was.

She'd said she owned Kirk Knowe, but he knew Kirk Knowe belonged to the church, a wayside chapel of ease under the care of the nuns at Ladyswell Priory. She'd also stated as owner of Kirk Knowe she owned the lands where he had found her. He knew they did not belong to Kirk Knowe, because they belonged to him, given to him by the king, as reward for his service, not two years since. The only way she could claim any connection to Kirk Knowe was if she belonged to it, and he'd never seen a nun who looked or behaved, quite like her.

Even now after her outburst, with reality settling in, she was still less afraid than he would have expected. He'd deliberately tried to intimidate her, if only to get a reaction, but despite his aptitude for the sport, he'd failed. He pondered on how far he would have taken the game if she'd not brought it to a close.

He thought again of spies, and now he'd seen her half naked, and knew to his cost how handy she was with her fists, he revised his opinion of her suitability. If he were to be pummelled for information, he could think of no one better equipped. He had experience of spies and they were usually well trained in the arts of deceit, but they were not usually quite so young.

She pulled the cloak around her shoulders and he sat back down across from her and watched as she waited patiently for his reply. She had questions, and he supposed that was to be expected; but he had questions of his own and he too required answers, for they could travel no further until he was sure she was no threat to his plans. He yawned, stretched his stiff muscles and rubbed his face with his hands.

"You have had a little accident, Mademoiselle," he replied eventually. "Do not concern yourself. You are safe now." He ran his thumb carefully along the flat of his knife, prolonging her torment against his better judgement. "What is your family name, Grace?" he asked, perhaps they were a local family and he would know of them. Perhaps then he could put his suspicions aside.

Grace dragged her gaze away from the knife. "Gardner," she replied hesitantly, "Grace Gardner."

"Very well, Mademoiselle Gardner," he said. Progress at last. He sheathed the knife and encouraged her with a crooked smile that put a sparkle in his tired eyes. "Perhaps you would like to explain why you were wandering alone in the forest. It's a dangerous place, particularly for someone so...vulnerable?"

"And it's not dangerous here?" she glanced about, avoiding the look in his eyes. He smiled as she noted the position of the door, marking it for escape perhaps. She'd have to get past him, but he supposed it was possible if she were determined.

He shrugged. "These are dangerous times, my lady. Scoundrels and lawbreakers prowl the land, who can say for certain where the true danger lies." He followed her gaze, smiled at her naivety. Did she really think she could outwit him?

"I was walking in the forest," Grace recalled. "I wasn't alone."

"There was no one with you when you were found. Your companions had abandoned you perhaps?" He cursed silently, had he missed someone else? He'd been so intent on leaving he hadn't thought to check for accomplices, a major error on his part. He was losing his edge, been too long on the road and he couldn't afford to be sloppy now, there was too much at stake.

Grace glanced at the dog. "Fly ran away. He's such a bad dog." her voice trailed away and Miles nodded.

Of course, the dog; he hadn't made the connection. There were no missing accomplices and no major errors. The dog, on hearing his name, bounded over and began licking the girl's face. She smiled, pushing him away half-heartedly. He settled himself beside her, wiry chin on her lap, his tail beating time on the dusty floor and she petted him distractedly.

She had an engaging smile, almost childlike, but the ache in his groin was proof his captive was far from innocent. And still, suspicion lurked in his gut. "So you were walking with your dog, picking flowers in the snow, with a noose around your neck?" There was a mocking tone to his voice now as he attempted to push aside unwelcome thoughts. It mattered naught to him if she had the smile of an angel or a hag. He raised a sardonic brow. "Where had you run from? Who wished to see you dangle from the end of a rope?"

"I hadn't run from anywhere. I don't understand what you're talking about. I don't understand you. What noose?" she asked, her words slightly slurred, her focus beginning to slip once more. She was either confused or a very good liar. Miles couldn't decide which.

He held it up then, the thin rope which had been tangled around her as she lay in the pool and he swung it slowly, deliberately from side to side. "It is of no concern to me what you have done as long as your trouble does not follow us."

Grace faltered, her fingers finding the raw spot on her neck. "It's Fly's leash, it must have become tangled." Her gaze dropped to her leg and she pulled at the covering cloak. She shot a glance at the wound which was crudely bandaged with strips from his shirt. The skin either side of the makeshift dressing was marred with bruising, the material stained with blood. She raised her bewildered gaze to him and blinked slowly.

"Look, I went for a walk in the woods and I woke up here with you. You'd better tell me what's happened, what's going on." She demanded. "I know I haven't been to some all-night party, so this," she gestured with a shaky hand to her head, "is not a hangover. Someone back there in the woods shot me. I know it was an arrow. Was it you? Are you some madman who lives in the forest and preys on girls?" She glanced quickly around the small building, a caged animal looking for escape. "Because if you are, then you can just forget it." She returned her gaze to his face. He retained an impassive expression, knowing his continued silence unnerved her further.

"What are you going to do with me? Are you going to kill me?" Her voice became shrill and her eyes finally grew wide with fear but she faced him bravely nonetheless. She clutched at the cloak as if it afforded some magical protection and at the little dog who sensed her fear and gave a low growl.

Miles ignored the dog and allowed the tension to grow. In all of his travels through the most exotic lands he had not met anyone quite like her and he wasn't sure whether that was good or bad. He thought he knew women and he thought he knew spies, but he was beginning to realise that when combined, he actually knew very little indeed. Her behaviour was so erratic he wondered which was genuine the fear or the fearlessness.

Perhaps she was not a victim of the noose, her explanation was plausible but he wasn't entirely convinced her sudden appearance was merely coincidental and still needed answers. He was more used to interrogating enemy soldiers however, not scared young girls, no matter how hard she might be trying to hide her fear. He could easily adopt the role of bully and tormenter, and indeed had done just that so far, but it did not sit well with him. He leaned forward again and the dog stood. The growl accompanied by the slight flick of its tail betraying the dog's immaturity and lack of confidence. He clicked his fingers, whistled softly and the dog approached on its belly. He scratched its ears and the dog grinned, its puppy grin and curled up next to him.

"I am no madman, nor do I prey on young girls. I merely came to your aid, Mademoiselle. You offend me by thinking otherwise."

"And yet you put a knife to my throat?"

"I am a cautious man and you incite bad behaviour," he replied with a smile. "I mean you no harm. You are quite safe."

"Well obviously you're going to say that," she answered. "You're not going to sit there and admit to what you're actually planning."

He shrugged. "Then why ask, Mademoiselle, if you do not believe I will reply truthfully?"

She looked at him, opened her mouth to reply and snapped it shut almost immediately; the realisation of the situation, evident in the scowl that soured her face.

When he realised she had no answer he smiled and began again. "Where do you really come from, you are not from these parts? I've been away for some time but still, I do not recognise the name of your family."

She stayed silent, swaying slightly before him, the tincture still present in her system. She had worn herself out with her tantrum. From where he sat he could see how her pupils dilated. He would be lucky to get much more out of her.

He was playing with her, avoiding her questions with ease, but he realised with growing frustration there would be no quick answers to his own. As with a wounded animal she needed sleep and she wasn't the only one. None of them were going anywhere while this weather continued, but he was happier knowing she was secure while he himself slept. There was something incongruous about her and he couldn't decide whether it was just her attitude or something more dangerous. Until he was certain of her identity she remained a threat. He could tie her up, although that seemed excessive given her size. Or he could give her more tincture and try again in the morning.

He considered his options, recalled her tenacity and well-aimed fist and sought the discarded rope. Reaching out he gripped her wrists in one hand.

"What are you doing?" she pulled away from him and he yanked her back.

"What I should have done earlier," he responded sharply as he deftly secured one end of the rope around her wrists and tied the other to the wooden beam supporting the roof.

"How dare you," she twisted wildly, whimpering with the pain in her leg and the frustration at being held captive. "You'll regret this," she spat at him.

"Perhaps." He withdrew the tincture, and avoiding her kicking feet with a raised hand, he offered it to her. "Do you want to fight the rope or fight the pain?"

"I want to fight you."

His grimy, battled-scarred face broke into a wide grin. "Master the pain tonight and tomorrow I will happily meet the challenge."

Grace scowled. "Tomorrow you'll take me back to Kirk Knowe," she muttered petulantly. "I demand that you do."

He was amused by her belief that she was in a position to demand anything.

If she was from Kirk Knowe, as she insisted, that would certainly explain the cropped hair and the fact he did not recognise her family. He wasn't sure about the tattoos or the undergarments, although as he'd never had occasion to look beneath a nun's habit he couldn't rule it out.

Perhaps she was from the chapel of ease, a runaway maybe. He'd heard how strict and frugal convent life was with the nuns at Ladyswell, but to be seconded to the tiny chapel at Ahlborett must surely be some form of punishment. He wondered what misdeed she'd perpetrated. Thought again of the butterflies, he could make a good guess. Or perhaps she'd told the truth all along and had merely wandered off the path. Either way it was good news. The Augustinian convent at Ladyswell was under the protection of the Bishop of Durham and the chapel at Kirk Knowe would surely benefit from the same protection. The bishop would be obliged to pay a substantial ransom for a little lost nun, especially one as odd as this. Things were looking up; Edmund had bagged a prize after all.

"Yer can't ransom her," Edmund cried indignantly when Miles outlined his plan. The girl had succumbed to the sleeping draught and Miles had taken the time to decide exactly what he would do with her.

"I can and I will," grinned Miles. "She'll be worth a tidy sum, and you will remember your place!"

"But I found her." His expression betrayed sullen displeasure.

"True, Edmund, you found her and almost killed her. What do you think she'll say when you tell her that, eh? You shoot her and steal her dog. It doesn't show you in the best light, does it?"

He found it amusing the boy was so smitten. He recalled with some relish the moment when he'd first noticed the fairer sex, but at the end of the day a religious who was bound to the church was no woman in his eyes. Not in the real sense, no matter how tempting. She was however worth something and that was ransom, and he was sorely in need of funds. Nearly two years on Crusade at the behest of the king and he'd barely the clothes he stood up in to show for it. Yes he had land, if he were prepared to fight for it, but land that had been neglected for the last ten years would require considerable investment.

Miles settled down on his blanket to rest while he had the chance. "Prepare for an early start Edmund. We leave for Wildewood at first light. We need to be safely at the Hall before I send a message to the bishop."

The boy kicked stubbornly at the straw, scattering a cloud of dust. "And what if he won't pay?"

"He'll pay."

"But if he'll not, what will yer do?" They both looked at her as she lay peaceful now in her drug induced slumber. Edmund saw her as his angel, conceded Miles, he, however, saw her merely as a good investment.

"Then I'll think of something else to do with her." If she were not a nun then she was surely a spy. Either way she would be worth something to someone. All he had to do was make the deal.

"But she is not yours, my lord. We must return her to the chapel." The boy stood before him stubbornly.

"We must first make sure she survives, Edmund. Then I will decide what is to become of her."

The boy tried again. "But, what if the sheriff comes seekin' her?"

Miles studied her as she slept. Perhaps the sheriff was already

31

looking for her. She was a strange little thing after all and he supposed if she were his, he would be out looking by now. The sheriff did not concern him; he could be outsmarted if necessary. What concerned him was making the best out of a bad situation and that meant not delivering her anywhere, until a ransom was paid.

Chapter Six

Grace woke again to weak sunlight filtering through the heavy, snow-filled sky. It crept valiantly through the tiny window illuminating the dancing dust motes. It was bitterly cold and despite the smoking fire, her breath was tight in her chest. She pulled the cloak around her more snugly and considered her surroundings.

There was only the boy, Edmund in the room. The building where they'd rested was little more than a shack; a shepherds hut maybe, with unfinished stone walls and a dirt floor. She didn't recognise it and couldn't even guess at where she might be. Though Miles said they were high on the Crags, she'd no reason to believe anything he said. They could be far away from her home or merely round the corner, how would she know the truth of it. All she did know was something very strange was going on. She was being held against her will and it was about time she did something about it.

She felt reasonably clear headed, the pain in her leg bearable and she was determined to end this today. She was Grace Gardner, she was in control. She repeated the mantra silently. She hadn't gone through the nightmare of the previous year without some measure of courage, and no way was she going to let some scruffy woodsman cart her off to goodness knows where and tell her what to do. She sat up gingerly and rubbed the sleep from her eyes. The boy smiled at her.

"Yer clothes be dry, my lady." He gestured to the trousers and woollen jumper which lay folded beside her. "I stitched yer hose." He added with a shy smile and Grace realised that despite the annoying Milady affectation he spoke to her in English with a rural burr, rather than a French accent. She reached for her clothes. The trousers had indeed been crudely stitched but they were stiff with dried blood and mud.

"Thank you...Edmund." Yes, she recalled his name and he seemed pleased that she had. "You're wearing my hat," she added with a smile. "It suits you." Edmund grinned. It was his hat now.

"You found me in the forest didn't you? Do you know what's going to happen to me? Where we're going? I really do need to get home."

Edmund glanced at the door. "Yer should be gettin' dressed, my lady, and takin' some refreshment. Yer need to eat before we leave." She sensed his reluctance to discuss Miles' plans, as if perhaps he didn't agree with them. She filed away the knowledge of his uncertainty for future use.

"Leave for where, Edmund? Where are we going? Are we going back to Kirk Knowe?" Perhaps she'd been worrying unnecessarily. Maybe it had all been a misunderstanding and at this very moment they were preparing to take her straight home. She checked the pockets of her trousers as she spoke. The assorted contents were still there untouched. They hadn't thought to search her, she smiled to herself. Perhaps they'd regret their oversight.

"To Wildewood," he offered eventually, as he began to pack away the cooking utensils and sleeping rolls.

"Wildewood, where's that?" The name was unfamiliar despite Miles' earlier mention of it, but it conjured up images in her mind. A Rapunzelian tower with giant vines and creepers. Her curiosity was piqued; she was no Rapunzel though and she wasn't going anywhere but back to Kirk Knowe.

"Tis, Miles' birthplace. We be takin' yer home. Please do not worry yerself, my lady. No harm will come to yer."

"And if I refuse?" she asked.

Edmund shrugged. "Miles has decreed it, so yer will go to Wildewood. Yer cannot refuse. Please get dressed, my lady and eat yer fill before he returns."

Edmund turned away from her and she dressed quickly in clothes that smelled. In fact as she wrinkled her nose she realised it wasn't just the clothes that reeked. The odour of stagnant water and sweaty horse clung to her hair and skin. She needed to wash.

Edmund ladled the last of the previous evenings stew into a wooden bowl and handed her a small knife for eating. She took it from him with shaking hands. She hadn't eaten since leaving the house with Fly. Her stomach was empty and she continued to feel nauseous, and more than a little apprehensive.

"What about you, aren't you hungry?" she enquired of the boy. She wondered why he wasn't eating; looked at her bowl suspiciously. If they'd wanted to finish her off, they could simply have left her in the forest.

"I have eaten."

"You look hungry."

"I'm always hungry," Edmund said simply. He grinned at her and gestured to the bowl. "Please eat yer fill, Miles will soon return."

"Why is he not taking me home? What does he plan to do with me, Edmund?" She picked at the food. Despite her hunger, she had no appetite. The strong taste of the meat and the way it had been boiled within an inch of its life, made her feel queasy. She put down the bowl, slipped the knife into her pocket and ran her fingers through the tangled strands of her short hair picking out blades of straw in a vain attempt to regain some semblance of normality.

"I will take you to Kirk Knowe eventually." Miles appeared suddenly in the doorway behind her. Propped casually against the doorframe, he added, "But first, I plan to collect some compensation for my trouble, from the bishop." He smiled at her, a crooked smile with a glint in his eyes. He looked younger. Less weary; more dangerous.

"Do not concern yourself, you'll soon be back in the safety of the convent and I will be a good deal richer. A satisfactory conclusion do you not agree?" He didn't wait for a reply. "Edmund put out the fire. Mademoiselle finish your food now, we must make haste."

What was he talking about now? What convent? Which bishop? But there was no time to ask questions. She was swept up by him and manhandled out to the horses. Real horses just as he'd said. Well, he could forget that. The last time she'd allowed herself to be manhandled she'd almost ended up in prison. She dug her heels into the snowy ground.

"Let me go," she insisted, as he made to lift her onto the horse.

"We need to make haste, the weather is set to turn again and we've a distance yet to travel."

"Do you really expect me to go with you?"

Did he think she was a fool, had no will of her own? Well perhaps she did have a foolish streak, her behaviour over the previous year had rather proved that, but she also had an iron will.

He cocked his head quizzically and removed his hands from her waist. "I do."

"I'd rather not," she said, in what she hoped was a self-assured voice, but came out a little less so and rather prim.

"You do not have the luxury of choice, Mademoiselle," he replied as he turned and tightened the horse's girth.

"You're a stranger, I don't know you, I'm certainly not about to wander off into the wilderness with you." She didn't appreciate having to address his back either. She resisted the urge to prod him.

Miles shrugged. "We have introduced ourselves, we are no longer strangers."

"Nevertheless, I think I'll just stay here, someone will find me eventually, someone who's prepared to take me straight home to Kirk Knowe." She took a hurried step away, as he turned quickly and she found him a little too close for comfort.

"You're already found, I have found you. What more do you want? This is not a well beaten path. There will be no more travellers this winter. If you wait here alone you will perish and no one will benefit from your ransom." He raised one brow and smiled his crooked smile. "Seems a waste, don't you agree?"

She hesitated, reluctant to go with this unknown man, to a destination, far from her home. Similarly, she had no wish to remain alone and injured in this remote place. He was cocky and arrogant, but was he dangerous she wondered, did he mean her harm? He was smiling now, a rather charming smile, but she hesitated nevertheless.

"I want to go home," she stated flatly.

"And I want to go on," he replied. "I have neither the time nor inclination, to retrace our steps through the storm."

"I don't care what you want."

He narrowed his eyes and smiled a little slyly. "A foolish move, Mademoiselle, I would also suggest rather reckless to admit indifference to the wants of your captor. Better by far to feign interest until you are more favourably placed."

Grace squared up to him, hands on hips, lips pursed indignantly. "Oh, so now you're admitting you're not actually helping me. You're kidnapping me. Well, you can forget that; it's not going to happen."

"How do you propose to stop me?"

"I'll think of something," she replied haughtily.

"We need to make haste, you can think on the way."

He offered his hand, the skin was tanned, the knuckles scuffed. Had he been fighting, she wondered? Or suffered injury digging the grave of his last victim?

She felt control of the situation slipping away and couldn't think of a way to recover it. He was waiting and the horses stamped their hooves impatiently.

She briefly considered the option of escaping, of evading his outstretched hand and starting to run. But the desolate moor stretched endlessly in all directions and she'd no idea where she was or how to get back. She tried to get her bearings, looked in vain for the unmistakable shape of Simonside, or the more distant Cheviot, but the low cloud obscured her view. Even with two good legs it would have been a foolhardy venture to set out into the unknown in this weather. Incapacitated as she was it was simply ridiculous. Even the short walk to the horses had brought tears to her eyes. She accepted reluctantly that for the time being she was tied by necessity to her battle-scarred captor. Perhaps she was overdramatizing. Maybe when they reached Wildewood, wherever that was, she would be able to get help; someone from the village would no doubt come and get her. Until then she would just bide her time, feign interest as he'd suggested. She could feign interest with the best of them.

When it became obvious to him that her resistance had crumbled, Miles affected a courteous nod, took her firmly by the waist and lifted her effortlessly onto the front of the saddle.

"Are you in pain?" he asked as he tied his pack to the horse. He looked up when she failed to answer and for the first time since their initial meeting they looked each other in the eye. "Pardon?" he asked in response to her expression.

"Quite frankly, I don't know where to begin," she said, bewildered and frustrated. "Yes, of course I'm in pain, what do you expect? I have a hole in my thigh, you put it there. However, I'll manage and when we get to Wildewood, will you tell me what's really going on?"

"There is nothing more to tell. I will send a message to the bishop and when he acquiesces to my request you'll be returned." He smiled again and his eyes crinkled with amusement. "Think of it as a little adventure, Mademoiselle."

An adventure! The man was mad. "But I don't know the bishop and he doesn't know me."

"No matter," said Miles, as he swung up behind her and clasped one arm firmly around her tiny waist. "He will not leave one of his little lost nuns in the clutches of a wayward knight. Who knows what might happen."

Grace tried to loosen his grip, but he merely tightened it further and she felt the shudder in his body pressed hard against her back. He was laughing, laughing at her. This wasn't really happening, it couldn't be. Knights and nuns, what on earth was he talking about?

It must be a dream. That was the only plausible explanation. She must have bumped her head and at some point when she was good and ready she would wake up, hopefully in her own bed in her own home, but waking up in the forest where she'd fallen, would also be acceptable if need be. Anything would be better than this.

Trouble was, if this wasn't a dream then she'd hooked up with a weirdo. So maybe she should hedge her bets and feign away until things worked themselves out. She wanted it to be a dream. It was definitely her preferred option when the alternative reality involved weirdoes who thought they were knights of olde. But it felt real, he felt real and the pain in her leg was very real. She turned her head to look at him.

"What year is this?" she asked.

Miles cocked his head. "It is February, my lady, in the year of our Lord 1275."

Oh yes, this was definitely a dream. How else could she have walked into the woods in 2012 and come out in 1275? She smiled to herself, blessed relief coursing through her. As far as dreams went, it could have been worse. She'd always wondered why knights in shining armour got such good press, maybe if she stayed asleep for long enough she'd find out.

Then again, a weirdo would say anything and a crazy girl might just believe him.

She closed her eyes gave a final shake of her head and decided regardless of whatever weirdness had befallen her, she may as well go along for the ride.

Chapter Seven

The sun broke through the clouds briefly and the landscape was transformed. The snow, treacherously thick in places, glistened like jewels covering the myriad of rocks littering the high ground. The brightness caused Grace to squint and she released her hold on the saddle to shield her eyes with one hand. She felt Miles' weight shift slightly behind her as he compensated for her unstable position. She'd dozed briefly, lulled by the gentle motion of the horse, but now she was awake and he was still there, large as life and not in the least dreamlike.

"It's beautiful up here," she whispered, despite her resolve never to speak to her captor again. Her voice was swept away by the wind across the moor and lost amongst the surrounding hills. She assumed she'd gone unheard until she felt his breath warm against her ear.

"Wait until you see the view from the top, it's breathtaking. If the sun holds out and the snow holds off, you'll see over the border and beyond into Scotland."

She turned her head out of the wind and into the shelter afforded by his chest so she could be heard, but mainly so she could avoid the feel of his breath on her skin. "Shouldn't I be blindfolded?" she taunted mildly, she lacked the energy for a fight. "What if I escape while you're not looking and retrace my steps back to Kirk Knowe? What happens to your ransom then?"

Miles smiled.

"I can blindfold you if you like, or tie you up if you prefer." He paused momentarily as she scowled her response. "But there is no need, beneath the snow, lie bog and marsh and deep crevasses which could swallow a horse. There are paths, safe paths known to those who need to travel them. You would never find your way. You would be lost and perish up here."

Grace knew the ancient lore associated with the high moor. This place high above the world, almost in the clouds had cost the lives of many unwitting travellers and it was said their ghosts travelled the moor at night looking for the right path. Some said the ghosts of Roman soldiers could be heard endlessly marching and drilling at the remains of the old roman fort at Chew Green. Locals knew the moor, knew where shelter could be had when the need arose, but even they were respectful of its ferocity and its history.

"Hmm, we shouldn't be up here at all," she muttered sourly. "Not while the army is on manoeuvres." She recalled the red flags she'd so stupidly ignored. By her reckoning they were probably slap bang in the middle of the ranges.

"Whose army?" he demanded. He pulled the horse to an abrupt stop and Edmund narrowly avoided piling into the rear of it.

"Whose army do you think?" She shook her head, made allowances for the fact he was a little alternative.

He gripped her chin firmly and forced her to look at him. "Whose army?" he repeated fiercely.

Grace jerked herself free, with a frisson of alarm. "Our army, the British Army, they've been all over the ranges the last few days, haven't you seen them?" How could he have missed them? The sound of their artillery rang through the valley on a regular basis.

"What do you know about soldiers?" he hissed.

"Nothing," she squeaked. "I don't know anything. They come and they run about and fire their weapons and then they go home."

"How many?" he growled.

He was in her face, so close she could have counted the scars marking his brow. So close, she could feel his breath against her skin. It wasn't pleasant, wasn't meant to be. She tried to pull back further, but he restrained her with ease, making no effort to conceal the menace in his expression. Whatever he was, whoever he was, he was dangerous. She didn't think it wise to reveal that hundreds of squaddies regularly played soldier on the moors.

"You're scaring me," she said finally. She pulled away with considerable effort and put what little distance she could, between them. Knowing full well, he could have snapped her back against him in an instant and snapped her neck just as easily.

"Good, it's about time. How many?" He cocked his head, curled his lip slyly and waited.

"Three or four..." *hundred* she added silently. She sent out a silent prayer in the hope that a whole battalion in full battle dress, would appear. She avoided his eyes, looked at her hands and twisted them nervously.

"Where did you see them?"

"I didn't see anyone, I just heard them. In the wood before we...met."

He stood in the stirrups narrowed his eyes against the glare from the snow and scanned the terrain. There were no soldiers to be seen in the vast, snowy wasteland. He shot her a suspicious look and let the silence between them grow. The horse pawed at the ground restlessly, the jingling harness and the soft wicker of the impatient beast, the only sounds in the vast emptiness. And still he waited silently as if considering his next move.

The snow began to fall again, softly at first in gossamer flurries, then thicker with gathering momentum. Grace pulled the cloak more securely around her shoulders, the hood over her head.

"How long will it take to get to Wildewood?" she asked eventually, desperate to dispel the sudden weirdness.

Miles gave her a slow, thoughtful look, the sly grin, gradually replaced by an altogether more charming countenance as if he'd finally arrived at a decision which pleased him. "We should be there by nightfall if we push the horses." He gave a final scan of the moor before kicking the horse on. "If this snow gets worse we may have to shelter and delay our journey. Are you cold?"

Grace shook her head. She was cold but that was the least of her problems. Deep inside her stomach churned with anxiety. She could play the fearless, couldn't care less charade for only so long. She'd made a mistake in admitting he'd scared her and couldn't afford to make that mistake again. The ache in her leg provided her with a well needed distraction. She concentrated on the pain, willing it to continue for the remainder of the journey, so she wouldn't forget what he'd done to her. Or what he was capable of.

If Miles felt the slump in her shoulders, her spirit, he gave no indication. Grace conceded, her frame of mind would be of little interest to him. He had a ransom to think about. As long as he kept her alive he would collect, that didn't mean he had to keep her happy. She was therefore surprised and more than a little apprehensive when he tugged her back against him. Wrapping both arms around her, he provided much needed protection from the wind. Despite her resolve, she settled against his warmth. With brisk commands in a language she didn't even try to understand, he urged the horse on at a faster pace. As the snow continued to thicken and the wind increased, he held her closer and she finally succumbed to the pain and futility of her situation, closed her eyes and laid her head gently against his chest.

* * *

By mid-afternoon it became apparent they could go no further. The wind was cruel, the snow unrelenting and the girl frozen and increasingly unresponsive, despite his efforts to shield her from the weather. The horses were disorientated and simply refused to move. Miles slid from the saddle leaving Grace to slump forward awkwardly over the horse's neck. He secured her with one hand and with the other he led the animal. Behind him Edmund did the same. The two murmuring encouragement to the exhausted beasts. By will power alone

41

they reached the shelter of a cave set high under the escarpment. The natural sanctuary was deep and had been used before for this very purpose. There were remnants of a fire and dry kindling left for such an emergency.

With the fire lit, Miles used the saddles and packs to create a protective shelter around it and then taking Grace's arm he guided her into the warmth. She'd been silent since their arrival, her face pale, cheeks sunken. She looked perished. He squatted down in front of her, smoothing the fringe from her eyes.

"Mademoiselle," he rasped, "you need to warm yourself. Remove the cloak and allow the fire's heat to penetrate your skin. We shall wait out the storm and complete our journey at first light."

There was no response.

"Grace!" He took her chin roughly and forced her to look at him. She blinked as if woken from a trance, her eyes rolled back in her head and the shivering began.

He muttered a curse. "Edmund get some water heated, she's frozen through."

"Worried yer won't be able to claim yer ransom?" asked Edmund, sullenly.

Miles shot him a sharp glance. He sensed Edmund's disapproval. Edmund was a child who should know better. They'd been through many trials together and it rankled Miles that the scrawny boy, now stood in judgement of his motives and morals.

"Edmund, I don't have time for this," he snapped. He glanced back at the girl and sourly conceded that Edmund was correct. He was not assured of the ransom yet.

He should have taken an alternate route, stopped off at a hostelry where her comfort would have been assured. He might need to do that yet. But he was reluctant to announce his return to the valley until he was good and ready, and safely ensconced at Wildewood. Not while there were soldiers on the moor, ready to cut him down before he could claim his prize. He rubbed her arms roughly with his hands to encourage the circulation.

Her eyes flashed open. "Ow, that hurts," she squeaked and Miles sent up a silent prayer.

"Mademoiselle, please do not make the mistake of dying." He forced a smile. "I will not allow it; I have a ransom to collect." A glowering Edmund thumped the pot of snow on the fire with a shower of sparks.

"Don't worry," Grace replied through chattering teeth. "I wouldn't give you the satisfaction. I have no intention of ending up in one of your shallow graves."

"My shallow...?" he shook his head, she was definitely mad.

Initially, she resisted his attempts to keep her warm, and he could understand her wariness. If she'd any inkling of what he was capable of, then perhaps she would have taken her chances in the snow. However, ignorance of his inglorious past, along with coldness and necessity drew her close and eventually in the dead of the night she laid next to him. Her head on his arm, her back to his front, and coldness was replaced by heat. He tried to move and she whimpered softly, turning to bury her face against his chest. Miles cursed. She was moving against him and he'd been a long time without a woman. He felt the stirring of need and groaned with frustration. Someone was making jest at his expense. A despoiled nun would be worth nothing at all to the bishop.

She slipped her slender hand beneath his shirt and released a soft sigh. She snuggled closer, her hand playing gently against muscles tensed in response. He couldn't decide if she was particularly unrestrained for a nun or particularly skilled for a spy. His indecision on the matter merely added to his torment. If he wanted the ransom, she was a nun and definitely out of bounds. As a spy however, she must take her chances. But right here and now, wound up tighter than a drum, he had no idea who or what she was. He rolled his eyes, glanced at the cave mouth and pleaded for an early dawn.

His thoughts strayed to Wildewood, his childhood home. He'd been away far too long. Ten years of battle, death and dishonour had transformed him from boy to man. He'd left with the outrage of youth and returned with a man's need for revenge. It sat in his belly curdling and demanding to be set free. He could taste it like bile on his tongue. Soon he would be in a position to exact a long awaited justice. Until then he needed to keep his wits about him. Nothing and no one could be allowed to get in his way.

He closed his eyes and succumbed to weariness. With the release of sleep he moved onto his back and the girl who he'd yet to decipher, moved with him, spending the rest of the night stretched languidly across him, her cheek nestled under his chin.

Chapter Eight

Grace woke slowly at first light, finally warm and rested. She stretched and snuggled deeper into a pillow which wasn't as soft and fragrant as it should be. Miles' shirt had come adrift in the night and she was laid upon the warmth of his skin, the firmness of his chest, the taut softness of his belly. She lifted her head groggily, opening her eyes as Miles woke with a start and they found each other nose to nose.

Raising her hand defensively, he caught it swiftly by the wrist

"What are you doing?" she cried, confused and indignant.

"I could ask the same question." Miles released her wrist, lifted her clear and dumped her on the cave floor at his side. "Mademoiselle, I believe you were the one on top."

Grace wriggled to a sitting position. She didn't know how she'd ended up straddling her worst nightmare but when she looked in his eyes, still glazed with sleep, she knew that nothing had happened. The fear she'd felt the previous day remained, but for some reason this morning it was dormant. She glanced at him, wondering how long it would be before his actions caused its reawakening.

"Okay," she said slowly, hesitantly. "I suppose I should thank you, for being such an obliging mattress."

"My pleasure, Mademoiselle," replied Miles with a slow smile. "And if you're a good girl today and behave as you should, I promise not to reveal your indiscretions to the bishop. Though perhaps in future, it would be wise to choose your bedfellows with more care."

Grace shook her head and ignored his attempt at humour. "You are mad," she said as she pushed herself away from him.

Miles got to his feet and reached out a hand as she struggled upright. "How is your leg?"

"It's okay, a little stiff perhaps." Grace flexed her leg experimentally.

He raised a brow. "Indeed. I am similarly afflicted this morning. Perhaps we share a malady."

She glanced up and caught the sly smile that brushed his lips. "I very much doubt it."

"And your leg is okay?" He sounded out the word, his accent transforming it somewhat.

"Yes...it means good, fine, alright...okay."

Miles considered her for a moment and she waited. She sensed from the look on his face he had further questions. She watched with rising indignation as he ran his gaze over the length of her.

"Yes?" she queried shortly. "You have a problem with the way I speak?"

He returned his eyes lazily to her face and smiled. "Not at all, Mademoiselle, I am well used to travel and the richness of language. I find your speech unusual...and interesting."

"Okay then," she replied shortly.

"Okay, indeed." He dropped his gaze once more. "I must take a look?"

"You must take a look at what?"

"At your leg, I must inspect the wound to ensure no bad humours remain."

She chanced a sly glance at him. That had to be the worst line ever. Had she really bedded down on his chest last night? She hoped she hadn't talked in her sleep-or worse. She wondered why he hadn't taken advantage of the situation; she was both relieved and offended. She gave a quick mental check of the current state of her belly. The fear was waking. Admittedly it was a late riser but it was still there and no amount of French schmooze could alter the fact that he had shot her, kidnapped her and scared the life out of her.

"I don't think that's necessary or proper," she replied tartly. Did he really think she was going to drop her trousers for him? Maybe she'd given him good cause to think she would. She cringed inwardly at the thought.

He raised his scarred brow and smiled again. "Proper, no. Necessary, yes."

"Oh for goodness sake, take a look if you must." She unbuttoned her trousers and lowered them just enough so he could reach the bandage around her thigh. Miles knelt before her, seemingly oblivious to the sight of her skimpy underwear and gently unwound the strip of material. She yelped as he pulled the final piece which adhered to the wound and found her fingers gripping the hair on the top of his head.

"You hurt me, I hurt you." she muttered through clenched teeth.

"Pardon," he winced. She had one hell of a grip. "The wound is fine and clean, it just needs to heal." He began to replace the bandage. "When we get to Wildewood you must remove the dressing and allow the air to cleanse it further."

"You seem to know a lot about caring for wounds." She kept hold of his hair, until he had finished and then pulled up her trousers self-consciously. Good God, of all the knickers she could have chosen to wear, she had to have on the tiniest, most frivolous scraps of nothingness. Why couldn't she have donned her girl boxers or her sensible sports pants?

He narrowed his eyes, dragged them away from her behind and back to her face. "I gained experience in the Holy Land."

"Oh, what did you do there?" she asked, anxious to dispel all thoughts of the appropriateness of her underwear. Was he really a knight? Had she really created herself a handsome knight in shining armour, not a bad dream after all? Although she'd seen neither armour nor crusader treasure and had yet to witness any display of chivalry. More likely he was simply so deranged he had created an alternate reality for himself in which he believed he was akin to Lancelot.

"I killed a lot of men," he answered grimly.

"Oh!" Said like that it didn't seem quite so exciting or romantic. She took a step back. He'd just admitted he was a murderer and if this wasn't a dream and he really was a crazy, forest dwelling madman then she'd better stop worrying about lingerie and start thinking about escape. She felt her stomach tighten, the fear was wide awake. She remembered his advice. Feign interest.

"I suppose that happens in wars," she suggested weakly. What did she know? She had no real concept of conflict, what it must be like to be in a position where you have to kill or be killed. She felt young and gauche and embarrassed. She wished she wasn't here, that she hadn't taken the dog for a walk. She wished she was home at Kirk Knowe.

Miles broke the awkward silence that followed. "Help me pack up our things, Mademoiselle and we can be on our way more quickly." He aimed a kick at the sleeping form in the corner of the cave. "Edmund, get a move on you lazy cur, Grace will ride with you this morning."

Grace shook her head. This was madness. She was in a cave at the top of the world with a medieval knight and his squire chatting about the crusades and yet she couldn't be. It was impossible, this simply could not be happening. The man, the boy, they weren't real, couldn't be real. They were in her head, and she was beginning to think she was going crazy. She'd called him mad, but she was the mad one. She had to put a stop to it, dream or no dream she was in charge and she would jolly well wake up. Maybe that was the answer, all she had to do was say no; click her heels together and it would be over and she would be back at Kirk Knowe.

"About that..."

"About what?" Miles picked up and shook his cloak.

"Well, about this whole business. You know; the ransom the bishop and Wildewood."

"Yes."

"Well, it's not really going to happen, is it? You're not even real, none of this is. It's all in my head. I know it is." She touched the fingers of one hand lightly to her forehead. "Or maybe you've drugged me. Who knows? I certainly don't. It's okay though, I'm used to everyone thinking I'm crazy. I suppose I've just gone a little too far this time."

He paused to assess her. "Pardon?" he said, this time heavily accented.

She thought distractedly how his accent became more pronounced when he was ill at ease, and if his expression was anything to go by, he was certainly that. She tried a different tack.

"Look, one of us is obviously crazy. You're either a weirdo or you're just in my head. Which would you rather be?"

Edmund took a step back, crossing himself fearfully while Miles stayed silent. Grace continued unabated.

"I've already told you that I don't want to go with you. I've played along so far, but my leg is much better, you said so yourself, and I have no intention of going any further with you. I appreciate what you have done for me, if you're real that is. But I don't know you. You could be anyone, and you're taking me further and further away from the people I do know. I want to go home. Either, you take me back or lend me Edmund's pony, and I'll go myself." She paused for breath. He was still studying her. Had he actually understood what she'd said?

"I don't believe a word of all that rot about bogs that can swallow a horse. Bloody hell you'll be telling me there's a dragon next! You can't keep me, and you can't make me do anything against my will." She set her hands on her hips ignored the frantic churning deep inside and looked him squarely in the eye.

Straightening, Miles let the cloak fall to the ground in a heap and stared at her. He was no longer smiling. Edmund looked anxiously from one to the other. Miles took a step towards Grace and she held him at bay with her open hand, which was deftly grabbed and held tight by the wrist. Suddenly, she was less sure of herself and even surer, this was not a dream.

"You think I am not real, Mademoiselle?" He squeezed her wrist. "Does this not feel real? Or what about this?" he added as he leaned into her. "Make no mistake, little one," he breathed slowly. "I am very real and whether you wish it or not, you will accompany me to Wildewood. Perhaps you are a little mad, touched by demons. Quite frankly I do not care, I carry demons aplenty. You will do as I say or suffer the consequences. You want me to treat you as my prisoner? Tie you up? I can do that if I really need to. Do I need to?" He raised a brow questioningly "You are coming with me, and you will be freed unharmed when I receive the ransom, and not before."

She stared at him; finally aware she was playing a very dangerous game and had no idea of the rules. She looked at his hand where he gripped her, his palm was warm against her skin and she felt the pulse in her wrist jump against him. She tugged her hand, her fear over ridden by his arrogance. Who did he think he was?

"Let me go," she hissed.

He yanked her closer instead and for a long moment they exchanged feral glares. She dropped her eyes to the jagged scar which followed the line of his jaw, cutting a silver swathe through his stubble. He glared back at her and they both took a deep breath. He dropped her hand and she resisted the urge to rub her wrist where he had held it too tightly.

"You don't scare me." She threw at him as she turned and limped out of the cave.

Miles watched her go. "I wasn't trying to scare you," he said to her departing back. "If I tried, you'd be terrified. You can be sure of that."

He turned to Edmund and shrugged his bewilderment at her outburst. Edmund looked back at him uncertainly.

"Are yer still wantin' her to ride with me, my lord?"

"Worried she'll overpower you, Edmund?" laughed Miles. "Of course she may ride with you. It'll give me a rest from her tongue."

Grace stubbornly limped past the tethered horses and kept going. She was headed back in the general direction of the way they had come the night before, though any tracks had been covered by last night's snow and she quickly veered off course.

"Will yer not go after her?" asked Edmund bewildered.

Miles shook his head. "There's no need she'll not get far." She stumbled and disappeared momentarily in a drift of snow. Edmund made to go after her and Miles caught his sleeve and held him. "Leave her."

Grace pulled herself up and took a couple more steps before admitting reluctantly to herself that it was madness to continue. Her thigh ached, she had no sense of direction and if her current run of luck was anything to go by, she probably would end up in one of Miles' horse-eating bogs. She had no option other than to go with him. She chanced a quick glance, they were already mounted. They were leaving her. She sat down on a boulder and studied her boots, fiddled with the loose threads of her jumper and wondered about curling up in the snow and going to sleep. If she didn't die of hypothermia maybe she'd wake up in a straight jacket on a psychiatric ward. She refused to call after them. How dare they leave her? She looked up when the legs of Miles' horse intruded on her peripheral vision.

"Mademoiselle?" He leaned down from the saddle and reached out his hand.

Glaring up at him she struggled to her feet and held up her hand reluctantly. Miles took her small hand in his and swung her, none too gently, up behind him.

"Hang on tightly," he said gruffly, as she reluctantly slipped her arms around his waist. He kicked the horse and cantered back to where Edmund waited, before dumping her back on the ground and leaving her to Edmund's ministrations.

Grace glowered at Miles from the back of Edmund's pony where she'd been swiftly transferred. Nodding back curtly, Miles turned away quickly before she could see the amusement in his eyes.

"Okay," muttered Grace. "So you're not the man of my dreams. That just leaves weirdo - and no bloody nutter is going to get the better of me."

Chapter Nine

"How did you end up with Miles?" Grace asked the boy as she sat behind him on the sturdy pony. Maybe Edmund could throw some light on the weird situation. Surely the boy wasn't also in on the charade? Yet, he acted the part perfectly and had the rustic accent and due deference one might expect from a medieval page. It would be a simple task to find out.

"I was in Palestine with Sir Guy; he was not a good lord, and Miles took me from him." Edmund pushed the pony on in an effort to keep up with Miles who was some way ahead.

"That's an awfully long way from here. How old were you, Edmund?"

Edmund turned to look over his shoulder, trusting the pony to follow without direction. "I'm uncertain, my lady." Grace watched, amused, as he counted fingers trying to work out the answer. "I was seven or eight summers when Sir Guy took me from kin to pay me father's debt. I spent mebbe one full year with him as page before we was off on crusade." Edmund flashed a shy smile. "He is mean spirited when in his cups. Miles and he did not agree on many things."

Grace returned his smile. Why did that admission not surprise her? Her recent experience had already proven that Miles did not agree on much at all.

"They fought at the tournament and Miles was victorious," continued Edmund, his smile transformed into a wide grin as he added, "and he took me along to train as his squire."

Despite her very real need to disbelieve everything the boy said, Grace found herself drawn in by his tale. She was appalled and fascinated in equal parts. To take a child from his family at such a young age was heart-breaking. But the idea of men fighting to uphold what was right was intriguing and seemed alien to her. Her experience of men had not been so noble. With the exception of her father and grandfather who had been exceptional men, all the men she'd encountered so far had their own interest at heart. She did not forgive or forget betrayal. She gazed at Miles far ahead on the path, and found herself pondering on what he'd fought about, instead of wondering how the man and the boy could possibly keep their stories straight...if it was all a pack of lies.

"Who is Sir Guy?" she asked, turning back to the boy.

"Sir Guy de Marchant." Edmund lowered his voice, making no

attempt to hide the nervous stammer, "An ... enemy and a...bad man."

"And Miles, is he a good or bad?"

Edmund seemed to consider for a moment before replying, slowly. "I reckon he be a good man, who sometimes does bad things."

What kind of bad things? She needed to know what he was capable of and who better to tell her but Edmund.

"How long have you been with Miles?"

"Three winters," he answered quickly, his small chest almost puffing with pride. He had no need to count on his fingers this time. "He promised to return me to me kinfolk once he'd enough funds to return to England, so we stayed in the Holy Land and Miles took payment for services."

Grace considered this. She knew nothing about the history of the crusades but in her experience no one did anything for nothing. "Didn't he get paid for supporting the king?"

Edmund shrugged and Grace supposed that squires were not meant to be privy to the financial dealings of their masters. "He amassed many wonderful treasures." The boy's eyes widened as he remembered, but just as quickly his expression changed and he lowered his voice. "But on our return through Normandy we be ambushed by Sir Guy and his men, naught but common thieves they be. Now he has nothin' but what ye see before yer. His armour paid our passage across the channel."

Grace tried to reconcile this last fact with the man who rode ahead. Strong and brave by Edmund's account, he'd already fought Sir Guy once and won, and then allowed himself to be robbed by the very same man, of everything earned during three years fighting in the Holy Land. It seemed a little careless. It didn't sound quite right. Maybe Miles had done something bad then? It was none of her business; she should really leave well alone. What good would it do to rake it up? But she was beginning to obsess and would continue to do so if she didn't get answers.

"What kind of bad things has Miles done?"

Edmund shrugged and stifled a sly smile. "I reckon yer'll have to ask him."

Hmm, thought Grace. She could just imagine how that conversation would end.

Edmund urged the pony onward. With the distraction of conversation he'd allowed it to dawdle. They'd fallen well behind and even Grace recognised the sense in staying close to Miles. He was the only one who knew where they were going. Shaken from its lumbering gait by Edmund's insistent kicking, the pony surged forward through the snow and Grace clung on tightly to retain her seat. She was grateful

51

she had, when the beast, in its eagerness to comply; stumbled over one of the many rocks hidden beneath the snow, and they were forced to dismount and temporarily halt their progress.

"Beg pardon, my lady," Edmund mumbled, forlornly.

"I distracted you, Edmund," Grace offered with a smile. He'd also provided her with some interesting snippets about her captor...ammunition should she care to use it.

Edmund scanned the horizon and Grace wondered at the anxiety on his face, perhaps he was worried at Miles' reaction. More likely she realised, as she followed his gaze, he felt vulnerable in the desolation of the moor. Miles was still some way off and although she didn't know why, she understood from the boy's attitude that it was not safe to linger.

"What's wrong, Edmund?" she asked.

Edmund turned back and pulled his own cloak tightly around his thin frame. "Yer should take heed of Sir Miles, my lady. He only means to keep yer safe. If he warns of danger, then I reckon there be danger lurkin'."

"Are you not a local, Edmund?" asked Grace.

"No, my lady, I was born in Lincoln, me father bein' a mason workin' on the great cathedral. He took a tumble from yon scaffolding and met his maker, God rest his soul. I left with Sir Guy shortly after."

Poor child, thought Grace, "Are you happy now, here with Miles? Does he look after you well?" she asked.

His anxious expression was instantly replaced by an infectious grin. "Oh yes, my lady, and I been hearin' great tales of Wildewood. It stands on a crag at the centre of a huge forest full of wild creatures. When yer stand at the top of the tower yer can see Scotland and all them heathens what be livin' yonder. There be deer and wild boar a plenty, herds of hill cattle and flocks of hardy sheep. Miles said, when he were a boy same as me, he would help with the sheep and his mother would nurse yon orphan lambs in a basket alongside the fire. Can ye imagine that, a fine lady helping with the beasts? I reckon Wildewood be a magical place, protected by woodland folk, wild beasts and suchlike. We will all be safe there."

"Safe from whom?"

"From our enemies," whispered Edmund.

* * *

Heartily sick of the weather, the mind numbing cold and yet another delay, Miles turned his horse and retraced his steps. He slipped from his mount, smoothed his hands down the pony's foreleg and then stood back and ran his fingers through his damp hair. The pony was lame and would have to be led. He glared at the girl suspiciously, more devilment no doubt. He was beginning to favour the witch theory. It was edging ahead of both nun and spy. His eyes fell automatically to the red wheals still evident on her exposed neck and he wondered again, at his decision to bring her along. The ransom would be no good to any man, if in the meantime she hexed everything he owned.

He turned back to the pony with a muttered curse. Typical of his luck, they were almost home and now obliged to walk the horses. He should've kept the girl with him and suffered her tongue. He doubted she'd have the will for trickery with his hands tight around her and a knife between her ribs. He felt her gaze upon him and shrugged it off belligerently. There would be time for reckoning later.

"What shall we do, my lord?" asked Edmund.

"Walk, Edmund, that is what we shall do," replied Miles shortly. Edmund nodded and shrugged apologetically at Grace.

"Perhaps they can help us?" said Grace and Miles followed her gaze to the far distance where the snowline was broken by a dark body of men approaching at speed on horseback. Miles pulled Grace roughly towards him placing her between himself and his horse. This was not good; it would not do to be caught out in the open by armed men. His own position was perilous to say the least and now he had the added complication of his travelling companion. If this were the sheriff and his men, then his chances of collecting any form of ransom were diminishing rapidly. He turned back to Grace, narrowed his eyes and scrutinised her expression, was this more trickery? Seeing nothing but bewilderment he raised the hood of her cloak to shield her face and pulled the flaps together tightly to cover her unusual garb.

"Stay close to me, do not say anything. Remember, if you will, who has tended you these past days, Mademoiselle, should this be the sheriff come to seek you."

"If that's the sheriff then maybe I'll ask for his help. Perhaps he will take me home," Grace replied defiantly.

"Enough!" hissed Miles, "This is neither the time nor the place; if you value your life you will say nothing." Her eyes widened and she snapped her mouth shut. He prayed she would keep it that way, for all their sakes.

Chapter Ten

"Good day, travellers," called the leader as he drew his band of men to a shuddering halt, mere feet away from Miles. His horse danced nervously. The sweat on its flanks spoke of a long, hard ride. The massive beasts milled about pawing the ground with their hooves, froth spraying from their open mouths as they shook their heads and fought the bit.

Miles stood his ground, hackles rising as he eyed the man who leered at him from atop the nightmarish beast. Grace opened her mouth to announce herself, he caught the movement out of the corner of his eye, but before he could take action to prevent it, the horses wheeled about and the two at the rear almost knocked her from his grasp.

The shock of the near-miss with the horses was nothing however compared to her reaction when she caught sight of the bodies slung across their backs. Men crudely bound with rough rope, their swollen tongues protruding hideously from their mouths. Eyes stared blankly from ashen faces and blood still oozed from their slit throats. She closed her mouth with a snap, and backed straight into his arms. He held her steady, absorbed her shock and turned back to the sheriff.

"Good day to you, sheriff," he replied as he edged back a little. The man encroached upon their space and Miles did not appreciate it. He was at a disadvantage stood as he was while the sheriff was mounted. He would stand a poor chance of defence from the sheriff's sword should he choose to wield it, while he had Grace attached to him like a limpet. "You have travelled far. What brings you to this God-forsaken place?"

The sheriff circled the group as he attempted to satisfy his curiosity. "I am in search of lawbreakers. Have you had sight of any Scotsmen on your journey?"

Miles shook his head, glanced at the bodies and his stomach clenched. He tightened his grip on Grace and willed her to be silent. They were after Scots rustlers not missing nuns, and the Scots could look after themselves, and yet, the man seemed determined in his efforts to get a look at Grace.

"You should not linger here, Sir, it is not safe." The sheriff yanked viciously at the reins and the horse fought the bit angrily, wheeling ever closer. "There are villains abroad and another storm is brewing. Where are you and your good lady headed?" He leaned down from the saddle for a closer look.

Grace balked at the sight of his florid, pockmarked features, the spittle spraying liberally from between flaccid jowls and broken black teeth. Miles felt her fear. He contained the quivers which shook her slight frame, within his embrace.

"We look for somewhere to break our journey," said Miles, he did not care to mention Wildewood. "The lady is unwell and the pony is lame." He tightened his arm around Grace's shoulders and prayed she would not betray him. To his surprise and relief she executed a perfect swoon and buried her face in his chest with a dramatic gasp. "We must seek shelter," he added and he turned and lifted Grace onto the back of his horse. "If you will excuse us, we will take our leave." He swung up behind her and taking the pony's reins from Edmund he gestured at him to follow on foot.

"But surely you do not expect that I would leave you out here at the mercy of the weather and the lawless. No, Sir..." said the sheriff with a glint in his eye, "my men and I will escort you and your good lady to The Wedder Inn. William Craig will have room, no doubt."

He called to one of his men to make room for the boy on the back of his horse and Edmund glanced quickly at Miles. Miles gave the slightest incline of his head. By necessity they were obliged to accept the sheriff's offer.

"What's happening?" whispered Grace. "Where are we going now?" She clutched the front of the saddle and for once did not resist as he tightened his grip around her waist. He turned the horse away from the sheriff and scanned the accompanying men quickly. Too many to fight and he had not the horse power to flee. He swallowed his unease, unwilling to reveal just how rattled he was.

"A slight diversion, Mademoiselle, I must ask that you continue this charade," he breathed hoarsely against her ear. "I do not trust the sheriff. We must ensure we do not give him cause to question our account."

"But...but isn't he the law?" Confusion and fear caused her words to stutter. "Shouldn't he be helping us?"

Miles laughed humourlessly. "He acts on behalf of the king but is in the pay of the barons. He upholds his own laws, those that bring the greatest reward."

"You know him?" She sounded appalled and Miles winced. He knew far greater monsters than this and recalled occasions when he'd behaved almost as badly.

"I know the likes of him but I do not know this man personally, and that is in our favour."

"Why?"

Miles smiled sourly "Because he is a collector of bodies and I have no desire to add to his collection."

Miles had little inclination to visit The Wedder Inn either. It would take them in the opposite direction from Wildewood and they were frustratingly close. However, he would rather that, than have the sheriff follow him home. He did not need the man's attention and didn't enjoy the man's obvious interest in Grace.

He was equally puzzled by the sheriff's lack of interest or knowledge in the missing nun from Kirk Knowe. He'd expected to be questioned and been prepared to feign ignorance. Perhaps the alarm was yet to be raised although that seemed unlikely. They must have missed her by now. He needed to keep her close, particularly at the inn; if they were separated he was unsure what she would do. He'd a lot to lose if she betrayed him, not least the ransom.

The sheriff rode frustratingly close, slowing his horse to keep pace with Miles. "Your good lady is very quiet," he stated slyly. "Is all well?"

"It will be when we are able to rest, sheriff. I fear we slow you down. Pplease feel free to continue your manhunt. We will find the inn ourselves." Miles wanted rid of the man but realised that would not be easy.

"I would not hear of it, Sir," replied the sheriff. He smirked and Miles held his gaze coolly. Something was afoot but caught up as he was with the mystery of the girl's identity he couldn't decide whether the interest of the odious sheriff was mere coincidence or more likely connected. He was certain of one thing. He couldn't afford to let Grace out of his sight at the inn. If the sheriff were to catch her on her own he would be unable to guarantee her story or her safety.

A shout came then from one of the men who stood in his stirrups and pointed north where the moor rose again. Riders could be seen in the far distance heading away from them. The remaining Scots raiding party no doubt and the sheriff glanced quickly from the Scots quarry to Grace, shrouded beneath her cloak, sheltered against Miles chest. His face was a torment of indecision and intrigue and it gave Miles a measure of power to know that the man's greed would naturally have him follow the bounty hanging on each Scottish head.

"If you are sure you do not need our escort then we will resume our chase," said the sheriff. "Perhaps we will meet at the inn?" He studied Miles for a moment, as if about to make further comment. Then he hauled the horse around with a cruel hand and headed north. He had Scots to kill.

Edmund was dumped unceremoniously onto the snowy ground, and with a curt nod, the hunting party were off at a gallop. Miles watched them go, waited until they were out of sight then dismounted and hoisted Edmund up in front of Grace. He passed the reins of his horse to Edmund, gathered up the reins of the pony and headed for Wildewood. When they reached the point where they had first encountered the sheriff he stopped and gestured for Edmund to dismount, he had walked far enough. It was time for the boy to stretch his legs.

"We will ride ahead, you will follow on foot with the pony. She must be allowed to take her time or the lameness will be prolonged." Edmund nodded, his disappointment at being left behind, and his anxiety regarding the sheriff, clearly evident in his pinched face.

"How far must I walk before I reach Wildewood?" he asked.

Miles took him by his shoulders and pointed him west, towards the tree line of a great forest which cloaked the hill before them. He pointed then at a dark shape which could barely be made out, peeping above the canopy.

"Do you see that, Edmund? There amongst the trees, do you see the stone of the tower?"

"Yes, my lord."

"That is Wildewood, Edmund, my home, and yours too now. Our trail will be easy to follow through the snow."

"And what of yon beasts in the wood?" asked Edmund anxiously.

Miles smiled. "I will ask them to let you pass safely."

He swung himself up behind Grace without comment, nodded once more to Edmund then kicked the horse into a canter. Despite the earlier altercation with Grace and the strange encounter with the sheriff, he was exhilarated. That glimpse of Wildewood had set his heart racing, it had been so long since he'd last seen it, and even the forest seemed more impenetrable. He wondered what he would find.

Grace clung onto the front of the saddle as Miles urged the horse faster through the snow. The horse seemed to have caught Miles' mood, picking up its pace and covering the distance to the tree line in long fluid strides. Soon they were in the forest with the trees closing in around them. Miles felt her alarm as she braced against him and for once he could understand where it came from. There was a sense of mystery and unease in the darkness between the trees. He slowed the horse and picked his way carefully.

"Where is the path?" she asked eventually as it appeared Miles was riding into nowhere.

It was the first time she'd spoken since leaving the sheriff and he guessed the words had slipped out accidently. He knew women; they could maintain a silence longer than any man for reasons known only to them. He smiled to himself. She had chosen to remain with him, despite her opportunity to escape. To be fair it wasn't much of a choice and

57

she'd obviously been influenced in his favour by the sight of the dead men, but he doubted the basis for her choice would be that straightforward.

"The path is right here, you just have to know where it is." He tightened his grip on her waist and felt her wriggle against him stubbornly. He tightened it further. He could be just as stubborn. As they broke through the trees into a large clearing he pulled the horse up sharply and paused to gaze at the place where he had spent his childhood; the place which held many happy memories and where he had first formulated his plans for revenge.

Chapter Eleven

Beyond the expanse of snow-covered parkland, Grace saw her first glimpse of Wildewood. Set against a background of impenetrable forest, the building was constructed from mellow cheviot stone and to Grace's untutored eye, it best resembled a small castle or fortified house. A castellated tower stood to the western end of the building. At the centre of a high retaining wall a stout pair of wooden gates led to an inner courtyard. The gates were ajar hanging unevenly on massive, rusted hinges. Ivy cloaked the outer walls halfway up to the stone slab roof. Some of the straw thatch on the smaller, adjoining buildings had fallen in and young trees were beginning to push their way through. An air of neglect enshrouded the entire place.

Miles urged the horse onward walking him slowly through the entrance and into the courtyard. Metal horse shoes sparked against the weathered cobbles, echoing coldly around the empty space. The place was deserted, had been for many years. Lichen hung eerily from the gnarled branches of trees and clung to the stonework as if in a bid to camouflage the place from the outside world. Miles slid from the horse and lifted Grace down. He remained silent and Grace saw the look of desolation on his face. She wondered what he'd expected. Perhaps he'd left family here and they'd perished in his absence. She reached out, despite herself, laid her hand on his arm and for a long moment he simply looked at her hand before blinking and pulling away.

"Did something happen here, to your family?"

"Yes, something happened to my family," he answered stonily, as he turned and walked away. The horse trailed after him, reins dangling.

No one came running to greet them. There were no welcoming noises from the buildings and no smoke from the chimneys, not even a barking dog or clucking chicken. Perhaps she'd made the wrong choice after all. Perhaps she should have thrown herself on the mercy of the sheriff. Miles had made it quite clear that all he was interested in was a ransom which she knew would not be paid. What would happen, she wondered when he realised she was worth nothing? She waited a moment in the snow, cold and hesitant but when he failed to return she made her way with difficulty up the stone steps leading to the first floor entrance and the heavy, oak door which led into the main building.

Stepping out of the brightness into the inner gloom, she paused awhile, waiting for her eyes to adjust. As they did, she realised she stood within a great hall, an oversized carved stone fireplace at one end and a stone staircase at the other. Massive oak beams held up the roof and mouldy straw covered the floor. She heard rustling and saw movement within the litter. The place smelled of decay and damp and the droppings of vermin living within the debris. She wrinkled her nose and tried not to inhale too deeply as she limped to the centre of the hall. Turning in a slow circle, she took in the sad spectacle before her. Tapestries depicting hunting scenes hung from the walls. Once vibrant with colour, they were shabby and drab, nibbled by rodents, their threads hung like sinister cobwebs. Near the fireplace a plain wooden table had been tipped over and a bench lay smashed.

Grace righted a chair which had once been placed to benefit from the warmth of the fire, and as she did her fingers found the delicate carving on the seat back. Flowers and fruits graced the mellow wood. A lady's chair. She crossed to the fireplace, taller than her, and could just make out letters carved in the stone, although she couldn't decipher their elaborate script. A basket lay upturned on the hearth; she imagined the soft, white wool of an orphan lamb. This had been a family home and something had happened to destroy it. She felt a great sadness overwhelm her and the unease in her belly grew.

This was no dream.

She glanced at the stairs but doubted her ability to climb yet another flight unaided. Her leg throbbed, a reminder of the strange circumstances which had brought her here. Weak sunlight tried valiantly to enter through a number of tall, leaded windows set high in the walls. Although glazed with coloured glass, the tints were muted with grime and allowed little heat from the sun to enter. The room was cold and unwelcoming. They would need a fire and Miles was nowhere to be seen.

She could attempt an escape while he was otherwise engaged or she could make herself useful. With a shrug, she chose the latter, picked up an armful of wood from the shattered bench and slowly deposited it in the empty hearth before casting about for some dry straw to help the fire catch. With difficulty she knelt on her good knee and arranged the wood and straw in a pyramid stack and then she rose and patted her pockets until she found the box of matches which she knew were there. She struck the match, set the straw alight and carefully pocketed the box. The straw caused smoke and Grace had a moment of doubt when she wondered at the state of the flue, but then the wood took hold and the fire drew as it should and the smoke went up the great chimney.

She looked about again. The straw was definitely alive and she didn't care much for sharing her living space with vermin. Fly would have some fun when he was let loose in here she thought with a smile, but he wasn't here yet and she felt the need to clear a safe area around the fire. Picking up another length of wood from the broken bench she used it as a makeshift broom to sweep away the straw from the area adjacent to the fire. Beneath the straw the floor was flagged with stone and although it was grimy, she could see that clean it would be beautiful.

She limped over to the table and with great difficulty dragged it to her cleared area. It was too heavy for her to right by herself.

"What are you doing?" Miles stood in the doorway. His eyes flashed from her, to the fire crackling in the hearth and the swept floor.

Grace turned and wiped the sweat and grime from her face with her sleeve. "Helping."

"I thought you wanted to go home?" He watched her moodily and she was suddenly uncertain.

"I do," replied Grace, pushing all thoughts of bad things to the back of her mind. "But I need to keep warm in the meantime."

He stepped towards her and she took a hesitant step back.

"Why did you not request help from the sheriff?"

"Because you told me not to." She edged back further until she felt the upturned table at her back.

"And of course you always do as you're told," replied Miles with a raised brow.

"You threatened me." Grace's indignation at the recollection was muted by caution. "You said if I valued my life I should say nothing."

"I did not threaten you, Mademoiselle, I merely warned you. You saw the bodies?"

"Of course I saw the bodies." How could she have missed them? Real bodies with blood and gore.

"You made the right choice."

"For whom?"

"For both of us." Miles crossed to where she stood, heaved the table upright and set the remaining chairs against it. "Where did you find the flint to start the fire?"

Flint? Grace stared at him as her hand closed around the matches in her pocket. She opened her mouth to respond but couldn't find anything sensible to say. Everything that had occurred since he'd revealed they were in the midst of medieval Northumberland seemed to prove his account. Crazy or not, she thought it wise to play along and pushed the matches to the bottom of her pocket. She caught his eye, briefly wondering if he could tell she was hiding something. He raised a brow questioningly and she guessed he probably could, but was content he would never guess why. They held each other's gaze and Grace waited for Miles to speak first. It took a few moments.

"You have no reason to fear me."

"I don't," she lied.

"I have no wish to hurt you. You must understand that. But I need the ransom. Look around, this place has been badly neglected in my absence. I suspect the rest of the demesne will be in a similar state."

"But do you not see? I can't get you the ransom. I've already told you, I don't know the bishop I don't know anybody here." Grace's voice was laced with frustration, why did he not believe her?

Miles shrugged as if she hadn't spoken. He cast his gaze to the stairs. "There are bedchambers above. My mother enjoyed her privacy."

She eyed him suspiciously. "How nice," she replied sarcastically as she shifted her weight from one leg to the other.

"Does the wound continue to cause pain?"

"A little, but I'm fine."

"You mean okay?" added Miles with a weary smile.

Grace wished she'd never asked Edmund about him, wished even more that Edmund had not mentioned about the bad things. Here he was trying to be pleasant and all she could think about was just how bad, he might be. She wasn't sure what was worse knowing what someone was capable of, like the sheriff and his bodies, or imagining the worst when you didn't know the truth.

She tried a different tack. "Look, I'm sorry about your family, I guess you were expecting this place to look better, but it won't take much to clean it up. Don't be disheartened."

"Why do you care about this?" He gestured with a sweep of his arm to the dishevelled hall. "I'm holding you against your will, I'm going to sell your hide for ransom, and yet..."

Grace shrugged. "You took care of me. I suppose if you hadn't I would be lying dead in the bog. I should be grateful, although I've no doubt you and your bow probably put me in the bog in the first place, but hey, I think I can do a bit of tidying up for you in return. So, are you going to show me the upstairs? I could do with some privacy."

He took her arm and she clung onto his soft woollen sleeve as they mounted the stairs. It was difficult, with only one good leg, trying to climb stone steps which were much steeper than she was used to. He slowed to her pace. He could have carried her more easily. She half-expected him to sweep her up impatiently but he seemed happy to let her be the martyr, and of course she would. She would not ask for his help.

There were two large rooms upstairs connected by a narrow passageway. It appeared that it had been created at a later date, perhaps in deference to the lady of the house and her desire for privacy. Grace considered that given the choice, she too, would not wish to share her accommodation within scent of beasts housed in the byre beneath the main hall. Along its length a series of small arched windows looked out over the courtyard. At the end of the passage a leaded bay window overlooked a walled garden. The first room they entered was gloomy and cold and Miles set about making a fire in the small stone fireplace. Grace noted how easily he struck the flint to create the flame, knew she would never have managed without the matches.

He turned to assess her slowly, seemed about to begin a conversation before giving a slight dismissive shrug. "Stay here until I've inspected the remainder of the property."

Unable to descend the stairs without help, Grace had no alternative other than to stay put. She did just that; not because he'd told her to, but simply because she had seen enough.

It was time to work out what had happened.

The room contained a large wooden bed with dusty drapes and a carved wooden chest under a window set so high in the wall that Grace would have had to climb on the chest to look out. She stripped the grubby linen off the bed and laid the cloak which Miles had wrapped around her on their journey, over the lumpy mattress. She needed to heat some water, and she needed a bath. She needed many things but top of the list was the need to get home. She lay down on the bed, worn out with the journey and the never ending confusion. Perhaps she would close her eyes just for a short while. Once refreshed everything might become clear.

She dreamt of the exhibition, her first, and of Will who helped organise it. Wonderful Will who had been so helpful, so encouraging, filled with belief in her talent. A rare find, he'd called her, a natural artist on a par with the early ecclesiastical painters. He'd made her feel like a star and she'd revelled in it. How easily she'd been seduced by this talk of greatness, of being special, unique and how easily he persuaded her to show how her talent compared against those great works. How easily that work would sell, he convinced her. It was her duty really, not everyone could afford something as rare as a medieval image, but hers were so convincing they would be a welcome substitute.

Not a forgery, never a forgery, she would never have agreed to that. Her work was her own. But the authorities were not quite so understanding and with her unique portrait of Edward Longshanks, identical in every brush stroke to the original, she was left with no defence. She'd chosen the one painting that stood alone from the usual flat two dimensional works of the period. She'd chosen a painting that at the time of its creation would have appeared scandalous, heretic even.

It had called to her in the strangest of ways and the image of the man beneath the crown, the father and husband, had empowered her to produce her greatest work with uncanny ease. Her career in the art world was shattered along with her trust in mankind. She had seen the smug look on Will's face when he'd left her to face the music. She'd crawled back to the home that had been hers since the death of her parents and grandparents. And she'd lived in that empty house, just her, the dog and a handful of chickens, until Fly had brought her here.

Chapter Twelve

She woke with a start, her cheeks wet with tears. The room was in near darkness with only the meagre firelight and one small candle struggling to illuminate the shadows. She watched the flickering light dance on the stone walls and took a moment to work out where she was. How strange this was, when she slept she dreamt of the real world and when she woke she was living a dream. Perhaps this was the real world after all? Maybe everything that had happened to ruin her life was merely a nightmare and she had finally woken from it.

She became aware of Edmund hovering at the open door and realised she'd been woken by knocking.

"My lady, we have food ready for yer to eat in the hall. May I escort yer?"

Grace swung her feet carefully off the bed and tested her leg gingerly. She was cold and starving and would have hopped down the stairs on one leg if necessary. "Thank you, Edmund, I could eat a horse!"

Someone had been busy in the hall Grace noted as she carefully descended the stairs, one hand securely gripping Edmund's surprisingly strong arm. It had been swept of the foul smelling straw and the table was lit with candles and set with bowls and a large dish of roasted meat. The fire was well alight and stacked with logs which burned far better and gave out more heat than the broken furniture of her earlier effort. The hall looked more welcoming than when she'd first seen it. A scent of pine logs and wood smoke filled the air, it reminded her of village winters when the fires were lit as soon as the sun's meagre warmth began to wain. She immediately felt homesick.

Miles rose from his seat at the table as she approached, pulling out a chair for her to sit. She avoided eye contact with him. His attempt at civility left her feeling awkward, as if they hadn't just spent the last two days in varying degrees of hostility. She took her seat hesitantly. She felt grubby, her hair hung in greasy strands and she was aware of an unpleasant pungency. She would never have sat down to eat in such a state if she were at home. She would have bathed in a bubble bath up to her chin, then dressed in pyjamas and snuggled up with Fly on the sofa in front of the fire.

She cleared her throat. "I need to bathe, is that possible?"

Miles indicated with a slight nod of his head, a bowl of clean water and a cloth next to her on the table and Grace raised one brow questioningly.

"I was hoping for something a little larger?"

"For your hands, Mademoiselle," replied Miles as he appraised her lazily. She wished he would stop. She wasn't vain by any stretch of the imagination, but she was a woman and bedraggled to say the least. "I'll bring something more adequate to your chamber later," he added slyly.

She shot him an appraising look of her own. Two could play at that game, and quite frankly both he and the boy fairly reeked.

"Thank you. Don't forget to keep some hot water for yourself. You know what they say: cleanliness is next to Godliness." He narrowed his eyes and she realised with a sickening jolt that maybe it wasn't wise to poke a stick at the tiger. "You don't need to carry water upstairs, down here will do," offered Grace in an attempt to recover some ground. "Just find me a tub and I'll happily splash in it." His grin widened and she marvelled at her own capacity for digging a hole and jumping in headfirst.

Miles glanced at Edmund who was paying far too much attention, his eyes flicking from one to the other as he followed the conversation.

"An interesting thought, Mademoiselle, however I would venture your chamber to be a more appropriate venue. He turned back to the boy. "Did you hear that, Edmund? We offend this fine lady with our stink." His smirk widened as Grace reddened awkwardly. That hole was getting deeper.

"That isn't what I said. I simply meant we'd all feel refreshed and fragrant after our long journey."

"And fragrant skin is naturally more appealing?" The amusement was clear now as he cocked his head and led her on, a lamb to the slaughter.

"Well, yes, of course."

"Yes, I would agree, Mademoiselle. When I lower my head, skim my lips across a woman's flesh and breathe the scent of freshly washed, pink and glowing skin, fragrance definitely encourages a...positive response."

She gaped at him, prepared to fling herself headlong into the bottomless pit she'd created. The arrogant twitch of his scarred brow saved her just in time and pulled her back from the abyss.

"So, as I was saying, yes, you stink and you've as much chance of a positive response as you have of securing a ransom."

Miles sat back with a snort of laughter, and Grace rinsed her grubby hands in the warm water and tried to ignore him.

"You think I won't secure a ransom?" he asked.

"I know you won't."

"And why are you so certain?"

"Because, I'm not who you think I am."

"Indeed." He sobered and studied her across the table. "Perhaps we should have a wager."

"Perhaps we shouldn't."

"Afraid you'll lose?"

Grace looked up at him then, and fixed him with narrowed eyes. "No, afraid you'll cheat."

He spread his arms wide, gave a self-depreciating shrug "I'm a knight of the realm, you can trust me."

"If you're so chivalrous, why didn't you take me straight home when I asked?"

"I didn't say I was chivalrous. I said I was trustworthy. If I say that I'll do something, then you can wager your life I will."

"And what are you going to do with me?"

He smiled and she caught the hint of something as it flashed in his eyes.

"Sell you to the highest bidder of course. I reckon you'll be worth a purse or two, fragrant or not. But in the meantime" he raised a cup in her direction, "I forget my manners, would you care for a little mead?" he asked. "It's been maturing during my absence. It may be a little strong for your tender palate."

Grace took the proffered wooden cup and against her better judgement, took a sip. It was strong and she was not much of a drinker but there was challenge in Miles' eye so she took another larger swallow and passed the mug back.

"Did you rest well?" he asked, as if he knew she had not. Grace wondered if he'd come to her room while she'd relived her nightmare.

"Not really," Grace replied truthfully, "I was dreaming of another place." She dried her hands on the square of cloth and helped herself to the food on the table filling her plate with as much as she could take without appearing greedy. The meat was identifiable only as a fowl of some sort, possibly pigeon by its size and there were a number on the platter. She glanced at Edmund who had taken a whole bird and followed suit. The nausea which had plagued her had finally lifted and it left her with a painful, empty stomach which she needed to fill. In the absence of cutlery she was unwilling to produce Edmund's knife from her pocket, so she picked at the meat and vegetables daintily with her fingers and licked the thin gravy from her fingers. Miles settled back in his seat and watched her.

"Another place, Kirk Knowe?" he asked as he passed the mug back and Grace wiped her mouth with the back of her hand and took another sip between bites.

"No. Just somewhere with bad memories," She wondered what Miles would make of the truth, if she ever got around to telling it. She chewed slowly and gazed into the fire. She was warm for the first time in days and there was something about an open fire that was comforting. Despite having just woken she was still weary and stifled a yawn.

"Was your father the gardener at Kirk Knowe?" asked Miles, taking the mug back from Grace and filling it from a pewter jug before taking his fill.

She reluctantly drew her gaze from the flames. Of course he had assumed her father's trade, because her name was Gardner.

"No my father was a teacher. He taught music at an academy in London. He was a talented violinist, you know, fiddler?" She mimed the action of fiddle and bow and ignored his blank look." He played in concerts. My mother was an artist a free spirit, rather like me really." She thought of them wistfully, hadn't really thought of them for some time. They had been gone so long and her memories were those of a child. She pulled at her fringe and twisted the ends between her fingers. It had been one of her childhood habits. Her mother had scolded her, warned her she would wake up one morning with no hair if she continued.

Miles studied her and poured another drink. "Why did they give you to the church? Surely you would have made a good marriage match, or did they have one too many daughters?" The mead was loosening her tongue, and he pressed another into her hand.

Grace smiled. She would have to put him straight. The whole situation was getting far too bizarre and the mead didn't help. She enjoyed it a little too much. Perhaps if she just came out and told him the truth they could sort out the mess she'd found herself in. Of course telling the truth wasn't the issue - having him believe it would be the problem...a time portal, a doorway, a passage to the past? She didn't quite believe it herself.

"No, they had only one child, although I always wanted a little brother." She glanced wistfully at Edmund. "They were killed in a fire at a concert hall when I was ten and I was brought up by my grandparents at Kirk Knowe." She paused to look at him. "I don't know who or what you think I am, but I'm certainly not a nun. No one is going to pay ransom for me. In fact there is no one here who would even care whether I exist or not. You may as well take me back to where you found me and let me go. I'm not worth anything to you." Or anyone else she added silently, and wasn't that the truth.

If she was expecting some blinding flash or whirlwind which would miraculously catapult her back to where she'd come from, she was disappointed. Neither did she find herself back in the forest with a bump on the head, or waking up in her own bed in her cottage. She was still in the great hall sat at the wooden table in front of the fire with Miles at one end and a slumbering Edmund at the other.

Miles took back the mug. She had recklessly drained the contents and he filled it once more. The mead was having an effect on him too. She could see it in his eyes; that mellow self-contentment and just a hint of wickedness. Perhaps her revelations had not come as an entire surprise, she did not behave as nun should, but if he accepted she were not a lost nun, then he must be wondering at her real identity. She watched as he toyed with his knife, slowly running his finger and thumb up and down the flat of the blade.

"So no one knows where you are and there is no one to care if they did. One must assume therefore that there is also no one to object if I decide to forgo the ransom and keep you for myself." He leaned towards her. "Or slit your throat and be done with you here and now." He blinked slowly and watched her.

"What!"

"Then again" he added with a slow smile, "you're not worth anything dead."

"Thank you, that's reassuring." She wasn't convinced. He had unnerved her, again. She took another drink and tried to consider her options, which was increasingly difficult as her options were limited and her ability to consider them impeded by the mead. She twiddled with her hair and attempted to concentrate her thoughts.

"There is more to you than meets the eye, I'll give you that." said Miles. "You may not think you're worth anything alive or dead, but fate crossed our paths and I'm a great believer in fate. I think you'll be worth a great deal to me, so no, I'm afraid you will not be returned to Kirk Knowe immediately. We will await the bishop's decision. If I am to believe the account of your father, then he will be known by many and your value will be even greater."

Grace shook her head. What on earth was she meant to do, to make all this go away? She drew a large breath. "But what about what I want? Why does no one care what I want? You can't just sell me. I'm a person - I have rights!" she declared as she struggled to rise from her seat. She'd had enough of his company. She was going to bed. She would worry about her rights and how to enforce them in the morning.

Miles caught her arm and steadied her. "That was perhaps a little reckless, my lady." he observed calmly as she swayed a little in his arms.

"I'm not a Lady," she hiccupped.

"Indeed."

"Don't you approve of women who speak their mind?" she tried to wriggle free and he restrained her with ease.

He shrugged. "You may speak as you see fit, Mademoiselle, however drinking to excess when you're patently not used to it, I would not recommend."

Grace pushed at his chest and with each prod she would have toppled if he hadn't held her fast. "Oh yes, well how on earth would I be used to ten year old mead when where I come from people don't drink mead, they drink ...." she struggled to string her words together, "cocktails? They're fun. Not that I can drink many of those either." She hiccupped and tried unsuccessfully to suppress a giggle with a hand over her mouth.

"And where do you come from, Grace?" asked Miles, amusement playing around his mouth.

"Well, Mr Miles de Know-it-all, that's for me to know and you to find out!"

"Are you throwing down a challenge, my lady?"

Grace hiccupped again. "Of course, but you'll never win." She slid back onto her seat, her head dropped to the table with a thud and Miles reached over her prone body and refilled the mug.

"One thing you should know, Mademoiselle, is that I never lose."

Chapter Thirteen

Grace didn't wake until morning and discovered someone had carried her to bed. She still wore her stinking clothes and the fire still flickered in the grate, though the room felt far from warm.

She lay for a long while, unmoving. Her head pounded. She regretted the mead. How had she allowed herself to end up with a hangover? Pulling herself into a sitting position she wrapped the cloak more tightly around her shoulders. She felt nauseous and dizzy again but tried to ignore it. This was Miles' fault; he should never have allowed her to drink so much. She was in his care and he was meant to be chivalrous. Some knight he was turning out to be.

Mind over matter, that's what was needed here. She studied the room, the way the weak sunlight danced with dust motes and illuminated the grimy walls and leaf strewn floor. Casting her eye to the stout planked door, she noted the heavy metal work hinges and latch. She wondered if he had turned the key and what she would do if he hadn't.

Under the high window lay the wooden chest she noticed the previous day. Rising slowly from the bed, she waited for the room to stop spinning and steadied herself before padding in stocking feet across the planked floor. She wondered absently where her boots had gone and who had removed them. The chest had been carved with the same intricate pattern as the chair in the hall. She ran her fingers gently along its surface and then gripped the edge and lifted the lid.

The smell of lavender caught her by surprise, and reaching inside, she discovered gowns of the finest fabrics stored carefully between layers of linen. The lavender scent emanated from bundles of dried flower heads placed carefully within the layers.

She carefully lifted out the nearest gown and held the garment against her cheek, the scent of lavender was still fresh. Returning to the bed she sat at its centre cross legged, the gown draped across her knees.

This was no dream, these things were real. Miles was flesh and blood, the wound on her leg actually hurt, and the tale Edmund told of the crusades had actually happened. She couldn't have made it up. She didn't possess enough historical knowledge for one thing, but there was only one other alternative and Grace was certain that it couldn't be possible.

Had she really stepped into the woods in 2012 and come out in 1275?

If it were true, she needed to get back immediately. Fear began to whisper down her spine. What if she couldn't get back? No one would believe her. They'd think she was crazy, or worse, a witch. Perhaps she'd already given too much away. She'd gotten drunk last night and couldn't remember much other than Miles' announcement that he was going to sell her to the bishop. She couldn't let that happen. Bloody hell, did they have the inquisition in the 13th century?

She had to leave before things went terribly wrong. Glancing thoughtfully at the gown again, she began to formulate a plan. Until she could make her escape it was imperative that no one suspected there was anything odd about her. That might prove difficult, she conceded, as she was considered odd by almost everyone she knew.

A commotion outside on the stairs interrupted her thoughts and she hurriedly covered the gown with the cloak. The door burst open, without so much as a knock, and in through the doorway bustled a rotund woman trailing a buxom young girl behind her. Both were carrying large ewers. Behind them in comic cavalcade came an elderly man with a grey beard and hooked nose and a man of similar age to the woman, wearing a patch over one eye. Between them they carried a large wooden tub, and as they held it upside down and over their heads, they had bumped their way up the stairs and through her door unable to see where they were going. Edmund followed with a slightly sheepish expression and a further ewer. Straggling behind at the end of the procession was, Fly, tail wagging, tongue lolling.

The woman set down her burden and clapped her hands together sharply.

"Get a move on yer want-wits. The mistress is askin' fer her bath and there's not enough water here to bathe a babe." The entourage deposited the tub in front of the fire and the ewers were emptied into it, with much splashing and sloshing. With the task complete, they scurried from the room.

"My name is Martha, mistress," said the woman who tipped a nod at Grace. Grace gazed open-mouthed. This was definitely not an invention. The dog jumped onto the bed alongside her and she drew him close.

"We all returned, yer see, when we heard Sir Miles was back."

Sir Miles? "Returned?"

"I'm the cook, housekeeper and nurse to Sir Miles when he was a babe and now I'm back and I'll look after yer, mistress. Just you tell me what ye need. The boy Edmund tells me you've had a run of bad luck, but you'll be just fine here, don't yer worry. Me and my husband Tom Pandy, that's him with the one eye - he lost it in a fight over his name, daft lummock, but that's another story…" She drew a breath. "Me and Tom will put this place to rights, just ye wait and see, and my granddaughter Belle, she's a good girl, mistress. She'll make a fine ladies maid."

Grace, was about to introduce herself when the cavalcade reappeared all carrying extra ewers of hot water which they added to the tub.

"One more round should do it," announced Martha and she shooed the others out of the chamber.

"Where is Miles?" Grace asked.

"Well, if he's got any sense, mistress, he'll be cleaning himself up, same as ye." She lowered her voice. "Though between ye and me, I'd say he looked slightly worse for wear when I seen him this mornin'."

Grace smiled. So she wasn't the only one with a thick head. She decided she liked this woman and her indiscretion. "I'm very pleased to meet you. Thank you for organising my bath."

"Martha, mistress, call me Martha, that's me name." She giggled and her whole body rippled rather alarmingly. Grace bit the inside of her mouth to prevent her own laughter.

"Well, Martha, in that case, you must call me Grace."

"No me dear, that would never do," Martha exclaimed. The water carriers were back and she ushered them about their business. "Do yer need me help, mistress?" she asked when the others had finally gone.

"No thank you, Martha." She was certainly capable of bathing herself. "Please close the door on your way out."

She waited until she could no longer hear them before crossing to the tub and testing the water with her fingers. It was deliciously hot. She ran to the chest and took out one of the lavender bundles - she was sure whoever they belonged to could spare one - then she stripped off her filthy clothes and stepped into the tub.

Her leg was surprisingly pain-free in the water, though the wound was not pretty and Grace hoped the scar would fade as it healed. She twisted her leg as best she could to see the wound at the back and acknowledged begrudgingly that Miles had indeed saved her life. If he had not brought her with him, she would have died.

By then, she realised, she was already on the other side of whatever strange gateway she had passed through and no one from her life would have been able to find her. She had to get back as soon as possible.

Finally clean, she picked up the russet gown and debated whether she should dare borrow it. It was either that or spend the entire day clothed in the sheet. She made a decision and slipped the gown over her head. It felt soft and gentle against her bare skin. She was surprised that it fitted and relieved at its length, as she couldn't risk a gust of wind revealing that she had found no underclothes in the chest.

There was no mirror in the room so she smoothed down her hair again and looked about for her boots. She couldn't run around barefoot in a freezing castle. She found them under the bed. Perhaps she'd kicked them off in the night or maybe Miles had removed them when he'd put her to bed?

Tucking Fly under one arm, she descended to the great hall carefully, conscious her leg was not fully healed and the stairs had no hand rail. Concentrating entirely on where she placed her feet, she didn't notice until she'd reached the ground floor that the hall was occupied. Miles sat at the table in front of the fire, deep in discussion with a tall, thin man with a shock of red hair, who was folded uncomfortably into a chair that was far too small for his frame. She was minded of a stick insect she'd kept as a pet as a child. At his feet a small boy with sallow skin and tight dark curls played happily with a carved wooden animal. Martha was correct - Miles had cleaned up. He'd also changed his clothes. Watching him, Grace thought he looked every bit the feudal lord and just a little tempting.

As she paused at the bottom of the stairs, the little boy looked up. His eyes sparkled when he spotted Fly, who wagged his tail furiously in welcome. Drawing the child's attention, she lowered Fly to the floor and beckoned him over. He ducked his head, giggling, as Fly tried to lick his face. Taking his hand she walked him back across the room to where the two men sat.

* * *

Miles watched her progress across the room, freshly scrubbed and pink-cheeked. Was this really the scrawny scrap he'd pulled from the woodland bog? To say she was beautiful was not entirely true. He'd known many beautiful women and, in fact, that was entirely the wrong word to describe her.

No, she wasn't a standard beauty. Her hair, though the colour of spun gold and fine as a babe's, was streaked with a peculiar shade of pink. Perhaps she'd unwisely strayed next to the dyers vat. It was worn far too short and had a mind of its own, sticking up where it shouldn't. In fact she was altogether too short with a quirky stubborn look, no acquiescence there, no willing compliance. And yet the gown, though a little long, fitted her body in all the right places, the colour brought out the golden streaks in her hair, and played down the pink, and despite the unlikely pairing of beautiful gown and muddy boots, she looked just right.

Miles swallowed and the giant who sat next to him said something which caused Miles to smile and shake his head in denial. He rose and stepped around the table to take Grace's hand which he brought to his lips. Grace tried to pull her hand back but he simply smiled and breathed against her skin so his companion could not hear.

"Humour me. I'm bewitched by your transformation, my lady." He held her at arm's length and turned her round. "You transform particularly well."

Grace smiled sweetly. "As do you, my liege."

Miles narrowed his eyes, immediately alert. There was something different about her other than her attire. Was she up to something? Was he to withstand another of her outbursts? Was the ransom really worth the effort?

"Let me introduce you to a good friend of mine, John the Mason. John is a master of the stone and has agreed to help me renovate the estate." He gestured to the child. "This is Linus Meek, his son."

"Meek?"

"Meek and mild," offered Miles by way of explanation.

Grace turned her attention from the tiny child to his father and smiled warmly at the man who now rose before her.

"My lady, I am pleased to be at your service. Linus will be honoured to know you."

"I'm very glad to meet you and your son, John. He's a delightful child." She ruffled the boy's curls and he smiled shyly and gripped his father's leg. "Edmund will also be delighted to meet you. His father was a mason too. He worked on Lincoln Cathedral. I'm sure he'd love to talk to you."

"Of course, my lady." The huge man tipped his head again. "I will speak with the lad."

"I hope I've the chance to speak with you again before I leave," continued Grace.

"You're leaving?" He glanced at Miles questioningly.

"Just as soon as Miles arranges it."

Miles interceded smoothly. "John, thank you for coming. We'll speak later. If you take Linus to the kitchen, Martha will get you both something to eat and arrange lodgings. Thomas of Blackmore should be with us in a matter of days and then we shall begin." He shook the man's huge hand and the giant hoisted the child on to his broad shoulder. "It has been a long time in the planning, John. I'm sure you're as anxious as I am to see this through."

"Cautious is the word I would use, my lord," replied the giant and with a nod to Grace he took his leave.

Miles returned his attention to Grace and considered her once more. "A word, if you please," he said and Grace smiled sweetly. "For your own safety please do not discuss with others the circumstances of your stay here."

"You mean the fact you kidnapped me and are holding me for ransom?"

"I did not kidnap you, I rescued you."

"Okay, you rescued me, then you kidnapped me and now you're holding me to ransom, yes?"

He sighed; she was off again.

"Why should I not discuss it? Why is it a secret? Are you worried your reputation will be damaged?" She faced him, hands on hips.

The size of her, squaring up to him. He had the urge to wrap his hands around her throat just to silence her noise. He kept his hands by his sides with considerable effort.

"No, I'm concerned, however, that yours might suffer. You will be here for some time before we get a message to the bishop and an answer back. It's safer for you if people think you are under my protection."

"Under your protection? What does that mean? That no one will think to steal me out from under your nose and sell me to the highest bidder?"

Miles sighed impatiently as if she were a small child, slow on the uptake. "There are those who would like nothing better than to thwart any plans I may have to reclaim this demesne. They would think nothing of using you to get at me."

"I see," said Grace slowly. "So they would use me?"

"Yes, exactly."

"And is that not what you're doing?"

Miles cursed under his breath. She was correct, he was using her, but she had no idea of the danger she would be in if she got in to the wrong hands.

"I suppose it depends on your definition of the word 'use'. I will not hurt you. I've already told you that. But others would not be so honourable. Just remember the sheriff and his bodies. Let people believe that you are with me until we decide otherwise."

"With you?" She took a step back and Miles shook his head with exasperation.

"Mademoiselle, you flatter yourself. I admit you look surprisingly tempting this morning and you smell particularly fragrant. Under any other circumstances I could think of far more satisfying things to do with you than argue, but you have the tongue of a harpy. I am worn out with you already."

"Then let me go home. I'll take the pony and be gone before anyone has the chance to use me."

"The pony is lame, do you not remember?"

"Then I'll borrow your horse or you could just take me back yourself." She tried her most winning smile.

He took her face firmly between his palms and looked her directly in the eyes. "No, Grace and that's an end to it."

"Edmund has told me all about you," she continued. "Yes, about the bad things you do."

"Has he indeed?"

He turned on his heels and left her before she could respond and force him to show her the full extent of his badness. She was not going to be an easy captive. She had bewitched Edmund already, and if she continued to charm those in the household, how could he be sure they would keep her safe in the grounds? Only Edmund knew of his purpose for her. He needed to maintain a constant watch if he were to prevent her leaving Wildewood. Unfortunately he had far more important things to do.

Chapter Fourteen

Retracing her steps to her room, Grace crossed to the door in the corner. Instead of the expected cupboard she found a steep set of stone stairs leading both up and down. She wondered where they led. Her curiosity took her upwards.

The stairs were narrow, dark and wound in a tight spiral. She counted the steps and after twenty-two had been trodden and her leg was about to give out, she found a door set in the inner wall. She felt in the dark and found the latch. The door opened with a creak of neglected hinges. The room beyond was surprisingly large, though smaller than her own, and took up the entire floor of the tower in which it was situated. It was furnished simply with a large bed, writing table, and a chair aside a small fireplace. On the back of the door hung a cloak she recognised. This was Miles' room.

There were three windows, one set on each of the walls not containing the chimney. They allowed sunlight to warm the room. She crossed to the bed and ran her fingers gently across the linen, wrinkled where he had slept. She lingered at the writing table where a parchment map was laid open to view. Perhaps this could help in her escape. The chart showed Wildewood and its surroundings, but she recognised nothing. The text was French and the lettering far too ornate to read. She guessed the river must be the Coquet, but as there were no roads drawn she could make no real sense of where she was. She remembered what Edmund had said about the view from the top of the tower. If she could see Scotland in one direction maybe she could work out where she was by the topography - surely that couldn't have changed.

Leaving the room, she closed the door behind her and proceeded up the steps to a smaller door opening out onto the roof of the tower. Although fearful of heights, she had to look. Carefully she made her way to the parapet and surveyed the view. Edmund had been correct - the panorama was indeed magical - and by ensuring she didn't look straight down, she was able to enjoy it without fear. On three sides woods stretched for miles, and beyond them lofty crags taller than the one on which Wildewood was built. To the side where they'd entered the day before, parkland was bounded by a much thinner belt of woods. Beyond that lay the snow-covered moorland they'd crossed with care. Realistically there was only one way in or out. They'd travelled towards the setting sun, so to return she must keep travelling east. There were no other landmarks to be seen.

Could she do that, she wondered, as she left the roof and descended the stairs. Would she have the nerve to set out on her own and cross those moors alone? She'd laughed at the thought of horse-eating bogs, but Miles was correct, the moors were dangerous.

She followed the stairs to the bottom and found a small door which was locked, much to her annoyance. No matter, she thought, as she climbed back up to her own room. She'd have plenty time to discover the secrets of Wildewood. Her leg protested and she rested a while, sitting on her bed. If she were to escape she would have to plan carefully. It had taken them two full days to get here, partly due to the bad weather, but Miles also knew where he was going. It would take her much longer, so she would need warm clothes, supplies and a pony. She also needed to be fully fit if she was on her own at the mercy of the weather.

She would wait one week. She would use that week to ensure she had everything she needed.

* * *

Miles spent the day out on the demesne assessing the state of his holding and visiting the folk who'd stayed loyal through trying times. His shepherd, Berryman, had tended sheep for the last forty years and continued to do so in Miles' absence. So despite the weather and the lack of adequate estate management, he'd retained a small flock due to lamb in the spring. There'd been a problem with rustling, Berryman told him, mainly from over the border, but he'd kept the flock safe by moving them onto the high moor where it was difficult for horse and rider. The cattle had all but gone to rustlers. Martha and Tom had retained a milking cow and calf, and a couple of oxen for pulling the plough, but the main herd had gone and would have to be replaced at market in the spring. The woods however were teeming with deer, according to Tom, and there were fish a plenty upstream, so they would not starve. The kitchen garden was overgrown, and although it could be dug ready for spring, they needed labour to dig and seed to plant.

Miles mentally totted up the cost of restocking the demesne and repairing the buildings. In addition to Wildewood Hall, there were a dozen or more cottages scattered throughout his holding and at least one stone bridge had fallen to winter floods. The folk who worked the land and maintained Wildewood had not been paid since he'd left. The total cost was massive. He shook his head with frustration. Even if he wanted to release Grace, he couldn't afford to. He needed the ransom.

There was no other way. He must send a message to the bishop. He was reluctant nevertheless. He'd told her fate had crossed their paths and he believed in fate. She'd accused him of using her and she was correct, but she really had no idea of just how safe she was here at Wildewood under his protection or what dangers lurked beyond the walls. It made him uncomfortable to think he might be putting her in danger by merely sending the message.

He wondered about her. She claimed she was not of the convent and he was inclined to believe her, if her behaviour was anything to go by. But if she wasn't a nun, who was she? The way she dressed, the way she spoke, were strange. Even the way she behaved towards him wasn't what one would expect. Yes, she'd initially been fearful, and who could blame her when one considered the circumstances under which they'd met, but now she appeared scared of no one and it was her self-confidence that worried him most.

She believed she could manipulate him by using her feminine wiles but she was naive to think it would work. He could see straight through her and as such would not be led along by her little games. But other men, men she might meet on her way to meet the bishop, may not be as self-controlled. He rubbed his palms across his cheeks. He could do without the added responsibility of having to worry about her but she was his responsibility. He had brought her here, after all.

He would give it a week. A week would allow her to calm herself and become more accustomed to her plight. A week would allow him to deliberate on the whole ransom business.

Chapter Fifteen

It was mid-afternoon and the weak sunlight was rapidly diminishing when he finally returned to Wildewood. He cantered across the snow covered parkland and in through the double gates which were closed and bolted behind him by Edmund.

"Where is our guest?" he asked as he dismounted and led his horse to the stables.

Edmund smiled. "In the kitchen garden with the little lad, Linus."

"Doing what? It's thick with snow."

"Go and see for yerself," suggested Edmund. Miles handed him the reins, and headed for the garden. In his mother's day it was a magical place. She'd a way with plants, growing many flowers, fruits and vegetables. He recalled idyllic days as a young child playing hide and seek amongst the plants. He closed his eyes briefly and could still see the beauty of it and smell the aromatic scent of the herb garden. Now, covered with snow, it had a different desolate kind of beauty. He owed it to his mother to bring it back to life.

A movement caught his eye, and there in the centre of the garden was Grace on her knees in the snow. Next to her, bundled up in a thick woollen shawl, was Linus and together they were making a figure out of snow. The figure wore a hat and had stones for eyes. Linus was trying to find more stones and Grace was showing him how to stick them into the soft face to make the figure smile.

Her gown was wet where she knelt in the snow and her fingers red with the cold. The little boy by contrast was pink-faced and snug under his many layers, a picture of happiness. She laughed, unaware he was watching. He approached them slowly, unwilling to spoil the moment.

"Here let me help you." He offered his hand. "You're wet and cold. Time to bring Linus in."

She slipped her hand in his and allowed him to help her to her feet. Her hand was frozen and he could see she held her leg stiffly. Perhaps not the best position for her wound to heal.

"I see you have found a playmate." Miles smiled at the boy who gave Grace an adoring look. Was no one immune to her charms? "Run in to the kitchen and ask Martha to get you something warm to drink. Tell her I said you were to have it."

The child looked to Grace, who nodded, and then he was off running in the clumsy way of a five year old, skidding and almost, but not quite, falling. Miles was unreasonably rattled that the boy sought Grace's permission to leave.

"This was my mother's garden," he said quietly as he considered letting go of her, then thought better of it and tucked her hand under his arm to steady her as they walked. "She liked to grow things, had a gift some would say. I would like to see it brought back to life someday."

"My grandfather was the gardener in our family. The garden at Kirk Knowe is beautiful. He planned everything and every corner was brimming with flowers. Of course the garden is still beautiful, but not the same as when he was there tending it. I think the garden knows he's gone." She glanced at Miles.

"When did your grandfather die?" he asked.

"A couple of years ago," she replied sadly. "When did your mother?"

Miles looked down at her and for a moment was reluctant to answer. "A long time ago. I was merely a boy. I think you're correct about the garden, it knows she's gone."

"It can still be made beautiful," said Grace. "Come the spring, all the new shoots will emerge and you'll see what's left and what needs to be replanted. Maybe you'll have ideas of your own to add to hers. My grandfather told me that's what gardens were all about, changing and evolving. My grandmother changed her mind so many times about what she wanted that in the end he scattered seeds to the wind so they grew where they fell. That way she couldn't blame him if they grew in the wrong place."

"Sensible man," said Miles, as they made their way indoors. "So, your grandfather was a gardener, your father a teacher and musician, and your mother enjoyed the arts. What about you, Grace, did you inherit any of their talents?"

Grace wrinkled her nose thoughtfully for a moment. "I do know a bit about gardening, I was brought up by my grandparents after all, and as for music, I know my way around a few musical instruments. But I don't paint anymore."

"Why not?"

She shrugged and looked away. "No time, I suppose."

Miles caught the delicate flush on her cheeks and said nothing. Twice now he'd caught her in a falsehood. Two lies about trivial things: the first regarding the lighting of the fire; the second about her painting. In his experience, people lied for a reason, usually to hide something. His curiosity was aroused; he would discover the truth eventually.

"Perhaps you can offer some advice with regard to the garden?"

"I won't be here long enough, will I?" replied Grace as they entered the kitchen.

Miles shot her a look. "Remember what I said this morning, Grace," he cautioned.

She sent him a teasing smile. "Oh yes, of course, loose lips. How could I forget?"

Miles shook his head with exasperation. By the end of the week she would have the entire household wrapped around her finger. He couldn't afford to wait a week. He would send the messenger tomorrow.

* * *

That evening Martha cooked wild boar and winter vegetables, and everyone dined together in the great hall. The fire was banked up, and despite the chill outside, the hearth was a warm and inviting place to be. Tom Pandy alternated between the pipes and the rebec, and John surprised Grace when he revealed himself as a master story teller. He held the youngsters spellbound with tales of other worldly creatures and in particular the mythical beast living at the bottom of the ancient Ahlborett Lake. Martha crossed herself at the mention of the beast and Edmund and Belle giggled at her discomfort. Belle sat next to Edmund and had eyes only for him. Miles smiled his approval; far better the lad be kept busy by the likes of Belle than waste his time making doe eyes at Grace.

The mead was free flowing and as the evening wore on the music got more soulful and the youngsters quietened, as first Linus then Edmund and Belle rested their heads on the table and slept. Miles said very little but when the story ended he leaned across and took up the instrument Tom had played earlier and placed it in front of Grace.

"Will you honour us with a tune, Grace?" he asked with a smile. Martha and John added their entreaties while Tom Pandy waited to accompany her. Grace fingered the warm wood of the small stringed instrument gently. She appeared reluctant and Miles wondered whether memories of her father caused her reticence. She glanced at him and he nodded his encouragement.

Picking up the bow, she appeared confused, as if unfamiliar with Tom's handmade rebec. Miles watched with growing interest as she first tried the instrument beneath her chin then settled it more comfortably, as it should be, on her knee and spent a few moments tuning the instrument. She chose to play a simple lilting piece that filled the cavernous space with its haunting purity. Tom soon caught the gist of it and joined in, on the pipes while Martha and John clapped and stamped their feet in time to the music.

Miles listened and watched. Mellow with drink he stretched out his legs, worked the kinks out of his shoulder muscles and relaxed back on his seat. Was there anything she could not do well? His mind began to wander as he pondered on her many talents and he wondered about those he had yet to sample. Imagination was wonderful, but there was no excuse for the real thing.

She finished to applause and returned to her seat, embarrassment at the fuss colouring her cheeks. She was flushed and no doubt thirsty, and despite an earlier vow never to tempt her with alcohol again, Miles produced a flagon of wine, and to his amusement she drank heartily from her goblet. Replacing the empty vessel on the table, she wiped a dribble of liquid from her chin with the back of her hand, and as she did so, their eyes met and what he saw in hers made his resolve falter. She had absolutely no idea how much danger she was in.

They both shared a glance far longer than was polite or decent, and he felt his loins respond as her cheeks pinked under his lazy review. He allowed his gaze to lower and imagine a little more. She should turn away. Could she not see how she tempted him? Did she not understand just how little encouragement would be needed? But she did not, and when his gaze returned to her face, she was still watching.

He leaned forward and took her hand, his eyes never leaving hers, oblivious to the others at the table. John had begun another tale which had Martha and Tom spellbound and they had gathered their chairs against the fire for effect more than warmth, for this tale was of a fiery dragon perched atop the Danestone guarding the valley. Miles and Grace heard none of the story.

"It's late," Grace eventually whispered, when the feel of her palm, and his lustful thoughts had become almost unbearable. He had the urge for her to squeeze more than just his hand, and the act of keeping his fingers still was turning into some hideous torture. This was not good, certainly not part of his plan, and he realised it was suddenly very important not to emit the wrong signals. He was teasing her, testing her and yet he realised it was his own resolve and self-control being tested. He wasn't sure of his ability to maintain control of the situation. He wondered at the power she wielded so innocently and thought again of witches.

"Mm," he murmured as he continued to watch, transfixed. Absently stroking the silken skin of her inner wrist with his thumb, he found himself obsessing about those indigo butterflies. She really was appealing and the more he considered her, the more appealing she became.

"I think I should go to bed now," added Grace breathlessly. The hesitancy in her voice could be taken two ways. He shifted between the two, uncertain whether she wetted her lips with a delicate tongue through fear or anticipation.

"Perhaps you should," replied Miles but he kept hold of her hand and wondered just how far she would play the game, the sound of her soft whisper playing havoc with the few good intentions he had left.

He watched as she swallowed and eventually dragged her eyes from his. He was left wondering who'd been playing who. He didn't even bother to hide the flare of amusement which flashed in his eyes in response to her lowered lashes. Time to admit defeat, he decided. Whether she was playing a game or not was debateable; whether she shared his reaction was not in doubt. The mistake she'd made was in believing she could control what had been started. She was out of her depth and unwittingly dragging him into the murky waters with her. He doubted his ability to save them both. He barely had the resolve to save himself.

He rose from the table with a backward scrape of his chair against the stone flags, slowly bringing her with him and as he did so the slightest tug of his hand brought her up against him. She had to tip back her head to look at him properly and she placed a hand against his chest to keep him at bay. He cocked his head and smiled at her. She was very nearly gone, but not quite...

"Enough," she said so quietly he barely heard, but he did detect the tremble in her voice as she asserted herself, and he narrowed his eyes and smiled to himself. *No, not nearly enough.*

"Good night, my lady," he said with a bow and a smile, and watched as she crossed the hall and hurried up the stairs. No, not nearly enough, but he had all the time in the world and she wasn't going anywhere yet.

"Another drink, my lord?" said John shrewdly.

"Is it that obvious, John?" sighed Miles as he slumped back in the chair.

"Indeed so."

"Then that is my dilemma, John, for I have a fancy I may want her, but I cannot keep her. Similarly, I cannot tolerate the thought that another may take her."

"You mean take her before you?"

"I didn't say that."

"But that is surely what you meant, my lord, and if that is so then what is to stop you. You do not need to keep her in order to take her."

Miles stared after her. John was correct, he was the lord here. He had rights and privileges if he chose to assert them. "And, John, do you consider that to be the honourable thing to do?"

"Since when did honour have anything to do with the cravings of a young lord?"

"You may be right, John. You know me better than any man."

John dipped his head in acknowledgement. "A dilemma indeed for you, my lord, but you will fathom the answer, I have no doubt. However, from experience, I would wager the answer may be found when considering not what you want but what she wants"

"I know what she wants, John. She wants to go home."

Chapter Sixteen

Miles rode out early next morning, alone. He was headed across the border into Scotland where he knew he could find a man willing to arrange for his message to be taken all the way to the Bishop of Durham, no questions asked. The same man would also be able to supply him with the information he needed about the man responsible for his mother's death.

A wanted man, Alexander Stewart had orchestrated many cross-border raids to rustle sheep and cattle. He was the bane of the English barons, costing them livestock and many men. A ruthless killer and a hero amongst his own kin, his biggest threat to the English was his ability to rally men to his cause. He had at his disposal many hundred kinsmen who, despite not being regular men at arms, were nevertheless experienced and fearless, and would drop everything at his calling. For these reasons Alexander Stewart was given a very wide berth by the English. There was a substantial price on his head but to date no one had found the courage to try to claim it. He was a very hard man to find.

The roadside ale house where Miles chose to wait was not picked by him at random. The Two Tups was a notorious haunt for villains, and any law abiding citizen who valued his skin would have avoided it at all costs. However, Miles knew if he'd any chance at all of a meeting, he would have to take the risk. The building itself was an aging timber framed structure that leaned perilously to one side. Word was, warring clans had pushed the structure off its foundations during a battle when one of the parties were holed up inside. In truth Miles thought it more likely the boggy ground had influenced the slippage, but the story was told and retold by those who frequented the place, and who was he to argue?

He left his horse with the stable lad, along with a tip and the promise of more to come if the horse and the tack were still there when he came back. The tip was significantly more than the lad could have got for the horse should he choose to steal it and sell it on. Miles was content his horse was safe while he waited inside.

Pushing open the heavy wooden door, Miles stood in the doorway a moment while his eyes adjusted to the dark and smoky interior. He counted six men at the bar and another ten sitting in groups of two or three at tables. They all turned to assess him and he rightly judged his position as precarious. He resisted the urge to grip the handle of his dagger as he made his way through the cramped space to the bar. The innkeeper broke off his conversation with two kilted clansmen.

"What can a git ye, stranger?"

Miles indicated the barrel of ale with a nod of his head. He was loath to speak as he would immediately be known as not only English but of noble birth and an enemy, but he had come here for a reason.

"I'm looking for Alexander of the Stewart clan." All eyes in the building turned to look and all ears tuned in to listen.

"Ah dinnae ken the man." The innkeeper slammed a jug of ale down onto the bar, slopping the contents over Miles' outstretched hand.

Miles ignored the animosity and nodded. "I'll sit and wait awhile. Perhaps he'll hear I need to speak with him."

"As ah say, ah dinnae ken yon man, but who are ye t'be askin' for him?"

"Miles, Miles of Wildewood." In his peripheral vision Miles saw two of the previously seated men rise and leave the building with a nod at the innkeeper. His message was sent.

He chose to sit at a small table with his back to the wall. One hand held the obligatory mug of ale while the other gripped his knife hidden beneath the folds of his cloak. The other drinkers viewed him with mistrust and he avoided eye contact with them. He was not there to start a fight which he could not win, he was merely waiting. It did not take long for word of his arrival to reach the ears of the man he wished to meet, and two jugs later Alexander Stewart pulled up a chair opposite and sat down.

Miles studied the man in silence for a moment. He was thickset, with a shock of carrot-coloured hair worn long and tied at the nape with a leather thong. He carried a jagged scar across his left cheek which parted his beard and continued under his chin. It was an old scar but still vivid, and it caught the eye of the casual onlooker. Those who knew the man saw it as a mark of his valour; those who did not would have been repulsed by its severity. He wore the traditional weave of his clan and carried a short sword tucked into his belt.

"I see you still prefer to wear a skirt, Alex," said Miles. "Aren't you concerned you'll be mistaken for a maid? This place is packed with randy men. I'd be watching my back if I were you."

Alex ignored the jibe. "What brings yer this side o' the border, Miles?"

"You owe me."

"An yer plan tae collect?"

"I do."

Alex gestured to the inn keeper to bring more drinks. He loosened his sword he placed it on the table between them.

"When did ye git back?"

"I've been back in England a matter of weeks, just a few days back at Wildewood."

"So, what can ah dae for yer, Miles?"

"I need two things, Alex, and then we'll call it quits. The first is the loan of a good man to carry a message to the Bishop of Durham. He must be discreet and trustworthy."

"Do ye no have such a man of yer ain?"

"I have men who are discreet and trustworthy, yes." He thought of Tom Pandy, Berryman and John. "But none are suitable for this task."

"Sounds like yer up to somethin', Miles. Does it have anything tae dae wi yon young lassie-and mibbe a ransom?"

Miles tried hard to hide his surprise. "How do you know about that?"

"Miles, Miles," he shook his head and smiled, "the whole o' Coquetdale kens aboot yer wee secret. It disnae tak much for news to trickle North. What's she like?"

"It doesn't matter what she's like," Miles replied shortly. *How had word got out?* No one knew but himself and Edmund and the boy had spoken to no one. He recalled the sheriff's interest. "What are they saying?"

Alex shrugged. "They're sayin' you've been fleeced, that yon lassie's a spy."

Miles stomach muscles tightened. "What do you mean a spy? She's from Kirk Knowe."

"Is she? Nay one there has heard o' her. Gerard thinks she's been sent by yer English king, Edward."

"Gerard, why would he think that?"

"Because Gerard is no yer king's favourite baron at the moment and he's become a wee bit mistrustful."

"Indeed?" Now that did interest Miles.

Alex leaned forward conspiratorially. "You've been away a lang time, Miles. Gerard was a wee shite then, an he's a bigger shite now. Folk never forgave him for what happened tae yer mother, even though he might protest it was an accident."

Miles knew it was no accident. He had been there, just a boy with his mother walking in the parkland, when Gerard and his hunting party had mown down his mother with their horses. Gerard claimed his horse was spooked but Miles had seen the look of triumph on his face.

"Why would that interest the king?"

"Gerard's been gittin worse, a bloated boar stuffed full o' his ain importance, and that yon king of yers is gittin a wee bit weary o' the complaints. There was a rumour some crusader booty destined for the royal coffers mysteriously disappeared on its way back from the Holy land an' Gerard's name was mentioned, but nuthin could be proven or found. Then he had Walter de Sweethope imprisoned at yon castle. God nays whit that was aboot, likely some pissing match between rivals, an' Edward was obliged tae intervene tae get him freed. That wisnae the first time either. Ye heard aboot William Douglas the year yer left? Gerard has developed a likin' for a full dungeon. Let's just say he wisnae best-pleased at Edward's intervention, nor was he enamoured the king gave Wildewood back tae yer, and he's been mekin' his mooth go. He thinks the king has him marked and somehow yon lassie is involved."

"She's not a spy."

"Are ye sure?"

Miles considered this carefully and the truthful answer was no, he wasn't sure. He sat back in his chair and swirled the dregs at the bottom of his mug. He'd come here with a simple plan to get a messenger to take his ransom demand to the bishop. If the bishop agreed terms then he would deliver Grace back to Kirk Knowe himself, picking up the ransom and using it to repair Wildewood.

It was a little too simplistic he realised.

Thinking back to when they'd found her, he'd been so sure no one had been in the forest. At the time he couldn't understand how she'd got past his trips and markers. If Edmund hadn't accidently shot her with his bow, would she have stumbled in to his camp anyway and made up a story to ensure she was taken to Ahlborett Castle, to Gerard? She kept insisting she wasn't a nun and she wanted to go home. Was that because she had a job to do for the king? If Grace had indeed been sent by the king to undermine Gerard's position of power then they actually had something in common, a score to settle with Gerard. And then there was the sheriff who was not out looking for a missing nun but had been more than a little interested in Grace.

"No, I'm not sure, Alex. Some things don't add up. She's certainly different and has been untruthful about things, trivial things, but she's lied nevertheless."

"You're holding her agin her will, Miles. Why should she respect yer wi' the truth?" answered Alex.

"You're right but I've always considered myself a good judge of character. I had my suspicions but deep down I believed her to be genuine."

"She may well be, Miles. Ah'm only repeatin' what ah've heard. Yer ken, people dinnae always tell the truth, for a variety o' reasons and no always bad yens. Perhaps she's a feared." He paused with a smirk.

"After all yer dae hiv a reputation..."

"Perhaps."

"Hiv yer heard from Hugh o' late?" asked Alex.

"Hugh?"

"Aye, Hugh de Reynard, ye ken, the man who took ye under his wing when yer mother died, the man who turned yer into a knight, who helped make ye the fine English lord ye are today."

Miles smiled, "Oh, *that* Hugh. No I haven't heard from him since I returned to England."

"Ah hear he's in Lincoln."

"You hear an awful lot, Alex."

"Yer should look him up. He can mibbe help yer wi' all o' this."

"Are you trying to say you can't?" asked Miles.

Alex spread his hands wide. "Miles, if ye want a messenger tae dae yer biddin', yer can have one, but ah dinnae ken it'll dae yer any good. It's no the bishop who wants the lassie, its Gerard de Frouville' an' somehow I dinnae ken you'll want to trade wi him. If yer short o' funds then we can always dae some business."

Miles shook his head. He knew the kind of business Alex operated and had no wish to be hung as a thief.

"Or go an' see Hugh, mibbe he can shed some light o' the situation. He has the kings ear now, by a' accounts."

"I thought Hugh was off Edward's list."

"Things change, Miles. Ye need tae learn tae keep up."

Miles stood and held out his hand; it was time he left. He could do no more here and Alex's theory that Gerard might be after Grace concerned him greatly. If the whole of Coquetdale knew of her existence then it would be reasonable to assume Gerard would know Wildewood had no men at arms and the girl was unprotected. "Thank you, Alex. I think you may be correct about the bishop."

"Whit dae ye plan tae dae, Miles?"

"I need to get back and speak to the girl."

"Rest a while. It's past dark. You'll travel nae further tonight."

Miles hesitated. Alex was right, it was foolhardy to travel after dark. He sat back down and accepted another drink.

"So what's the second thing ah can dae for yer, Miles?"

Miles grinned. "I need a pony, one that won't get me hung if the sheriff looks upon it. A lady's palfrey, something finely built. Do you have anything?"

"For yer young lassie, Miles?"

Miles nodded.

"Whit size?"

Miles gestured to just under his chin. "She's about this tall and light as a feather."

Alex grinned. "Ah meant the pony, what size pony? You've got it bad, Miles. The sooner yer decide whit tae dae wi' her the better."

Miles scowled. "Have you anything suitable or not?"

Alex narrowed his eyes as he considered. "As it happens, ah have a wee grey filly. She's young an still a wee green, but wi' a gentle hand she'll make a fine ladies mount. She's yer's if ye want her."

"Thank you, Alex, that would be grand," he sighed wearily. He hadn't had any real rest, not since he'd got caught up with Grace. He rubbed his eyes and scanned the room distractedly. Most of the men had left and a serving girl was collecting the empty jugs. She looked at him from beneath lowered lashes and her invitation was unmistakable. Miles shook his head; he was not in the mood. Alex gestured one of the men over and spoke quietly to him. Nodding, the man pulled his cloak around him and left the inn. Miles assumed he'd gone to get the pony.

"So ah still owe ye, then?" asked Alex and it took a moment for Miles to register he'd been spoken to.

"No, you don't owe me. The information and advice were payment enough. The pony is an added bonus."

"Ye once saved ma life, Miles," answered Alex and his hand strayed to his scar. "Ah think ah still owe ye. Let me know if ah can return the favour."

"Let's hope I never need to call it in."

"A word o' advice, Miles, though ah doubt ye'll take it…"

"Go on."

"Be careful. Yer playing a dangerous game, wi' people who have far more tae lose than ye. Make sure ye dinnae get caught up in the thrill o' the game an' lose sight o' the prize."

* * *

It was just gone dawn when Miles left the ale house. He was bone weary and certainly not alert after an evening of drinking ale with Alex, but it was a clear morning with a touch of frost and he followed a well-trodden path. Even so, it took all of his willpower to stay awake and in the saddle for the long journey back.

He led the grey pony on a long lead rope tied to his saddle and it was indeed a pretty filly. It kept pace with his horse with no real effort which was just as well as he pushed both animals hard to get back. He had an increasing sense of urgency. Things were beginning to unravel. He had to get back.

The sun made its appearance as he entered the great forest which protected Wildewood from the north. The horses were weary and gratefully slowed their pace to negotiate the hidden trails between the trees. Miles slid his feet from the stirrups and stretched his legs trying to regain some circulation. Although it hadn't snowed, the morning remained frosty and he was chilled to the bone. He imagined the hot bath he would take when he eventually got back and he forced his drooping eyelids to stay open, not much further to go. The horse, having no further impetus from its rider, slowed to a walk and Miles closed his eyes and slumped against the horse's neck.

He woke when he slid from the horse's back and hit the ground with a thump. His left shoulder took the full force of the fall and he swore as he staggered back to wakefulness. Rising slowly he gathered up the reins of his horse and the filly. The horse whickered softly and Miles was suddenly aware he was not alone in the forest. He willed the horses to stay silent and crouched still, straining to hear.

The soldiers passed within ten yards of where he hid, and so busy were they with their conversation and so ineffectual in their observations, they saw neither him nor his beasts. By their livery he could tell they were Gerard's men. They were on foot and they totalled eight men at arms.

He quickly tried to assess his position in relation to Wildewood. He'd been travelling through Gerard's land since he'd crossed back over the border. Had Gerard been alerted, were these soldiers looking for him? He was still an hour's ride from Wildewood. He couldn't afford to get involved in an altercation with Gerard before he had a chance to speak to Grace. He remained still and silent, and after what seemed an agonisingly long time, the soldiers moved on and Miles was able to remount his horse and press on to Wildewood.

Chapter Seventeen

Miles made it back by mid-morning. He spent the remainder of his journey turning over in his mind the seeds of doubt which Alex had inadvertently sown. It left him in poor humour and irrationally suspicious of Grace. Who was this cuckoo in the nest, what was her purpose? Pulling his horse to a standstill in the courtyard, he barked at Edmund who was busy in the stables.

"Edmund, get these gates shut and barred. Where is Grace?" He swung down from the saddle, the horse skittering away from him in alarm. "Where is she?" he snapped.

"In the kitchen, my lord, she be helpin' Martha..."

He would get the truth if it killed him...or her. He'd come home to Wildewood with his own plans, to re-establish the estate and exact his revenge on Gerard. He'd initially been distracted by the ransom he could get for Grace, then he'd been similarly distracted by the notion of keeping her for himself and foregoing the ransom. She was a distraction, there was no denying it. But was that her ultimate plan all along? He recalled the night in the great hall. He'd thought himself the victor of the game. The idea that he may have been the one being played and bested did not sit well. He had played the chivalrous knight on that occasion, but the rules had just changed. He would not make that mistake again.

Bursting into the room, he found her seated at the table with Linus, painting. She, the child and Martha started with fright as he slammed the door closed behind him. Ignoring Martha and Linus he crossed the room, gripped Grace firmly by her arm and pulled her to her feet.

"I would speak with you, in private."

Grace's protestations went unheeded as Miles marched her back across the courtyard and into the great hall. Tom Pandy rose from tending the fire to stare in wonder as Miles strode across the hall without comment and proceeded to propel Grace up the stairs to her chamber. Grace finally came to her senses as they approached her door and tried to slow his progress by setting her feet against the floor, but he simply pushed her harder. Once in her chamber he flung her aside and slammed the door, drawing home the bolt with a resounding clash.

He narrowed his eyes, cocked his head and drew a long calming breath. It would not do to lose control.

"What on earth do you think you're doing?" cried Grace, fury and fear competing on her outraged face.

"Mademoiselle, what do you know of the king?"

Grace stared back at him blankly. "The king?"

"No more games," he said coldly, his composure reined in and held with an unsteady hand. "What is your connection to Edward?" He caught the revealing look of alarm on her face before she controlled it. Her continuing deceit caused his gut to twist along with his patience.

"I don't know what you mean. I'm not playing games. I've never met any king."

Miles could barely look at her. It seemed Alex had been correct and he had been fleeced after all. He dropped his gaze, studied the weathered boards beneath her feet and counted to ten silently. She was treading a hazardous path between falsehood and truth, but not quite carefully enough. He could easily force the truth from her; it would be a simple task for one as well trained as he. A hand at her throat, a blade between her ribs, it could be done in seconds and she would be begging to reveal all she knew. Instead he raised his head and said softly, "You are not of the church?"

"I told you I wasn't. You didn't believe me."

"Yet you say you come from Kirk Knowe?"

"Yes."

"Kirk Knowe is a chapel. What is your purpose there, if you are not a religious?"

"It's complicated," replied Grace. "I live there in a cottage. I told you this. I haven't lied to you. I also told you I want to go home." She faltered as he shook his head dismissively. "What's happened? Why are you behaving like this..?"

"What do you know of Gerard de Frouville'?" he asked, and again caught a flair of recognition in her eyes. She couldn't lie to save her life. It was time she understood that only the truth could save her.

"I know nothing," she replied.

He sighed with weary acceptance of her duplicity and Grace glanced away, avoiding his gaze. Reaching out an impatient hand he caught her chin and forced her to look him in the eye. "Try again, Mademoiselle."

"I know the name...I must have read about him somewhere," she stammered.

"You read about him?" He raised a brow. Yet another falsehood. The only women he knew who could decipher the written word were nuns and high born ladies, and she'd already denied being either.

"Miles, why don't you just tell me what you think I've done." She batted his hand away, stepped towards him and he took a sudden step back. He was not about to fall into that trap. He knew his current state of mind was undisciplined and wasn't totally convinced he wouldn't fall

95

beneath her spell. Wary of doing something he would later regret, he shrugged away thoughts of witches, took a breath and circled her menacingly.

"I have it on very good authority that Gerard believes you to be a spy in the employ of the king. He considers you a significant enough threat to necessitate your removal. He is currently planning to remove you by force from Wildewood. I passed a number of his men at arms in the forest on my return this morning. If he succeeds in gaining access to Wildewood, you can rest assured you will not last the night. He will have no qualms about slitting your throat, nor will he baulk at slaughtering the household or putting a sword through Linus."

Grace stared at him wide-eyed. He doubted she'd ever been speechless before, but he'd certainly shocked any response right out of her. He conceded his appearance along with his words might have caused the reaction. He was unshaven, dishevelled and still carrying the effects of a night spent drinking and a long morning in the saddle. He leaned in with a snarl, pushing his advantage, awaiting her response. When it eventually came, it was not as expected.

"Get out of my room," she hissed, eyes flashing, cheeks flushed. Miles drew back in surprise. He'd anticipated denial or more lies, not defiance. Did she really consider herself a match for him?

"Get out," she repeated, attempting to step past him toward the door. He moved quickly to prevent her and she pushed angrily at his chest. Catching hold of her arms in a firm grip, she wriggled in vain to break free, kicking wildly with her feet. "Let me go. Just leave me alone. You're nothing but a bully," she panted.

Forcing her back against the barred door, he did just that, releasing his grip and slamming his hands flat on the door either side of her. She flinched and he leaned into her. Despite the anger sparking in her eyes and the reckless show of defiance, he could almost smell the fear leaching out of her pores, and for the first time in a very long time, he had the urge to do something bad.

"Did you hear a word I said?" he growled, suppressing with considerable effort the self-loathing rising from his gut which threatened to overwhelm him. He had been so close, a mere heartbeat away from resurrecting his inglorious past. Resting his forehead wearily against the door alongside her, he closed his eyes dragged in a ragged breath and slowly gathered his composure.

"I shall spell it out for you. Gerard, a very unpleasant man, is on his way here to take you by force. He will have the manpower to succeed and the arrogance to suppose he can do as he pleases with you. He believes you will bring about his downfall, so naturally he will wish to exact some revenge."

He pressed close against her, drawn like a moth to the very flame that threatened to ignite him. He could feel her heart pounding through her clothes, matching the erratic beat of his own. She was soft, warm and fragrant and he was filled with the scent of her. He tried to ignore it, to steer his thoughts away as his breath burned a trail against her neck. His lips almost touched her ear as he continued in a hoarse whisper.

"He will kill you, but not before he has enjoyed some sport." He pulled back slightly so he could see the moment when she finally realised he was deadly serious. When he saw her pupils flare, he continued.

"And when he has satisfied his extremely distasteful appetites, he will offer you to his men and then punish everyone at Wildewood who provided you with hospitality. He will slaughter the children in front of their parents, and he and his cohorts will take pleasure in every moment." He watched as Grace's eyes registered horror and her complexion paled. For the first time he saw real terror and was uncertain whether her fear was caused by his own behaviour or the threat of Gerard's.

"Have you nothing you wish to tell me?"

His eyes fixed upon her soft mouth as she gasped, tried to speak but seemed unable to get the words past her lips. He shifted his gaze, fascinated as her eyes pooled with unshed tears. She gave an ineffectual struggle but he held her fast and waited. Finally the bravado began to crumble.

"I...I am not this person...this spy...," she stammered. "I...don't know anyone here...least of all the king or this Gerard. I don't belong here. I just want to go home." She shook her head desperately. "If you really believe I'll bring danger to your home, then let me go now before he arrives so the children will remain safe. You choose to disbelieve everything I say and yet I've never deliberately lied to you. I didn't ask to come here, you forced me. This is none of my doing." She held his gaze determinedly, despite the tremor in her lower lip, "This is your doing," she added softly. The tears spilled over and slipped softly down her cheeks.

He heard the break in her voice as she fought for control and his gut twisted with shame. He witnessed her inner struggle, saw the way her chest heaved with the task of keeping her sobs in, felt how her whole body trembled against him with the effort of restraining herself and he was filled with self-loathing. He was a fool. What had he become? He'd set out to scare her, indeed had taken some measure of satisfaction from it, and succeeded in terrifying her. She was correct, he was a bully. He was worse than Gerard.

Whatever the truth, and he was certain it would remain a mystery, he did not believe her a spy. She might possess guile, she might have feminine wiles to ensnare the unwitting, but under real pressure she buckled easily. There was no way he could allow Gerard near her. She was no match for such evil. How he would achieve that was yet to be determined. He'd no men to speak of, very few weapons, and from experience, he knew Gerard to be a ruthless foe. But he himself was trained in warfare and the killing of men, he just needed a plan.

He closed the gap and drew her away from the door. Her resistance quickly dissolved as he placed his hand against her back and pressed her gently against him. He let her cry until her fists unclenched and she had worn herself out, and when her tears were finally exhausted, he led her to the bed, sat down next to her on its edge and sought to undo the hurt.

"Mademoiselle, please forgive me. I did not intend for this. I fear we find ourselves at the mercy of events beyond our control. Please do not alarm yourself further. Gerard will not gain entry to Wildewood."

He gently brushed her fringe from her eyes and his hand lingered, absently stroking her hair, soothing her. She leaned into his hand.

"Gerard and I have a shared history, perhaps this has allowed a confusion to grow and flourish." He faltered, "Like you, I am tired of it all, and today I am especially weary." He lifted her chin so he could look her in the eye and see for himself the damage he'd caused, the trust he'd destroyed. "I am truly sorry, Mademoiselle. I beg your forgiveness." His heart sank when he recognised her disappointment.

He should have stayed where he belonged, amongst the dead and dying on the battlefield. Perhaps it was too late for him to make amends.

Chapter Eighteen

The fiery blush had long since left her cheeks. In its place, her skin carried the pallor of resignation and quiet determination. He watched as she reached out an unsteady hand and placed her palm against his cheek. He held his breath enjoying the touch as her hand slid hesitantly across his unshaven jaw and hovered over his scar. She'd no reason to fear him now, but perhaps it was too late. She'd witnessed the strength of his emotions when he feared for those close to him. Pity then, that she did not realise she was closest of them all.

"I forgive you," she whispered softly, her tears spent.

His heart lurched with hope. "Why?"

She shrugged gently. "Because, if I don't, if I believe instead the glimpse of hell I saw in your eyes when you held me, then I may as well accept the fact that you're as evil as Gerard." She inhaled softly and raised her head to look at him. "I don't believe you're an evil man, but I suspect you've experienced evil in the past. In that respect we are alike."

They held each other's gaze for a long moment and he saw his own indecision mirrored in her eyes. Her hand gently cupped his chin and she drew him closer. Miles hesitated and while he considered this surprising turn of events she reached up and hesitantly brushed her lips across his. They were warm and moist.

He closed his eyes briefly. Was she playing the game again? He wasn't sure, wasn't certain about anything to do with her anymore. He had bullied her, terrified her, hurt her beyond forgiveness and yet here she was playing with fire, with no concept of how badly she could be burned. She considered them alike, yet she couldn't be further from the truth. He lowered his mouth and gently took her lower lip between his teeth, tugging. He covered her lips with his and she obliged, parting hers to allow his tongue entry. Miles growled as the kiss deepened. If this was a game, then it was a good game and he was happy to play. But if it was merely a reaction to his appalling behaviour, then he wanted none of it.

He paused, the effort in doing so caused his muscles to knot, his hand to shake. She had initiated this, but still, he was uncertain. He took a steadying breath and lifted his head to look at her. Her face was flushed and her eyes clouded with confusion. Did she think this was all she had to offer in exchange for her safety or did she imagine she could manipulate him to her own tune?

Of course she wanted him, he reasoned. *Who wouldn't*, he thought derisively. Wasn't he every woman's dream, the un-chivalrous knight with dubious morals who thought nothing of bullying girls half his size, the soldier of fortune who thought more of revenge than forgiveness, and of lust rather than love? He watched her, seeing through the shell of confusion and indignation to the passion which simmered beneath the surface. She was a mass of contradiction and secrets.

He needed a reason to change, to put his past behind him once and for all. Perhaps that was why fate had brought her to him, to test his resolve and prove his worth.

He drew a breath and smiled slowly at her. It was time to start a new game where he would make the rules and ensure that he won.

"Mademoiselle, I am a scoundrel, with the manners of a rabid dog. You must excuse me." He pulled away and stood, putting much needed space between them.

She frowned at him, puzzled perhaps by his withdrawal. He took some pleasure from the obvious flicker of disappointment which accompanied her furrowed brow.

He was not an animal, even if she caused him to behave as one. She was a lady, whether she realised it or not, and he should treat her as such. He'd spent all morning in the saddle, he reeked of horse, sweat and fatigue, and she deserved more. More importantly he had no wish to discover that her acquiescence was merely a reaction to his behaviour and her fear.

"Be assured, I will never hurt you."

"You flatter yourself, Miles," she murmured. "No man could ever hurt me." Her strained voice was at odds with her words. Her hand strayed to her hair, the nervous gesture revealing far more than she could have guessed.

"I assure you, I could," he replied silently.

Her earlier confidence, though frustrating and amusing in equal measures, was suddenly revealed as a fragile shell and he had no wish to shatter it. He stepped away, keen to put some space between them. His self-discipline had limits.

"I have things I must do now, but later we might discuss the subject in more detail."

He resisted the urge for a further kiss and crossed to the door, drew back the bolt and took a steadying breath. He was halfway out of the door when he remembered the pony.

"I almost forgot. I have a surprise for you."

"You do?" Grace smiled tentatively. "What kind of surprise?"

"A big one."

Grace raised one brow.

Miles shook his head slowly, almost gave in and re-bolted the door, but held onto his resolve. "Your surprise awaits you in the stables, my lady."

"The stables?" She crossed to the chest, climbed clumsily onto it and looked out through the window.

Miles followed and steadied her around the waist. He resisted the urge to run a hand beneath her skirt, to feel the smooth skin of her thigh. His heart rate increased and his stomach knotted with anticipation. He resisted them both.

"How is your leg?" he asked hoarsely.

"It only hurts when someone decides to manhandle me."

"Mm, then I'd best desist."

* * *

He escorted her to the stables and was surprised by the look of genuine pleasure on her face when he led out the palfrey. He had to admit the filly was stunning, a little taller than Edmunds pony but much finer in proportion with a sweet Arabian head.

"You got this for me?" she asked, bewildered. "Why would you do that, I ...I don't know what to say."

Miles handed her the lead rein and winked. "You can thank me later."

Grace smiled at him. "Is that where you've been for the past two days, getting this pony?"

"Amongst other things," he replied carefully. He didn't think it prudent now, to let her know he'd been trying to make arrangements to sell her hide to the bishop.

She allowed the pony to nuzzle its velvet nose against her cheek; closed her eyes and breathed in its scent like a mother with her new child. Miles was captivated. Everything she did made him want her more. He shifted his gaze and thoughts to the hay loft and abandoned them just as quickly in favour of a soft mattress and the privacy of a locked chamber. He could wait.

"Aren't you worried I'll use her to make my escape?" she asked.

"Should I be concerned?" He wouldn't put it past her to head off into the wilderness.

Grace laughed. "No, at least not until after you give me my next big surprise."

Miles cupped the back of her neck and pulled her to him. "Now there's a challenge." He lowered his head and kissed her. He intended it to be a fleeting taste but her husky response was his undoing and he angled his mouth and crushed her lips with his own. "In that case, I shall ensure I make myself a little less resistible."

"Edmund was right. You really are bad, aren't you?"

Miles held his hands out in mock surrender. She had no idea how bad he could be. The thought chilled him but he was determined not to spoil the moment with unbidden memories. "Guilty as charged, my lady," he replied softly. "Now, I must go and wash. I see your nose wrinkling ever so slightly. You may return to whatever it was you were doing before I scared you in to my arms."

"I was painting," she said, "with Linus."

Miles studied her, caught the change in her tone, and felt what she'd said was significant in some way but wasn't sure why. "Good, you may show me later, but in the meantime stay indoors. Edmund will see to the pony and if the weather holds you may ride her later." He led the pony back in to the stables and Grace watched as he bolted the door and turned to leave.

"Miles..." she called after him softly and he turned. "You do believe me, don't you?"

"Should I?"

"Yes."

"Then I believe you." He turned back and started across the courtyard.

"Miles..." He stopped and turned again. "Nothing."

He smiled at her as she gathered her skirts and walked away. Later couldn't come soon enough.

Chapter Nineteen

Grace returned to the kitchen and Martha's questioning look. The woman was agog with curiosity. Grace had, after all, been dragged to her chamber by Miles.

"He's a fine figure of a man, is he not?" stated Martha shrewdly.

Grace rolled her eyes. That was definitely an understatement.

"I barely know him," she replied cautiously as she gathered up the crude colours she'd managed to create from the available raw materials. Linus had made hand prints on the scrap of white linen she'd left him with. He was curled up now, asleep on a basket of rags in front of the cooking range, a mud-coloured thumb stuck in his little cherub mouth. She dipped a finger in the paint and carefully scrawled his name beneath his artwork.

"But I'd wager you'd like to know him a little better, Mistress," pressed Martha.

Grace recognised a born gossip when she saw one and reckoned if there was a tale to be had Martha wouldn't be above using any means necessary to ensure she had the full story. Two could play at that game.

Apart from the undeniable physical attraction they shared, she wasn't really sure of her feelings for Miles, or of his feelings for her. He had an air of danger about him, which might well be necessary in this hostile place but it scared her nevertheless. There were obvious additional complications to their relationship which she certainly didn't want to discuss with Martha.

She smoothed a large square of linen and taking a piece of charcoal from the fireside she began to sketch the sleeping child.

"He's not had an easy life, yer understand, what with his ma bein' so tragically taken from him."

Grace glanced at Martha. "What happened to his mother?"

Martha settled her mammoth bulk in a fireside chair. Grace realised she'd swallowed the bait and sat back to allow Martha to tell her tale.

"Well, I'll start at the very beginnin'."

"That's a very good place to start," hummed Grace.

"Miles' mother, Katherine, was the cousin of Gerard de Frouville's father. She lived at the castle with Gerard the Elder and his wife, Lady Maud, since childhood. When Gerard died, Maud banished Katherine here to Wildewood."

"Why?" asked Grace. She began to delicately colour Linus' image and despite the lack of palette the little portrait began to take on a life of its own.

"She was with child, of course," answered Martha in an exaggerated stage whisper.

Grace looked up. "Miles?"

"Yes," answered Martha. "Miles was born here and I cared for them both."

"So Miles is Gerard's half-brother?" That's what Miles had alluded to when he referred to his past with Gerard.

"Maud believed so," answered Martha. "Katherine would not speak of it, only to say the one she loved was lost to her. She mourned him every day. Miles was her reason for living. They lived a simple life here, she with her garden, Miles with the horses. She was a gentle and honourable lady. Miles is very like her."

Grace wasn't sure about gentle and she was equally unsure about honourable.

"It's very sad," she murmured. The poor girl, taken advantage of by her own cousin and cast aside when she became pregnant, and yet she still loved him?

Martha nodded but she'd not yet finished her tale. "Young Gerard took against Katherine and her son, jealous no doubt. Miles was such a bonny, happy bairn. Gerard wore a permanent scowl. He, bein' older and bigger, used any opportunity to bully him."

Martha grinned and Grace realised she was missing half of her teeth.

"Gerard was nay match for Miles, though, yer see, Miles bein' a clever child and quick-witted. He took many a beatin' but he always got the better of Gerard."

Grace imagined Miles as a child. She could understand how he'd find it easy to outwit someone as lacking in intellect as Gerard appeared. She also knew how galling it would be to the outwitted one. She wondered if that's what Miles had just done to her.

"So what happened?"

"When Miles was neither child nor man, Gerard brought a huntin' party out to Wildewood. Truth be told, they were a mob of drunken louts, Gerard's cronies bought with Gerard's money. Ran amok in the woods and park, so they did. Katherine was trampled by Gerard's horse. Miles was with her, saw what happened and accused Gerard of murder."

Grace put the finishing touches to her painting and turned to give Martha her full attention. "So how come Gerard didn't hang?"

Martha puffed with indignation. "Well, me dear, that would never do, would it? Hanging a baron on the say-so of a bastard upstart? Miles swore he'd kill Gerard himself, but at the time the lad was more at risk from Gerard and his cronies and needin' protectin' for himself. He was sent to Sir Hugh to be trained as a knight."

"Sir Hugh?"

"Sir Hugh de Reynard, of Normandy."

Grace pulled her legs up under her, wincing as her thigh rubbed against the wood of the seat. Martha noted her reaction and sucked at her teeth.

"Have ye suffered an accident, mistress?" she asked shrewdly.

Grace had no wish to discuss the cause of her discomfort and wondered why she felt it necessary to protect Miles' reputation. She'd no doubt either he or Edmund had been responsible, but she believed it an accident and best forgotten.

"It's nothing," she replied. "Who is Sir Hugh?"

Martha rose with some difficulty from her chair as her bulk had moulded to the shape and it took some jiggling to release herself from its grip.

"Sir Hugh be a friend of Gerard the Elder. When he heard the terrible news, he agreed to take Miles." She crossed to the fire where a pot was bubbling and lifted the lid to check the progress. "He went away a boy and has returned a man."

"And he still wants Gerard's blood?" asked Grace.

"He's an honourable man. He'll avenge his mother."

At what cost? thought Grace, sadly.

This really was a mix up and she'd landed right in the middle of it. With so much bad blood between Miles and Gerard, her presence would only serve to make matters worse. Miles was right; Gerard would use her to get to him. Miles was no longer merely a bastard child. If he were to accuse Gerard of murder now, people might listen. King Edward might listen and Gerard may yet hang. Gerard would have to act quickly. No wonder Miles was suspicious of her. She wondered whether he believed her now or was merely blinded by lust. Time would tell, no doubt.

"Do you think my presence here is a good thing or not?" she asked Martha.

"Well, of course it's a good thing me dear," cried Martha. "Why else would Miles have brought ye here?"

To sell me to the highest bidder, replied Grace silently. "I don't know, Martha. Why do you think I'm here?"

Martha gave a toothless grin. "Because Wildewood needs a mistress and Miles is a good judge of character. Yer young and spirited and will provide him with sons."

I don't think so, she thought and rose stiffly from her seat. "On that note, Martha, I think it's time I left."

"Left?" Martha looked aghast.

"Just as far as my chamber," laughed Grace. "I would like to bathe later, if it's not too much trouble. My leg's a little stiff and warm water will no doubt be beneficial."

"Of course, mistress, nay trouble at all," replied Martha and she began bustling with the cauldron. "I'll have it sent up."

Grace smiled as she recalled the water cavalcade. "Thank you, Martha." She gathered up her painting things, and using a basket loaned from the kitchen, she carried them up to her room. She left the painting of the child on the table to dry.

She wondered at Miles' plans and if there was anything she could do to assist? Who was Gerard's primary target after all, Miles or herself? She rather thought the outlandish story of her being a spy said more about Gerard's insecurity than anything else. Perhaps he wasn't as untouchable as he perceived. Maybe there was a way around this mess after all? She thought again about Miles' demand for ransom money. Looking around she had to admit his need was real. He saw nothing wrong in what he'd done and believed by handing her to the bishop he could kill two birds with one stone. Return her to Kirk Knowe and get paid for his trouble. Was there actually anything wrong with that? Hadn't she been asking from day one to go back?

She wondered if he'd sent his messenger and what she'd do when it was time to go.

* * *

The men came into the kitchen to warm up at midday and Martha fed them with pottage. Miles caught sight of the painting and drew it carefully towards him across the table. Grace was remarkably talented, he decided, but nevertheless he could not ignore the feeling of unease as he looked at her work. He'd never seen anything like it. He could have been looking at the child himself rather than an image. He held it up to the light and the colour on the child's cheeks came alive. He hurriedly replaced it on the table and thought again of witches. He wondered why she'd lied about her painting, or indeed about the other things. She'd no flint, he was sure of that, yet she'd lit the fire. She said she had no link to the king, yet her expression when he was mentioned belied her denial. He wondered what it would take to get the truth from her. She had proved to be persuadable. Perhaps that was a more enjoyable method to use.

"Look, John," he said as he carefully passed the cloth across the table, "see what Grace has created. It's a perfect image of Linus."

John admired the cloth with fearful reverence, his big hands gently holding the corners of the cloth. He glanced at Miles. "Perhaps it is a little too perfect. Blasphemous, some might say." He folded the cloth carefully and tucked it beneath his shirt next to his skin. "I shall keep it safe."

Miles nodded, distracted "Yes, John, a wise move. It would not do to have it fall into the wrong hands."

"She has many talents, my lord," continued John. "A valuable asset to Wildewood, do you not agree?"

Miles met his eye. "An asset to be protected at all costs." He forced a smile. He was not confident in his ability to protect her against Gerard. It was time to call in some favours.

Chapter Twenty

Miles found Grace at the stables with the filly. He stood in the shadows and watched her briefly as she calmed the flighty youngster with a soft murmur and even softer caress. He was no closer to understanding her, to knowing who she really was, but no matter her identity or true purpose, she would be his before the night was out.

"Have you chosen a name for her?" he asked, enjoying her nearness as he saddled the pony.

"Not yet. I need to get to know her first."

Miles lifted her onto the saddle and allowed his hand to stray and his mind to wander as he handed her the reins.

"I thought about 'Ransom', what do you think?"

Miles ignored the jibe. "How well do you ride?"

"Well enough." There was mischief in her tone and it drew him back from his contemplation.

"She's young, and unschooled. You'll need to be patient." He glanced up and caught her smile. "Can you be patient, I wonder?"

"I have the patience of a saint."

He too, could be patient when required. Had he not waited more than ten years to avenge his mother? But today he found his patience sorely tested. He could think of nothing but her.

"Take her round the courtyard and let me see how she responds to you."

"Aren't we going out into the park?" Grace's disappointment showed on her face. "I thought we'd ride out together."

Miles patted the pony's rump. "It's not safe. Stay within the wall."

"For how long?"

"Until I've attended to Gerard."

"And how do you plan to do that, you're only one man?"

"He is also, one man," replied Miles. "An over-confident man who will make a mistake."

"And you, Miles, are you confident?"

"Realistic. That's the difference between us."

* * *

In the loft above the stables Belle lay on her stomach alongside Edmund and watched the boy silently as he in turn watched Grace and Miles with the pony in the yard.

"She is beautiful," said the girl slyly as she pulled out a strand of straw and chewed one end. Edmund shrugged. "They make a good pair, don't ye think?" she pressed, rolling on to her back.

"No."

"Ah, but they do, Edmund, he bein' so handsome and rich. Look at the pony he's given her. A fine beast. It will have cost him, nay doubt."

Edmund scowled. "He is not rich and she be far too good for him."

"Surely not, Edmund? A gallant knight, master of an entire demesne - what woman could resist? Just look at the way he watches her. I'll wager he's not thinkin' of ponies and such like."

Edmund spun, anger sparking in his young eyes. "She's not like yer other women. She will resist. He's playin' with her."

Belle continued to study the couple from her lofty vantage point.

Miles stood at the centre of the yard and watched as Grace trotted the pony and then pushed her into a canter. She grabbed at her skirts as the pony picked up pace and Miles smiled at her attempts at modesty.

"Why does he not take her out into the park to ride?" asked Belle. She glanced at Edmund, irritated at his obvious infatuation.

"In case she buggers off, I reckon," replied Edmund. He stood up and brushed the straw from his clothes.

"Why would she run off?" questioned Belle, a sudden gleam in her eye. There was definitely something odd about this whole situation. "I thought she was here under Miles' protection?"

Edmund shot a quick glance at Belle. "The pony, I meant the pony. She's young and still green. It's safer keepin' her enclosed until she settles down." He let out a held breath.

"Is she a good rider?" asked Belle.

"Good enough." He smiled and added, "though she hung onto me tightly enough when she shared my pony." Belle shot him a withering glance.

He crossed to the ladder and lowered himself onto the top rung. "You may have time to spend the day up here, but I've got things to do."

Belle stayed a while longer in the loft watching the couple in the yard. They were indeed a handsome pair, although Belle thought Sir Miles far too old and battle-scarred for her own taste. She'd seen him stripped to the waist at the water trough and been shocked by the number of scars. Edmund told her the worst was from a sword which almost cost his life. Her grandmother hinted he'd brought Grace here to wed and carry his children. And that was fine with Belle. Edmund would soon get over her when she'd a full belly. She could help him if he'd give her a chance. But if Sir Miles was just playing a game and Grace remained here and unattached, then Belle would have to take

109

matters into her own hands. She wanted Edmund's attention on her and her alone.

* * *

Miles sought out Edmund after supper and they walked together in the growing gloom by the stables. He'd barely had time for the lad since they'd arrived and he'd not yet dealt with the boy's behaviour regarding Grace.

"How do you find Wildewood, Edmund? Is everything as you expected?"

"T'is grand, my lord," replied Edmund. "The way it sits, hidden like, and can only be seen if yer know where to look."

"And the others – Tom, John the Mason - have they made you welcome?"

Edmund nodded. "John's been tellin' me 'bout his time in Lincoln. He worked with me father, did ye know that?"

"Yes, he told me, Edmund. He said he was a fine man. It's good for you to talk with someone who knew him. I'm sorry that despite my best efforts I've been unable to take his place, but a father's place is very special and should remain so." It was unfortunate he could not say the same about his own father.

"You've been very good to me, my lord. I'd not be here if it weren't for you. I know that and I am in your debt."

Miles sighed and considered his words carefully, "We have become close, Edmund. I rely on you for many things. Do you know the reason for that?"

"Nay, my lord."

"Well, because you are loyal and trustworthy, and I know you'll always be truthful." Miles could just make out the boys expression and he looked wary, uncertain. "Do you trust me, Edmund?"

"Of course."

"Do you trust me to do the right thing for Lady Grace?"

Edmund was silent for a moment. Miles waited and the boy scuffed at the dirt beneath his feet.

"She is very lovely, is she not?" continued Miles, and Edmund nodded. "She's a very fine and clever lady and she thinks highly of you, Edmund." The boy looked up. "She's been scared and alone and you have been a friend to her, she's very grateful and hopes you will continue to be her friend." Edmund stayed silent. "But you need to appreciate, Edmund, you are as a brother to her. A brother do you understand?"

"And you, my lord," Edmund's voice was barely a whisper. "What is she to you?"

Miles shook his head. "If I'm honest, Edmund, I don't know. I find her exasperating and annoying, and at the same time I want her. What do you make of that?"

Edmund shrugged "Do yer still plan to sell her?"

"No, Edmund, I do not intend to ransom her. You were correct. It was an ill-conceived plan."

"Do yer swear?"

"Swear on what?"

"That ye won't sell her?"

"You have my word, Edmund."

Edmund grinned and Miles sensed his relief.

"I have been made aware of certain things which lead me to believe she may be in danger, Edmund, and I need to know I can count on you."

"What danger?" cried Edmund in alarm.

Miles shushed him and glanced around warily. "Can I trust you, Edmund? Are we together on this?"

"Of course, my lord, I would do anything necessary."

"Good, there are some things you need to know."

Chapter Twenty One

It was late when Miles eventually climbed the spiral stairs to his room. With the exception of young Edmund, the rest of the household were sleeping and the gates were bolted against unwelcome guests. He'd left Edmund on first watch with a promise to relieve him when the moon began to wane. Miles felt secure in the knowledge he would be alerted in good time if anything untoward should happen during Edmund's watch. The boy would not fail him. Little more than a child, he had the heart of a lion and would make a good knight one day. Though he was lowly born, Miles was determined to make good the cost of Edmund's training. Circumstances may have caused the loss of his own valuable destrier and armour but it was a temporary situation. Fortunes could be reversed if there was will and determination, and Miles was not short of both.

He'd arrived late to supper and been so intent on other matters it was not until after the meal he'd realised the reason for his distraction. Grace was no longer there. He wondered at the reason for her absence. Perhaps she'd had second thoughts.

He paused now on the spiral stairs outside her bedchamber. He needed to speak with her, and although it could have waited till morning, he saw the light from beneath the door and decided he did not wish to wait. He knocked gently but received no response. She'd likely fallen asleep with the candle burning. Nevertheless he pulled the latch and opened the door to her room. He had to duck to enter through the small doorway, and as he did, he realised she was indeed sleeping. He closed the door behind him to stem the inevitable draughts, and quietly crossed the room.

This had been his mother's room and he recalled how she'd decorated it with many bed hangings and tapestries. From spring through to autumn she'd brought in wild flowers, and the scent hung sweetly in the air.

He looked about now in the dim candle light. The bed linen had been cleaned, as had his, and the room smelt of lavender. Unlike his mother however, Grace was untidy and clothes were scattered about, draped over the chest and hung over the posts at the end of the bed. He gently touched the flimsy garments suspended above the now dying fire. They were still damp; she had been washing her clothes. He noticed the tub in front of the fire and imagined her languishing in the water. Imagination...it would be the death of him.

Leaving his thoughts along with her undergarments, he crossed to the wall opposite the window where she'd hung some pictures of her own. There were three, all painted on squares of linen. In the dim light he saw the image of Edmund his youthfulness captured perfectly. Although he could not make out the colours, he knew he was looking at the work of someone with great talent and despite of his discomfort at her irreverence, he found himself in awe.

The second picture, of the filly, was full of movement and excitement, the pony an image captured in mid-flight. Nostrils flaring, mane and tail flying, the background a blur as the pony galloped through it. He reached out and traced the pony's outline with his fingers. He could almost feel her flinch beneath his touch and the flickering candlelight served to animate the creature with movements which he knew were impossible but were nevertheless real. He drew a breath and crossed himself.

The last could not be described as a painting, merely a collection of random charcoal lines. A nose, eyes, an expression, a taste of something to come, yet he recognised every line.

"It's not finished yet," said Grace. Miles smiled, turning slowly.

She sat up in bed, her knees under her chin the covers pulled around to keep out the cold. Her hair was messed as if she'd just woken but her eyes were bright and held a glint of mischief.

"I thought you were sleeping," he answered.

"So you thought you'd sneak into my room?"

Miles considered his position, why had he come to her chamber? It certainly wasn't to talk. "Is this why you dined in your room, so you could continue to paint?"

Grace shrugged. "Yes and no. I had things to do," she paused and smiled. "I was washing my hair."

"You have a remarkable, if somewhat dangerous, talent," he said as he approached the bed, "Who is the handsome knight on the left?"

Grace narrowed her eyes. "Oh, just someone I met on the road, a bit too clever for his own good, you know the type. Thinks the world revolves around him, that women will fall at his feet."

"And will they?"

"Perhaps..." She revealed her naked arm from beneath the cover and patted the edge of the bed next to her. "Sit down. You're blocking what little heat there is from the fire."

Miles smiled, "Excuse me, my lady" and he stretched out next to her on top of the covers.

"Are you going to finish the painting?" he asked.

"That depends on whether I'm here long enough."

"Do you want to finish it?"

"I like to finish everything I've started," she replied as she watched him in the candlelight.

He smiled and returned her gaze. The game was back on. "Does it matter how long it takes to finish?"

Grace drew one slender hand through her hair, delicately taming the long strands of her unruly fringe. She twisted the hair slowly, seductively and Miles paused entranced. "I suppose it depends on what you've started. Some things are best over as quickly as possible." She sent a smouldering glance in Miles direction, "But other things are so good...you don't want them to end."

"Such as?" Miles swallowed with difficulty, watching as she pulled the tips of her hair across her lips. He remained transfixed as her tongue delicately swept the strands into measured obedience. Imagined the feel of her tongue on his skin and fought the urge to reach out.

"Mm, I can't think of anything right now, can you?" She watched him through lowered lashes. He heard her slight intake of breath, the whispered softness as she exhaled and his eyes were drawn down to the coverlet caressing her shoulders and the soft inviting swell of her breasts.

"I can think of one at least." He raised himself up on one elbow and turned towards her, resisting the urge to touch. "Trouble is, it takes two and some considerable effort, if you want it to last as long as possible." He paused, fighting the desire which threatened to overwhelm him, determined not to make a move without her assent.

Raising one brow she inched closer, allowing her hair its untidy freedom as she reached out an unsteady hand to gently caress his cheek. "Is this where you make me want, what you want?" she asked provocatively.

Miles swallowed the groan that began deep in his chest and threatened to spill out. He turned into her palm, felt her fingers draw delicately between his lips, and tasted her briefly before pulling away with a ragged breath. "Only if you wish it..."

She gave a slow smile, an almost imperceptible nod of her head and he lowered his head and kissed her. This time there was no hesitation, her lips felt familiar and they responded instantly to his. He held himself above her and moved his lips to her neck and the soft skin beneath her ear. She was fragrant her skin was like silk and he wanted more.

He smoothed down the covers and groaned as he revealed her nakedness. She arched against him, and he drew back and gazed down at her in wonder. The candlelight danced off her skin, she was beautiful, bewitching and he was almost undone.

He pulled himself up off the bed, trailing his hand gently across her skin as he stepped away. She watched him through lowered lashes as he dragged his shirt over his head to reveal a torso bearing evidence of many battles, he heard her soft gasp, as he kicked off his boots and slowly unfastened his trousers. He cocked his head and a slow smile escaped, as he watched Grace's reaction as the rest of his clothes slithered to the floor.

"Bloody hell....," she muttered when the extent of his desire was no longer in doubt. She dropped her eyes and Miles grinned and pulled back the bed clothes.

"Now where were we?" he murmured hoarsely as he slid beneath the covers and took her in his arms.

The feel of her softness beneath him, the touch of her hands on his skin sent his heart racing, the blood pounding in his veins. She writhed against him and he took his fill. She kissed his neck, ran her hands across his back, and his muscles rippled in response to her featherlike touch. He dragged in a breath. He wanted to spend the whole night showing her just how positive his response could be, but she'd bewitched him with her sweetness and passion. He tried to pull back and take a breath, kissing her gently while attempting to regain control but the feel of her soft skin against his body as she moved beneath him, and the sound of her passion and soft laughter as she goaded him on, were his undoing. With his mouth on hers, he swallowed her sweet, velvet breath.

Miles felt her gasp as they came together for the first time and was overwhelmed by the sense of rightness that buzzed throughout his body. He held her still in his arms, felt the rhythm of her heart matching his, beat for beat, her skin hot against his. Breathing hot and heavy against her ear he paused; allowed the moment to stretch tantalisingly, and then he dipped his head and with a lazy smile kissed her open mouth and the games began again.

Later as she lay sleeping, curled in his arms; Miles considered the treasure he'd almost given away. He'd bedded many women but he'd never experienced anyone like Grace. She was a strange and wonderful creature, her mystery, her secrets both frustrating and endlessly tempting. She was the most delicious forbidden fruit and he couldn't help feeling he might yet be damned for allowing himself so much pleasure. He held her, unable to let her out of his grasp, let alone his sight. She was beautiful, passionate and different, and they were perfectly matched. God help anyone who came between them.

Miles slept eventually, entwined with Grace. The moon waned and still he did not wake. He finally stirred at the sound of insistent knocking at the door.

Stretching languidly, the feel of Grace's warm silken skin against him caused him to react before the reason for his waking registered in his brain. He came fully awake with a start and his eyes shot open. Light streamed through the window. He had missed his shift change with Edmund and there was someone at the door. He leaned over and kissed the tip of Grace's nose. She was still sleeping and irresistible, but resist her, he must.

He slid from beneath the bed clothes leaving her covered, and pulled on his trousers. Fastening them as he opened the door, he realised his appearance in her chamber in a state of undress would do little for her reputation.

He found Edmund on the other side, hand raised for another round of knocking. The boy took in his master's appearance without comment and Miles carefully shifted his position to block any view Edmund may have of the bed. No need to rub the boy's nose in it.

"Is there a problem, Edmund?"

"Yer were meant to relieve me."

"I'm sorry...I became distracted." He remained distracted. He kept a straight face with great difficulty.

"Yer promised me."

"I promised you what?"

"Yer swore an oath that yer wouldn't sell her to yon bishop."

"And I won't," said Miles, confused.

"Then why is yon bishop's man at the gate?"

Miles stared blankly at the boy and the boy glared back. "On my life, Edmund I have not done this."

He turned, grabbing his boots and shirt and followed the boy down the stairs. Pausing at the bottom he hopped from one foot to the other pulling on his boots before following Edmund out to the courtyard dragging his shirt over his head as he walked.

John waited by the gate a heavy mason's hammer in one hand, he nodded to Miles as he approached but instead of feeling encouraged by the obvious support shown by the man, Miles felt only guilt. What had he done? The whole of the household would now know he and Grace had shared a bed. Would they also believe he intended to sell her out to the bishop? The timing could not have been worse. Even he would have believed he'd taken advantage of her knowing she was to be handed over the next morning. God knows what she would think.

"Open the gates," he called to Edmund "and close them after I'm out."

Miles took a calming breath and stepped outside to meet his visitors.

Chapter Twenty Two

Miles expected an entourage and was relieved they numbered only three. Two men at arms were mounted on heavy chestnut horses; they had a look of the plough about them, and were certainly not built for speed. The rider's, young men in their early twenties looked bored, as if when told of escort duty they'd expected something a tad more exiting. He was momentarily distracted by the thought they seemed familiar, but they wore the livery of the bishop and he knew no one from Durham.

The man whom they escorted sat astride a small highland pony, best suited to a child. The sight all the more ridiculous because the man was grotesquely overweight and his girth appeared to overlap the pony at either side, akin to fleshy saddlebags. Miles knew these mountain ponies were extremely strong; nevertheless he had sympathy for the beast. The man was without hair and wore a velvet cap which matched his crimson robe. The latter marred by a good deal of mud, no doubt thrown up by the horses as they progressed through the snow melt and muddy tracks of the forest. He wondered how they'd navigated their way through the dense woodland.

"Philibutt of Mayflower," the man announced himself with a flourish of spittle and an alarming ripple of blubber. The pony, dozing in the morning sun, awoke with a start and shied against the first escort, who in turn nudged the next. Miles waited for them all to topple, but by some fortuitous act of God, they managed to retain their seats.

"Miles of Wildewood," answered Miles formally. "What brings you here at such an early hour?"

The man peered at Miles through cloudy eyes. "I represent His Eminence the Bishop of Durham. I have come to discuss the release of a young innocent whom I believe you have captive here. I demand you allow us entry, in the name of the church. We require vittals and repose and our horses need tending."

Miles stared at the man and considered his position. "Who has sent you? Where have you gleaned this information? I have no captive here."

Mayflower narrowed his eyes and sucked at his wet lips.

"How I came upon this information is no concern of yours, what should concern you is the fact I am here to negotiate a ransom. A sizeable ransom if the girl is unharmed," he added slyly. "Now, I demand entry."

Miles looked from the escorts to the odious bishop's aide. He could see no real threat from them and it would be foolish not to allow them to rest before sending them on their way. He scanned the distant tree line, conscious this may be a plot of Gerard's and there may be men hidden out of sight within the trees. He saw no one.

"Edmund," he called loudly. "Open the gates and allow our visitors entry." As he passed through the open gates ahead of the trio, he pulled Edmund and John to one side. "Be watchful, this may be a trick. Edmund, take their horses; make sure they cannot make a speedy exit. John, keep watch across the park, something is amiss here. I sent no messenger, how has word of Grace reached the ears of the bishop?"

Tom Pandy emerged from the kitchen. He glanced from the new arrivals to Miles and raised a curious brow.

"Tom, see these men are fed and ask Martha to bring a platter for the bishops aide, we will be in the great hall." He turned as Mayflower dismounted his steed in a flourish of velvet obesity. The pony gaining inches with the weight removed.

"Come this way, Master Mayflower and you can tell me what it is you think you know."

He escorted him into the hall and bade him sit at the table. The fire was kept lit all night during winter and the flames were bright and hot. Mayflower declined his seat and stood instead with his back to the fire and toasted his behind. A pungent odour rose from the man and Miles used considerable will-power not to gag.

"It has come to His Eminence's attention that you have misappropriated one of the nuns from Kirk Knowe and are demanding ransom for her return."

"Who has made this declaration? I have demanded nothing of the sort." The only person he'd spoken with, other than Edmund, was Alex Stewart and he'd not have betrayed him. Alex had however told him knowledge of the girl was commonplace. Perhaps word of mouth was responsible for this situation. He glanced at the stairs and willed Grace to stay in her chamber out of harm's way.

"I am not at liberty to divulge my source," said the man with an accompanying spray of spittle.

"Then you've had a wasted journey, there is no nun from Kirk Knowe here."

Philibutt of Mayflower scowled. "Do you not wish to know how much the bishop is prepared to pay?"

Miles certainly didn't want to know how much he was prepared to pay, how much he was sacrificing. If he'd been offered the money three days ago he would have accepted and shook the man's hand, but not anymore.

"I have no need to know the value of your purse, Master Mayflower, and if you continue with this, I will relieve you of your coin, regardless of whether I am able to fulfil my end of a ransom bargain."

"You would steal from the church?" The man was aghast and crossed himself piously with podgy fingers tipped by filthy finger nails. He settled himself precariously on a chair.

"No, I would not," replied Miles. "But I could, particularly if I thought you were not, in fact, acting on behalf of the church."

Mayflower fluffed out his ample chest like a bird realigning his feathers. He filled his mouth with a selection from Martha's platter and glowered at Miles.

"I know you have a girl here." He spat food over the table as he spoke and Miles leaned back in his chair to avoid it. "I must see her and ascertain she is not from the religious order. I cannot in all honesty allow a defenceless innocent to remain unchaperoned in the home of an unmarried man. It is unseemly."

Miles knew she was neither defenceless nor innocent, nor did she require a chaperone, but even so the turn of events concerned him.

"I have no nun here. The members of my household remain here of their own free will and none of them should interest you or His Eminence. I would ask that you enjoy my hospitality before it's withdrawn and leave when your horses are rested."

"What of the ransom?" Mayflower withdrew a bag from his voluminous robe and clashed it onto the table. "Think what you could do with that, Miles of Wildewood." The corners of his mouth were white with drool, the man was repulsive. Miles pitied the maid who would have to lay out his cold, naked body when it was time for him to meet his maker.

Miles gritted his teeth, the bag was large the contents heavy. If only. If only she'd been ugly or stupid or cruel - or even a real nun. But she was none of these things and there would be no sale.

"You may keep your ransom, Master Mayflower I have nothing to exchange."

A movement on the stairs behind the bishop's aide caught Miles' eye and he froze. Grace had paused on her downward journey to scan the room. She must have woken and wondered at his absence. She was wrapped in a coverlet which had slipped to reveal one bare shoulder. Her feet were also bare and he noticed distractedly how she hopped from one foot to the other on the cold stone. She opened her mouth as if to call to him and in that split second before a sound was made, he willed her to stop. She closed her mouth slowly and locked eyes with him. Over such a distance he wasn't even sure she could see the warning in his.

Mayflower began to rise. Fortunately his bulk made any movement laboriously slow and as he heaved himself to his feet and made to reclaim his loot, Miles tried to communicate across the expanse of the hall. Grace shrugged her shoulders questioningly and casually retrieved her cover as it slipped to almost reveal one naked breast.

Mayflower dipped his head to give thanks for his food and Miles took the opportunity to run his finger across his own throat, an explicit warning for Grace. Grace either misunderstood or chose to ignore him for she merely smiled and continued down the stairs. Was the girl mad thought Miles wildly. She would be seen; any second, the odious whale of a man would turn and see her. He ran his fingers through his hair in frustration and looked from one to the other.

At the exact moment that Philibutt of Mayflower turned and set eyes upon her, Grace's face lit up with a beautiful smile and she descended the last of the stone steps in a ruffle of linen. Miles groaned inwardly. What now? - What was she up to?

"Aha!" Exclaimed the bishop's aide, "My missing nun no doubt?" He noted her state of undress with a shudder. "I trust she has not been compromised."

Grace fairly skipped across the stone flags. "Good morrow," she trilled, offering her small, pale hand which the man snatched and kissed wetly. Grace smiled, looked at the drool and then wiped her hand delicately on her sheet.

"My dear child, I have come to rescue you from the clutches of this wayward knight." He huffed and puffed with the excitement of having outwitted Miles. "His Eminence the Bishop has kindly provided the required ransom; you will soon be safely, back at Kirk Knowe."

Miles looked questioningly at Grace and shrugged.

"I see," replied Grace as she rearranged her coverings, rather inexpertly observed Miles, as the swell of her breasts was clearly visible. She shuffled on the cold floor balancing one foot on top of the other in turns. "I'm sorry. Miles is remiss as a host and has clearly failed to introduce us." She glanced at Miles and he was sure he caught the ghost of a smile.

"This is Philibutt of Mayflower," said Miles. "He comes on behalf of the Bishop of Durham with a ransom which he claims I have demanded in return for a nun, whom I don't have."

Grace arched one delicate brow. "How very thoughtful of the bishop," she cooed and Miles swallowed his disbelief. She was playing the man. Some innocent!

"I am Lady Grace, niece of Sir Hugh de Reynard of Normandy, no doubt you will have heard of him."

Both men stared at her open-mouthed.

"I am a guest in the home of my uncle's favourite protégé. He is such an honourable man." She turned to bestow a grateful smile on the bewildered Miles. "Like you, I too am here on Gods business, you might say."

She took a seat opposite the bishop's aide who also reclaimed his seat with an alarming creaking of wood under considerable stress. Grace leaned forward provocatively, and the man went a peculiar shade of puce.

"I seek funds for the benefit of the orphaned children of Normandy, poor children. Without an orphanage and the strict care of the church I fear they will all be lost to the devil. The bishop will no doubt share my concern."

Mayflower wrung his hands, his face a picture of confusion.

"Perhaps word of my arrival and my charitable undertaking to secure funds for these poor children has become confused in the telling. We all know how peasants love to embellish a tale. Do we not, Philibutt?" she inclined her head coyly, "May I call you, Philibutt?"

Mayflower spluttered and Miles shook his head in disbelief.

"I see a solution to this confusion, if I may suggest it?" Grace continued.

The bishop's aide dragged his protruding rheumy eyes from her flesh. "Of course, my dear, any confusion must be hastily clarified."

She gently weighed the ransom bag in her delicate hand. It was heavy, rather too heavy for one nun. "It occurs to me that His Eminence the Bishop, would think highly of anyone who could recover such a delicate and embarrassing situation; and you must agree, Philibutt, you're coming here and making scurrilous accusations against a fine and honourable knight, a knight who has fought at his king's side; is embarrassing for his eminences reputation?"

"Yes of course," muttered Mayflower. "I can see how this situation could be perceived."

"Then I suggest that as the bishop has already allowed for the giving of these funds on behalf of the church, that we do not deny his generosity but allow their donation to the orphan children of Normandy."

Miles stared at her in growing wonder; Mayflower, merely stared.

"Are we in accord?" She drew the bag towards her, "Of course if you do not have the authority?"

Inner turmoil was written all over the man's face. "Madam," he snorted. "Take the bag. I will inform the bishop of your gratitude."

He struggled to his feet and knocked over his seat. Miles bent and set it to rights. As he brushed past the bishop's man, Mayflower caught his arm and held him fast with an icy glare.

"This is not finished," he spluttered.

Miles returned his glare with one of his own. "Then I look forward to our next meeting." He took the man by the arm and frog-marched him out of the hall.

John was waiting by the gate.

"Have Edmund saddle the horses. Our guests are leaving."

John nodded and went in search of Edmund who waited by the kitchen and watched the men at arms who supped at Martha's table. They had far too much of an interest in Belle. She fluttered her eyelashes and swished her skirts, enjoying their attentions. Edmund kept out of sight, but near enough should he be needed. He had to speak to Miles.

The bishop's aide and his escort left Wildewood shortly after, the gate soundly barred behind them. Edmund caught up with Miles as he crossed the yard.

"Those men, I recognised them, my lord."

Miles stopped and looked at Edmund. He too had thought them familiar but could not place them, "From where, Edmund?"

"Normandy, my lord, they are Guy's men."

Miles hand went subconsciously to his side where he carried the mark left by Guy's sword. "How did I not remember them?"

"Yer did not recall much after ye suffered yer wound, but they were the ones who robbed ye when yer lay bleedin' from Guy's sword."

Miles did not recall much from that episode. He had spent many weeks recovering before their journey home could be resumed. If Guy's men were in Northumberland then it seemed apparent that Guy was in league with Gerard. If Philibutt of Mayflower was in fact the Bishop of Durham's aide, then he must be currently in the employ of Gerard and it was therefore Gerard's money lying in a velvet bag in the great hall.

"Good lad." He patted Edmund's shoulder. "Keep your wits about you, and make sure no one comes through that gate."

Chapter Twenty Three

The velvet bag was still on the table when Miles re-entered the great hall. Snatching it up, he crossed to the stairs and taking them two at a time, he went in search of Grace.

"I didn't send for him," he announced as he entered her chamber, to find her dressing in the clothes in which she'd arrived.

"I believe you." Grace buttoned her trousers and turned to face him. Her breasts barely covered by lace. She reached for her vest laid on the rumpled bed and began to pull it over her head.

Miles found himself distracted by her state of undress, the soft glow on her skin, and the glimpse of indigo butterflies, that fluttered tantalisingly as she stretched. He shook himself. "Where are you going?" He gestured at her clothes.

Grace smiled and crossed the room. Reaching up she placed her palms against his chest and planted a long, wet kiss on his lips. He tried to prolong it, instantly and shamelessly distracted, but she pulled away with a grin. "I'm not going anywhere; I just want to be comfortable when I ride the filly."

Miles stood perplexed. She'd just schemed her way into a fortune and she was going riding? She was far too sure of herself.

"How much is there?" Grace reached for the bag.

"Enough for more than a few orphans," replied Miles holding the bag aloft. "What do you know of Hugh?"

Grace grinned.

"Just what Martha told me. His was the only name I could come up with on the spur of the moment. That awful Philibutt creature, what an arrogant little man, he needed taking down a peg or two, and now you have the money for Wildewood." She paused at Miles expression, "What's the matter, did I do the wrong thing? I thought you'd be pleased."

"Pleased? Stunned is the word I'd use. I didn't realise you were so accomplished an entertainer." He recalled how well he'd been entertained in this very room. His eyes strayed to the bed, a wicked smile spreading slowly across his face.

He should be pleased. He now had the money for Wildewood. Money to pay for the renovations, to restock, and do all the things he wanted. Unfortunately, he also had more trouble than he cared to have. If Gerard had Guy and his henchmen on side and was willing to pay out the kind of money Mayflower was carrying, then he'd be unlikely to give up and go away. Particularly when he realised he'd been bested by a girl. Gerard was not a good loser.

"That was Gerard's man you just fleeced. He won't be pleased about it and neither will he believe your story, anymore than Mayflower."

"Philibutt believed me. Why else did he give me the money?" exclaimed Grace. "That was the whole point; to make him believe I was someone else, not the nun he was looking for."

"He wasn't looking for a nun. He was looking for the king's spy. He gave you the money because you outwitted him, it doesn't mean he believed you. Do you really think the bishop cares about orphaned children?" He cocked his head and studied her. "The bishop cares for naught but spreading the word of Christ. If you'd asked for coin to further the Crusade and crush the Saracens, then, Mayflower would likely have swallowed your tale. But he'd not sully his hands to save one child, let alone a litter of parentless Norman brats. You did, however, confuse him by mentioning Hugh. He likely believed that, no reason not to, I suppose. But he's not going to return to Gerard and admit he gave the ransom to a pretty girl because he couldn't keep his eyes off her flesh."

Miles paused, his gaze also drawn to her flesh. His grin widened when he caught her raised brow. He shrugged his apology. Temptation and imagination...twin sins...and he was guilty of succumbing to both.

"I don't know whether bringing Hugh's name into this has made things better or worse." He closed the door behind him and stepped closer to the bed. "By all accounts Hugh is back in favour with the king and that may well play into Gerard's paranoia. If he continues to believe you've been sent by Edward, he may think all three of us are in collusion. I may resort to using Gerard's money to pay for our own defence."

"Have I made things worse?" asked Grace. Concern flitted across her face.

Her sense of alarm affected him, in ways he couldn't explain. His first response to hold and protect, was fuelled by their closeness the previous night, and his continuing desire for its repeat. But deep in his gut, caution warred with passion and together they churned mercilessly.

"No, not worse, just more complicated." He reached out a hand and let it play down her bare arm, caressing gently. She'd been so convincing, as she played the coquette with Mayflower, it unsettled him. Aware she had secrets, he wasn't sure whether they should concern him or not. Truth was, he'd more than enough to worry about without adding Grace to the list. He watched her eyes widen as he let his fingers stray to the nape of her neck and she inclined her head with a soft sigh.

125

He still didn't know the full truth about her, wondered whether what she'd told Mayflower was in fact the truth and she was in some way connected to Hugh. He thought it unlikely, sure he would have known of her, would perhaps have met her in Normandy and he was sure he'd never had that pleasure. He lowered his hand and hooked a finger in the front of her vest.

"Come here." He pulled her gently and she placed her arms around his waist, her head on his chest. "We just need to be careful," he whispered hoarsely as he pressed a kiss on the top of her head. Very careful he added silently.

He moved his mouth to her ear, "Tell me Mademoiselle; are you...well this morning?"

Grace smiled. "You mean did I survive that incredible night of wild passion with yours truly?"

"Yes, but more particularly did you enjoy it?"

"Mm I suppose so," she pondered with deliberate slowness. "I expect I'll need to repeat it though...just to be sure." She squeaked as he grabbed her.

"We'll see what we can do about that later, but first I have things to do."

"You always have things to do."

"I need to be ready for Gerard's next move."

"No, we need to be ready for his next move," replied Grace.

Miles sobered, restrained his imagination with difficulty and concentrated on what he needed to do rather than what he wanted to do. She really had no idea, and may well have been brought up in a convent for her alarming lack of common sense.

"Ever killed a man, Grace?"

"Of course not."

"Do you suppose you could if it were necessary?"

"No I don't."

"I think you could," said Miles. He stroked her cheek gently with his palm.

Grace swatted his hand away. "That's rubbish. No one is going to get killed, least of all by me. I'm just a girl, not a soldier, I couldn't kill anyone. And I wouldn't want to."

"Not even to save your own life?"

"No," replied Grace determinedly.

"Not even if it meant saving someone close to you?"

"Absolutely not." She pushed at him. "You don't need me to save you!"

She'd thought of him first as the, someone close to her, he liked that.

"You're correct I can look after myself. I was thinking more of Linus or Edmund; could you kill to save them?"

Grace shrugged. "No - I don't know. Who would want to kill a babe like Linus?"

Miles sobered instantly. "Hmm, you would be surprised."

"I wouldn't know how to," continued Grace

"You could use the knife you took from Edmund."

"How did you...?"

Miles shook his head.

"Grace, Grace I know all your little secrets." He caught the almost smug look that flitted across her face and accepted reluctantly that his statement was probably far from the truth. "What did you plan to do with it?" he asked.

Grace stared at him, guilt colouring her cheeks in an alluring way. He was momentarily distracted by the notion of how interesting it would be to persuade the truth out of her. He cleared his throat and continued. "The knife, what did you plan to use it for?"

"I don't know, I just thought it was a good idea at the time," replied Grace hesitantly.

"You took it because you feared for your life and thought you might need a weapon to protect yourself...yes?"

"I suppose so."

Miles smiled. "Maybe you had a mind to protect yourself from wayward knight's...and that's how I know if you really had to, you could kill. All I need to do is teach you how."

"Are things really so serious?" Grace asked. "Can't you just talk to Gerard, explain it's all a mistake?"

"It's gone beyond that I'm afraid. I have a score to settle with Gerard. I've waited a long time and he knows I must have my revenge. He'll use any means possible to avoid it, including using you to get to me. If he didn't believe you to be a spy, then he would manufacture some other reason to involve you. As I've said he's a dangerous man, and now he has some equally dangerous allies."

"Who, Philibutt?"

Miles shook his head.

"Mayflower may have the ear of the church, which carries some element of risk, but the only thing in real danger from him, is his pony which is at risk of being crushed beneath his incredible bulk. No, Gerard has Guy of Marchant and his entourage on side, Guy's men escorted Mayflower this morning and no doubt they are at this very moment discussing their next move."

"Tell me about Guy?"

"It's a long story. I'll give you the abridged version."

Miles stepped away from her and leaned casually against the back of the door. "Guy is a bully. His family own half of Lincolnshire. I first met him in Palestine, we didn't get on. We are not cut from the same cloth. There's something about him, that's difficult to explain. He's not quite right; he has a predilection for cruelty particularly where small boys are concerned. We had a difference of opinion over Edmund, and settled our disagreement at the tournament. Guy was well and truly beaten."

He smiled at the recollection. The picture of Guy, unseated from his horse and humiliated, was one to savour. "Did I mention, he's also a poor loser? The king was present at the tournament. Guy was therefore honour-bound to hand the boy over, but he was not enamoured. He festered for over a year until he could stand it no longer. On our return home through Normandy he and his merry band ambushed us. Took everything I'd earned and the few treasures I'd managed to collect." He recalled the amber necklace; it would have been perfect around her neck. "He thought he'd killed me, would have too, if it weren't for Hugh. That man always manages to be exactly where he's needed, thank God."

"Is that how you got your scar?" Grace asked. Stepping close, she smoothed his shirt away from his warm skin and he felt her fingers gently trail across his puckered flesh.

"Guy's sword. The cowardly son of a she-devil attacked at night. He didn't give me the chance to draw a weapon. He would have skewered Edmund also if the lad hadn't the presence of mind to hide. Edmund sought help, sent a message to Hugh. Hugh is remarkably skilled in the healing arts."

Grace paused to consider. "Okay, so on the one hand we've got Guy, the child molester who made the mistake of trying to kill you, and on the other Gerard who hates you because...?"

Miles sighed. "Gerard is a complicated person. He doesn't like to think a bastard could have him hanged. He killed my mother, I saw him do it and I intend to have my revenge."

"Will you kill him?"

"Eventually. One way or another he'll pay for what he's done. He's worried now I've acquainted myself well with the king, Edward will concur when I proclaim his guilt. He sees the fact the king has given me title of Wildewood as a sign of his own disfavour. He's deranged." He tapped his head. "A little touched, and by all accounts he hasn't matured as he's got older. There are probably a fair few people who would enjoy the sight of him dangling at the end of a rope."

"Are all the men you know like this?" asked Grace. Despair flitted unchecked across her face.

"You mean, are they all ruthless killers with no moral code?"

"Something like that."

"Most of them are ruthless killers, but the ones I count as trusted friends all know right from wrong. You'd like them if you met them."

"Is it likely I'll meet them?"

"I've sent a message but can't be sure they'll get it, there are complications. I think we should assume we hold Wildewood alone."

"So it is serious."

"Truthfully, I cannot be certain, but we plan for the worst."

"Is that the soldier talking?"

"It's the soldier who came back from the crusades in one piece. I think I know what I'm talking about."

Chapter Twenty Four

Within the chest, hidden within the folds of linen were the things Grace had brought with her from home. The matches, half a packet of chewing gum, a safety pin, half a packet of sunflower seeds and the remains of a roll of red electricians' tape, a very ripe apple and Edmund's knife. She felt Miles' steady gaze on her back as she pulled out the knife and re-covered the other things. She wondered if he'd discovered her stash, and what he would make of the strange assortment.

"What do I do with this?" she asked as she held it aloft.

"Not holding it by the blade would be a good start," he replied.

The knife was small and sharp enough to cut food but scarcely sharp enough to break the skin. It did however fit perfectly in her small hand and was light enough for her to carry concealed.

Miles took her hand gently and showed her how to hold the knife. "If you need to use this, you can guarantee it will be against someone taller and stronger."

"Everyone is taller and stronger than I am, I'm used to it." She remembered how easily he'd held her down on the bed. She'd not found his strength threatening, far from it, she'd found it arousing. She let her gaze travel the length of him, recalling deliciously. Catching his amused expression, she shook the image from her mind.

"Maybe so, but you have proved to be clever, Mayflower will certainly vouch for that, and clever can outwit strong."

Grace recalled Martha's account of Miles and Gerard, how he had outwitted the bully.

"I can do Judo," she offered.

"Pardon?"

"Judo, self defence." She'd never got beyond blue belt, but remembered being smaller was an advantage.

He shrugged; by his expression he'd no idea what she was talking about. Grace stepped back and beckoned him with her hands.

"Come towards me," she said. As he stepped forward on his right foot, she turned beneath his centre of gravity and swiftly rolled him over her shoulder on to his back. Miles hit the floor with a thud.

"I think I like Judo."

Grace grinned, holding out her hand to pull him up. "I thought you might."

"Okay," he began with a smile. "Perhaps you'll get your man on his back but you need to make sure he doesn't get you on your back.

Whoever it is, will have more weight behind them.

Grace's grin faded, she may have enjoyed being held down by Miles, but he was the exception.

"Lunge upwards with the knife with as much force as you can. Go for the throat." He reached for her hand, tightened it around the hilt of the knife and forced her hand upwards till the tip touched his throat. Keep pushing even if your assailant gags and you think you have him. Don't stop till he drops."

Grace gazed fascinated at the red mark she'd made on Miles' skin. If the knife had been sharp he would have bled. He pulled up his shirt, moved her hand and aligned the knife with his abdomen.

"If you go for his gut then push the knife up to the hilt, turn it if you can. It still may not kill him, but he'll fall." He released her hand and without his guidance the blade trailed slowly and gently down his belly creating a line which matched the shadow of dark hair starting below his navel and disappearing below the waist of his trousers. His muscles flinched and Grace watched mesmerized, it took considerable self control to prevent her hand from following the knife.

Grace tried for a smile and failed. "I don't know whether I can do this."

Miles took the knife from her. "We prepare for the worst remember, you may not need to do anything, but if you do, at least now you'll know what to do. I'll make sure the knife is sharp, but you must keep it with you. It's no good to anyone if it's left in the chest."

"Unless it's in his chest of course," Grace quipped. She felt a sudden hysteria bubbling inside, like the urge to laugh in church, totally inappropriate but irresistible nevertheless.

Miles grinned. "His chest is good, but you've got to get between the ribs, like this." He poked her in the side and she squealed and tried to pull away, laughing. He pulled her back and held her tight against him. "You'll be fine I won't let anything happen to you."

Despite hugging him back, feeling his strength and inhaling his scent, she didn't feel fine. She was out of her depth and she knew it.

"Just remember, don't leave the grounds unless you're with me."

"Don't worry I won't."

"Promise?"

"I promise," replied Grace.

Miles turned to leave. "I need to make some enquiries, see what people know. I'll be gone for the rest of the day. Stay in the grounds. I'll be back by nightfall."

Grace watched him go and considered her position. Last night with Miles had been wonderful, but she wasn't naive enough to think it meant anything to him other than sex. She'd been available, more than willing and they were both consenting adults. They found each other attractive, and the state of danger they were experiencing had perhaps heightened the attraction for her. Grace conceded, Miles was a very appealing protector, an inventive and experienced lover and under other circumstances she'd be hanging on very tightly to him. But the whole situation unnerved her.

He'd told her to stay at Wildewood, but he wasn't here to keep her captive. He now had the money he needed to repair the estate courtesy of her, which was his original reason for bringing her here, but he may end up having to use it to ensure her protection. Perhaps the real answer was for her to take control of her own destiny and leave now while Miles couldn't stop her? It was a simple enough solution, just go back the way she'd come and get on with her life leaving Miles to get on with his. She hesitated nevertheless and wasn't sure why.

She crossed to the chest, took out the apple and decided to go and see the filly. Perhaps a ride around the grounds would clear her head and make decisions easier? She looked at the other things and wondered again whether Miles had discovered them? She couldn't risk losing anything; they were her link with home. She scooped them up and distributed them in her many pockets.

She called at the kitchen, which was strangely empty of people, but filled with the aroma of freshly baked bread. Martha must be in the dairy making butter. She borrowed a cloak from the back of the door and slipped quietly from the room. The weather had warmed marginally. There had been heavy rain throughout the morning, but the rain had moved east and the sun broke weakly through the clouds. She wrapped the cloak around her and crossed to the stables.

There was no sign of Edmund. Perhaps he'd gone with Miles? The girl Belle hovered and Grace couldn't help feel that her friendliness masked other, real feelings.

"Are ye riding today, mistress?"

"Yes, Belle, could you help me to saddle the filly? I intend to take her round the yard."

Belle nodded and proceeded to tack up the pony before leading her out to the mounting block. "It's a fine day for a ride, yer should take her into the park, let her have her head."

Grace considered the girls words. She obviously hadn't been made aware of any external threat to Wildewood from the Messers Gerard and Guy.

"Miles didn't want me to take her out of the grounds,"

"It's quite safe, mistress. Why even Linus and Edmund have gone

132

out today. The snow is almost melted from the park and they've gone with the dog to catch some supper."

Grace was surprised that Miles had allowed the boys to leave, if the danger was so imminent. She recalled what he'd said earlier about whether she could kill to save Linus. She felt a tightening in her stomach.

"Which way did they go, Belle?" she asked.

"I'll show you, mistress." She waited while Grace mounted the filly. Once mounted, she led her through the walled garden where overgrown ivy concealed a door in the outer wall.

"This leads around the side through the pasture to the park, the boys will be in the wood. Edmund has set some traps. The ground is quite steep, it falls away to the river on the south side, but if ye keep in next to the wall ye'll eventually see the track to the woods."

Grace hesitated suddenly unsure whether Miles had exaggerated the threat. But if he'd been telling the truth, then Edmund and Linus were in danger. Belle noticed her indecision.

"Yer can't get lost, follow the track, cross the park to the woods and Edmund will bring ye back. The pony will thank yer for the exercise."

Grace nodded, mind made up. "Will you close the door after me, Belle and make sure John knows where I've gone please?"

"Of course, My lady," said Belle, with a smile.

* * *

Belle closed and bolted the heavy oak door. She dawdled her way back to the kitchen where Martha was sawing slices of bread and ham.

"What have you been up to?" queried Martha. "You look like the cat that's got the cream." She thrust some parcels of food at Belle. "Make yourself useful and take these to Edmund and John. They're working on the dairy roof. Bring Linus back here while you're at it. He's been getting under their feet."

Belle took the food without comment and went to find Edmund.

* * *

Grace edged the pony along the narrow path beyond the wall. As Belle advised, the drop to the river was steep and she'd no wish to tumble down it. Once past the danger, the track opened out and the pony began to prance at the sight of the open parkland. Grace held her in check as she scanned the park. She could see no sign of the boys and as the snow was melting there were no footprints to alert her to the direction they'd taken. She glanced back at the hall. The only windows looking this way were in Miles' room and he was not there to watch. She scanned the park again. It was empty. There were no enemy soldiers lurking in the undergrowth. She would give the pony her head, cross the park to the tree line and call for the boys. If there was no sign of them she would return and seek help from John or Tom Pandy.

The filly was fast, an exhilarating ride and Grace was glad of the fresh air and the feel of the wind in her hair. She'd been cooped up too long. She pulled her up at the edge of the wood reluctant to enter, remembering too well what happened the last time she'd wandered into the forest. She called to Edmund and Linus, but to no avail. Trotting along the tree line she called softly into the darkness and as she travelled further from the protection of Wildewood her stomach began to knot with apprehension.

Grace whistled in an effort to attract Fly's attention. Perhaps he would hear her and lead the boys back, but a few moments of waiting brought no result. The pony began to mither at the bit and stamp with her forelegs, fighting Grace's attempts at restraint. She spun on her hind legs in an effort to unseat her rider, Grace clung on doggedly. She'd not ridden for some time, but was not inexperienced, and as long as she kept the filly in check she retained control. She pulled at a whip thin branch and used it to chastise the pony. Allowing her to trot a little further along the edge of the wood, Grace became aware of a track leading in to the forest. Perhaps she would find the boys if she followed it just a little way?

She glanced back at Wildewood. Despite threatening to leave at every opportunity, now she was outside the walls she felt vulnerable and a little afraid. For the first time she wished Miles was there. He would know what to do, he would not be afraid. She nudged the filly, and followed the track into the cover of the trees.

Chapter Twenty Five

Gerard sat astride his grey stallion as the beast fidgeted impatiently. He should have waited at the castle for news from Mayflower, but of late he seemed unable to play the waiting-game. There was too much at stake to remain in idle expectation. He felt the need to be taking action, doing something, even if it did entail sitting in the pouring rain. He felt old, weary of the tangle of his life, but the more he contemplated, the more tangled he became. It was his way.

A well-built man, he sat hunched against the weather, fair hair plastered against his head. His grey eyes were hooded, his skin similarly grey with the cold and the effects of the previous nights heavy drinking. He'd always considered himself a handsome man, like his father before him, and in his younger days he'd no shortage of partners to share his bed, willing or otherwise. But lately his obsession with the bastard Miles had overtaken his thoughts and he'd no room left for any semblance of normal life. He needed this to be over and he would do anything to ensure the outcome turned in his favour.

"For pity's sake, Gerard, does it ever stop raining in this Godforsaken place?" Guy urged his horse to the dubious shelter of a nearby stand of trees.

Younger than Gerard, his black hair was worn longer than fashionable for a Norman lord. He considered himself an individual, believing his father's wealth allowed him certain status, certain rights. An attractive young man, he held a certain appeal to the fairer sex. Tall and dark with a rakish smile and a lean and toned body he was every maidens dream. But the cold cruel eyes gave him away. They revealed his true nature, his lust for danger and misuse of his questionable power. His partiality for the unsavoury and his need to control those weaker than him, marked him as a person to fear. He and Gerard made a good partnership. Neither could see beyond their own wants and needs, but on this occasion they both wanted the same thing, Miles of Wildewood.

Gerard turned to look at Guy and spat derisively on the ground. "This Godforsaken place is worth more to the security of England than the flat green swathe from whence you were whelped." Despite his numerous faults Gerard was proud of his land, the land of his forefathers, the rolling hills, the crags, moors and deep woods, which made it all the harder to stomach; now the king had handed some of it over to Miles. Wildewood should have been his, was his, after he'd gotten rid of Miles and his mother all those years ago. What right had the king to interfere and give it back?

"Perhaps, but at least we are blessed with the sun. How in God's name do you get crops to ripen and harvest in all of this infernal rain?"

"It is not yet spring, Guy. Come in the summer and you will see the sun on the hills and the maidens in the fields."

"I shall be home well before then. I do not expect this business to demand much of my time. I have beaten Miles once remember."

"As I recall he did not stay beaten. A word to the wise, Guy, Miles is a clever opponent. I know this to my cost. He would not be sitting on my land with the king's blessing, and warming his bed with the king's spy if he were not."

Guy acknowledged Gerard with a scowl that marred his fine features.

"Pray tell, what is she like; this spy whom you seek?" he asked. "I am keen to know more about the girl who has taken Miles' fancy."

"We will know more when the bishop's aide arrives with her," answered Gerard shortly. He did not wish to discuss this spy business. It made the tangle in his head more difficult to unravel.

The noise of approaching horses drew the men's attention to the main tree line of the great forest that encompassed Ahlborett and stretched as far as the eye could see. Beyond the bounds of the forest lay Wildewood and it was from there the approaching travellers came. Philibutt of Mayflower and his escort emerged from the forest as wet and miserable as the two who awaited them. When Gerard realised they carried no captive, his agitation grew.

"Where is the girl?" he demanded as the riders approached.

Mayflower had the grace to look sheepish. "My lord, there is no nun at Wildewood, there is however a young woman. She claims to be the niece of Sir Hugh de Reynard."

"The Fox! What has he to do with this?" Gerard questioned. Reynard was another who was close to the king, were they all conspiring against him?

"I know only what I was told. She is a shameless maid, my lord. She came to meet me straight from his bed, barely dressed, with the scent of him still on her skin." He crossed himself piously.

"Sounds like my kind of wench," sniggered Guy.

Gerard silenced him with a look. "And what of Miles, what did he have to say for himself?"

"He reiterated that he held no nun, and had demanded no ransom. He was suspicious, I believe."

"So you still have the money? He wasn't tempted to take it?"

Mayflower began to sweat, his florid forehead fairly dripping. "Perhaps, my lord, we could continue this discussion back at the castle, out of the weather. We have travelled for some time in this appalling precipitation and I must confess I cannot think straight because of the cold."

Gerard ignored him. "You still have the ransom?"

"Not exactly,"

"You either have it or you don't."

"The girl has it, my lord. She confused me with talk of collecting funds for orphans in Normandy. She convinced me His Eminence the Bishop would donate the money to that worthwhile cause. Of course I could not reveal the funds were not in fact the bishop's, but, belonged instead to yourself. She is very clever, very plausible...she bewitched me."

Guy laughed. "Why you horny toad, she played you and you gave it up didn't you?"

"Shut up you fool," snapped Gerard. "What did you say, Mayflower? That she bewitched you?"

"Yes, my lord...I...I was not in my right mind."

"No your mind was in your codpiece I'll bet," said Guy.

Gerard glared at him. "And you would be prepared to testify to that?"

"To what, my lord?"

Gerard gave a sly smile. He knew his tendency to incarcerate people at the castle, was well known. He had even given the toad Mayflower a guided tour of the dungeons despite his reluctance. He knew the man would not choose to join the current inhabitants. "To testify that she is a witch," he retorted.

Guy snapped to attention. "Miles is bedding a witch? No wonder I couldn't kill him."

Gerard swung his gaze from the jibbering fool Mayflower to the arrogant knight at his side.

Of course. How else could Miles have survived a fatal blow, seduced the king and ended up with Wildewood. He turned back to Mayflower and smiled, his mind becoming clearer.

"Make haste, Mayflower we will soon have you warm and dry at Ahlborett. You have done well. You may rest and eat your fill tonight. Tomorrow you have a long journey ahead of you. You must carry a message to the bishop."

"My Lord?"

"You must inform His Eminence that Sir Gerard de Frouville' requests his attendance here at Ahlborett Castle for a forthcoming witch trial."

Mayflower paled and dropped his eyes. His hand strayed to the cross hung from his neck.

"Can I rely on you, Guy, to bring me the witch?" asked Gerard, turning to Guy.

Guy nodded his agreement. "Now that's what I call a good days hunting!"

"Well don't let me stop you, Guy," said Gerard as he turned his horse for home, "The day is still young. Your men will show you the way."

Scowling at the weather, Guy scanned the sky. The clouds were moving in the direction of Ahlborett away from Wildewood and the sun was struggling through. He turned to his men.

"How far to Wildewood, Percy?" he asked the first who sat slouched in the saddle.

"A half day, there and back, my lord."

Guy narrowed his eyes in consideration. "What militia does he have?"

"None to speak of. A number of peasants, women and children," replied Percy "He still has the boy," he added.

"Does he now..." Self-interest flickered across Guy's face. "Were you recognised?"

"Miles did not give any sign of recognition," replied Percy, "but the last time we met, he was not at his best." The man smirked.

"And what of the boy?" He turned to the second of his men "Do you think he recalled you, Simon?"

"Possibly, he did not speak, or reveal anything to us, but he was with you, for some time and would have seen us around camp often."

"He feared you, my lord, I do not think he would risk himself by revealing anything," added Percy.

Guy shook his head. "You would be surprised what the little brat is capable of. By all accounts it was he who sought help for Miles after we failed to kill him. Do not underestimate him or Miles." He looked again at the sky. If Miles had been warned it was even more important to strike quickly before he could prepare. He turned to Mayflower.

"What does she look like? How will I recognise her?"

Mayflower swallowed nervously. "She is small, and her hair is as short as a boy."

"What colour?" asked Guy.

"The colour of sun ripened corn, my lord, streaked red with the devils blood."

Guy smiled and turned his horse.

"Come boys; let us catch ourselves a witch."

Chapter Twenty Six

Miles was reluctant to leave Wildewood. Gerard was unstable at the best of times and Grace's little performance with Mayflower would have inflamed him further. However, Gerard was no fool and Miles doubted he would show his hand without considerable thought to the repercussions. It would not do for him to get on the wrong side of the king permanently.

What concerned Miles more was the fact Guy was suddenly part of the equation. Unlike Gerard, Guy believed he was untouchable, his father's wealth and standing providing protection to him regardless of his actions. Miles had seen first-hand, his cruelty and his unsavoury fancies. Guy was the child who pulled legs off spiders and he had yet to grow up. The biggest threat, however, with Guy, was to those who knew no better, he appeared so plausible, likable and sincere. Miles could not take the risk of Grace falling into his hands. She was so incredibly reckless, despite what he'd already revealed about Guy, she might not recognise the danger he presented.

Leaving John to keep watch, he'd intended to seek out Alex Stewart with a request for help, but the further he got from Wildewood his sense of alarm grew. Finally when he could ignore his unease no longer, he detoured onto the high moor and sought out Berryman, who was still tending his sheep away from the risk of rustlers. Berryman would take his message the rest of the way. The old man was fearful of the Scottish war leader. He knew of his reputation, but Miles assured him he would be safe and Wildewood needed his help. The man subsequently secured his flock and set off for the Two Tups. Miles headed back by way of the moor which was quicker though less travelled. With the weather still ever present on the high ground he was careful as he guided his horse at a pace marginally faster than was safe for the conditions.

He arrived back at Wildewood to discover Grace had gone.

No one had seen her leave, though the girl Belle suggested she'd been desperate to take the pony out. John was mortified he had failed in his duty to keep watch, but Miles waved him away. The man could not be blamed, he did not realise that as well as keeping intruders out; his role should also have been to keep Grace in.

Had she really gone, escaped? She'd confided her intention; made it clear she wanted to go home and he couldn't keep her against her will. But that was before they'd lain together. He assumed things had changed, stupidly perhaps. He found he couldn't speak to John and turned away from Edmund. He couldn't bear to look at the fear on the lad's face. Leaving them in the great hall, he took the stairs two at a time. Had she taken her things? The things he knew she kept in the chest? He lifted the lid. They were gone. Why take them if she intended to return? He sat on the edge of the bed amid the rumpled sheets, inhaled her scent and rested his head in his hands.

Edmund stood for a moment in the doorway watching, before knocking and waiting to enter.

"Not now, Edmund," said Miles wearily.

"My lord, she has not left yer."

Miles raised his head and looked at the boy. "What do you mean?"

"She would not have left the grounds without good reason. Something caused her to leave." The boy looked Miles squarely in the eye, and Miles thought distractedly how he had grown over the past few days.

"She is clever, ye said so yerself, she understood the risk of leaving the protection of the grounds. She wouldn't have taken that risk unless it was necessary."

"You're right, Edmund, why did I not see that?" Miles stood.

"Because yer concerned for her," said Edmund.

A commotion on the stairs drew their attention and John entered with Linus' hand clasped tightly in his.

"My lord, Linus saw her leave."

Miles took a calming breath and crouched before the little boy. He'd never interrogated a five year old before.

"Linus, we have mislaid the Lady Grace. You like, Grace, she plays with you, doesn't she?" Linus nodded. "We need your help to find her, can you do that?"

Linus nodded again, and Miles hoisted him into his arms. It felt strange carrying someone so small. "Can you show us where you last saw her?" again Linus dipped his head and Miles wondered if he ever spoke.

He carried the child outside accompanied by John and Edmund and when they reached the courtyard Linus pointed to the walled garden.

"Yes, that's where you made the snowman with Grace, but where did she go?"

"Through the door," whispered Linus and he pointed to the far wall where the ivy had been pulled back to reveal the door in the outer wall. Miles recalled it now from his childhood, it led to the river. Why would she have gone out there?

"Belle shut the door," added Linus and everyone turned to look at him.

"Belle! What has Belle to do with this?" asked Miles. He controlled his voice with difficulty he didn't want to scare the child, but he had a growing sense of unease.

"She led the pony and locked the gate," said Linus.

"Linus, you are a good lad." Miles ruffled his hair and nipped playfully at his nose, before turning away, his expression hard. "Edmund, take him to the kitchen and bring Belle back with you." He turned to John, "What has gone on here, John, what has happened to her?"

The girl, Belle, was high spirited. Miles was aware of that, and he knew Martha despaired of her at times. He also knew she had a youthful eye for Edmund. He'd caught the sly looks she'd sent his way, even if Edmund hadn't. He pulled back the bolts and flung the door open. Outside in the mud were the unmistakable tracks of a pony.

"Fetch my horse, John," said Miles impatiently as he stood and looked at the trail. She'd headed across the park into the woods; she should be easy to follow. But why had she gone? She'd promised she'd stay till he got back.

Before John could return with the horse, Martha arrived, dragging Belle by the wrist. Tom and Edmund followed at a safe distance. Martha was puce with rage and Belle, white with fear.

"Tell his lordship what ye did, yer ungrateful wretch." The girl whimpered but Miles had no time for sympathy, let her grandmother deal with her.

"I thought Edmund and Linus had gone out," she lied. "The mistress was worried, she went to fetch them. I only showed her the way," she pouted.

"How long ago?" demanded Miles and Belle shuddered.

"Not long, the sun was high."

John arrived with the horse, and Miles swung himself into the saddle, the horse danced in anticipation of the ride. He turned to Martha, his rage barely contained.

"Deal with your granddaughter madam, or I will do it myself."

He pushed the horse on through the gate and warily along the narrow river path. Once the path widened he forced the horse on as he took the expanse of parkland at a gallop, one eye on the tracks she had left, the other on the tree line ever watchful. He had another few hours of day light. He needed to find her before dark.

Chapter Twenty Seven

Grace was lost in the woods for the second time, and the irony of the situation did not escape her. Once again she'd thrown caution to the wind and was unprepared for the consequences. She found the filly increasingly difficult to handle, her own anxiety transmitted through the reins and caused the pony to jump and skitter. Grace struggled to control her. With no sign of the boys she began to wonder whether Belle was playing a game.

With a determined effort she tried to turn the pony and follow her own tracks back to the park, but the pony baulked and began to rear and spin. The commotion created uproar in the slumbering forest as all manner of woodland creatures vacated the proximity in fright. The pony's stamping hooves and squeals of frustration raised a pheasant which flew out beneath its nose, and no amount of skill on Grace's part could hold her fast. She did well to stay in the saddle as the pony reared and bolted.

* * *

The commotion alerted more than just the pheasant. Nearby, Guy and his men halted their horses to listen and strained their eyes to see through the tangle of trees. Whatever was causing the disturbance, it was coming their way. Percy, standing tall in his stirrups, was the first to catch a glimpse of the runaway pony and rider, but it was Guy who kicked his horse and raced to head them off. He was an accomplished rider and the thrill of the chase was a welcome release from the monotony of the ride through the damp forest. He quickly levelled with the grey pony. Leaning over he grasped the rein with one hand, pulled his own horse to a shuddering halt and the pony along with it. Only when both beasts finally stopped did he turn to look at the rider.

Good Lord above, he was the luckiest man alive, for sitting atop the runaway pony was the very girl he'd been sent to catch. Miles' witch girl had literally landed in his lap. She was as Mayflower had described: petite and fair with the peculiar devil's hair, but he had neglected to mention how young and attractive she was.

"Thank you," she cried, breathlessly. "Thank you so much, I thought she'd never stop." He watched as she attempted to catch her breath. She was shaking, her hands almost frozen to the reins she'd been hanging on so tightly. She beamed her gratitude at him.

He returned the greeting with a wolf-like smile. Nudging his horse closer he looked down on her from the taller beast. "Are you hurt, Mademoiselle?" He spoke with the slight French accent of a Norman lord.

"No, just a little out of breath," she replied. "The filly is young. I thought I could handle her. I was wrong. She's stronger than she looks."

She was an unusual little package, thought Guy, as he took in her petite features and heaving bosom. He could see how Mayflower had been seduced by her and he could easily appreciate what Miles saw in her too. She was different from the women he knew from court with their elaborate coiffure, their silks and dazzling jewels. She was unfinished. The wind and rain caused her pink streaked hair to stick up, and her fringe to flop untidily over one eye. Her clothes were a crime but there was no contrived coyness, no fluttering of lashes.

She may have been scared atop the bolting pony, but she certainly wasn't the quivering wreck he expected. She was alive, vibrant, exhilarated and he found her very tempting indeed. He wondered how she would feel beneath him. She pushed her fringe back from her face with an unsteady hand and an almost apologetic look. As if regretful of any trouble she may have caused. He found that even more tempting, in the way that a wolf is tempted by the succulence of a fresh lamb. He licked his lips and leaned closer.

She had beautiful eyes and long lashes, and when she smiled openly at him again he knew she was his. She'd absolutely no idea who he was. Edmund had not alerted Miles. This was going to be the easiest job he had ever undertaken.

"You are a long way from anywhere, here in these woods. Where are you headed, my lady? I would escort you to ensure your safety."

Grace took another breath. "I'm meant to be at Wildewood, only I've managed to get myself lost. I was looking for the children and I'm afraid I've got a terrible sense of direction."

"You're a long way from Wildewood, my lady."

"Am I?" Grace looked about her, taking notice of her surroundings for the first time.

"It will soon be dark," said Guy. "We are headed for Ahlborett Castle, it is not far. I suggest you accompany us. We can have a message sent to Wildewood if you're concerned they will miss you."

Grace faltered, one hand straying to her damp hair as she twisted the strands nervously. "I don't think that's a very good idea actually."

Guy raised his brow questioningly. "You will be made very welcome." He thought of the very special welcome awaiting her and smiled.

"I'm sure you're right. It's just there's been a bit of a falling out between Wildewood and those at the Castle and I'm not sure Miles would be happy for me to visit." She stopped herself with a hand across her mouth, "Oh dear, you're not Gerard are you?"

Her rescuer smiled again, genuinely amused now. "No, I am not Gerard. I hear he can be a little tyrannical, but as a host he is second to none." He thought of Gerard's most recent guest. Walter de Sweethope had complained rather loudly about his incarceration. He nudged his horse onward through the wood taking Grace's pony with him.

Grace looked around her. "Be that as it may, I think Miles would rather I went straight back to Wildewood."

Still the horses continued.

"And Miles is your...husband...brother...?"

She paused and he watched as she struggled to find the correct term. "Miles is my friend...my protector."

Guy wondered if she really was as naive as she appeared. If he kept her talking they would be at the castle before she realised it. "In that case I'm sure Miles would want you to be safe."

Grace leaned away from him and attempted to look back over her shoulder at the way they had come. "Well that's the thing, I'm not sure I would be, not at the castle, you hear such stories."

Guy nudged his horse closer causing the filly to skitter sideways and ensuring Grace's attention on their forward progression. "You do, my lady. Stories to titillate the masses, some folk lead such drab lives they feel the need to spice them up. Rest assured I will be there to protect you, should the need arise. However, I'm sure any difference of opinion between Miles and Sir Gerard would not extend to you. They are both honourable men and have a code to uphold."

The horses continued and Grace tried again. "All the same, I wouldn't like to intrude unannounced." She glanced behind her again and his men slunk some way back. She shifted her gaze to the surrounding forest warily. Guy saw the growing apprehension on her face.

"My men are good honest soldiers. We will ensure you are returned to the safety of your home, once you have rested." He waited with heightened anticipation, for her reaction when she finally realised the situation.

Grace hesitated. "I really am very grateful for your help but I'm fine now, and I do think perhaps it would be best if I just made my own way home, I've taken up enough of your time. Perhaps you could just point me in the right direction." She attempted to take back her reins but he held them fast.

Cocking his head to one side, Guy smiled at her. For a long moment he said nothing and let the uncomfortable silence hang between them. "I'm afraid that's impossible...Lady Grace," he finally said. He studied her face, the widening eyes, confusion and then the fear and he felt the warm glow of satisfaction ignite in his belly.

"You see, my lady, you have the devil's hair and our mutual acquaintance, Philibutt of Mayflower has unfortunately marked you as a witch. I have my orders to take you to Ahlborett Castle for trial. Sir Gerard awaits us."

He marvelled at how her pupils dilated with shock, and the way she fearfully moistened her lips with the tip of her tongue. It gave him an urge which he toyed with. Did he have the time, he wondered, to take her, here in the forest? It seemed such a waste not to; after all if she were found guilty she would burn regardless.

"Of course if it were up to me," he added with a sigh, "I would endeavour to save you from the flames, but alas I am merely a tool of my lord."

She tried to snatch the reins back once more but he retained a firm grip and merely shook his head and tutted at her.

"Now that's not going to work, is it?" he said patiently. "I'm bigger and stronger than you."

Grace glanced about her frantically and Guy watched as her panic rose along with his arousal.

"At the end of the day, my lady, you will be coming with me. What you must decide is whether we leave the forest as friends or enemies." He leaned towards her conspiratorially. "A word of advice, Gracie - may I call you Gracie? It has a certain ring to it. Anyway, as I was saying, friend is always better than enemy. I'm sure Miles would vouch for that. He knows first-hand what happens to my enemies." He smiled at her. "As friends we could amuse each other, I could even offer you a character reference when the bishop and his inquisitors come a calling. But as an enemy, well as an enemy, I am sorry to say I would be more inclined to light the pyre beneath your feet when they tie you to the stake. Take it from me, friend is more useful to both of us."

Grace stared open mouthed, as the colour drained from her cheeks.

"Our ecclesiastical friend Mayflower tells me you're warming Miles' bed, if it is pleasure you seek then you need look no further. As a friend I can guarantee you a far more exiting ride than you'll get with your protector Miles. I confess, I prefer a more voluptuous maid, but I find you refreshingly different and it interests me to know what Miles finds attractive in you."

Grace took a ragged breath. "After that little speech I assume you must be Guy, the man who bullies little boys. Miles did mention you." She glared at him but he merely grinned.

"Is that not what little boys are for? Little boys grow into little men unless their mettle is tested as a child. I merely provide them with adequate tuition."

"You are evil," she declared.

"Oh yes, definitely...," he replied with a smirk. "Deliciously so..."

"Let me go, now. Miles will not be far away and when he finds you, I'll not be responsible for what he'll do."

Guy laughed out loud. "Do you hear that boys? Miles is coming to get us....Are we fearful?" He turned back to Grace. "I have already beaten Miles once. Perhaps he neglected to tell you that?"

"He told me you came in the night like a sneak thief. Were you scared to meet him face to face, Guy?"

Guy narrowed his eyes shrewdly. "It's called cunning, knowing thy enemy, and anyway, I still beat him. And while we're on the subject of your lover, have you ever seen a knight with more scars? It rather begs one to question his prowess on the battlefield. I shall be generous and we shall call him a trifle clumsy."

"If you'd beaten him he would not still be alive," snapped Grace.

Guy snorted dismissively.

"If you had beaten him he would not be standing behind you now."

Guy turned instinctively and in that instance Grace swung out with her makeshift whip and struck him across the face. She yanked at the reins and the filly squealed angrily, but still Guy held on and with a howl he turned and she took the full force of the back of his hand across her cheek. The blow was enough to unseat her and she tumbled backwards from the saddle, landing in a painful heap on the forest floor.

Guy dismounted slowly and stood over her where she lay in the dirt. The angry red mark of the whip marred his perfect face. His smile gone, his eyes were cold and cruel. He shook his head in disbelief at her daring.

"You should not have done that, witch. Did you not understand my explanation of friends and enemies, about making the right choice?" He shrugged and began to unfasten his belt.

"No matter. Enemy works for me."

Chapter Twenty Eight

The ground was damp beneath her. The smell of leaf mould and decay filled her nostrils, permeating her senses and dragging her back to the time in the wood when the arrow had claimed her. Grace felt her heart rate hike, and nausea born of fear churned inside. She remembered Miles' words: don't let him get you on your back. She tried to wriggle away before he dropped his weight upon her.

"Hold her." Guy barked the command to his men who covered the distance from their horses to grab her arms and hold her down. Grace swallowed the screams that welled from deep inside. She instinctively knew that revealing her fear would feed Guy's warped fantasy and incite him all the more. She was defenceless against one, never mind three, but she struggled nevertheless, terror lending strength to her puny efforts.

"Let me go," she snarled. "Let me go, or you'll really find out if I'm a witch or not? Do you want your pricks to shrivel and drop off?"

The men holding her arms immediately let go and jumped back. "For God's sake she's no witch," shouted Guy in frustration. "She's a little whore with paint in her hair."

* * *

"Let her go." Miles' voice rang out clear and strong immediately behind Guy. Grace almost sobbed with relief. "Let her go and step away, Guy," he repeated. Guy took a step back, his hands in the air.

"Are you well, Grace?" Miles asked calmly. "Has he hurt you?"

Grace struggled to her feet. She was dishevelled and her right cheek had begun to swell but she favoured him with a brave smile. "I'm fine, Miles," she answered weakly.

He momentarily slid his gaze from Guy and assessed her. What he saw reassured him and strengthened his resolve. He felt the sliver of something decidedly bad begin to weave its way through him and he tightened his grip on the bow. He had an arrow aimed at the back of Guy's head, the string of the bow taut, the arrow ready to launch. He steadied his breath. She had scared him and he hadn't been scared for a long time. Hearing the commotion as the pony bolted he'd been too late to stop Guy. Instead he watched and positioned himself with one arrow ready, but knew by the time he released it and readied to fire another, he would be taken down by one of Guy's men.

"Get behind me, Grace," he called and Grace gingerly stepped past Guy.

"You can't take all three of us, Miles," taunted Guy. "And when you go down, be assured your little whore will follow."

"You tried to put me down once before, Guy. You couldn't do it then, and you certainly aren't going to do it now." Miles flicked a glance at Grace. She was moving too hesitantly and remained far too close to Guy. Her fear was palpable. She was still in danger.

Guy locked eyes with Miles and inclined his head suggestively. "Does she whimper in your bed, Miles?"

"You will whimper, Guy," snarled Miles. "You will whimper and beg, before I'm finished with you."

Guy shifted his gaze to Percy whose hand hovered over the knife at his belt. He raised a brow and Miles amended his aim. The arrow struck Percy in the chest and he thudded to the ground.

Taking the opportunity of Miles' distraction, Guy made a grab for Grace, pulling her against him, one arm tightly round her waist, the other at her throat, his own knife now in his hand and pressed against her soft skin. He spun round to face Miles, but he was no longer there.

"Where did he go?" he snarled at Simon, who had dropped to the ground for cover.

"I know not, my lord. One moment he was there, the next he was gone. There is witchcraft afoot." He cast a wary eye about the clearing.

"Forget witches, you sorry son of a pox ridden whore. Find the bastard or it will be you who will burn." He spun around, dragging Grace with him as he scoured the trees for a trace of movement.

"I'll slit her throat right here if you don't show yourself," Guy spat into the surrounding woods. "Or maybe I'll have her first. Would you prefer me to do that, Miles?" Grace struggled vainly against him. "Would you like to witness how loudly she whimpers when I take my pleasure...?" He increased the pressure of the blade and her pale skin pricked with the crimson of fresh blood.

Simon fell a moment later with an arrow in his chest and a dull thud as he hit the ground. Neither he nor Percy remained of any further use to Guy. Miles stepped out from behind a tree and held the bow out to his side.

"Let her go, Guy, she is not part of our fight." He called on his reserves of self-control and hung tightly to the bitterness which swirled in his head and pulsed through his veins. He could not bear to see the man near her, let alone with his hands upon her. His eyes locked on the trickle of blood at her throat.

"Ah, but that is where you're wrong, Miles. She is at the very centre.

Gerard reckons you are all in league with each other. You, Hugh and the king. She is the glue which holds you together, the power keeping you alive and invincible. He intends to cut off your power source. He plans to burn her as a witch. He awaits the bishop as we speak."

"That will never happen, Guy, and you know it. Let her go and I'll give you your fight if that's what you want. Fair and square. Just you and me. Not a sword in the belly in the middle of the night but one on one, hand to hand combat here and now." He glanced at Grace and held himself in check. "Whoever wins takes the girl."

"Do you think I'm a fool? As soon as I release her, you'll put an arrow through my heart."

"No, I won't," said Miles. "You have my word, as a knight." He placed the bow on the ground before him, and Grace stared at him, open mouthed.

Miles knew Guy thought him the fool for giving up his advantage, as if he didn't realise the knife currently pressed against Grace's tender flesh could just as easily be flung at his own chest after slitting her throat. He was, however, wagering that Guy would be unable to resist the lure of a fight which he was sure he would win.

"It seems your lover is keen to be rid of you my dear." Guy pushed Grace to the ground and turned a cold glare on Miles. "I will happily take her off your hands when you lie beaten and bloody on the ground. The last thing you will see in this life will be me thrusting between her thighs."

"Grace, wait by the horses," called Miles with a reassuring nod. He clenched his fists as he shot Guy a murderous look. He had an urge to cut out the man's tongue. "We will be leaving soon."

"Oh, the confidence of the man," laughed Guy as they circled each other. Miles did not share his laughter. A cold calculating look transformed his face as he sized up his opponent and unsheathed his sword.

Miles bided his time while Grace moved the filly alongside his own horse, standing beneath the trees away from the ensuing fight. He watched her edge carefully past Guy's fallen men. When he judged her to be safe he turned his attention back to his opponent and began.

Each held their sword in a two handed grip. Guy advanced first and swung for Miles. The weight of the parried sword caused Miles to steady his stance following the blow.

"You see, Miles, you are getting too old for this," taunted Guy. "Give up now and I shall kill you swiftly and save you the sight of me taking your whore."

Miles brought his sword down and then, Guy too, was required to defend himself from the weight of the blow. The inertia knocked the breath from him, momentarily silencing his taunts.

"With age comes experience, Guy. Experience and intelligence. You have neither."

Guy sneered.

"Intelligence? You had the chance to kill me with your bow and declined. Where is the sense in that?"

Miles shook his head derisively. "You have neither brains nor the stamina for the game, Guy, admit it." Miles was the stronger. He assumed he would soon have Guy beaten, but the swordplay went on at length without either man seeming to take the advantage. Guy was the more agile and, despite his bravado, Miles began to favour one side, protecting his belly from a further blow, conscious of a weakness and unwilling to allow Guy to monopolise on it. Yet, Miles' own skill with the sword was second to none and Guy spent a great deal of his time and energy avoiding the weight of the blade. On balance it was an even match and Miles wondered how long they could realistically keep it up. He needed to change his tactics.

Miles caught Guy off guard and ripped Guy's sword from his hand, sending it crashing to the ground. He paused and both men took ragged, desperate breaths. A sudden stillness encompassed the clearing. The horses stilled and Grace closed her eyes, the fight had reached a conclusion.

"Come, Guy," taunted Miles as he dropped his own sword and gestured with his open palms. "I said it would be a fair fight. Not scared to get up close are you?"

Guy spat venomously on the ground before Miles. "Scared of a bastard like you? I think not, Miles." He charged at him. Miles sidestepped him easily and landed a crushing kidney punch that left Guy gasping. Guy caught his breath, hands on his knees while Miles waited. When he swung round and launched his return attack, Miles was ready and sent him sprawling.

"You'll have to do better than that," said Miles and then regretted his jibe when Guy rose up catching him on the side of the jaw with a gloved fist. He felt his teeth rattle. He caught hold of Guy by the shoulders and head butted him. Guy's nose burst in a spray of blood as did Miles' brow; the blow merely served to inflame Guy further. He flew into an undisciplined manic rage landing punch after punch, until one lucky blow caught Miles in the belly and he dropped to his knees, clutching his abdomen.

Guy whooped with delight. He aimed a kick which caught Miles cruelly under his chin and sent his head flicking back. Miles lay for a moment, stunned. Pain and rage swirled madly together. His vision blurred but his focus remained intact. He shook his head, swung his gaze as he sought to clear his vision and caught a glimpse of Grace's terrified face.

"Is that good enough for you?" taunted Guy and he landed another booted foot in the small of Miles' back. Miles rolled over with a groan. He needed to finish this quickly.

Guy continued to circle him, landing a kick at his shoulder, another on the side of his head. Grace stepped forward, away from the safety of the tethered horses, as he delivered a further brutal kick. Miles groaned, aware, despite his condition, that Grace was vulnerable and Guy, so easily distracted. He expected her to do something foolish, he willed her to desist. He had everything in hand.

Miles watched in dismay as she ran to where his sword lay in the dirt and grasped it with both hands. She tried to lift the weapon but struggled to manage the weight. All she could do was drag it along the ground. He opened his mouth to deliver a warning and received a further kick to his belly which knocked the words and what was left of his breath right out of his mouth. He focused on her again as she lifted the sword and attempted to swing it at Guy. Guy ducked out of her way and as the effort of the swing spun her round, he put his foot on her derriere and sent her sprawling.

"Got your little lady fighting your battles for you now, Miles, what is the world coming to?" Guy aimed another kick at Miles prone body.

All the while, Miles waited and he took the blows. Then, when it appeared by his stillness that he had lost consciousness, Guy made to kick him again and Miles caught hold of his booted foot with both hands, one at the heel and the other at the toe, and with a quick twist of his wrists and a considerable amount of strength, he snapped Guy's ankle with a satisfying crunch. Guy's scream of pain resonated throughout the forest. Grace stifled a sob and ran to Miles.

Struggling to rise, he waved Grace away as she tried to help him. His face was slick with blood. One eye was swollen shut and he spat blood onto the ground. With difficulty he stooped, picked up his sword and bow, and straightened himself before walking slowly to where Guy writhed on the ground. He held the point of the sword at Guy's throat and allowed its own weight to indent into the soft flesh.

"Take a message to Gerard," he growled.

Guy opened his eyes and captured Miles with a malevolent glare.

"Tell him that Miles of Wildewood is back - and I will have justice."

Despite much verbal abuse, Miles ensured all three men were

secured in their saddles before he applied a whip to the horse's rumps and sent them back to Ahlborett. Finally he turned to look at Grace.

She had placed herself in danger to try and protect him but it could have gone terribly wrong. He drew an arm around her shoulder and tucked her into his side.

"We must get back, it will soon be dark." He was weary, his body racked with pain.

"We can't go back," cried Grace, "Not yet, the boys are missing. I came to look for them, I called for them, I looked everywhere, I couldn't find them. They could be out here, lost."

Miles attempted a tired smile. Edmund was correct. She had not been leaving him. "The boys never left Wildewood."

"But Belle..."

"Belle deceived you."

"Why? Why would she do that," she faltered. "I could have been killed...You could have been killed."

He shrugged painfully. "Who knows what goes on in her head, I certainly don't. Her grandmother will no doubt get to the bottom of it." He glanced at the darkening sky. "We must leave now; I will not relax until you are safe within the walls of Wildewood." The wound dissecting his eyebrow reopened and he wiped the blood from his eye with the back of his hand.

"Sit down a moment," said Grace. "I have something that may help to stop the bleeding." She pushed Miles gently onto a log and he sat wearily as she rifled in her pockets. "Do you have a sharp knife?" she asked as she pulled out the roll of electricians' tape.

"I have your knife, freshly sharpened."

"Shame I didn't have it with me earlier."

Miles shook his head slowly as he pulled the knife from his belt. "I take back what I said earlier, I don't want you killing anyone. I don't want you near any of them again."

Grace took the knife from him and he realised that despite her bravado her hands were still shaking. He took hold of them gently. "You're safe now, Grace. You did well, but they've gone now, they cannot hurt you." He smiled as he recalled her attempt with the sword, it was almost as heavy as she, and yet she had tried, risking her own life for him.

"If you hadn't come along when you did then, Guy would have...." she bit her lip to stop its involuntary quiver.

Without a doubt she looked more scared now than he had ever seen her. Even her reaction to his appalling behaviour the previous night as he forced her up against the chamber door, was nothing compared with what he saw in her face now. The idea that anyone would want to do her harm ignited flames within him that seared his soul. But the realisation this had become personal and was gathering momentum, lit far darker flames of revenge and deadly retribution. He wondered at his own self-control.

She took a calming breath and used the knife to cut thin strips from the plastic tape. She wiped the worst of the blood away with the corner of her sleeve and when the edges of the gash were visible she used the sticky tape to pull them together. She did the same with the wound on the side of his head.

"I'm afraid you may have a few more scars to add to your collection."

"That's useful stuff." Miles observed wearily, distracted equally by her soft touch and the thought of other scars, those he would inflict on his enemies. "What is it?"

"Just sticky tape, nothing special."

"Another one of your secrets?"

Grace smiled, "Perhaps."

"You have others?"

"One or two."

Miles dragged himself up and took Grace's small hand in his. He pulled her to him and simply held her, gaining immeasurable strength, from the feel of her in his arms. He dipped his head and sighed regretfully when he noticed the thin mark of Guy's blade on her skin. He pressed a gentle kiss before pulling away.

"Do you plan to share them with me?"

"You wouldn't believe me anyway."

"Try me."

"I'm a time traveller from the future..."

Miles looked at her blankly. His head hurt and he could make no sense from her words. He opened his mouth to respond to her nonsense and for once was too weary for her games.

"Of course, Mademoiselle...and I am the King of England."

Chapter Twenty Nine

It was well after dark when Miles and Grace crossed the park and finally reached the safety of Wildewood. Their return shocked the household, and brought home to them all the seriousness of the situation they faced.

Edmund had watched for them all afternoon from his position on the wall. John had attempted to replace him but he would not give up his post. He strained his eyes in the growing dusk not certain of their approach until they were almost upon him. He yelled to John to open the gate.

Grace had not the energy to withstand any of the filly's recent antics. Miles anticipated trouble from the youngster and attached a lead rope to her bridle; as a result the journey was surprisingly uneventful. The horses, like their riders were dispirited and craved the security of their stable. Grace was in a state of shock. Her eyes glassy and her cheek swollen and not even the welcoming torchlight atop the main gate or Edmund's excited shouting could shake her torpor. They passed through the entrance and the gate was quickly and securely bolted by John. Tom looked on in horror at the state of them.

Nodding his gratitude to the men, Miles pushed the horses the last few yards to the stables. He could barely dismount, his muscles seizing up, his body wracked with pain. His face was a mass of bruises and wounds, one eye completely closed. He dismounted slowly and Edmund ran to take the reins.

"My lord, you are injured," the boy cried, as he attempted to shoulder Miles' weight.

Tom rushed to help, grabbing Miles' arm as he staggered back, sharing the burden with Edmund. "What has happened?"

"Does our lady require assistance?" added John as he took hold of the filly's reins.

Miles waved away the many questions. The men were naturally concerned but there would be time for that later. They both needed to rest. He shook off his attendants and helped Grace from the pony.

"Edmund, see that the horses are well looked after tonight - they are hungry and tired." He smiled crookedly at the boy. Edmund's concern was plain to see.

Gerard would not come tonight. All the same he bade John and Tom to mount a watch. "Place some fires a short distance from the gate," he suggested, "that way you'll be able to see if any unwelcome guests

154

come a calling."

"Do you expect them?" asked John gravely.

"No, but we must always prepare for the worst."

"And hope for the best?" added John.

Martha rushed from the kitchen wringing her hands in dismay. "Lord above us, what has happened?" she fussed around Grace. "Poor child, she is struck dumb with shock." She bustled her out of Miles' reach and he had not the energy to prevent it.

"Your face, my lord; who has done this?" she cried. They all looked awkwardly at the mess of Miles' face. No one made comment on the unusual strapping.

"See that Grace is made comfortable, Martha," said Miles, wearily. Martha nodded and placing an arm around her shoulders she shepherded her indoors.

"You are injured, my lord, do you need anything?" asked John, quietly when the women had left them alone in the yard.

Miles grimaced. "I expect I'll be pissing blood for a week, but other than that I'm fine, John. In fact better than that, I am focused, and tomorrow we will all be focused. For now though Grace and I both need to rest. I know I can rely on you to watch our backs while we do so." He reached out and patted the giant's arm, then turned and entered the house.

Martha boiled water, her remedy for all ills. She ran both of them a bath and they soaked in the scented warmth together, in the privacy of Grace's room. Neither of them spoke, there was no need. As the warmth seeped into their bones; Miles in particular felt the benefit in his protesting muscles. He gently washed her hair and she used a soft cloth to clean the blood from his face. Food was provided, but neither Miles nor Grace could stomach it. No one asked the whereabouts of Belle. Later, when the household was finally quiet, Grace lay in Miles' arms and he held her gently, warm and safe. She wept silently against his bare chest and the feel of her tears against his skin scared him. He had almost lost her. He could never let that happen again.

* * *

Throughout the following afternoon the valley folk began to arrive at Wildewood. First came the brothers, Sam and Joseph, lanky young men straight off the land with calloused palms and heavy picks. They were not alike in looks but their relationship was unmistakable in the way they walked and in the humble way in which they offered their services. They had heard from Berryman, the Lord of Wildewood needed help

155

and they had come.

From the deep woods came the Foresters, a father Jack and his son Robert, rugged well-built men, they carried mighty axes and possessed the strength to wield them fearlessly. With them came Jack's wife Peg a daughter May and a cartload of poultry: chickens, geese and capons. Raised in the woods, they were fat and content and were released into the walled garden where they would be safe from foxes. Peg and May joined Martha in the kitchen, where they set about cooking for the growing household.

The Scots arrived next: six young men led by an elder dressed in the weave of his clan. They had come as Alex Stewart's representatives to join the defence of Wildewood. They did not socialise immediately but nodded curtly to John, who manned the gate, and settled themselves outside the stables where their shaggy horses were tethered and fed by Edmund. Like their horses, they were fearsome looking, wild and otherworldly.

Late afternoon brought four families, all of them farmed within the bounds of Wildewood but closely bordering the vast holdings of Ahlborett. They feared Gerard's retribution and came for the safety of Wildewood's stone retaining walls and brought what little produce they had left after such a hard winter. Foodstuffs went straight to the kitchen where Martha now presided over a growing band of helpers. The livestock which included four pigs and a pair of goats went into the walled garden and the children, who now numbered eight, were set the task of tending them. The nanny goat was an instant hit, the billy goat less so as he had a tendency to butt and had a dreadful odour.

Each man carried a weapon of sorts, be it a knife a pitchfork or hammer. All carried a bow and a quiver of arrows, and all were expert in its use. Their survival depended upon them being able to hunt and kill, be it rabbit or Gerard's deer.

By evening Wildewood had twenty additional men capable of maintaining a defence and after they had all been fed, the Scots, minus their elder, Angus Baird, melted into the forest to keep watch. John told the children a story around the fire in the great hall and when they were sufficiently sated they were put to sleep on clean straw by their mothers. The men gathered at the table with Miles to discuss the plan. Grace sat at his side. Miles still carried the evidence on his face of his encounter with Guy, but both he and Grace were rested, focused and heartened by the support shown by the folk who had given themselves to defend Wildewood. If Gerard thought he would find them dispirited and beaten underdogs, then he was mistaken.

The men listened in silence as Miles described the previous day's events and one or two did glance warily at Grace when mention was made of Gerard's plan to have the Bishop of Durham condemn her as a witch. However, Miles' unquestioning loyalty to her, seconded by John, was enough to convince them she was no more a witch than they were. Those that may have harboured doubts reasoned it was far better to have her power on their side if that was indeed the case.

They had to assume, explained Miles, that the bishop's aide, Philibutt of Mayflower, had a day's head start on his journey to Durham. At the rate his tiny pony travelled, though, Miles estimated he would have got no further than Hexham.

"He must not get to Durham," said Miles.

"Consider it done," replied the Scotsman and he rose to leave the table.

"He must not be killed," added Miles. "Detain him and bring him here, we need his evidence to condemn Gerard and Guy." He found it difficult to say Guy's name. He regretted not running him through when he had the chance. His regret festered and threatened to intrude on his strategy. He reluctantly pushed thoughts of Guy to one side. Revenge was all the better for waiting.

"Who will believe such a man when placed against such a great nobleman?" asked Jack Forester. "If he is as easily corrupted as you say, then he will not stand as a good witness."

Jack was right, they needed more than the odious Mayflower, but he was all they could hope to have for the moment.

"We could petition the king," suggested Grace and was met by stunned silence. Miles smiled patiently at her. She obviously did not understand how things worked.

"Why not? Is the king not involved in all of this in a roundabout way? Gerard has been making accusations against him. Wouldn't he be grateful for the chance to finally put him in his place?" she pressed on. "The king gave you Wildewood. He took it from Gerard and gave it to you. He must hold you in some regard. Surely any judgement made by him would have to be upheld by Gerard."

Miles conceded she was correct, but things were never that simple.

"The king is in London. By the time we got word to the royal court, Gerard would have an army encamped around our walls and a stake positioned at the gate."

As soon as the words were out of his mouth he regretted them. Grace was putting on a brave face, but he knew her experience with Guy affected her more than she was prepared to admit. She'd cried herself to sleep the previous night and in her dreams she relived her fear. He'd held her as she'd whimpered and fought the nightmare. He watched her visibly pale at his mention of the stake. Taking her hand in his, he squeezed it reassuringly.

"John, how quickly do you think a man could get to London on a swift horse?"

"Not quickly enough, my lord, for he would also need to get back with the king's reply and I doubt Gerard would find it difficult to stop him."

"Yer do not need to go to London."

All heads turned to seek out the owner of the voice, who lurked in the shadows beyond the reach of the candlelight.

"Who goes there?" called Miles. "Come forward into the light and show yourself."

Belle stepped forward nervously and there was a collective murmur. Miles silenced them with a raised hand.

"What have you to say for yourself, Belle?" asked Miles quietly, so quietly she was forced closer to hear him.

The others held their tongue. They too were interested in what the girl had to say. Miles had chosen not to deal with her since their return. He'd left her to her grandmother, accepting Martha would exact an appropriate justice. He did not quite trust himself. She'd endangered Grace and he could not forget that, no matter her youth or whatever excuse she may offer.

Grace watched as the girl stood fearfully before Miles. It had taken courage for her to present herself at such a gathering. The animosity directed toward her was palpable.

"Come closer, Belle," she requested kindly. "You're quite safe, no one will harm you, and we just need to hear what you have to say."

Miles glanced at Grace, she may have the capacity to forgive; he doubted he shared it.

"Yer don't need to go to London to petition the king, he's coming here - to Alnwick."

"How do you know this?" suddenly Miles was hopeful, Alnwick was a mere twenty five miles away.

"The men who escorted the bishop's aide, I overheard them talking. They said King Edward was coming to Alnwick and Gerard was beginning to unravel. I didn't know what they meant." She glanced at Grace who smiled encouragingly.

"When did they say he was arriving?" asked Miles.

"When they were in the kitchen, yer asked grandmother to feed them and I served them their food."

Miles shook his head. "No that's not what I mean, Belle. Now think, when did the men say the king would arrive at Alnwick?"

Belle frowned as if trying to remember, her answer could prove vitally important.

"I don't think they mentioned what day he would arrive but they did say he would attend Sunday High Mass. I remember, because they said Sir Gerard would be expected to attend at Alnwick, rather than take mass at Ahlborett, and he was fearful it may be a trap. They were to join Sir Gerard's escort just in case."

Sunday, was four days away, they had to hold Gerard off till then, but that was not so bad. He no longer had Guy and his henchmen at his disposal and four days would give them time to pull all of the pieces of their plan together.

Miles sat back in his seat and considered the girl before him.

"Belle, I don't know why you misled the Lady Grace and put her at risk. It was a dangerous and wicked thing to do, to betray a member of your own household. You must be punished for your actions. If you were one of my men I would not hesitate to take a whip to your back or put a knife to your throat. But you are not one of my men. You are a child who mistakenly believes she is a women. Your grandmother will no doubt find an appropriate punishment for you. You must grow up, Belle, and learn responsibility for your actions. Everything you do in life has consequences. Yesterday you nearly cost the life of an innocent woman..." He paused to let his words sink in. He trembled with emotion, Belle trembled with fear.

"But today you have shown courage and you may have saved the lives of us all. Think on that, Belle."

The girl, who had been studying her feet, looked up then, relief evident in her soft gasp. She glanced at Grace who smiled and nodded.

"You may go to your grandmother now," added Miles. She fled the hall gratefully and he let out the breath he had been holding.

"We have a chance," he said to the assembled men. "Let us not waste it. Those who are not on first watch should get some sleep." He turned to the Scot who was readying to leave. "Do you need anything from us?" The man shook his head. "Then will you pass my thanks to Alex, I am in his debt."

"Nay son, we are in yer debt and will remain so as lang as Alex lives. If it wisnae for ye an' yer courage in defendin' him agin the Saracen Horde then we widnae have a leader capable o' leadin' us in the defence of oor lands against yer English barons." He gave Miles a wry grin, "Of course yer English noblemen may come tae regret yer actions, but we Scots never shall." He crossed to the door." Tae ye and yers ..."

"And you and yours," answered Miles. Life continued to amaze him. He felt humbled. One life saved in the heat of the Palestinian sun and he had gained lifelong support from over the border. Although the border region had been fairly settled for some years now, with the exception of the occasional rustling, who knew what would happen in the future? As he had tried to explain to Belle, every action had consequences.

The gathering dispersed, with the majority seeking comfort on the floor alongside the rest of their families. Miles wondered absently whether perhaps some of the outbuildings could be made weatherproof and adapted for the families. He knew too well the discomfort of sleeping on a cold stone floor and there was no privacy for those couples who did not choose to go straight to sleep. He would speak with John maybe a little work would keep everyone's minds off the predicament they found themselves in. Now he had Mayflower's money he could afford to pay them, which would go some way to recompensing them for the time spent away from their land.

He hoped they would soon be able to return to their homes, but until his feud with Gerard was settled, nothing was assured.

Chapter Thirty

"We need more than Mayflower," Miles confided in Grace later. "We need more evidence to take to the king."

Grace drew her bottom lip between her teeth, her face a study in concentration. She sat on the bed cross-legged, covers pulled up around her, a goblet of elderflower wine in her hand, courtesy of the Foresters. It was her second and almost finished. For someone who couldn't take her drink, Miles reckoned she was certainly getting some practice. He paced back and forth across the room, with the flagon. As he gestured with his hands, he sloshed the wine, over the floor and the toes of his leather boots.

"Sit down. You're making me dizzy just looking at you," she demanded. He acquiesced, taking space at the bottom of the bed his booted feet on top of the covers. Grace looked pointedly at the boots and he moved his feet to the floor without comment.

"We need to put Edward in a position where he cannot fail to decide in Wildewoods favour. He'll not want to stand up to such a powerful family unless it's advantageous for him to do so. He relies upon the power of the de Frouville's to keep his northern border patrolled and safe from Scottish attack."

"Is it likely, he'll do anything at all?" asked Grace. "How far back does his connection with the de Frouville's go?"

"Generations; It was King Henry II who first instructed the de Frouville's to build a castle at Ahlborett. To be fair they have managed the land well, and defended the border as instructed, Alex would no doubt vouch for that. The region has enjoyed an extended period of peace which is largely due to the de Frouville's. The fact Gerard has behaved like a prick since he was old enough to piss straight, is neither here nor there as long as he continues to protect the king's border and doesn't do anything to damage the king's reputation. Edward will not allow Gerard to make a fool of him, but I doubt whether he'll go so far as to hang him for murder."

"And yet your mother was a de Frouville' and so are you. Surely the king could act as arbitrator in what is essentially a family disagreement?"

Miles narrowed his eyes.

"I do not care to think of myself as a de Frouville'. I have never been a part of that family. They maltreated my mother when she most needed their support. They murdered her when she was at her happiest. And I know Gerard would see me dead."

Grace hesitated. "What of your father?"

"I know nothing of my father," Miles replied curtly. That subject was not for discussion.

"What else has Gerard done that might anger the king?" asked Grace.

"In addition to the murder of my mother?"

Grace winced. "Um...yes."

Miles thought about it. In his opinion everything else seemed insignificant. "He imprisoned Walter de Sweethope. Edward was forced to intervene to get him released."

Grace drained her goblet and clinging onto the covers with one hand, twisted around looking for the flagon. "Who is Walter de Sweethope?" she asked, leaning perilously over the side of the bed as she reached out blindly with her hand.

"A landowner, from some way west of here. Kirkwhelpington, I believe." Miles cocked his head and watched as the covers slid away and she hovered closer to the point of no return.

"Why?"

"Why did Gerard imprison him, or why did Edward intervene?"

"Well, both I suppose." She pulled herself back from the brink and ran her fingers through her hair.

"Not sure to both, I assume he pissed Gerard off for some reason, and I assume Gerard subsequently pissed Edward off. I don't know the man, Sweethope, so I couldn't really say."

Grace studied Miles. "Do you know your swearing is increasing, rather alarmingly?" He raised a brow and opened his mouth to reply but she beat him to it. "I think you're mixing with the wrong people," she giggled and he returned a grin of his own.

"I think you've had enough to drink, I wouldn't care to be accused of corrupting you."

"That's better," she said. "You look so much nicer when you smile."

"There hasn't been much to smile about recently," he replied. His eyes trailed over her, "Apart from you of course."

She crossed her legs again and rested her elbows on her knees, her chin pensively on her hands. "Okay, anything else?" She yawned softly.

Miles tipped his head back, closed his eyes and put his boots back on the bed. He needed to stretch out. His thoughts were beginning to wander and his concentration not helped by glimpses of flesh and white lace. His imagination took hold as he visualised her stretched out next to him. "There was the business of the missing treasure," he muttered.

Grace leaned forward. "Treasure?"

"Something Alex mentioned, Gerard was suspected of misappropriating some loot from the crusades. It was all supposed to

162

come back to the king's coffers and apparently Gerard's didn't. He claimed it was stolen."

"Wasn't that your excuse?"

"No, it wasn't an excuse, it actually happened. Guy and his associates took it while I was otherwise engaged."

Grace let that go with a smile. "But if no one knew what Gerard had in his possession in the first place then it would be hard to prove."

Miles shrugged. It was late, his thoughts were already elsewhere.

"Do you remember what you had, before Guy took it?"

"Not everything." It had been three years' worth after all. "A collection of gold and jewellery, merely what could be carried on the back of a horse."

"Do you think Guy and Gerard might possibly have pooled their ill-gotten gains?"

Miles considered it. They were both self-centred men and he doubted they would have the capacity to share anything unless they had a specific plan and purpose. The fact they were now working together, led him to believe there was indeed a plan afoot. "You think if they have, Guy may have included the valuables he took from me and I might be able to identify them?"

"Possibly."

"But we'd have to find it first."

Grace's face changed as something important finally dawned. Miles saw the excitement sparkle in her eyes. "I may just be able to help with that," she cried excitedly.

"You're telling me you know where Gerard has hidden the treasure?" he raised a sceptical brow. "I thought we'd already established you aren't a witch."

She glanced at him through lowered lashes, mischief lacing her words. "I think I do ... but who knows what powers I'll need to unleash, in order to be sure."

He shook his head. "Don't - not even in jest, Grace. There are people not so far from here who would hang you from the nearest bough simply because you're ... unusual. Don't give them further cause. Anyway, how do you know?"

Grace scrambled out of her cocoon of covers and left her empty goblet at the side of the bed. She crawled up the bed to him on all fours, sat astride his out stretched legs in her underwear and shuffled up onto his knee.

"Careful," he winced as she adjusted her position with a hand on his still tender abdomen. "We were talking about the treasure...I think."

She kissed the end of his nose and he put his hands on her hips to keep her still. "How do you imagine you know where it is?"

"My grandfather told me." She shivered delicately, goosebumps spreading over her bared flesh and reaching behind her she attempted to pull up the covers.

Miles shook his head. "You expect me to concentrate while you writhe half naked on my lap?"

"I'm testing your chivalry," she replied with a grin, and continued to wriggle.

"And I've told you, chivalry is dead. Long live – lust, revenge and pleasure -" He dipped his head and caught her mouth with his.

"You underestimate yourself," she said softly as she pushed him half-heartedly away.

He helped her to pull the covers around her shoulders, allowed his palms to linger on the soft skin at the nape of her neck. "You said your grandfather told you?"

"Yes. I don't know why I didn't think of it before, that's why the name de Frouville' was familiar when we first met." She leaned into him conspiratorially and hushed to a soft whisper. "Apparently one of the de Frouville's hid his stash in the crypt below the chapel at Kirk Knowe, or so the story goes. It must have been Gerard; it's too much of a coincidence."

"And your grandfather, the gardener at Kirk Knowe, told you this - when?" asked Miles. Something didn't add up. Her conflicting stories were beginning to overlap. His mind strayed back to spies and witches.

Grace shrugged. He couldn't tell whether her cheeks pinked as a result of subterfuge or something else. She wriggled closer and he cast all thought of spies from his mind.

"But you haven't seen it?" he croaked. She was doing things she shouldn't and he should probably stop her, but his self-discipline was ebbing at a surprising rate.

"Well, no of course not. It was just a story, but where better to hide something you didn't want found?"

Miles looked at her, weary scepticism creeping back into his expression. "A story? We need a little more substance than that."

"But it makes sense doesn't it." She smiled her sweet smile and slid her hand beneath his shirt.

"Not entirely, but if it means we can forgo talking and move onto other things. I expect we could go and look."

* * *

Grace faltered. Go to Kirk Knowe. How could they do that? Wasn't it on the other side? Or was that just her Kirk Knowe, her cottage? It was complicated. What if they returned to Kirk Knowe and she was back in 2012 and he was with her? Or would he cease to exist if they crossed the divide? She looked at him and worried. She had demanded he take her back, and certainly after the incident with Guy she'd been more than ready to leave, this life was altogether too dangerous. But was she ready to go back and leave Miles behind?

She backpedalled a little, suddenly scared and not entirely sure why.

"But it's miles away. It took us days to get here. We haven't got days."

"It took us days," replied Miles, "Because it was necessary to navigate a course to avoid Ahlborett Castle, and partly because of the weather, but mostly because of you. Your injury naturally slowed us down."

"Of course," replied Grace. "I'd forgotten all about the fact that one of you tried to kill me. I'm sorry I caused you so much trouble."

Miles held her face gently between his palms and kissed her, lingering a little longer than necessary. "My lady, it was not I. Edward mistook you for a deer. Those large, doe eyes of yours obviously had something to do with it. And I would argue we did take care of you. We could have left you where we found you."

Grace kissed him back slowly, her mind not quite in the same place as her lips. If they travelled a different route then maybe the divide would not be crossed at all? She had no idea how these things worked and tried to remember how she'd slipped through the first time. One minute she'd heard the artillery fire and the next it was silent. Recalling the spot in the ancient wood when she'd first noticed the silence, she wondered if she'd be able to find it again if the need arose either to avoid, it or use it.

"You took care of me very well," she agreed, still distracted and concerned. "We would still need to avoid Ahlborett. It wouldn't do to bump into Gerard." She couldn't quite work out in her head where they were in relation to the castle. Because of the arduous journey they'd taken to get to Wildewood, she imagined they were located many days ride from Gerard. She tried to recall the map she'd seen in Miles' room, the images made little sense then, but now perhaps they would.

"Not if we went after dark," he replied. "We could pass quite close to the castle without being seen."

"How would we see where we're going?" Grace imagined them lost in the great wood, bumping in to trees. There were no battery powered torches here, and despite having a myriad of other things in her pockets, a torch was not one of them.

"We wouldn't need to see, you're not coming."

"But you said we."

"I meant John and I, there's no way you're going anywhere near Gerard, not after what happened with Guy."

"It was my idea," Grace exclaimed indignantly.

"And it's a good idea," Miles agreed. "But you're not going. John and I will ride over, recover whatever's there and deliver it to Edward on Sunday."

Grace shook her head, "You can't take it, Edward has to find it himself or Gerard will just say you set him up. All we have to do is make sure it's there."

"I told you, you're not going."

"You need someone small to get in to the crypt."

She was clutching at straws and she knew Miles recognised it when he humoured her with a crooked smile.

"We could just use the door."

"There is no door." Although, she realised, it would have a door in the thirteenth century and it would also have a chapel above it. She shook her head. This was getting far too complicated. Her knowledge extended merely to a tiny opening below the foundations of her grandfather's cottage. She remembered clearly the time his terrier, Skip had strayed through the aperture. The dog went in and didn't come out for two days. Grace had been convinced he'd been eaten by monsters. Her grandfather however, simply left food outside the opening and waited for him to re-emerge. He'd turned up at the bottom of the steep dene at the back of the house where the ground dropped steeply to the river. Her grandfather reckoned Skip had come out on day one when they weren't looking and been off chasing rabbits for two days.

The old man kept her entertained for years with tales of what might lie beneath their feet. As a child she'd imagined skeletons and ghosts, and of course, treasure. There were remains of graves in the garden and years before her grandfather's time, workmen unearthed a skeleton beneath the drive. She wondered now whose skeleton it was. Wondered if it was anyone she now knew. Glancing at Miles, she worried again.

"You told me you were never going to let me out of your sight. What if Gerard turns up here while you and John are digging for treasure? What if he brings his witch-finder and a big stake? What if you come back from your little adventure and find me burnt to a crisp in the courtyard?" She left a dramatic pause.

He shook his head at her. "There's probably nothing there anyway."

"Then why was Gerard so interested in me, once he knew I was from Kirk Knowe? Don't you see, this is not about witches, or spies, or even about his history with you? Although Guy probably thought he could use the situation to finish what he started, and it would suit Gerard to be rid of you at someone else's hands. No, Gerard thinks I know about his hidden treasure. Treasure he should have given to Edward. He thinks I'm going to tell the king. The fact that Edward has suddenly decided to pay him a visit must be making him very nervous. Surely that would be enough for the king to lose patience with him. No wonder he wants me dead."

* * *

Miles looked away. He couldn't concentrate when she was seated on his knee in her underwear. It gave her an unfair advantage. It made sense though, what she was saying, and it would explain Guy's involvement. Guy wasn't interested in treasure, his father was the richest man in Lincolnshire, but he was interested in revenge and he'd still not managed to achieve it, not to his satisfaction. Every time he'd tried to exact it, Miles ended up the victor. He again regretted not running him through when he'd the chance. He was an extremely dangerous man, maybe more so now he'd suffered a further humiliation.

"Maybe there's another way."

"Such as?"

"If Gerard has secreted the booty at Kirk Knowe and he does believe you know of it, and thinks you will reveal its location to the king; then he has two choices. He has you silenced, or he moves the treasure."

"So?"

"He knows I will thwart any attempt on your life. He's seen firsthand what happened to Guy's attempt to kidnap you. So he has to move the treasure. He has to move it before the king gets to Alnwick, and we have to make sure someone the king trusts, sees him do it."

"What if he's already moved it?"

Miles shrugged he was tired, his brain hurt. "Then we lose."

"Wrong answer, we put it back."

Miles watched her. She seemed exhilarated at the thought of beating them at their own game. It was rubbing off on him. "We'd need to go soon, we only have four days till the king arrives and Gerard may have already decided to move it."

"We could go now," suggested Grace. "There's a full moon to light our way."

Miles glanced at the window. The moonlight illuminated the room. He was torn. She was correct, the sooner they got this done the better, but he was tired and reluctant to remove himself from what was

167

becoming an increasingly attractive position. She was warm against him, her skin soft and scented.

"It's late. It will take us half the night to get there, the rest of it to get back and we still need to plan. What shall we do if Gerard has beaten us to it? Do you really want to leave this warm bed and go out into the night on that wayward filly? Perhaps it would be wiser to delay until tomorrow evening."

Grace grinned at him and snuggled closer. "Or we could hurry and be back by dawn and still have time to finish what we've almost started." She reached up and kissed him softly, allowing her hand to trail across his belly.

Miles groaned, made to remove her hand then thought better of it. "Or we could finish what we've begun and then go treasure hunting...?"

Grace laughed. "You'd need to be quick."

"I can be extremely swift." He returned her kiss, turning soft and gentle into hot and steamy within a couple of breaths. "I'd prefer not to, but under the circumstances one has to make sacrifices."

Chapter Thirty One

They left an hour later with thick cloaks to guard against the night chill and John at their side. Miles and John were well armed and Miles ensured Grace had Edmund's knife. Only Tom Pandy, Edmund and the Forester men were aware of their departure and they positioned themselves to keep watch until their safe return.

The moonlight served them well. They travelled quickly past their Scottish sentries and on through the forest spread out to the South East of Wildewood. They followed hidden trails, which cut many miles off their journey and brought them to the outskirts of Ahlborett a little after midnight. They halted by the Danestone on the rise above the village and Miles dismounted, climbed the great prehistoric monolith and scanned the castle from this vantage point.

Grace stared down at what could be seen of the village in the moonlight. It was unrecognisable to her. It still hugged the narrow road that snaked through the valley floor and the dwellings on the north of the road still sat precariously on steeply rising plots of land, which reached a pinnacle, before they dropped hazardously down to the river running behind the village. But the village itself was merely a collection of wooden and stone dwellings enveloped in darkness, slumbering. No sign of the sturdy stone houses she knew. No welcoming lights at the windows, no sign of the pub, the converted church or the village hall or school. There were no quaint cottages with lovingly tended gardens and flowers tumbling over dry stone walls.

The castle which she knew only as a ruin, stood tall and proud with watch fires lit and guards on sentry duty at the main gate. If Grace still harboured doubts about the reality of her situation, they were instantly dispelled. This was medieval Ahlborett, of that there was no doubt.

Reluctant to travel the main thoroughfare in case the sound of jingling harness might waken sleeping dogs, Miles led them with considerable care down the steep slope to the south of the great stone and skirted the village.

The landscape changed as they approached the eastern edge of the village and Grace's sense of direction became confused. The layout of the road here was unfamiliar. Many trees encroached from all sides and the road was merely a track wide enough to allow the passage of a cart, petering out to a pedestrian or single horse width before winding its way downhill to where the river could safely be forded during the summer months.

Miles halted beneath the trees and they dismounted and secured their horses. He pressed his finger to his lips and beckoned for his companions to follow. It was a strange experience for Grace when she first caught sight of the tiny chapel of ease which stood on the very spot where her own cottage should be—would be. Somehow it didn't seem to be as high from the path as her cottage was from the road, but as one had been built upon the other this explained the topographical difference. The building itself was small and built in the random stone that Grace recognised from the foundations of her cottage. This was the right place.

"Where is the entrance to the crypt?" asked Miles quietly.

Grace scanned the front of the building. The small entrance known to her was at the south west corner of the building and below the level of the cottage drive. Only the top lintel of the aperture had been visible above ground. She looked for it now and realised the aperture was in fact a tiny, glassless window opening and as the ground level was much lower now, she could see, positioned to the left of the window, stone steps leading down to a small wooden door. Her grandfather had been correct there truly was a crypt beneath the cottage and here it appeared in all its glory.

"There," she pointed. She squeezed past the men, excited by the prospect of what they might find. Miles held her back, placed a finger at her lips, and they stood silent for a moment listening to the stillness, straining to hear beyond it.

"John, take a look about, see if there's anyone resident, a monk or priest. We don't want to alert the whole village with his cries of alarm." John nodded and picked his way through the tangle of yew trees with remarkable ease for such a large man.

"We shall await his return," breathed Miles against her ear as he stood and took stock of the situation. "So, this is your home?"

Grace considered her response, in light of his confused expression. "In a way yes, it's complicated."

"Everything about you is complicated. I look forward to the time when you have the opportunity to uncomplicate matters. Now however, we have more pressing demands on our time."

A rustling to their right had Miles reaching for his dagger but it was merely John returning from his search.

"There is indeed a priest. He's in a room at the back of the chapel sleeping off a large flagon of wine. He'll not awaken this night, but just in case I have barred the door."

"Good man, John. Come then, let us see what Gerard has hidden."

They crossed with care to the stone steps and Miles took the lead. He tried the door with no success and turned with a muttered curse to John who grinned and held aloft the ring of keys which he'd taken from the sleeping monk's belt. Grace could barely contain her excitement. She'd been brought up on stories of this place, unsure of its actual existence. She wished her grandfather were there with her.

The door opened on surprisingly well-oiled hinges to reveal stone steps continuing for a further six feet or so, which placed the floor of the crypt approximately twelve feet below ground. The invading moonlight barely saw them safely to the bottom of the steps before they were shrouded in inky blackness. There was a damp smell of earth and wet stone and Grace had the uncomfortable feeling they were somehow intruding.

"There must be wall torches. Feel along the wall, John until we find them," said Miles. Both men set off in opposite directions. There was much cursing and clattering about as they bumped into the unseen.

Grace felt in her pocket and brought out the matches. She had to use them. She would explain later. She struck one match against the box and held the flare alight illuminating the room briefly.

"Dear Lord ...!" exclaimed Miles. John took a hurried step back, and crossed himself in fear, at the sight of flame leaping from the end of Grace's fingers. Grace ignored them and scanned the walls for the torches. She located one behind Miles but before she could light it, the match burnt her finger and she let it drop to the floor with a curse.

"What are you doing?" he demanded into the darkness.

"Never mind that," hissed Grace. "Where are you? Hold out your hand." She didn't want to waste another match. She cast about in the darkness and he grasped her hand and pulled her to him. Rather roughly, she thought as she banged into his chest. She struck a second match and reaching up on her toes lit the torch. The room was slowly illuminated as the torch took hold. Miles looked at her questioningly. She shrugged and looked for the next torch. He could question her later.

"John, get that door closed and see if you can cover the window we don't want any light to spill out and alert whoever might be out there." John nodded. He gave Grace a momentary glance before attending to the door.

They turned then, and scanned the room. Still shadowy despite the torches, the large space occupied the full footprint of the chapel above. The vaulted stone ceiling was held aloft by stone pillars set at intervals along the periphery of the space. John laid one hand against the masonry in deference of a fellow craftsman's work. One wall was made up of stone racks hewn out of the wall itself and edged by a mason's hand. They ran floor to ceiling each being approximately four feet wide and arching to three feet high. Their depth into the wall; could only be guessed at six to seven feet, for on the racks were the caskets belonging to those interred within.

Grace stifled a squeal and stepped back against Miles with such a start he was forced to steady her against his body to prevent them both from falling backwards.

"They're already dead. They can't hurt you," he whispered.

Grace slipped her hand in his and he squeezed it comfortingly. She wasn't afraid of ghosts. There'd been enough strange goings on at the cottage to have cured her of any such fear. She'd regularly heard voices in the house; the young mother calling her child, the old man who would grumble at her grandfather's dog to be quiet. The rooms were prone to sudden chills which caused the dogs to sit alert until the temperature returned to normal. So no, Grace was not afraid of ghosts, but the sight of all these caskets, and the knowledge she had lived scant feet away from them for most of her life, unnerved her.

Not all of the niches were occupied, some remained eerily empty. Black voids waiting their turn to swallow the dead. The majority of the caskets were aged and decayed. Some had collapsed upon their occupants. Grace averted her eyes not wishing to see what might be visible through the splintered wood. One or two seemed more robust and had presumably spent less time in the place. She wondered at the state of the inhabitants, somehow the idea of skeletal remains seemed less frightening than those not completely decomposed. She wrinkled her nose but could detect no offending odour.

Turning slowly, it took a moment for her to realise her preference for the skeletal, rather than fleshed occupant, was premature for the entire east wall was stacked floor to ceiling with skulls and thigh bones. She tightened her grip on Miles' hand and he gave an involuntary wince.

"You've got a good grip on you, Grace," he said quietly. "I'm sure it will come in useful sometime, but just now I could do with my hand back in one piece."

She relaxed her grip but kept his hand. "What is this place?" she breathed. She'd never seen anything like it.

"You know what it is." He glanced at her strangely. "It's a crypt, a charnel house, a place of the dead."

"But there are so many..."

"Some have been interred here - he gestured to those in the caskets. And some have been brought here from a previous burial."

She looked again at the pile of bones. "Where are the rest of their bones? Why are there only skulls and thigh bones?"

"That's all that is necessary, my lady," said John. "For the afterlife."

Grace shuddered.

"So where is the treasure, Grace?" asked Miles, as a cursory inspection of the space revealed nothing but cobwebs and the remains of the dearly departed.

"It must be here," she exclaimed, as she recalled the reason for their presence and frantically scanned the room. "Why else would Gerard have been so concerned about Kirk Knowe?"

She steered well away from the wall of the dead and the bone pile and peered into the shadowy corners of the subterranean vault. Beneath a mound of dusty robes she saw the glint of metal.

"Look - look! Miles, what's that?" she grasped the corner of the robe excitedly and yanked at it revealing what lay beneath and showering them all in suffocating dust in the process. "What is it?" she asked, as they all looked at the jumbled pile of tarnished metal.

Miles squatted down and pulled at the nearest piece. "It's armour."

"Is it Gerard's armour?"

Miles shook his head slowly. "No this is Saracen armour, taken from a dead man no doubt."

Crouching next to him, Grace ran her fingers gently over the surface. "A dead man, are you sure?"

"If he were still alive then his armour would not be rusting here on the floor of a Northumbrian crypt."

"Has it come from the Holy Land? Is it part of Gerard's haul?"

"Probably," replied Miles.

Grace was disappointed. "I'd expected treasure to be exactly that, gold and jewels and precious things, not pickings off fallen men."

Miles smiled grimly. "It was certainly precious to its owner. Unfortunately not well made enough to save his life this time, but judging by the many dents and distortions it did its job well a number of times before."

"Did your armour have many dents?" she asked quietly.

"My armour had so many holes you could have used it as a sieve, so many dents I had to breathe in just to put it on. Did Guy not tell you that I was the clumsiest knight on crusade?"

"He did, but I didn't believe him."

"You should have, I was glad to see the back of that armour."

In the background John shuffled his feet. "Time marches on, my lord, we must make haste if we are to be away before dawn."

John was right, it would soon be light again and they needed to be well away before the castle guard changed and Gerard got wind of their visit. Miles pulled the dusty robes clear of the corner, perhaps the treasure was concealed beneath the armour, but there was nothing but more armour and weapons. Lots of armour and lots of weapons and not all of it was Saracen. Miles carefully pulled at the uppermost pieces and stood back confused.

"I don't understand. This is English armour."

"My lord, look above the door." John gestured to the racks above the entrance, which they'd not noticed on entry. Displayed neatly along the length of the space were perhaps thirty helmets some with plumes intact some without. Some carried the scars of terrible conflict, one was even cleaved in two; the two mangled halves alongside each other. Others seemed entire and unmarked.

Miles spun about taking in the sight of the armour and the helmets, displayed like trophies, in this place of the dead. "What has gone on here?" he asked no one in particular. "Saracen trophies although unsavoury, are questionable, however ultimately understandable, but these are English trophies taken from fallen English knights." He looked at the helmets again and his face displayed his revulsion. "Look, John, the colours of Gilbert of Broxham, a comrade who fought bravely and died for his king and his God. This is the work of a madman."

"Gerard?" asked Grace.

"No, this is not the work of Gerard; I cannot believe that. Yes, he's a fool and a greedy one at that. Yes, he's tried to cheat the king, plotted against you and I. Committed murder to regain Wildewood, but this is different this..." He gestured with a sweep of his hand, "This is evil. This goes against the grain of every noble knight. Gerard is one of a long line who has held and maintained this land for the king, although he does not portray himself as honourable, in matters such as these, I can assure you that he is."

"Then, if not Gerard, who is responsible?" asked Grace.

"Guy de Marchant is a man with no honour," John said, simply.

"Then we must ensure Guy is held to account. First we must find what we came for." Miles scanned the room again. "Here is proof this place has been used to store artefacts from the Crusade, but Saracen armour will be of no interest to the king. The collection of the English armour needs further investigation before it can be fully understood. We must look more carefully, there has to be more."

They set about the place then, systematically checking each corner and each of the empty casket niches but there was nothing but bones and armour. Miles took one of the wall torches from its holder, walked the length of the wall of the dead and studied each casket. He paused at one engraved Fortune de Frouville' and smiled.

"John, help me," he called as he handed the torch to Grace and reached up to pull the coffin from its perch. It took the two of them to dislodge the heavy casket and when it had been pulled more than halfway from its niche in the dead wall, its own weight brought it crashing to the flagstone floor where it split apart spilling its contents and causing all three to leap out of the way. The noise reverberated around the stone room and Grace dropped the torch and covered her ears. Good Lord, they would hear the din all the way to the castle. They waited in the eerie hushed silence that followed, until they were certain the only sound still to be heard, was their own pounding hearts. Miles stooped and held the torch aloft.

Spilling out of the shattered coffin, cascading onto the stone flagged floor, sparkling and glittering in the flickering torchlight was treasure of the kind that Grace had only dreamt of, had only heard of in her grandfather's stories. Gold plates and goblets littered the ground. Chains and necklaces tangled and twisted amongst the larger items. Statuettes and tiny marble and ivory carvings and a myriad of coins of all denominations, lay amongst religious artefacts, crucifix and bejewelled daggers and knives.

John stared in stunned silence.

"Oh bugger," exclaimed Grace.

"Indeed," agreed Miles. "You were correct." He pulled her to him and swung her around. "You were right all along. How did you know?"

"I didn't know, not really. It was just a guess, a wild guess."

Miles stooped and pulled an amber necklace from the treasure trove. He held it up to the torch and turned it to catch the light. "We have him," he declared. "We have all the proof we need."

"My lord," John hushed him urgently. "I hear horses in the distance, we must leave now."

"What about all of this?" Grace gestured at the mess they'd made. There was no time to put it back.

"John, hurry to the horses, take them around to the ford make sure they remain safe and unseen, we will be right behind you."

John looked questioningly at him. "You need to come now."

"We are behind you, John, now go." He caught at John's arm as he made to leave. "If anything happens," he added quietly, "Go straight back to Wildewood and get a message to Alex and Hugh." John nodded reluctantly and slipped out of the door closing it behind him to prevent spillage of light.

Miles pushed the necklace into the front of his leather jerkin and put out the torches.

"You can't take it with you," said Grace. "If it's proof then it needs to stay here, so the king's man will find it. If you take it, then there's no proof it was ever here, nothing to link it to Gerard."

"Come here," he called. "We must leave now." He reached for her in the dark and grasped her hand pulling her towards the moonlight that crept in through the narrow window. They both froze at the sound of voices nearby. The voices were alarmingly close and drawing nearer. They were going to be trapped.

"Whatever happens next you must stay silent," he breathed hoarsely and then lifted her by the waist and shoved her feet first into the nearest empty niche. "Move over," he hissed as he grasped the stone work above the opening and swung himself in on top of her.

"Ouch." She stifled a groan as his elbows and knees dug into her and she wriggled out from under him as best she could in the narrow space.

"Move back as far as you can," whispered Miles and they both shuffled back into the darkness. Grace's heart began to pound.

If they were caught they would be killed. It was as simple as that.

Chapter Thirty Two

The door burst open seconds later and light pooled into the room. Six men at arms barrelled down the stone steps. As flickering torches picked out the shattered casket and spilled treasure, their faces displayed a mix of wonder and horror. This was not a knowledge they wished to be party to. Men had died for less. They glanced at each other and shuffled uncomfortably.

Hunkered back in the darkness of the niche, Miles considered his options. The men were hesitant that was obvious, but could they be turned? He made to move but Grace gripped his arm and held him. She breathed against his cheek; her breath short and ragged. He may have taken a gamble with his own life, but not with hers. Pulling her close he bided his time.

"What now?" she whispered.

He opened his mouth to respond, but paused when a movement at the entrance drew his attention. Gerard had entered the crypt.

Grace released a soft gasp that Miles recognised as confusion. He had created a vision of a monster in her mind, deliberately so, as he'd no doubt as to the man's capacity for evil. But it was obvious by her reaction, that Gerard was not what she had expected. In fact, even he was distracted by the decline of the man. His memories were that of a young, arrogant Gerard, who employed subterfuge and trickery to get his own way, a spoilt brat grown to a spoilt man. But now, as he scrutinised him in the flickering torchlight, he appeared much older than himself. His hair was beginning to grey and although a tall and well-made man, his muscle was turning to flab. He cut an almost sad figure in his finery. He looked weary; tired of whatever game he'd been playing but unwilling or unable to desist. Gerard's gaze swept the room, and Miles, with great relish, saw in his face, realisation that once again he had been bested. As Gerard turned and took in the armour and the helmets, Miles recognised confusion followed swiftly by fury.

"Bring me the priest," Gerard barked, his voice resonated within the stone chamber. The familiar, demanding tone brought Miles' memories sharply back into focus. His gut churned with dark emotion.

"And search this place inside and out, they cannot have gone far, I can still smell the torches." Gerard paced back and forth as the soldiers jumped to his bidding. They swept light into every corner checking for the intruders.

"There is no one here, my lord," said the first soldier, warily.

"Then look outside. I will have Miles and his witch before this night is out."

The soldiers eagerly took the opportunity to vacate the oppressive place, tripping over each other in their haste to leave.

Gerard kicked at the treasure with his boot and glanced again at the English armour. "What has that fool Guy, done now?" he muttered sourly.

Turning back to the treasure, he crouched, running his fingers through the scattered smaller items. Miles watched as he seemed to ponder for a moment before glancing up at the wall of the dead with a sly grin.

"Little brother, I know you are still here," he said softly. Rising to his feet he drew his sword and turned slowly. "Come out—come out— where ever you are." He reached for one of the burning torches and held it out in front of him as he approached the wall of niches. Grace drew back fearfully and Miles tightened his grip around her, shushing her gently with a silent breath against her cheek.

There were twenty four niches in total. Three rows of eight. Only six were empty. It did not require a genius to work it out, nor would it take long for them to be discovered. Miles tensed as Gerard approached the first and held the torch aloft.

"Too high I imagine, for a little witch," he mused and passed by that and its partner on the top level. He squatted slowly by the first of two on the lower level.

"And too low I warrant, for a knight who does not bend easily to the will of others." He moved slowly along the row until he stood alongside the two remaining empty niches on the middle row. He stepped back a pace and swung the torch between the two leaving a trail of sparks in the darkness.

"Eeny...meeny...miny...mo."

Inside their niche, Miles and Grace lay trapped, unable to move any further back. Miles gripped Grace to him, her fear was palpable. He tried to reach his sword but the tightness of the chamber made it impossible for him to manoeuvre. He silently cursed his stupidity in delaying when they could have left with John. He would not be caught like a rat in a pipe.

He felt then, a small hand at his groin. Good God! What was she up to now? This was neither the time nor the place. He felt his sword slide against his thigh as she gently worked it free and pushed it out of its scabbard and up towards his out stretched hand. He squeezed her gently with the arm that held her against him, and readied himself.

Gerard thrust the torch into the first of the niches, dust and cobwebs flared instantly and spiders scuttled for cover. The void was empty. He moved to the last niche and called for his men. Three of them crowded through the small doorway and stumbled down the stone steps.

"Miles, you can climb out like a man - or be dragged out like a rat? The choice is yours, it matters naught to me." He gestured to two of his men to position themselves either side of the entrance.

Miles had no intention of making it easy for them. He crept forward, sword outstretched before him and when next the torch swung by he reached out and slashed wildly at it, knocking it from Gerard's hand.

Light danced around the crypt as the torch bounced to the floor and Miles took advantage of the momentary chaos, to dive from the niche and roll onto the hard stone floor. Two soldiers pounced, knocking the sword from his hand and the air from his lungs. The third soldier quickly reached into the blackness. He yelped when his hand was stung by the very small but very sharp knife in Grace's hand. Staggering back, he gripped his hand to stem the flow of blood. Miles grimaced wryly as he was dragged upright by the soldiers and held tightly with his arms pinioned behind him.

"Be careful who you back into a corner, Gerard," he hissed. "She has claws and can use them."

Gerard studied him, and Miles met his gaze defiantly. It mattered naught that he was cornered, outnumbered and well and truly beaten, he still managed to exude an air of victory, of righteousness. It was important he didn't back down and that Gerard understood he had more than met his match.

"So I understand," replied Gerard shortly. "Guy, has recounted the highlights of your last encounter. I am afraid he does not speak highly of you or your witch. He is still smarting from the outcome."

"He's lucky to be alive," growled Miles. He flexed his shoulders testing the soldiers grip but the more he resisted the more painfully the pressure was applied.

"Yes. Lucky for Guy, perhaps, but not so fortunate for you, Miles. You should have killed him while you had the chance. As we speak, he imagines every evil thing upon you and your witch. He is a man beset with fury and bitterness."

"He is a man with a broken leg and shattered pride. I have nothing to fear from him."

Gerard cocked his head. "Then you are a fool. There is nothing more dangerous than wounded pride. So, you claim you hold no dread for Guy, but what of me, Miles? Do you not fear my retribution? You break into my sacred property and desecrate the final resting place of these poor souls. Are you a thief, Miles, or is there more to this?"

179

"You are misguided, Gerard. It's you who should fear me. I will have justice for the death of my mother and demand you recognise what has already been made so by royal decree."

"I did not murder your mother, Miles. You were merely a child, and your memories of the situation are warped by time and emotion. Do you imagine if I had committed such a crime the king would have left me unpunished these last twelve years?"

"I know what I saw, Gerard, and when the king hears my account he will believe me."

"Oh, yes of course, because the king is such a good friend of yours now isn't he, Miles. Now why is that I wonder? Is it something to do with, Reynard perhaps?" He stepped nearer, pressed his face close and curled his lip into a smirk. "Why did Edward take Wildewood from my holdings and decree it to you?"

Miles narrowed his eyes, refused to give an inch despite his inclination to break Gerard's nose with a swift thrust of his head. "I was of service in the Holy Land, when Edward was but a prince in waiting for the crown. He gave me Wildewood in payment."

"But Wildewood is mine, Miles."

Miles twisted again and pain lanced up his arms. "You never wanted Wildewood. I've been away for twelve years and in all of that time no one has lived there. The place was deserted and in a state of disrepair when I returned. Why can you not let it go?"

"My family has held this land for generations I will not let any of it go, not to a bastard usurper such as you."

Miles railed against his captor's despite the pain and spat his disgust in Gerard's face. The crippling punch delivered to his stomach in return was small price to pay for the reward of Gerard's outrage. Miles gasped at the blow and doubled up.

"Time to take a look at your little witch, I think," said Gerard as he wiped his face clean. "Guy was rather enamoured until she used her whip on him." He turned to the niche entrance. "Come out, Mademoiselle. I wish to make your acquaintance." Grace stayed as she was, crouched like a feral animal in the back of the void.

"Come out or I'm afraid Miles will pay the price." He delivered another punch and Miles' knees buckled under him. The soldiers held him up but only at the expense of his shoulders and he swallowed the pain beneath a string of muttered curses.

Grace crawled hesitantly to the edge of the entrance. She twisted her legs around in the tight space so she could hang them over the edge and then she let herself drop to the ground. She landed in a heap at Gerard's feet and he reached out his hand and gently pulled her up.

"Good evening, Mademoiselle," he said, dragging her reluctant hand to his lips for the briefest touch.

Miles bristled and Gerard smiled and studied his captive. She was a tiny thing, Miles realised, as he too watched and awaited her reaction. She had a dirty face and dusty clothes and in the torchlight her eyes seemed larger than they probably were. Her short hair stuck up on end and she chewed nervously at her bottom lip. It was true she was no lady, but nor was she a witch no matter what Gerard might choose to tell the bishop. She pulled her hand from his grip and rubbed the back of it against her clothes. Miles noticed then the little knife in her other hand and she brandished it fiercely, as she turned slowly and backed away from Gerard.

"Let him go now!" she demanded of the soldiers, and even Miles smiled at that. The soldiers grinned and looked to Gerard.

"Or else?" asked Gerard, patiently.

Grace took a breath and jutted out her chin. "Do not underestimate me...I have a blue belt in Judo!"

Miles shook his head.

Gerard shrugged. "And this means what, exactly?"

"It means if you come too close, I could have you flat on your back in an instant."

Gerard laughed. "So that's what Miles sees in you, I can see how that could be an interesting trick."

Grace scowled. "You won't be saying that when I slit your throat from ear to ear."

Gerard nodded slowly. "No, I agree that would be difficult, but you see my dear there is a flaw in your delightful plan." He paused and Miles held his breath and watched as Grace struggled to maintain her stance. She was shaking and yet she stood her ground. It was easy to show bravery when you had no fear, a different matter entirely to face an opponent who you know you cannot hope to beat.

"You see, supposing you get me on my back and supposing you succeed in slitting my throat, how do you then intend to overpower my men and free your lover?"

Grace looked from him to his men and back again. She looked from Miles to the door and back again. Miles recognised the tell tale threads of panic as she chewed at her lip once more to stop it from quivering. One hand strayed to her fringe, the strands tangled mercilessly between shaky fingers. He desperately needed her to do the right thing, but he doubted she would choose sensible over reckless. She glanced at him questioningly but held tight as he was, he could do little to help. Her knuckles were white around the handle of the knife and it was taking some effort of concentration to keep her arm straight out in front of her. She swallowed nervously. Miles knew her head would be full of all the terrible things he had told her about, Gerard and her fate should she be caught. He wished now that he'd held his tongue. Could Gerard tell, he wondered, did he realise how scared she was, how easily he could have taken the knife from her.

Gerard interrupted his thoughts.

"We could stand here all night until one of us falters, but to be honest, and I think even Miles would agree, you my dear would fall long before any of the men before you. Give me the knife or would you prefer me to take it from you?"

She glanced at Miles and he gave a barely discernible nod, far better she gave it willingly, he did not want Gerard to take anything from her. Slowly she pulled back her hand and the knife hung slackly by her side.

"I think I'll just hang onto it while we discuss this situation." Her voice shook but she maintained her position and hung onto the knife, "and then you can let us go and we'll all be on our way."

Gerard considered her for a long moment, flicking his gaze between her and Miles thoughtfully. Finally he turned, nodded to his men and they released Miles, causing him to stumble to the ground, his upper arms numb from being held. He flexed his shoulders and grimaced as the blood came rushing back in a wave of pins and needles. Gerard inclined his head to Grace and stood aside so she could join Miles. She crossed the room on shaky feet with her head held high and slipped her hand in his. Her gentle warmth within his strong grip renewed his resolve and he pulled himself to his feet and squared up to Gerard.

"Miles, it pains me to admit it, but if this girl is your chosen one, then you have chosen wisely. Her courage in the face of the inevitable is quite impressive."

Miles stayed silent. Now free from restraint they had a chance. He glanced quickly around the room, noted the position of the soldiers in relation to the steps and the doorway.

"Gerard, the king will want his treasure, what do you hope to achieve by keeping it from him?"

"Edward knows nothing about it, and never shall."

"But why? You don't need this, you have wealth and land. Why do you align yourself with the likes of Guy de Marchant? Look about you. Do you not see what he's done?" Miles gestured to the English trophies. "This is the work of a madman, if you do not condemn this and him, then you condone it and the king will finish you."

"I do not condone this," growled Gerard. "I know nothing of this and I will not pay the king's price for Guy's actions. I will deal with Guy, but Edward must remain in ignorance."

Miles shook his head in frustration. "Listen to me. You say my mother's death was an accident, if that is so, why do you resist my title to Wildewood? My mother was a de Frouville' she was originally gifted Wildewood by your mother. Why do you deny me my birthright?"

"Wildewood was never gifted to your mother. It was simply a convenient place to put her when it was no longer possible for her to share my mother's roof. You have no rights to de Frouville' land," stated Gerard flatly.

"What about the rights as my father's son?" hissed Miles?

"A bastard has no rights."

"The king thinks differently, and when he discovers what has transpired, I have a fancy he'll ensure you change your mind. Gerard, for God's sake think man; you risk losing everything, everything your forefathers have fought hard to retain, and for what, some ridiculous childhood hatred?" Miles shook his head "You know Grace is no witch and yet you instigate investigation, send for the Bishop, bay for her blood...why? Gerard, what threat does she pose to you?"

"She is connected to Reynard, is she not?"

"What has Hugh to do with any of this? What is he to you?" This was the second time Hugh had been suggested as an answer to the current situation. What was it that both Alex and Gerard knew and he did not.

"If you have to ask the question then you know less than you think." Gerard narrowed his eyes thoughtfully, "Considerably less than you think. I almost pity you, Miles. The people around you, whom you believe you can trust, have not been entirely truthful. Ask Hugh to explain it to you...although on second thoughts perhaps it's better that you don't. The king arrives at Alnwick in three days. It is in all of our interests, that you do not reach the king or Reynard for that matter. Which of course leaves me with a dilemma... what shall I do with you?"

Miles tightened his grip on Grace's hand and she sidled closer to him.

"I could just kill you both now and be done with it, but I'm impressed with the courage of your lady and when all's said and done I may have use of you both yet. So I think, on balance, I will leave you both here with the dead until the king has gone. If you still live by my return then we will reconsider your future. If you do not then you will unfortunately be remembered as an irreverent thief. An inglorious end for such a noble knight, the king will be disappointed, and Reynard, well he will wonder if the time spent teaching you the chivalrous arts were worth his effort."

He climbed the steps and paused at the open door. "See how you enjoy spending what time you have left, in the house of the dead, Miles. If you've not been driven mad by your ghostly cellmates I may call on you after the king has left Alnwick. It is a pity you and the little witch will miss him. Pity too he will miss the burning. Let's not forget the Bishop is on his way."

He closed the door as he left and shouted at his men to nail it shut. "I want a round the clock guard on this door," he barked as he mounted his horse.

Now it was time to deal with Guy.

Chapter Thirty Three

Miles stood for a moment listening as the door was barricaded to prevent their escape and pondered on Gerard's words. What was afoot? Who could he trust? He turned to Grace, she had not been entirely truthful with him, but that didn't mean he did not trust her.

The room was once again in darkness but for the weak moonlight filtering through the high window. They needed to light another torch.

"How are you?" he asked eventually and in the darkness Grace shrugged. "You were remarkably brave we would both be dead if it weren't for that."

"What did Gerard mean?" she asked.

Miles had no idea and was not inclined to discuss it. "We need some light, are you going to perform your little trick again?"

"It's not a trick. Hold up the torch and I'll show you," replied Grace and she pulled the box of matches from her pocket. She struck the match and lit the torch. When there was sufficient light for him to see, she showed him what to do. "It's simple, just like tinder really. Strike the coloured end of the match against the rough side of the box and hey presto...flames."

Miles was intrigued and tried it repeatedly. "Don't waste them," said Grace as she made to take them back but he held them out of reach.

"Where did you get them?"

"I don't remember. Keep them if you must, but don't lose them, we may need them again."

They sat amongst the bones with their backs against the wall and Miles put an arm loosely around Grace's shoulder.

"Will John get help?" she asked.

"Eventually," replied Miles, "but I imagine we are in for a long wait."

Grace rifled in her pockets once more. "Here," she said tearing a strip of chewing gum in two and offering him half, before popping the remainder in her mouth.

"What is it?"

Grace smiled. "Something to keep your breath sweet, just in case we get so bored down here that we end up snogging."

Miles chewed and tasted mint. "Snogging?"

Grace reached up and kissed him. "Snogging."

"Okay, snogging's good."

Miles remained deep in thought; he couldn't help but go over and over in his mind what Gerard had said. He trusted Hugh; he trusted all those around him. In fact as the only person he didn't trust was Gerard, why did his words unsettle him so?

"Tell me about Hugh," asked Grace. "Martha said he taught you how to be a knight."

Miles smiled. "He taught me many things. He's a good man, and you'll like him. He'll like you, in fact in some ways you are alike. He doesn't always do the expected either."

"He must be well respected if he's close to the king."

Miles considered. "That wasn't always the case. In fact I was surprised when Alex told me he was. He's always been a rebel, on the edge, an outsider but a marvellous soldier and tactician. He can see things from a different perspective, which is useful especially during conflict."

"How long were you with him?"

"Almost ten years intermittently. He wasn't always in Normandy when I was there, but he was, when I was younger. He's an adventurer, he'd disappear for months on end, turning up when you least expected him."

"He looked after you when you were wounded by Guy?"

"Yes— fortunately. I don't imagine I would have survived if it hadn't been for his skill." He smiled at her. "I'm looking forward to seeing him again."

"Will you ask him about what Gerard said?"

"If I need to."

"I think Gerard is playing with you. He resents the fact you're well liked and have people who support you of their own volition, not because they're forced or scared of you. I think he fears your relationship with Hugh because he sees him as a powerful man who is close to the king and this is his attempt to undermine that relationship."

"You've done a lot of thinking."

Grace shrugged. "Sometimes it's easier to look at situations as an outsider."

"Do you think of yourself as an outsider?"

"I've known you for little more than a week, Miles. There are lots of things that I don't know about your life and lots you don't know about mine."

"You seem to know ample about mine, courtesy of Martha," replied Miles.

"She does like to gossip." Grace smiled. "And Edmund talks a lot about you because he admires you."

"But there's no one to tell me about you, is there?" Miles stretched out his legs and Grace rested her head on his shoulder.

"There's nothing to tell."

"I don't believe that," said Miles. "We're going to be here for some time, perhaps you should tell me about your life."

Grace settled herself against him. "I've already told you my parents were academics. They were killed when I was ten and I was brought up by my grandparents. When I was eighteen I went to university to study art and people reckon I'm pretty good at it."

"University?"

She faltered and he watched as colour heightened her cheeks and a flicker of concern crossed her brow. She was hiding something, yet again, but it suited him to let her continue her tale. The truth would out eventually and currently he had not the energy, or will, for picking over the details.

"Um...a place of learning...a school...a very big school."

"You're very skilled," he said. He thought again of the lifelike images. They would surely condemn her in the bishop's eyes, if Gerard succeeded in his quest for a trial.

"Skilled at what?"

"Painting..." He closed his eyes and let her words roll over him "Amongst other things."

"Anyway, I got my degree in fine art and a man I knew got me involved in this business he ran. It didn't work out so I came home. By then of course my grandparents had died, so the cottage was mine and that's basically it. Not very exciting I'm afraid."

Miles dragged his attention back. "What man?"

"He was nobody, I thought I could trust him." She shrugged. "But sometimes people are just out for themselves and don't care if they hurt other people in the process."

"Did he hurt you?" Miles asked quietly.

"A little," she replied.

"Where is he now?"

Grace smiled. "Too far away for you to worry about. I don't need you to uphold my honour or anything like that, Miles. He was a selfish idiot, a liar and a cheat and he lost his business because of it."

"Is that why you stopped painting?"

"I suppose so."

"But now you've started again, what does that mean?"

"I suppose it means I'm happy."

"Good," was his simple reply but it hid a tumult of emotion. He would get to the bottom of what had happened, maybe not now, but eventually, and the man would pay. Revenge was so...liberating.

"Were you happy with your grandparents?"

187

Grace smiled wistfully. "I remember one time my grandfather got drunk on homemade bramble wine and he tripped over Skip and blacked his eye. My grandmother was so cross with him she wouldn't sit next to him at church."

"Skip?"

"My grandfather's jack russell terrier. He only had three legs; he lost one in an illegal trap when he was a pup—" She stopped suddenly and struggled to her feet.

"What's wrong?" asked Miles.

She crossed the room glancing up at the window and down at the floor, it was at least an eight foot drop. "There's another way out," she said slowly and then more confidently. "There's got to be another way out."

Miles stood and took her arm. "What do you mean, how do you know?"

"Skip. Of course why didn't I think of that before? Skip strayed through the window up there and he didn't come out for two days. He couldn't have come back out through the window it's eight feet off the floor and the door was blocked. We found him on the river bank. He must have got out another way." She spun round, "Somewhere in the back wall, there must be a tunnel."

"A tunnel?" asked Miles.

"Yes, somewhere low down, he was a little dog and he only had three legs..."

The back wall was lined with niches; there were only two empty ones on the bottom row. Grace scooted down on all fours and took the torch from Miles. She crawled halfway and shone the torch the rest of the way but it was blocked with a sheer stone wall at the back.

"This one's blocked, it must be the other." She reversed back out and Miles took the torch, knelt down and peered into the next one. The blackness seemed to go on forever there was no stone wall at the end.

"It's here," called Miles softly and he put his finger against his lips and gestured to the door. The guards were still outside. They could not afford to draw their attention. He retrieved his sword swept a final glance around the darkened crypt and turned to Grace. "Follow me."

The niche went back about seven feet and then narrowed slightly and they had to crawl on their bellies for at least another ten feet, before the floor dropped away suddenly and Miles would have plummeted if the torch had not illuminated the way and shown him the roughly hewn stone steps leading downhill. He wriggled round with difficulty in the tight space burning his arm on the torch in the process and cursing out loud.

"What's wrong?" whispered Grace, close behind him.

"Nothing. Here let me help you, there are steps here, they must lead down to the river."

He stepped down until he was beneath her on the stone steps and then turning he lifted her out of the tunnel beside him. The steps were steep and Grace had to tread slowly. The roof of the tunnel was low and Miles had to stoop to prevent his head from cracking off the stone.

The steps were wet with water that seemed to be running. Miles held tightly onto Grace's hand to ensure she didn't slip. The smell of dampness, moss and wild garlic, clung to them as they descended. The tunnel seemed to go on forever.

"I can hear the river," called Grace eventually, the rushing sound was unmistakable. "Be careful we have no idea where the tunnel exit is."

"I think I just found it," replied Miles with an accompanying splash. "You're going to get your feet wet." He doused the torch in the water and left it on the last step.

The exit brought them to the very edge of the river bank and the high level of the river due to melt water had flooded the first few feet of the tunnel itself. They waded through the icy water, stumbling on the river bed boulders. Shrouded by plants and bushes they pushed their way through to the other side and stopped to catch their breath. They were to the west of the ford maybe one hundred yards from the crossing.

"You took your time." Came a voice to their left and as Miles turned hand on sword he realised it was John, sat astride his horse. "I'd about given up on you," he added.

"You've been waiting here all of this time?"

"This was the only way out, I just had to wait for you to find it."

"But how on earth did you know?" asked Grace.

"It was merely speculation, my lady. It is never wise to build, without considering the need for a swift exit."

Miles took the reins of his horse from John and helped Grace to mount the filly. "Come, we must ride hard and fast. Believe it or not, we have an advantage. Gerard thinks we are safely locked up out of harm's way, which leaves us free to plan our next move."

The journey back to Wildewood was one Miles would not forget. Once they were clear of Ahlborett it was a wild exhilarating dash, a race to beat the sunrise. The filly, for once unrestrained, flew across the uneven ground, her hooves barely making contact with the earth as she kept pace with the bigger horses. Grace clung on crouching low over the pony's neck guiding her around the many obstacles the woods had to offer. Miles galloped ahead, John behind, both men constantly on alert for any followers or possible ambush.

The rain began again and the animals splashed through the wet forest floor, the rain from flying manes spraying back on their rider's faces. Grace's fringe clung wetly to her face and she closed her eyes and let the pony carry her home.

Miles slowed his horse as they entered the deeper wood and pulled alongside her. He had forgotten she was not an experienced rider, but as he glanced across and saw how she sat the pony despite the terrain, the weather and the speed he was struck not for the first time at how much she meant to him. She was definitely unique. He would never understand her, but she was his. It was as simple as that. She opened her eyes conscious perhaps of being watched and swept her drooping fringe out of her way with a quick flick of her head. She grinned at him and above the noise of the snorting heaving horses and their splashing hooves, she called to him.

"Race?"

He shook his head; no way could she stay on board if they were to race. The filly was excitable enough. She nodded back at him and pressed the filly on.

"Slow down," he called maintaining his position alongside her. The girl was mad. She laughed at him and continued to press the filly onwards. Leaning across he caught hold of her reins. "I said, slow down." He slowed the filly to a canter and finally as they came out of the wood and into the park, they all slowed to a walk and all three animals and their riders caught their breath.

"Are you crazy?" he asked as he rode to her right, John to her left.

"No just having fun. We did well tonight, didn't we?"

"We did," agreed Miles, very well, and it was all down to her. Guy said she was at the very centre of everything, and Gerard had intimated the same. Since the day he'd come across her in the wood the course of his life seemed to have been orchestrated in some strange way by her. She was his talisman, his lucky charm. Guy had called her his power source, and he was right. When he had Grace with him he was energised and believed all was possible. He felt emotion tighten his chest and he looked away from her, lest she notice how his eyes glistened. He could not, would not lose her.

The household was still sleeping when they returned but Edmund was at his post atop the gate. Eyes glazed with the effort of keeping awake.

"He is a good lad," commented John. "His loyalty to you is unwavering."

Miles dismounted and watched as the boy took Grace's reins, struggling to stay on his feet.

"His loyalty is to the lady, John," replied Miles as he followed Edmund into the stables and unsaddled his horse. "Edmund leave that. We will see to the horses, away now to your bed you have put in a long shift and we will need you bright eyed when the sun is up."

"Did everything go as planned, my lord?" the boy asked. "Ye were long awaited. I was concerned."

Grace took the boy's hand, her face alive with excitement. "Edmund, we had such an adventure. You would not believe what we have seen." Edmund gazed at her hand in his and smiled.

"Everything went as planned, Edmund," Miles answered the boy and took his arm turning him towards the ladder that led to the loft above the stables where he slept. "We will talk further tomorrow, but now sleep."

Miles unsaddled the filly and then leaving John to feed and water all three beasts he and Grace finally retired.

"What next, Miles?" she asked as she closed the door behind them and leant back against it.

Miles gave her a lopsided grin, she may not be tired, but he craved the comfort of his bed. Like Edmund he was having trouble keeping his eyes open. He sat on the edge of the bed and pulled off his boots.

"Sleep, that's what's next." He threw off his leather jerkin and dragged his shirt over his head, lay back against the pillow and patted the mattress next to him. Grace followed him, unlacing her own boots; she kicked them off and wriggled her toes. She slipped off her trousers and pulled her sweater over her head. Miles watched as she stretched and revealing her slender waist. He reached out and caught her arm, gently pulling her so she fell back into the space beside him. She curled up against him one hand idly played with the short hairs on his belly, and he flinched and stopped her hand.

"I said sleep." He kissed the top of her head and closed his eyes.

* * *

Grace watched him as he slept. She ran her fingers gently across the tanned skin of his chest and noted the assortment of scars that peppered his torso and upper arms. She recognised what looked like an old arrow wound in his shoulder and a long jagged scar on his left arm which could have been caused by a knife. The sword wound on his side given him by Guy was by far the worst and she placed her small palm against it and rested her head against his chest.

She thought about what his life was really like, away from Wildewood, where battles were an everyday occurrence and life was cheap. She wondered how far he would take the fight for Wildewood and who might fall in the process. He turned away from her in his sleep, wincing as he did so and she realised he was covered in ugly bruises from his fight with Guy.

She curled against his back, one arm around him her breasts pressed against his warm skin and found herself reliving the past few days. She'd no idea what had happened to bring her here but it was as real as any place she'd visited, the people more sincere than any she'd known. She could make no sense of it. All she could do was live it, for however long she remained.

Chapter Thirty Four

The Scotsman, Angus Baird, returned late next morning with a reluctant Philibutt of Mayflower in tow. He'd caught up with him as he left the protection of Hexham with a group of travellers enroute for York. Although large in number, the group had no men at arms and consisted mainly of pilgrims heading for in the largest city outside London. No one was prepared to stand in defence of the Bishop's man who had proved a surly companion.

The fat man had coveted his rations greedily while others had little, and forced foot weary women and children off the road with the ill-mannered riding of his equally fat pony. Naturally the man baulked and threatened all manner of retribution against the travellers for not coming to his aid and at the Scotsman for interfering with his mission, but the travellers merely bowed their heads, stifled their smiles and continued their journey. Angus closed his ears to the man's whining and took a stick to the idle pony. The Scotsman kept him riding throughout the night and it was a weary pair, both Mayflower and his pony who found themselves back at Wildewood.

Miles, by comparison, was well rested and in good spirits. Wildewood was suddenly alive with activity and industry. He'd sent John away with some of the men to begin the restoration of the dilapidated ancillary buildings. Under John's instruction the unstable and fallen stone was cleared away and stacked for reuse. The Forester's were sent into the wood under the protection of the Scots clansmen, to fell the timber required for the repair of the roof and the construction of new timber framed dwellings. Under Edmund's watchful eye all of the children were set to work fetching and carrying whatever they could to assist.

Grace sat with John, protected from the biting wind against the shelter of the stable wall, and together they poured over the plans Grace had sketched. John had never seen the like of the buildings Grace had drawn, but she assured him with his skill they were possible. John had an eye for detail and as a master mason he also possessed mathematical abilities far beyond Grace's, despite her university education. He poured over the measurements and quickly calculated the amount of additional stone required to complete the first phase of Miles' plans.

"Where shall we get what we need?" asked Grace.

"The nearest quarry is on Gerard's land," replied John. "It may therefore prove problematic."

"Miles will think of something."

John smiled. "I have no doubt, but in the meantime there is plenty that can be done before we need worry about stone." He took the plans from her and rolled them carefully and placed them inside his shirt for safety. "Next to my heart, my lady," he joked.

"Your work means a lot to you, doesn't it?"

"My work yes, but knowing it is appreciated by people I respect means more."

"I know how you feel," replied Grace a little sadly as she thought of her painting and how her best intentions had gone terribly wrong.

* * *

Martha and the rest of the women were setting food out in the great hall for all of the workers when Angus Baird and Mayflower arrived. The aroma of freshly plated fare was enough to cause the man to visibly salivate. So obsessed was he with the demands of his stomach that his anxiety over his immediate predicament was temporarily forgotten. His eyes darted about furtively as members of the household took their fill and returned to their labours. He eyed the rapidly decreasing feast with alarm and the Scotsman observed his growing discomfort with relish as they awaited Miles.

After what seemed an age to Mayflower but in reality was only moments, Miles appeared and greeted the Scotsman warmly.

"Did you have any trouble?" he asked as he watched the bishop's man drool over what remained on the table.

"Nae, no one in his party was inclined tae offer any resistance."

I wonder why? thought Miles.

"Please eat and rest awhile before you return to your men. I am grateful to you. I am in your debt."

The man shrugged. "The food from yer table is payment enough." He proceeded to fill a platter which he took with him as he left the hall.

They were alone then, Miles and Mayflower, and Miles let the silence between them grow as he studied the man who ogled the remains of the food. He was indeed a fool thought Miles; he thought more of his belly than any danger he may be in.

"We have some matters to discuss, Master Mayflower."

The man dragged his eyes reluctantly from the food and Miles was sure he heard the giant belly howl its protest.

"Indeed," said Mayflower indignantly. "My abduction, for one. You seem a mite partial to kidnapping if I may be so bold."

Miles shook his head. The man truly was a fool if he thought he could redeem himself with that attitude. He relaxed back in his seat.

"Forgive my manners, Mayflower you must be hungry after such a journey, please eat your fill. We will discuss the ways in which we can assist each other when you are sated."

The relief on the man's face was palpable and he moved with surprising speed as he filled his plate with enough to feed an entire family. Miles chose not to watch as he ate. The act of guzzling and slurping was enough to make the strongest stomach churn. He studied the remains of the tapestries on the walls instead and considered idly whether they could be repaired or replaced. The room lacked the warmth that had abounded in his mother's day. He wondered how far Grace's skills extended. To date she had surprised him with her many talents. He would speak with her later when she'd finished with John and he was finished with the porcine fellow seated before him.

"You are in an unfortunate predicament, Mayflower," Miles said at last when the man had eaten his fill.

"On the one hand if you align yourself with Gerard in this little witch hunt pretence, you may save your skin now, but lose your soul in the hereafter, for causing the death of an innocent; and Mayflower, you do know she is innocent. When your subterfuge is made public, and be assured that it will, you will be cast aside by your bishop who will see this charade for exactly what it is, and may well end up hung for your troubles. On the other hand you may consider you have no option, for fear of Gerard's wrath, if you do not carry out his wishes. Gerard does not care what you may suffer as a consequence of your lies. He cares only for his own position."

Mayflower squirmed with discomfort. "What do you intend to do with me?"

"I intend to offer you a solution to your problem, an alternative course of action that will see you exalted by your bishop and rewarded by your king."

"And what might that entail?" asked Mayflower, eager now to wriggle out of Gerard's clutches.

"Firstly, I need you to bear witness to the fact that Grace is no witch. To confirm that in your presence she behaved exactly as you would expect a young lady to behave, and at no time did you hold suspicions she could in fact be in possession of the dark arts. That, all talk of witchcraft was instigated by Sir Gerard as a way to get to me."

Mayflower regarded him gravely. "Do you consider she behaves as a young lady should?"

The man had a point. "I do. Perhaps, Master Mayflower you are not quite as informed on the behaviour of young ladies as you would like to think."

"That is all well and good, but if I denounce Sir Gerard and his accusations, how then do I protect myself from his inevitable retaliation? Having already experienced a tour of the dungeons at Ahlborett, I have no wish to end my days languishing in a subterranean cell."

"Gerard has made an unfortunate error in retaining for himself a large amount of Crusader spoils which by rights were destined for the king's coffers. I know of its location and need a witness to collaborate this."

"And what's in it for me?"

Even now the fat toad of a man was attempting to line his own pockets. A greedy man was easily turned.

"The king will no doubt reward the finder and restorer of such wealth. It is entirely up to you whether you decide to carry out your righteous act on behalf of your bishop and add your reward to the church's coffers, or keep the loot for yourself. Either way you will be made for life. The king's gratitude, and a sizeable reward, or the king's gratitude and your career enhanced by a beholding bishop."

Miles watched as Mayflower assimilated the options and considered his response.

"And what's in it for you? Why do you not just take the loot for yourself and say naught?"

"I have a score to settle with Gerard, and it is best served this way. The king, when he learns of Gerard's deceit, will deal with him appropriately and you will be protected from any retribution."

"And no doubt you will be very much in the young lady's favour for saving her from the stake. She will be very much in your debt, will she not?" Mayflower gave a sly smirk and Miles shrugged.

"It doesn't hurt to keep on a woman's good side."

"Where is the treasure?" asked Mayflower.

"The location of the treasure will be revealed in the fullness of time. What I need from you now is an answer. Will you help us and redeem yourself or do you choose to remain aligned to Gerard?"

Mayflower considered in silence, and Miles watched the indecision reflected on his face. The man clearly held no affection for Gerard, and judging by his reaction at being outsmarted by Grace, he did not hold Miles in high esteem either. The difference between the two of course, was one offered fear, pain and possible death and the other riches and the notoriety he so craved. There really was no decision to make. Miles smiled lazily and waited.

"Are you certain, Sir Gerard will not exact his revenge?"

Miles could not be certain of anything at this stage, but he needed this man. "I give you my word I will protect you."

"Then, Sir Miles of Wildewood, you have my word that I will assist you in your plan."

Miles rose and took the man's hand, it was greasy with food and Miles stifled his initial response to draw back his own. He shook Mayflower's hand firmly.

"We have an accord then, Master Mayflower and may God look favourably on our endeavours."

"Amen to that," replied Mayflower. "Amen to that."

"The king is in residence at Alnwick Castle. He will be attending High Mass at Alnwick on Sunday; I intend to seek an audience with him after the service. I will require your testimony as soon as required, during or following that audience. You must be prepared by then."

"And when will I see the treasure?"

Miles looked at him, considered the risks involved in returning once again to the crypt.

"You do not need to see the treasure, you only need to know it is there and testify to that when questioned by the king."

"And what if you are mistaken and I am caught in a falsehood?"

"I am not mistaken. I have seen it with my own eyes, along with Grace and John the Mason. We will all back up your testimony. I cannot run the risk of showing you the treasure before we meet the king. Time is short and Gerard must not know you are here and that we have formed an alliance."

"I must at least know where it is, the king will expect me to know of its location."

Mayflower was correct but it pained Miles to reveal the location, he did not entirely trust the man. "I will reveal the location in good time, Mayflower. For now, be happy in the knowledge that you are safe from Sir Gerard and you have only two days before you become a rich man."

Chapter Thirty Five

Gerard returned to Ahlborett Castle, safe in the mistaken knowledge, that the thorn in his side, the bastard Miles of Wildewood, was safely secreted at Kirk Knowe under armed guard and could pose no threat to him while the king was in attendance at Alnwick.

There was no earthly reason for the king to know about the treasure, he had vast wealth. He was not in need of any more, whereas Gerard had a specific reason to accumulate as much as was possible. The uneasy peace that existed between the English and the Scots for the better part of the 13th century was beginning to grow stale and there had been mutterings for some time about a resurgence of hostilities from across the border. Despite his family enjoying a history of co-operation with the Scot's in times past, he himself suffered losses from his outlying farms and had not the resources to police the entire border. The Scot, Alex Stewart was behind it all, he was sure of that, though despite dispatching his men as soon as reports of sightings were made, he failed to catch the man.

He would not be beaten by an outlaw. His family had kept the border land safe for generations and he expected his son, Robert, and in time his son's son would follow on after him. If he were to nip this in the bud he needed more than adequate militia and that demanded more funds than he currently had. He could not go cap in hand to the king and admit he could not manage the defence of his own lands. It was his responsibility to ensure appropriate funding and his alliance with Guy de Marchant had done just that until the discovery of Guy's sordid little secret.

He'd no idea what Guy had been doing, how or why he collected so many trophies of the dead, but he would make it his immediate mission to discover the truth. He would not have his honour tarnished by Guy. He'd suspected Guy was a little touched. Hell, people thought that of him, but it bothered him naught. Everything he did had reason behind it. He simply chose not to reveal his motives to all and sundry. Guy however was different, he had a reckless streak, a penchant for cruelty and Gerard heard things about him that made even him, shudder. However, he found his obsessive hatred of Miles useful and cultivated it for his own ends.

Miles had been an irritation to him, since childhood, but even more so while he held the title to Wildewood. Wildewood with its remote location was crucial to Gerard's plans for defence and yet he could not contemplate what was planned, with Miles and his hapless band of followers ensconced there. Rumour had it that Miles was sympathetic to the Scots; he could not allow a sympathiser to hold a strategic position within his domain.

He thought of the girl. Miles' girl. Who was she? Where did she fit in to this? She claimed she was related to Hugh de Reynard and they did share some characteristics, courage and outrageous behaviour, but he did not believe her claim. Either way she was daring, and her spirit, teamed with Miles' bloody self-righteousness, was not a match he could allow to flourish. But that was for later, after the king had gone. He may even let Guy loose on them, as long as his own hands were not bloodied, Guy could have his fun.

The surgeon had seen to Guy's leg and he was splinted and a little high on opium when Gerard returned to the castle. His wife had cast him a withering glance when told Guy would be staying. Gerard knew she found him offensive and did not think him a suitable guest with a young child in residence, but Gerard also knew despite this, she would not voice her opinion and it irritated him to think how spineless she was. The girl, Grace, would have let her opinions be known; he had no doubt about that. He wondered distractedly how Miles dealt with her forthright nature. He himself thought it refreshing.

He found Guy ensconced in his chamber, fire blazing, his trusted cohorts Percy and Simon at his side. Both had been wounded by Miles and attended by the surgeon at considerable expense to himself. He found them in a delicate state having imbibed rather too much of his wine along with the opium and he was furious with all three. What a pathetic display, Miles had taken all three of them and still managed to save the girl and find the treasure. His admiration of the deeds vied with his dislike of the man and almost outweighed his contempt for these so called knights.

"Get out," he bellowed at the two hangers-on as he hauled them out of the door by their collars. He called to the men at arms. "Take these misfits to cool off in the barracks I will not have them in my home."

He turned then to Guy who gazed at him with bleary eyes.

"What news, Gerard, have you captured our errant knight?" He grinned and raised his glass.

"Forget Miles, I am more interested in your little hobby, Guy."

Guy shrugged and blinked so slowly Gerard thought he had fallen asleep. He caught him by the front of his shirt and shook him violently; Guy startled out of his stupor, snapped to attention.

"Tell me about the armour, Guy?"

"The armour?"

"Yes, the armour stashed at Kirk Knowe, you ignorant toad. What have you done? And don't lie to me, Guy, or I'll snap your neck here and now."

Guy smirked. "Just a collection, Gerard. Did you never collect things?"

"Yes, I collected bird's eggs as a child. It was something I grew out of when I became a man. Are you not yet a man, Guy?"

"Of course I'm a man," grinned Guy. "And I have developed a man's hobby. It's good to have a hobby, Gerard, it expands the mind."

"I will be more than happy to expand your mind, Guy, with a sweep of my sword, unless you tell me what is afoot. The English armour, how did you acquire it?"

"From the battle-field, Gerard, where else?"

"And the owners, were they fallen knights or pushed knights?"

Guy laughed, "I like that, Gerard—did they fall or were they pushed— how droll. Well I'll tell you, Gerard, just between you and I." He leaned forward conspiratorially and almost fell from his seat. "Some were fallen, but most just got in my way."

"But they were on our side, Guy, why would you take out your own men?"

"Not my men, Gerard, the king's men. And who are you to criticise, do you not plan to take out your own brother?"

"My dispute with Miles does not come in to this. On what basis did you take these knights?"

"Why, Gerard, where did you think your treasure came from? Do you think I merely asked and they happily gave what they had? Now that would have been altogether too easy. No, Gerard, I believe it was what you may call a mutual agreement. You got the treasure which you so crave while I got the pleasure of taking it and when the gallant knight was no more, I also got his armour to add to my collection."

Gerard stared at him in disbelief. "You murdered all of those men in cold blood and kept their armour as some kind of sick trophy?"

"Why not? I did think about keeping their heads, but after a while they do have a rare pungency. I couldn't have the ladies thinking it was me."

Gerard stepped back stunned by the depravity of the man, and then as his head cleared, and his thoughts became more focused he was equally stunned by the stupidity and arrogance of the man.

"Are you mad? Every trophy you have taken ties you to a murder which in turn ties you to the theft of the king's treasure."

Guy narrowed his eyes. "I think not, Gerard, for where does all of this evidence lie?"

"Kirk Knowe."

"And who does Kirk Knowe belong to?"

Gerard flew at him then. "You son of a shrivelled toad, I'll kill you." He back handed him across the face and Guy's lip burst in a spray of blood.

Gerard shook with fury. How had he allowed this to happen? He had been well and truly outmanoeuvred and as a consequence he stood to lose everything. His heart pounded in his chest but with considerable effort he managed to control himself. He may need Guy alive yet.

Miles and his woman were locked in Kirk Knowe. They had seen everything, the treasure and the trophies. It was now even more imperative they did not get to the king. There was no alternative. They would have to be killed. Who else knew? He cast about wildly, the men at arms had been in there, Guy's men no doubt knew all about it. Perhaps he was the only one who did not. He spun around and delivered a crunching blow to Guy's grinning face dispelling the grin along with his consciousness. Gerard strode from the chamber and slammed the door behind him.

Things were beginning to unravel again at an alarming rate. He would have to move the treasure and get rid of the armour. But he had two days and Miles was going nowhere. Tonight he would lie with his boring biddable wife and tomorrow he would rewrite his future.

* * *

Word reached Gerard the following day, that tree felling was being undertaken in the forest at Wildewood and the Scot's were somehow involved. It concerned Gerard that his trees were being taken without his permission, it mattered naught to him that Miles considered Wildewood and its timber to be his. Wildewood would never be his. Of more interest however, was the news that Alex Stewart's right hand man, Angus Baird had been spotted with the Scottish outlaws.

Today would be a good day, mused Gerard as he set off for Wildewood with a dozen men at arms. Guy was under house arrest, Miles and his whore under armed guard at Kirk Knowe, the king safe in his ignorance at Alnwick and Alex Stewart was now within grasp. What more could he ask?

Chapter Thirty Six

The Foresters had felled six large trees in response to John's request for long straight timbers and their Scots minders assisted in the trimming of the ancillary branches. The giant logs were chained one at a time to the two heavy horses who dragged them back to Wildewood. It was not safe to linger in the wood to cut the beams, so the work was done within the safety of Wildewood's walls.

It took time however for the logs to be hauled and the horses to return for the next load and all of the men were jumpy. The return of Angus Baird however, lifted the spirits of his men and they rested together while they awaited the return of the horses. Jack Forester returned to Wildewood with the penultimate load so he could begin work on the timber immediately. He left his son Robert to bring back the last log. They had worked hard, as had the Scots, but for Jack and his son there was a sense of pride in being a part of the rebuilding of Wildewood. Under John's guidance they hoped to create something that would last for many generations.

The horses were weary and reluctant to head out for yet another haul. It took some effort on Robert's part to get them out of the courtyard and into the park. Miles, keen for some fresh air after his less than fragrant discussion with Mayflower, mounted his own horse and joined Robert for the final journey. Robert allowed the horses to idle back to the forest knowing they would naturally quicken their pace on the homeward journey with the lure of fresh hay and a bucket of oats. Miles rode alongside keeping watch, but his mind was on other things. Treasure and revenge.

The two lumbering giants alerted Robert initially to the notion something was amiss. It began with the flicking of their ears and gentle snorting through velvet flaring nostrils. Robert halted their progress and reassured the beasts with gentle words. Miles raised his hand to silence him and they paused under the shelter of the trees, harness jingling gently as the horses fidgeted. Miles strained his ears as he listened acutely; and then far in the distance he heard the sound of approaching horses, many of them, travelling at speed. He gestured to Robert to remain where he was and set off at a pace towards the felling ground. If he were not mistaken, the Scots were about to be ambushed.

The Scots were taken by surprise, much to their chagrin. Heavily outnumbered they scattered into the trees to avoid a one-sided fight. Determined not to be deprived of his prize, Gerard set his men to root out those they could find. The soldiers pushed their horses far faster than was safe within the confines of the forest and the noise of the squealing frightened horses and the yelling of men as they bullied the beasts rang horribly through the woods.

Angus avoided the stampeding horses with the ease of a man who lived a life in the shadows. He called to his men using the language of the forest; the call of the fox and the screech of the hawk, sounds that could only be recognised, by those who knew how to listen. It was inevitable however there would be an altercation. The Scots, who were masters at guerrilla warfare, did so love a fight.

Miles arrived at the logging area to find a furious and bloody skirmish raging. Despite being outnumbered two to one, the Scots were letting rip with short swords and axes and some of the men at arms had already fallen, hacked to death. He yanked his horse to a sudden standstill, drew his own sword, and quickly assessed the situation.

As he'd surmised, they were Gerard's men and no matter how skilled the Scots were, they could not hope to win such an uneven fight. He noticed Gerard then, calmly observing the skirmish, looking for someone in particular. Miles cast his gaze across the fighting men, looking in the direction that so interested Gerard. At first he saw nothing but the clash of swords, the heaving of bodies and the spray of blood. Then he caught sight of Angus squaring up to one of Gerard's men. Glancing quickly back at Gerard he realised Angus was Gerard's target. He could not allow Alex's right hand man to be taken.

Miles had neither armour nor helmet to protect him, but he did have his padded leather jerkin and a sword that had served him well so far. He thought of Grace, of their plan and how it could all go awry if he were to fall here in the wood, but could not turn his back on the man who delivered Mayflower into his palm. He kicked his horse and charged through the melee, hacking wildly with his sword at anyone who came between him and Angus.

The blow that unseated him and sealed his fate was in fact meant for another.

* * *

It was only later when those not killed outright were bound and tethered to their horses for the return journey to Ahlborett, that Gerard realised not only had he managed to capture Angus Baird, but the bloodied and unconscious scoundrel at his feet was none other than his nemesis, Miles of Wildewood.

Gerard shook his head, baffled. How had the man managed to escape from Kirk Knowe? He had left him under armed guard. No matter, he had fallen into his lap now and he would certainly find it a challenge indeed to escape from the dungeons of Ahlborett.

* * *

Robert delivered the terrible news back to Wildewood, but it was John who took Grace to one side to explain how Miles had been taken. Grace found herself strangely numb. This man who she'd known for so short a time had influenced her life greatly and she was bereft at the thought he was now gone from her. She paced the room pale faced, hands twisting together as she fought to keep control of the panic rising inside her.

"Was he alive?" she whispered.

"Robert saw him felled from his horse and taken away. Sir Gerard would not have taken him if he were dead."

"So, he is alive and at the castle?"

"It would seem so, my lady."

"Then we must rescue him."

"How? The castle is heavily manned and the dungeons will be guarded further."

She shrugged at him. "I don't know, John, but we have to try." She fought back fearful tears. "Ask everyone to gather in the great hall, have Martha cook for us all and we will decide what to do."

Three young Scottish warrior's had fallen in the wood and their bodies were brought back to Wildewood by the Foresters', carried reverently on the backs of the giant horses and laid temporarily to rest in the walled garden, awaiting retrieval by their kinsman. Mayflower surprised those who had gathered to pay their respects, by leading a prayer and Grace thanked the man with a weary smile.

The mood when the household gathered was sombre. Without Miles they were adrift and anxious, fearful the fight would be brought to Wildewood. They had all volunteered to defend Wildewood when they believed they would be led by Miles, the brave knight who fought alongside the king. There was no one to lead them now and they cast furtive glances at each other. No one wanted to say out loud, what was being thought by all.

"We must rescue Miles and Angus and any others who may still be alive," Grace said simply. "We just need to think of a plan."

"If they are held in the dungeons then we have no chance. I know of no one who has come out of Ahlborett alive."

Grace looked at the man who'd spoken. He was one of the brothers who'd been the first to volunteer their support. She was disappointed. She'd assumed she could rely on him.

"What of Walter de Sweethope?" asked Jack Forester "Was he not imprisoned and released on the king's word, would he not be able to assist with a plan of the layout?"

"And who will travel to him and bring the plan back?" said another. "The woods will be crawling with Sir Gerard's men waiting to pick us off."

Grace despaired. If Miles were here he would rally them, encourage them. She had nothing to offer. She was a silly girl from another time who would get them all killed given half a chance.

"I have knowledge of Sir Gerard's dungeon system," said Mayflower calmly. "In fact, I was given a guided tour quite recently."

Grace turned to him. "Could you draw us a plan?"

"I fear I am no artist," replied Mayflower, "But I understand you have a certain skill in that area. Perhaps together we can create something useful."

Grace could have hugged him. "So, we will have a map to follow once we are in the castle."

"How do you propose we gain entry to Ahlborett?" asked Robert Forester. "We are a ragtaggle band of peasants. The men at arms will laugh at us before they cut us down."

"We're a force of twenty, and have horses for us all. Surely, twenty, galloping towards them will cause some reaction other than laughter?"

John shook his head wearily and Grace saw the defeat on his face.

She could not give up. It was not in her nature and knew if the situation was reversed Miles would not abandon her.

"We have a plan of the dungeons, so we know where they are within the castle. We need to get someone inside to locate the prisoners and be ready to let us in when we get there. Who is allowed in the dungeons, Mayflower? Who did you see when you were given your tour?"

Mayflower paused, "My lady, I confess, I was less concerned with those incarcerated, and more concerned about leaving. I regret I took little notice of anyone other than guards."

"How many?"

"There were two at the entrance to the dungeons."

"Anyone else? Are they allowed visitors? How do they get their food?"

"The food is taken in by the relatives of the captives," said Martha. "They receive no food unless they are fed by their own, but anyone who enters will be searched, I expect."

"Would they search a boy?" asked Edmund. All eyes turned to him, the scrawny twelve year-old who looked younger than his years.

"No, Edmund, I won't allow you to put yourself at risk, it's far too dangerous." Grace couldn't bear the thought of anything happening to Edmund. Miles would never forgive her. She would never forgive herself.

"The boy could do it," said John. "No one would suspect him."

"And what if he should bump into Guy?"

"Guy has a broken leg, he will not be abroad."

"I am not afraid." Edmund looked at Grace. "It would be an honour to help. I can do it."

"Not alone, Edmund, never alone," replied Grace.

"I will go with him," said a voice from beyond the gathering at the table. Belle stepped forward from the shadows. She glanced at Edmund and smiled nervously. "I'll distract the guards, while Edmund locates Sir Miles and the others. "We can do it together."

Distract the guards? Grace didn't like the sound of that. Belle was a child with the body of a woman, and she too would be in danger. Despite her foreboding, she nodded reluctantly. They were both children, but here in this place, they were all she had.

Jack Forester spoke up again. "So, the youngsters get into the dungeon, smuggle in a knife or two, manage against all odds to release the men; what then? We are still an untrained band of peasants with no weapons to speak of and no armour to protect us from Sir Gerard's wrath. Do you think he will run from us when he sees our army advance upon his castle?"

Grace looked to John, catching his eye. He gave an imperceptible nod and she smiled. Turning back to the gathering, she rose to her feet and with all eyes upon her she declared.

"We will have armour and weapons and Sir Gerard will think the army of the damned has come a calling."

Chapter Thirty Seven

Miles woke sprawled in the straw on the floor of the dungeon. He lay face down where he had been thrown by the guards, his cheek flattened against the filth. Dragging reluctant eyes open he viewed the cell from his horizontal position. He'd found himself in far worse and more dangerous places in his time and learned from experience it did not pay to move too quickly when regaining ones senses, you never knew who might be watching and waiting for an opportunity to strike.

The smell from the rancid litter was foul and the straw moved with vermin and lice. It was no good, he could not lie amid the piss and shit of other men, nor could he stand anymore of the stink. He groaned and raised his head. The room swam and he paused until he regained his equilibrium. Spitting blades of straw from his mouth he rose up on hands and knees.

"Ah wouldnae stay lang in that position, if ah were ye," said a gravelly Scottish voice. "Some o' these men hivn't had a woman in years an' they're no choosy."

Miles swung his head and the grinning face of Angus Baird came in to view. He grimaced and sat himself up with his back against the support of the cold damp wall. The cell was not large and it contained at least a dozen men. The low ceiling made the space feel smaller. One wall was barred with iron work beyond which was a passage which led to the guard room. Torches lit the cell dimly, but there were no windows and no circulation of fresh air to relieve the stench.

They were well below ground level and Miles could only guess at the thickness of the walls which enclosed them. He glanced around at his fellow captives and recognised three of Angus's men, their faces showed evidence of battle but they were alive and watching him with interest. The others were a collection of men unknown to him. Some looked as if they had been there for some time. They were undernourished and their skin carried signs of disease and poor diet.

"What happened?" asked Miles as he attempted to brush the fetid straw from his clothes.

"Yer brother happened," replied Angus.

"Gerard?"

"Aye. Gerard and a dozen men at arms. They knew we wir there. Caught us nappin' ah'm afeared, but they were armed an armoured tae the hilt."

"I don't remember a thing," admitted Miles.

"Ye did try tae rescue us," grimaced Angus and his men grinned, "Unsuccessfully as it happens. Ah caught sight of ye gallopin' tae me through the mess o' men; how ye survived in the Holy Land is a mystery tae me, not a bloody thought as tae who was at yer flank. You're lucky tae be alive."

Miles shrugged. He'd never said he was a skilled fighter, but he'd never been short on determination. "How many did you lose?"

"Three, one o' them was ma nephew."

"I'm sorry," said Miles.

"Tis Gerard whae'll be sorry, "replied Angus with a grimace.

"Do we have a plan?" Miles enquired.

"Nah,"

"Does Gerard?"

"Ah expect he plans tae see us all swing."

Miles considered this. "Well, he won't do that until the king has returned to London, so we have a few days grace." He held his head in his hands. He was getting too old for all this fighting. He'd come home to Wildewood for some peace and quiet after the rigours of the crusade but it seemed since he'd returned he'd had nothing but grief. First from the girl, then Guy, and now Gerard, it was beginning to get a little repetitious.

"Is ye head still botherin' yer lad?" asked Angus. "Ye took an almighty blow; if it had been the blade you'd have lost yer head for sure. We thought yer were dead."

Miles smiled, "I've felt worse with the drink."

"Then ah suggest we maintain a state o' readiness. When the guards come tae take us tae the scaffold we'll make oor move."

Miles nodded and yawned. "Wake me when they get here."

He was kicked awake a short while later by the guards who dragged him to his feet and hauled him from the cell. He shot a warning glance at Angus; this was not the time to make a move.

He tried to take note of where he was being taken but his head was forced down by the guards and when he struggled to right himself he received a blow to the belly for his trouble. Pushed forward, he stumbled when down a flight of stones steps leading further into the bowels of the earth. He tried to resist the pressure of the soldiers at his back as a sense of alarm crept through him. He'd been singled out for some purpose and he could only assume Guy was at the root of it. He took a steadying breath. Guy was a madman, he could not be anticipated in the way a normal man could. He wished, yet again, that he'd run him through when he had the chance.

"Where are you taking me?" he asked the soldiers.

"To hell," replied one. The other laughed humourlessly.

"I can show you hell, right here if you release me."

The men merely grinned. "Save your bravado for Sir Guy, you're going to need it."

Miles exhaled slowly. He was familiar with torture. He had been captured and suffered at the hands of the Saracens who were masters at the art, but despite that, or perhaps because of it, he felt the beginnings of fear curling deep inside. The trick he knew was in hiding it. Torture was a game played out on a knife edge, a balance between courage and fear. He could not afford to allow his self belief to falter.

"You are mistaken in your allegiance with Guy de Marchant, he is a madman and soon the King will know of it. Do you want to be tried for treason?"

It was worth a try, but he doubted the guards would act against Guy. If he, an experienced knight could be rattled by the thought of an encounter with the man, then the guards would definitely be fearful of his displeasure. They exchanged a nervous glance.

"Keep your mouth shut, bastard."

The first guard jammed his elbow into Miles' ribs with such force Miles dropped to the ground and tumbled down the remainder of the stone steps reopening the wound above his eye and splitting his lip on the unforgiving stone. Dragged upright by the guards, he spat the coppery taste of blood from his mouth. He stifled a groan as one of the guards slammed him hard against the stone wall at the foot of the stairs, opened a heavy wooden door and flung him into a room flooded with light. Temporarily blinded and immediately at a disadvantage, he sucked in a ragged breath, slowly opened his eyes and relaxed his clenched fists.

His nemesis was not immediately visible. The glare from the many torches caused Miles to narrow his eyes as he scanned the space. This was indeed a torture chamber. His heart quickened. He'd seen many of the devices before and been the victim of one or two in his time. Hideous memories re-emerged unbidden from the depths of his mind.

He steeled his expression, heard movement and turned to look squarely at Guy. He was seated, with his foot propped on a wooden stool. He wore an amused expression.

Finally, thought Miles, he has me exactly where he wants me and I have no one to blame but myself.

"We meet again, Miles," said Guy, "and after our last meeting I've been so looking forward to this." He gestured to his splinted foot. "I would have come a calling, would love to have met your good lady once more, but unfortunately I'm a trifle incapacitated."

"Likewise," replied Miles. "We have unfinished business, do we not?"

The guards held his arms loosely. Perhaps they thought as there was no escape, he would be resigned to his fate. They were incorrect. If there was a way out of this place he would find it. He had no wish to end his days being pulled apart by a madman. Miles scanned the room for something to assist him. There were many tools of the torture trade that could be turned upon the torturer. If he were free to utilise them. He bided his time.

"You made a mistake, Miles. Finally, after all this time, you let a woman get under your skin and weaken you. You're slipping. You should have killed me when you had the chance."

"I couldn't agree more, Guy." He wished he had, didn't really know why he hadn't, other than the fact that Grace had seen enough brutality for one day.

"They say the time brings its reward, Miles, and I have waited some time for this, so you must excuse me if I make the moment last." He gestured with an open hand to the array of despicable contraptions. "Where would you like me to start? The rack? The hot iron? Or perhaps the thought of rats gnawing at your belly appeals?" He gave a sly grin and the soldiers winced at his obvious sadistic enjoyment.

Miles glared back and shook his head. "Do you really think you'll get away with this? Do you think the king will not hold you to account for murder?"

"Miles, you have an inflated opinion of yourself. The king cares not for what happens to a bastard such as you."

"Perhaps, but I wager he will question what has happened to the many other knights you have seen fit to dispatch. Knights, who rode under the king's banner and defended his realm. Your crimes are about to be revealed, Guy. The king will have your head."

"Another mistake, Miles, once again you've played your hand too soon. Who is going to inform the king when I have you here?"

"Others know of your perversion, and they'll do what is honourable, regardless of whether I live or not." He thought of Mayflower, would he have the guts to carry out the plan without him being there to cajole him? He doubted it, but John may have the presence of mind to persuade him.

"If you refer to your whore, then I would not rely too heavily on her. You forget, Miles, while you are here as my guest, Wildewood remains unguarded and the girl unprotected. I have no doubt in her naïveté she will seek to find you and I will take great pleasure in assisting her, we too have unfinished business."

Miles seethed with rage. The thought of the man getting anywhere near Grace made his stomach churn. He silently counted to ten and forced himself to relax his bunched up muscles. Guy was baiting him and he refused to give him the reward of a reaction.

"What is she like, Miles? Do you think she will warm to my particular style?"

"I believe she is far cleverer than you, Guy. She will run rings around any attempt you may care to make."

She was clever but she was also headstrong. Guy was correct, she may well try to find him and believe herself capable of interceding on the outcome, but any attempt she may make was doomed to failure. She had no concept of Guy's capacity for evil.

"It's a shame then you'll be unable to protect her, unfortunate you put the lives of the Scots before your good lady, but I'm sure she'll understand. I'll take the time to make her understand. I'm a patient man after all."

Miles glowered at him. He wondered if he'd already dispatched men to Wildewood and whether Gerard had assisted. It seemed the two of them were inexorably linked but driven by different goals. Gerard would not allow himself to be drawn into the debacle of the murdered knights, but he might happily utilise the unprotected state of Wildewood for his own ends.

"Does Gerard know you have me here?" he asked, uncertain as to whether Gerard would also collude in his torture.

Guy laughed. "Don't hold your breath waiting for Gerard to come to your aid. He's off to Alnwick with the good Lady Maud, to meet the king. A little anxious to make a good impression, I believe. But even if he knew you were here, providing my entertainment, he would not intervene. You've rattled too many cages, Miles, with all this talk of spies and secret allegiances. Gerard considers you far too dangerous to keep alive. You seem to find comfort on all sides of the blanket these days and it concerns him as to where your true loyalty lies. Perhaps the girl is not the spy after all."

Miles shook his head. "You talk nonsense, Guy. My only allegiance is to the king."

"And yet you fraternise with the Scots."

"We are not at war with the Scots."

"And your closeness to Reynard is questionable, considering his own position is far from clear. He seems to have the ear of the rich and powerful of Europe."

"Are you envious, Guy?"

"No, merely curious. It's all rather perplexing, since no one knows of his background. Perhaps he is another bastard, Miles. They say like attracts like, and of course now there's your dalliance with the little witch girl. Did you know, Gerard thinks you three have hatched a plot and are in collusion with the Devil?"

"You're not wrong, Guy. There is the devils' work afoot here, but I assure you it has naught to do with us. I would say you are more closely aligned to the horned one than any acquaintance of mine."

"So, she is not a witch after all?" laughed Guy, "And yet she bewitches every man who lays eyes on her? How do you account for that? Mayflower was practically drooling at the mouth, Gerard was ready to exchange his wife after his encounter with her at the crypt and I must admit I was more than tempted to take a bite of the forbidden fruit. How about you, Miles, are you also under her spell? Are you positive your actions are yours alone and you are not merely a puppet being manipulated for another's purpose."

"You know nothing, Guy. You see conspiracy and intrigue where there is none. Grace is beyond suspicion and I am my own man."

"Good for you, Miles. So, who is little Gracie and from where does she hail? Is she the missing nun from Kirk Knowe whom no one has heard of? Or the niece of the infamous, Hugh de Reynard, as she informed Mayflower? Or perhaps she is someone else who we have yet to discover. What do you think?"

Miles remained silent. Guy had an uncanny knack for finding raw nerves, and where Grace was concerned his nerves were very sensitive. He too would like to know the truth but he would not give Guy the satisfaction of knowing that.

Guy smiled, and Miles realised he was not sufficiently adept at concealing his feelings. The tightening of his jaw and the slight narrowing of his eyes had betrayed him.

"Myself, I think if she is not a witch then such a foxy, little strumpet must be the niece of Reynard and whatever game she is playing will be known in due course. Such a shame therefore you will not be around when the truth is revealed, Miles."

Miles wearied of Guy's baiting and it seemed Guy had also grown bored of being the baiter.

"Enough idle banter, Miles, it's time we got down to business." He gestured to the guards, "Strip him to the waist. Let's see if we can find some flesh that hasn't already been claimed by a scar."

Miles was not about to allow himself to be manhandled and readied himself. He did not however expect the blow to the back of his knees which dropped him like a stone, or the vicious kick to the back of the head which left him stunned while his shirt was ripped from his back.

"Oh my," exclaimed Guy. "Is that my handwork?" He rose to his feet and with the help of a crutch crossed the room to inspect the wound left by his sword. He reached out and drew a finger down the length of the scar and the guards were hard pushed to hold Miles back.

"How are you still alive?"

He cocked his head and circled Miles, viewing his handiwork from all sides. The guards glanced awkwardly at each other.

Guy stood back leaning heavily on the crutch.

"Forgive me, I digress. Which do you prefer, Miles? The rack or the lash, the choice is yours?"

Chapter Thirty Eight

Edmund and Belle left the safety of the forest and paused before descending into the valley, somewhat in awe at the castle revealed in all its glory beneath them. The sun was waning and Ahlborett was bathed from the west in a soft orange glow. Light glinted off the metalwork, the portcullis, the giant studs on the castle gates and the swords and shields of the men at arms. Soon the castle would be lit by torch light and Edmund realised they needed to be inside before that happened.

Between them they led Mayflower's tiny pony which had been smeared with mud to disguise its appearance, should anyone recall it from Mayflower's last visit, and draped with a rough blanket which served to hide a short metal bar. On the pony's back sat Linus. It had taken an enormous amount of argument and negotiation before Grace had agreed to his inclusion in the plan. Jack Forester had argued, the younger the child the less suspicious the group would appear and the guards less likely to search them. John had reluctantly agreed his son would be safer with Edmund and Belle than left at Wildwood unprotected while the men folk were away. Grace had listened and understood their reasoning but was mortified they were about to use this child, this baby. She agreed simply because she could see no other way to ensure Miles' release, and because, like John, she recognised Wildewood was currently not a safe place to be.

Edmund led the pony carefully down the steep track from the Danestone and Belle held Linus tightly and ensured he did not slip. The two older children were nervous, but Linus was oblivious to danger and merely excited at being allowed to ride the little pony he so coveted. Perhaps if he were a good boy and did exactly as he'd been told, Mayflower would let him ride the pony again. He knew exactly what to do and repeated it in his head lest he forget. He was to hold tightly to Edmunds hand. That was very important. When Edmund squeezed his hand he was to howl and cry as loudly as he could. He had practised in the great hall at Wildewood and everyone agreed his was the loudest voice they'd ever heard. He looked forward to doing that again.

Belle held a basket in her free hand and beneath its cloth cover it held fresh bread and roasted fowl, winter stored apples and a stone flagon of mead. Beneath her skirts she carried a knife strapped to the outside of each thigh. Edmund glanced at her as they negotiated the narrow path, he hoped she would do as she had been instructed and only that. She was inclined toward recklessness and he feared her doing something ill-advised in a vain attempt to impress him. He was already impressed that she'd volunteered to accompany him.

Edmund hefted a heavy, yew staff, which at seven foot long was far taller than him. He carried one knife against his back beneath his clothes which he felt against his skin as he moved. He would have chosen to carry more, but John advised the only safe place to hide a weapon was at his back and there was only room for one.

They reached the road and before they crossed and entered the castle approach, Edmund stopped and took hold of Belle's sleeve.

"Are yer sure of what ye are to do? Are yer sure ye want to continue? Stay here with Linus if yer wish, I will understand."

Belle smiled nervously. "We shall do this together or not at all, and we're not about to let everyone down are we?"

Edmund nodded and they continued over the drawbridge and paused before stepping into the outer bailey. They were stopped by the guards as they knew they would be.

"We bring food to our father, he awaits God's mercy in yer dungeon we seek leave to visit him with yer good grace."

The soldier looked at the dirty children, wrinkled his nose and waved them through, turning away to confront the next visitor. Edmund slipped the iron bar from beneath the pony's blanket and jammed it unseen into the drawbridge mechanism. He paused then, as if unsure of the way. He glanced right and left, up and down as he stood hesitantly beneath the raised portcullis, then he propped the staff up against the wall and left it there. Once behind the walls of the inner bailey, Edmund lifted Linus from the pony's back and tethered the pony to the metal catch which held the inner gate ajar. He soothed the pony and gently placed a teasel from Belle's basket beneath the pony's blanket.

"We will return for yer," he whispered in the pony's ear.

"Come," he said, and taking Linus firmly by the hand, he led the way to the dungeon entrance. He had memorised the plan which Grace and Mayflower had produced and he knew exactly where to go. The next set of guards gave them a cursory search paying more attention to the contents of the basket than anything else. As expected, they took out the flagon of mead and one of the roast fowl before letting the children pass. The only remaining guards were those who attended the cells and they were currently engaged in a heated argument in the guard room. Belle sashayed past swinging her skirts and they paused in their debate. She smiled at them as Edmund and Linus continued on into the passageway. The soldiers smiled back, eyeing her with sudden interest.

Edmund ignored their lechery and peered into the dimness of the cells. The first held only one man who was chained and desperately thin.

He looked blankly at Edmund. Edmund wondered how long the man had been there, wondered at his crime, and if his family knew he still lived.

The next was empty but smelt of death. Edmund imagined he saw the shape in the straw where a blood stained body had lain. He pulled his eyes away with a shudder and moved on.

The third was full and Edmund stopped and looked in vain for Miles in the gloom. He had to be there. The plan relied upon it. He turned, unsure as to what he should do.

Suddenly, his wrist grabbed from within the cell and yanked against the bars.

"Why, Edmund, lad, what have ye brought us?"

Edmund let out the breath he'd been holding at the sound of Angus' thick course brogue. The Scot smiled at him reassuringly from within the cell.

Edmund glanced at the guards. Belle had them both entertained. Retrieving his hand he pulled the knife from beneath his clothes and slipped it through the bars.

"We need mair than that son. We need the keys," added Angus and Edmund nodded.

"Belle, give me a hand with this 'ere basket," he called.

Belle skipped to the cells and brought with her the youngest guard who had keys attached to his belt. She leaned back against the bars and as she flirted with the guard she slid up the back of her skirts to reveal the hidden knives. They were carefully and quickly retrieved by calloused but gentle hands. She wrapped her arms around the guard and swung him around, so he was the one now pressed against the bars.

Belle reached up with the promise of a kiss and then dived for cover as his throat was slit from behind and blood spurted into the narrow space. More hands yanked the keys from his belt before he was allowed to fall.

Edmund dipped Linus' finger in the gushing blood and squeezed his hand tightly before handing him to Belle who ran with him to the entrance. Linus bawled loud enough to split the heavens as he held his blood stained finger aloft.

"Beg pardon, the child has caught his finger, I would take him out if yer please," pleaded Belle. The racket of the screaming child echoed around the subterranean labyrinth. The remaining guard grimaced and unlocked the door to let them through, By the time the noise had gone from the place the cell was open and the final guard dead.

"Where is Sir Miles?" asked Edmund fearfully.

"Yer too late lad, he was taken, tae be tortured by Guy nae doubt."

Edmund shuddered at the thought of Guy. "Then we must find him, we cannot leave without him."

* * *

Below in the torture room, Miles hung from shackles which were pitched at such a height, he was required to stand on the tips of his toes to prevent his shoulder joints from dislocating under his full weight. He would be unable to hold the position for much longer. The heat from the hot coals in the centre of the chamber had him sweating; rivulets ran down his face unchecked. The salts from his body leached out with the perspiration on his back and created further torment as they invaded the raw wounds newly created by Guy. Guy circled him slowly. He had delivered one stroke of the lash and noted how Miles had stifled his curse.

He cracked the lash in the air causing the guards to jump, but Miles barely flinched. He flicked it again toward the men and they glowered at him. Guy turned back to Miles and delivered another lash which caught him across the chest, the tip whipping a line of blood across his chin. Miles teetered precariously on his toes and willed his self-control to hold fast.

The sound of the child's screams reverberated suddenly in the small space, drowning out Guy's laughter. Guy paused and lowered the lash.

"Spawn of a whore, who in God's name allowed a child in here?" He threw the lash to the floor, "Go and see what's happening," he said to the guards. The men took their opportunity and fled.

Miles held his breath and listened carefully. A child in the dungeons was unlikely and as such offered up a unique opportunity while Guy was distracted. He stretched with his fingers and succeeded in wrapping his hands firmly around the ropes which held the manacles in place. As his hands and the muscles in his forearms took the strain from his shoulders he thanked the Lord for screaming children.

Guy turned back to him and smiled. "Now where were we?" He bent to pick up the lash, balancing with one hand on the crutch and as he righted himself, Miles pulled himself clear of the ground swung his booted feet with all of his weight behind him and caught Guy full in the face. He dropped as if pole axed and lay unmoving on the floor.

Chapter Thirty Nine

The sun had almost set when Linus' shrill cry was heard, carried on the wind to those who awaited its signal behind the safety of the Danestone. As the last rays of the sun disappeared they lit their torches, mounted their horses and with a signal from their diminutive leader the riders began their descent.

Twenty riders came down the hill at a charge, with torches blazing and hooves pounding. Behind them the sound of banging drums, clanging metal and banshee screams filled the air. All the folk of Wildewood had gathered at the stone to lend what support they could to their lord. The children banged and rattled whatever they held in their hands and the women keened into the darkness. The torches lit the sky, eerily dancing back and forth and up and down as the riders who carried them, clung valiantly to the galloping beasts. The horses screamed in fear and anticipation, plunging into the darkness anxious to escape the terrible noise from the rear.

The guards at the castle swung their gaze from the screaming child and his bloody finger, to the advancing spectacle and crossed themselves in fear. The vision that stampeded toward them out of the night was the devils army. Horrifically, lit by orange flames, the horses screamed and pawed the air with their giant hooves. Their flowing manes were stained blood red and their heaving flanks similarly streaked with white, transformed them into horrific skeletons in the dancing light.

The riders of these deathly creatures were armed to the teeth, with weapons which they brandished aloft. Armoured in a mongrel assortment of styles each more exotic and horrifying than the next. The bloody skins of animals flapped against the metal and the stench of death clung to them. Each rider was unique in their fiendish garb, yet each wore the same blood red plume which marked them as one entity, one horde. The noise of their approach was both deafening and terrifying.

"Close the draw bridge!" A desperate shout came from within and men ran to carry out the order. But no matter how many tried they were unable to raise it. The mechanism was jammed tight and in the dim light no man could see the cause of its failure. Another turned with an axe and with one swift blow cut through the rope that raised and lowered the port cullis. It dropped like a stone under its own weight until it met with Edmund's staff and its downward plummet was suddenly stopped by the iron like strength of the yew wood, to leave it hanging impotently seven feet from the ground.

The riders and their fearsome mounts thundered as one mass over the drawbridge. They ducked their way under the port-cullis and then they were in the outer bailey and Gerard's men swarmed among them.

The sound of clashing metal reverberated around the castle. A shout went up to close the gate to the inner bailey. The man who tried to do just that, pushed at the pony stood in his way and inadvertently pressed the barbs of the teasel into its flank. The pony reacted as Edmund had expected by rearing and kicking out with its hind legs wheeling this way and that to rid itself of the stinging barb. The man was kicked to the ground and the gate stayed open to allow the riders through.

Grace pulled the lead horse to a sudden halt at the entrance to the dungeon complex and the horse pranced with fright and frustration. The little, grey filly tossed its blood red mane and froth sprayed from its mouth as it wrestled the bit. Grace fought to control the beast while all around men on foot and on horseback fought with swords, axes, knives and horrific spiked iron balls wielded on lengths of chain. Weapons clashed against shields and the metallic clang jarred her ears. Where they clashed against flesh and bone there was merely a sickening thud.

She slid with difficulty from the horse. Despite choosing the smallest and lightest of the available armour from the crypt at Kirk Knowe, it was over large for her and heavy. She lifted the visor on her helmet so she could see more clearly.

Glancing around, through the melee, she was relieved to see Belle and Linus crouched safely out of harm's way. She gestured for them to retrieve the pony and leave. Their job was done and they needed to escape while they could. The advantage which they'd initially had was wearing off. Up close it was easy to see they were not the army of the damned, but merely a ragtaggle band on painted horses that lacked any real fighting skills and were no match for trained men at arms. She had to find Miles and get everyone out before the plan went horribly wrong.

Grace made for the door as it burst open from within and Angus and the Scots came barrelling out with Edmund. Angus raised the sword which he'd taken from the fallen guard and was only stopped from cleaving Grace in two by Edmund who leapt between them.

"No, she is ours, Angus. This is the Lady Grace."

Angus pulled back stunned.

"Good God, yer right. What are ye doin' lassie, yer'll be killed, come away." He took her arm and tried to pull her away from the door.

"I'm here for Miles, where is he?" she breathed heavily, stifling beneath the weight of the armour, she had difficulty keeping the visor raised.

"He's lang gone, lassie, taken tae thon torture chamber, ah dinnae ken where."

Grace pushed at him. "I know where that is. I'll not leave him." She forced her way past leaving the bewildered Scotsmen to defend the entrance from Gerard's men at arms who had regrouped and were now mounting a concerted effort to vanquish the invaders.

"Wait for me. I must escort ye," cried Edmund, but Grace stopped him with her hand.

"You must see to Belle and Linus - they're by the pony. Make sure they get out. Edmund I'm relying on you."

Edmund was torn, he glanced across the courtyard where the pony was tethered and where Belle was desperately trying to untie the terrified creature. Linus clung to her skirts wide eyed. "But what about ye?"

"I'll be fine Edmund," Grace assured him. Then she turned and entered the dungeons.

The passageway was dimly lit by torches. She trod slowly and carefully, her breathing so heavy she feared she would be heard before she was seen. She gingerly stepped over the bloody bodies of the gaolers who lay slain in her path, and hurried past the rancid empty cells.

Pausing by the door at the end of the passage, she steadied herself. The killing of these men had been part of her plan; integral to it. She may not have wielded the knife but she was responsible nevertheless and she felt her stomach knot with shame and remorse. She no longer recognised herself.

She returned her attention to the door. According to the plan provided by Mayflower, through this door lay the stairs which led to the torture room. She took a breath, tried to ignore the muffled sounds of the battle raging outside, and opened the door. The stone steps were dark and she felt for the edge of each riser with the heel of her boot. She held the sword out in front of her, dropped her visor and used her left hand to feel her way against the damp stone wall. Her breath misted against the metal face guard, and she dearly needed to rub her eyes but kept going until she saw light leaching from beneath a door at the bottom of the steps.

Halting outside the door she waited, listening for any sound from within. She heard nothing. Reaching out she touched the door then drew back uncertain. She had no idea what was on the other side, what might be lying in wait for her. But if she were to find Miles she had to open the door.

She tightened her grip on the sword and flung open the door. Miles hung suspended from the ceiling by ropes which held his wrists. His head drooped limply. He had been whipped and bled from the lash. She stepped towards him and raised her sword. She must cut him down. She took a long calming breath and stepped back. She prepared to swing the heavy sword and at that precise moment Miles raised his head.

* * *

He thought he must be in some terrible nightmare. That he was back on crusade in some Moorish prison. Why else would a Saracen stand before him, sword held high making ready to take his head from his shoulders?

He sent up a silent prayer, if this was to be the end then let it be swift. He looked his executioner in the eye. The soldier was small and held the sword two handed, Miles grimaced, perhaps he was the soldier's first kill; so be it. He too had killed many.

He dropped his eyes, resigned to his fate. He was tired, weary of fighting. The Saracen swung the sword upward, slowly. There was not enough power in the movement to do the job cleanly and Miles winced in anticipation of a slow end. He looked one final time at his killer and noticed a tall knight appear in the doorway behind, sword held aloft in a perfect killing position. Miles heart surged as he recognised the Templar, perhaps today was not the day he would die.

The knight's sword descended and the Saracen's rose, as if in slow motion. In the same long moment, Miles registered the outrageous pairing of English and Eastern armour, the stinking animal pelts, and finally the boots on the Saracen's feet; good boots with unusual fastenings - Grace's boots. His brain clicked into gear and he roared his warning.

Grace faltered. Half turning, her sword collided with the downward thrust of her attacker's weapon. The force behind the blow flung her sword from her hand and knocked her across the room where she collided with Miles' legs. The knight crossed the room with two strides, kicked her prone armoured body out of the way and taking Miles' weight he unhooked his shackles. Miles crumpled to the floor in a heap. He dragged himself to Grace's still body and pulled the helmet from her head.

"My God," exclaimed the knight. "It's a girl."

"Yes, Hugh, this is Grace. Pray to God you have not killed her." Miles brushed her hair from her face and as he did her eyes flickered open and she smiled weakly at him.

221

"You're alive," she said breathlessly.

"And so it seems are you, though no thanks to our friend here who took you for one of the Saracen horde." He pulled her up then and held her, breathing her scent in grateful gulps. She leaned against him and he shifted his gaze to the knight who stood before them.

His white tabard bore the scarlet Templar's cross. Pulling off his helmet he knelt before Grace taking her hand and pressing his lips to the pale skin.

"I am Hugh de Reynard, my lady, and I am at your service."

The handsome man with graying hair and striking blue eyes winked at her mischievously before rising and turning to Miles. "We must leave now, before the army of Wildewood are over run. I have a dozen men with me, but I fear the Horde are tiring and need to retreat."

"What army?" asked Miles. He gathered up Grace's sword and helmet and his own weapons from the floor and followed Hugh to the door, "Wildewood has no army?"

"It has now. Wait till you see it, Miles. It will be the talk of Christendom, but come we have no time for banter we must leave now, if we are to see you all safely home."

The Templar knights, mounted on their huge destriers held Gerard's soldiers at bay while the Wildewood Horde regrouped and made their retreat. John, mounted on a prancing fearsome skeletal beast handed Miles the reins to his mount and Grace was fairly thrown on to the saddle of the filly. Miles looked about in awe at the men of Wildewood, these simple peasants, woodsmen and farmers as they milled about the bailey, struggling to contain the excitable mounts amid the awful noise. He marvelled at the macabre and terrifying dress, the painted devil horses they rode; and the look of pride on their faces when they caught sight of him and realised they had succeeded. He glanced at Grace. She had done all of this.

His own horse appeared as though it had galloped all the way from hell. Its eyes made all the more fearful by the white paint daubed around them, its blood red mane dripping dye which sprayed like an open jugular as it tossed it's head. He hushed it quickly, then swung himself up onto the saddle. Wheeling the horse around to follow Hugh, his thoughts returned to Guy.

"We must go back," he called from the saddle. "I must finish Guy."

Hugh forced his bigger horse against Miles' so he could be heard above the din. "There is no time, Miles, we must get all your folk including your good lady to safety. Your feud with Guy will keep."

Miles acknowledged the sense in his words though it did not sit well to leave Guy alive - yet again. He nodded at Hugh, wondered distractedly at the man's uncanny knack of appearing at just the right time and kicked his horse into action.

"Come," yelled Miles, raising his sword triumphantly, and together the Wildewood Horde and the Templar knights fled the castle and disappeared in to the night.

Chapter Forty

The men retrieved their women waiting at the Danestone and swung them onto the backs of their horses. The women clung to their men with desperate relief. The children, hoisted excitedly behind the Templar's, would retell the story of how they played their part in the rescue of their lord for many years to come. John plucked Linus from the back of the little pony for the child had not the skill to remain seated unaided and Edmund tied its reins to the saddle of his own pony.

They rode hard through the forest, led by Miles down hidden paths, with the Scots bringing up the rear, but no one from Ahlborett Castle followed. Stunned by the outrageous attack, Gerard's men no doubt, waited in trepidation for the return of their lord, and the inevitable backlash to follow. Would he believe they had been attacked by the forces of the Dark Lord? Probably not, when he realised that during the attack, Miles of Wildewood and the Scottish prisoners had been released.

Miles kept Grace within sight the entire journey. He needed to see her in order to believe they were both still alive. Her visor had slipped down over her eyes and he doubted she could even see where she was going. Her breast plate flapped against her overlarge padded aketon and she'd foregone the chain hauberk, which would have reached past her knees and been far too heavy for her to heft. She was like a child playing dress-up, but she had led these men in extraordinary circumstances and he was in awe of her courage.

Martha Pandy and Peg Forester had stayed behind at Wildewood. With the setting sun, the women had set a pig to roast and by the time the weary fighters returned, the great hall was laid for a feast and the wine and ale flowed to the accompaniment of music and shared tales of danger and heroics.

There had been some injuries but fortunately no fatalities, a miracle indeed considering the odds. The injured were tended by the women. Miles shrugged off Grace's attempts to treat the marks of the lash, with a weary smile.

"Do not concern yourself, Grace. I've had far worse than this and survived to fight another day." He took her hand, pulled her close and hid the pain as she assessed him with a worried frown. He dipped his head to kiss her, but was dragged from her grasp by knights filled with the adrenalin of battle, eager to celebrate success and renew acquaintance with an old friend. They jostled him, heavy arms embraced him. Fists raised in comradery landed mock punches and he took it all with weary resignation.

He cocked his head and shrugged his apology to Grace, as she too, was whisked away by the womenfolk, who jabbered excitedly for details of her account. Relief at the outcome of the rescue, masked their usual reserve in Grace's company, and they clamored to hear her story.

He knew she watched him as he greeted Hugh's men. He felt her gaze, and suppressed the longing. Despite the humour in his expression as he regaled some tale or other to the raucous men, his heart was not in it. Nevertheless he played the part and suffered their good natured banter while he bided his time until he and Grace could be alone.

Propelled to a seat next to Hugh at the table, he drank what was offered. Momentarily distracted, he lost sight of Grace and reluctantly turned his attention to his mentor.

* * *

Grace watched Miles and Hugh as they caught up on recent events. She hung back, distracted by the endless twittering of the women, and unsure of this charismatic newcomer. She judged him to be about fifty years, perhaps older, though he had the countenance of a much younger man and there was something about him other than his charm and good looks that attracted her. She was curious about him and thankful he'd arrived when he did, for without his men they would not have made good their escape.

She watched him covertly from beneath lowered lashes as she broke from the women and circulated the hall checking on the children and congratulating the fighters. She was mortified when he caught her glance and smiled slowly at her. She turned her back, tried to look busy and disinterested but when she turned again he raised his drink and nodded in her direction. Damn the man, he was as bad as Miles.

She turned her attention to the rest of the room, searching for Linus and was surprised to see him perched not on John's knee, but that of one of Hugh's knights. The child's face was lit with delight as the man regaled him with a tale of sorts. She saw humour on the man's tired face and great tenderness in his eyes as he gazed at the child. John stood behind and placed a hand briefly on his shoulder, causing him to turn and receive the slightest of nods, an unspoken word. With a quick glance in Grace's direction, he handed back the child, almost reverently, and returned to his comrades, gathering admiring glances from the unattached ladies. He had a ready smile for each but managed to resume his seat at the table with the rest of the men without offending the ladies too greatly.

Momentarily distracted by the notion that she had witnessed something she was not meant to see. Grace threw off her curiosity with a smile. These knights certainly had a way about them.

Fly approached her then, tired from playing with the children, his belly full with scraps from the table. He wagged his tail and wiggled at her feet, tongue lolling as puppy tongues are prone to do. She bent and picked him up. It had been some time since she'd been honoured with his presence. He was in demand here at Wildewood such was his cheerful disposition and his uncanny record for catching rabbits. She buried her face in his rough coat and sighed.

"We're a long way from home, puppy," she whispered against him and she felt his tail thud against her. "How will we ever leave this behind?"

The wagging increased dramatically and she looked up to see Miles approaching. "Traitor," she muttered to the dog.

"Come join us, Grace, I would like you to meet Hugh." He reached out a hand and tucked her fringe behind her ear. "You look deep in thought..."

Grace smiled at him. She had lots to think about. She reached out and took his hand, glad that they were together again, amidst the noise and crush of the celebration. But unsettled by the sudden invasion of Miles' other life—the life she had inadvertently become a part of.

"Do I have to?"

He returned her smile. "Like you, I would like nothing better than to escape this melee and seek the privacy of our own chamber, but I think we must await our reward a little longer."

Grace shrugged. She felt helpless. She sensed a shift in what had become normal in this strange situation, and sought to restore the balance.

"Who is the charming knight who is enchanting all the young ladies?" she asked as she cast her eye toward the gathering of men.

Miles followed her gaze and chuckled. "Thomas of Blackmore, a reluctant Templar...a far bigger rogue than I, but a good loyal friend."

"He seems to have taken a shine to Linus, and the child to him," commented Grace.

"Indeed." Miles shrugged off her interest. His gaze flicked briefly between Thomas and John. "Thomas has that effect on most people. I shall have to keep him away lest he steal you from under my nose."

Grace raised a brow. "I'm not that easily stolen..."

"Oh, I don't know, I didn't have too much trouble." His accompanying grin saved him as he added quickly, "Enough of Thomas, come meet Hugh."

"I've already met him, remember," she replied, the memory of his attack still clear in her mind.

Miles grinned, "He thought you were going to kill me."

"Well, if I had, you'd have only yourself to blame. I learned everything I know about killing from you." She glanced down at her clothes. She couldn't sit at the table dressed as one of the devils army, although no one else seemed at all bothered about getting out of their armour. "I need to change first. My rabbit skin stole, although rather fetching is beginning to smell." She wrinkled her nose.

"Go then, but make haste, Hugh is waiting to speak with you."

Grace stretched out her arms to the sides and looked at him helplessly. "I think I may need some help. John fastened me into this and I've no idea how to get out."

"That's why knights have squires." He sidled closer and gave a crooked smile. "Shall I be your squire this evening, Lady Grace?" Taking her hand he escorted her across the hall and up the stairs to her chamber, unaware that their progress was being watched. From his seat below in the great hall Hugh gave no hint to his thoughts.

* * *

"You were stunning today, Grace, absolutely stunning." Miles breathed against her ear, as he unbuckled her breast plate

"And I could be equally stunning tonight if you have the will." She smiled at him with the merest hint of mischief.

"My will is without question." Miles gave an answering grin. He was high on adrenalin and in the mood to play despite his wounds. He helped her to pull the aketon over her head and added it to the pile of rank smelling armour on the floor.

"Well, they say where there's a will there's a way." Grace teased him.

"Now...?" Miles voice whispered gruffly in her ear. No one would notice if they didn't go straight back down to the hall. He ran his hand down her bare arm

"Miles you have guests." Grace raised a brow in mock horror at his suggestion.

"And they will understand. They are men." It had started in jest, but now he found that it was not, and he wanted her more than anything. He wished they were alone, but they were not and he wondered how long he would need to play the dutiful host before retiring.

Grace squeezed his hand, "The best things are always worth waiting for."

And don't I know it, thought Miles as he watched her strip down to her underwear and wash with a cloth soaked in the warm water left out by Martha. The water ran down her neck and he watched as it slipped between her breasts.

"Is this going to take long," he asked...hopefully.

She threw the wash cloth at him "Your turn, you smell of...."

"Piss and shit, I know," he replied "The hazards of hanging around in dungeons."

"You have such a romantic turn of phrase," muttered Grace.

It took a little longer to get ready than if she had been left alone to dress, but not long enough according to Miles who felt he needed a little more practice in the art of lacing or more specifically un-lacing ladies undergarments.

Chapter Forty One

Unaware of Hugh's calculating gaze, Miles and Grace descended the stairs together. They had succumbed to distraction and kept their guests waiting much longer than intended. Dawn was fast approaching. The celebrations had mellowed. The men were stated and those not already sleeping, listened as Tom Pandy played a final haunting melody on the pipes.

"My lady," Hugh said as he rose slightly, took Grace's hand and brushed his lips across her skin.

Miles grinned as he placed an arm loosely around Grace and leaned past her toward Hugh. "Hugh, finally I can introduce you formally to my guest, Lady Grace from Kirk Knowe. Grace this is Hugh de Reynard my good friend and mentor."

Grace gave a cautious smile.

"So, is this the diminutive Saracen warrior whom I almost beheaded at Ahlborett? Or the niece that slipped my mind?" Hugh's voice rumbled pleasantly from deep within.

"Neither I'm afraid. I'm just Grace; a little prone to dramatics when the need arises, Miles will no doubt agree."

"You make for a convincing Saracen."

"I can play a part when required," she replied. The look they shared was one of mutual curiosity.

"I can imagine." He gave a slight shrug as if casting off some puzzling thought and bestowed her with a charming smile. "I must apologise for almost taking your life, Grace, but the lad here looked like he needed my help. He's prone to getting himself into scrapes which require the intervention of others. I can see now, however, you had everything in hand and I need not have concerned myself as to his safety."

He turned to Miles with a slow smile, "Miles, the plan with the armour and horses was masterly. If you'd seen them hurtling out of the night you'd have believed the very gates of hell had opened. The painting of the horses was quite unique, I may borrow that idea myself sometime."

Miles caught Grace's hand and squeezed it gently. "It is not only horses that Grace paints, she is an exceptional artist."

"So I understand," replied Hugh. "Why even the king himself has learned of your skills."

Miles spotted the familiar frisson of discomfort in Grace's

expression, the quickly downcast eyes, the hand straying to her hair, and felt an unwelcome churning in his gut. Once again secrets lay between them. He didn't want this tonight. Tonight was about celebrating victories not harbouring doubts and suspicions. In an effort to divert the conversation away from Grace he turned back to Hugh.

"How did you know to come to our aid?"

"Mayflower..."

"He sought you out?"

Hugh shook his head. "Not entirely, Inspired by your good lady he was enroute to deliver a message to the king. I intercepted him."

"So, the message is not yet delivered?" asked Grace. She glanced at Miles who merely shrugged his confusion. "What about the treasure and Gerard? How can Miles expect to retain Wildewood if our ace card has not been played?"

Hugh smiled at her and his blue eyes twinkled with mischief. "Fear not, my lady, Gerard will keep and the treasure is in safe hands."

"Whose safe hands?" she muttered, as she moved closer to Miles.

"Where is Gerard?" asked Miles, confused by her unwarranted suspicion and at pains to diffuse it. "Guy said he'd gone to meet the king."

"Everyone wants to meet the king," sighed Hugh. He took a long drink and set down his flagon. "The king is a busy man and although the plan was astonishingly ingenious," he turned to Grace. "Your idea I believe."

Grace shrugged. "Not entirely."

"Hmm, well from long experience of dealing with more than one king, I have found it unwise to be so...honest."

"What do you mean, Hugh? Would you rather we deceived the king? Personally, I value my head more than the treasure."

"No, I do not recommend deceit, Miles, merely an economics of the truth." Miles stared at him bewildered, Grace with continued suspicion. Hugh gestured them closer.

"What did you hope to achieve with your plan to expose Gerard's greed to the king?"

"Gerard's compliance with the king's decree, giving title of Wildewood, to me."

"And what of Guy and his predilection for perversion," asked Hugh.

"The king does not need to concern himself with Guy, I will finish that myself," stated Miles vehemently.

"I don't doubt it, Miles, and therein lies the answer and the reason why I intercepted your message."

"I don't understand," said Grace, swinging her gaze between the two

230

men.

Hugh raised a brow at Miles. "Perhaps this would be better discussed later, in private."

Miles gave a quick shake of his head. "You may speak freely, Hugh. Grace is one of us. She has earned her place at this table." He reached for her hand again and held it firmly.

"Very well, after talking with Mayflower, this is what I surmised." Hugh settled back in his seat leaving Miles and Grace to lean close to hear what he had to say.

"Gerard used Guy to accumulate funds and Guy used Gerard's need of funds to feed his own urges, both for the murder of good knights and the growth of his bizarre collection. They use each other but the only thing they have in common is you, Miles. Gerard wants you off his land and Guy wants you dead." He paused to consider Miles.

"You're a popular young man, Miles and not just with the ladies. You have two men fighting to get at you. However, if you inform the king about the treasure then you may cause the wrath of the king to fall on Gerard, albeit it would be temporary, for the de Frouville's are powerful barons and the king relies upon their ward-ship of this land. So, you would make a mortal enemy and gain nothing."

"I would gain Wildewood," stated Miles.

"You already have Wildewood, Miles. The king has decreed it. What you need, is to remain here unhindered by your neighbour, and that will never happen if you betray him to the king."

"What are you saying?"

"Gerard needs additional funds to protect his land from the Scots, but does not wish the king to know of his financial predicament. If he is allowed to retain those funds without the king's knowledge then he will forgo his claim on Wildewood and leave you in peace."

"But why would I make peace with the man who killed my mother?"

Hugh winced and shook his head. "Because it is imperative you remain at Wildewood, Miles. Things are beginning to happen, to change. This period of relative calm with the Scots will not last forever. Gerard will vehemently defend the border on behalf of the king and so he should, but without you and your affinity with the clansmen we will have no lines of communication and the country will be forced into bloody conflict. You speak of your mother, of defending her honour, but, Miles, apart from you this place is all that is left of your mother. She would not want you to do anything in order to retain it. She would want you to do what is right."

"And you believe this pact with Gerard is right?"

"I do."

"What if Gerard does not agree?"

"I have already spoken with him, he is in full agreement."

"You spoke with him without first discussing with me?" Miles frowned, unsure now as to Hugh's motives.

"I took an opportunity to broker peace and avert disaster."

"And if he reneges?" asked Miles.

"He will not renege. Who do you think sent me to Ahlborett this night? He put his own men at risk in order to facilitate your escape."

"In order to salvage his position, more like," muttered Miles. He looked from Hugh to Grace. He needed time to think. He was not entirely sure he could put the future stability of Wildewood before his need for revenge against Gerard. He was surprised Hugh had orchestrated this, dismayed by what appeared to be his lack of regard for his mother's memory.

"You obviously do not hold my mother's memory as dear as I, Hugh," stated Miles coldly.

"You have no notion of what I hold dear, Miles," replied Hugh with equal chill and the men considered each other in silence for a moment.

Grace shuffled uncomfortably. Both men were silently squaring up and the atmosphere becoming charged.

"And what of Guy?" she asked in an effort to break the deadlock.

Hugh visibly let out a breath and turned to her with a tight smile. "The evidence against Guy is here now at Wildewood, on the backs of your own men, scattered on the floor of your chamber, my lady. If you declare it now to the king then you may condemn Guy but you will also shatter the myth of the Wildewood Horde and I fancy you will have need of it again."

"And so what of Guy, is he also to escape justice?"

"That is a matter of honour between Miles and Guy. You do not need the king for justice to be done."

"So, you will allow me to finish Guy, but I must forgo my revenge on Gerard?" muttered Miles. He reached for his drink, drained it in one and slammed down the flagon with irritation.

Hugh shook his head with frustration. "Miles this is not about you, it's about doing what is right for the majority of those who have been, or will be affected by your actions. You are a good man, Miles, when you have time to consider this you will agree that a truce with Gerard is currently advantageous to all concerned. Guy is expendable, do as you wish with him."

Hugh rose and pushed away from the table. "Please excuse me, I am not as young as I like to imagine and I am weary." He turned to Grace with a wry smile, "Perhaps, Grace, you could show me where I may rest and I'll leave Miles to deliberate on the situation."

"Of course," replied Grace uncertainly. She looked at Miles who shrugged and pulled himself to his feet reluctantly.

"Martha has prepared the guest chamber, Hugh. Grace will show you the way," He nodded at her raised brow. "Hugh, don't think I'm not grateful for your intervention, I know you mean well and your motives are honourable but it is not easy for me to align with Gerard, we may be linked by blood but that is where the similarity ends."

Hugh considered him in silence a moment before nodding curtly and following Grace from the hall.

* * *

Allowing him to take her arm as they mounted the stone stairs, Grace paused at the top to look down on those gathered below. There had been much merriment throughout the evening and it was good to see the hall filled and being used as it should. Miles however sat alone as he had been left; pensive he gazed unseeing across the room. She knew he was obsessing about his feud with Gerard and it would do him no good. Hugh interrupted her thoughts.

"What do you think, Grace, about all of this trouble with Gerard and Guy? Would you not rather have Wildewood at peace?"

Grace looked at him, "It's really nothing to do with me," she answered carefully, aware that anything she said was for some reason of great interest to this man.

Hugh shook his head slowly as he propelled her onwards, his hand firm on her arm. "You're mistaken it has everything to do with you."

Grace pulled her arm away and stopped outside the guest chamber door. "I don't understand," she shrugged. "Everyone talks in riddles here, why don't you just come out with it and say what you mean. You've been watching me all evening, don't think I haven't noticed." The man made her uneasy and she'd no idea why, but she'd grown tired of secrets and hints. Everyone seemed to think Hugh knew more than he was letting on and she wanted to know what it was.

"You are very direct, my lady," answered Hugh with a twinkle in his eye, "and you are different...," he paused "and yet familiar."

Yet another riddle. "I'm not your lady. My name is Grace, please use it. And yes I am direct and I believe that you're up to something," she added bluntly "And if you mean to hurt Miles then you will have me to answer to."

"I have no intention of hurting Miles. My intention is to protect Miles, Wildewood and all who reside here including you if you intend to stay," he paused again, seemed distracted by some sudden notion. "Do you intend to stay?"

"I have no idea."

"Do you have somewhere else you would rather be? Family who will be wondering where you are?"

"Not really."

"Not really? What does that mean?"

"It means that at present I have nowhere that I need to be."

"And what of your family, is there no one desperately seeking you?"

"I have no family, I'm an only child," she found herself admitting reluctantly, she didn't want him to think she was alone and defenceless. She could manage perfectly well on her own.

"Then why not stay? Miles is a good man, you have the respect of all those at Wildewood even Gerard speaks highly of your courage, which is not a bad thing if a truce is to be upheld."

"It's not as simple as that." The words were out before she could predict how they would be received. She wasn't even sure she was really here, that her whole existence wasn't about to disappear in a puff of smoke. That she wasn't going crazy.

He leaned against the door frame and studied her. "Sometimes we make the mistake of imagining things to be more complicated than they actually are. If ever you need help to simplify things then you need only ask."

"Why is what I do, of so much interest to you?" asked Grace. Despite her suspicion, she found herself almost wanting to confide in him. He was very persuasive. Perhaps he was the witch.

"Because you make Miles happy, and I want him to be happy."

"Why?"

Hugh grinned then and wagged his finger slowly at her, "Why not?"

She'd had enough. She had the strange feeling that she knew him from somewhere, which was impossible but disconcerting nonetheless and she wanted away from him, before she was tempted to reveal more than was sensible or safe. "This is your room, Hugh," she gestured to the door. "I hope you'll be comfortable. If you need anything ask Martha.

And for your information," she added. "I don't make Miles happy. I annoy and frustrate him and cause him all kinds of trouble, so on reflection perhaps it would be better if I didn't stay. He'll soon meet a nice biddable little lady who will happily do as she's told and stay where she's put and fill this place with nice biddable children."

"Miles doesn't do biddable," laughed Hugh. "That's why he has the good barons of Ahlborett queuing up to finish him off. Like you, he annoys and frustrates and causes all manner of trouble. I don't think a lady who did as she was told and stayed where she was put, would necessarily be Miles' first choice. There's just no challenge in biddable is there?"

Grace stared at him, realised this man knew Miles, really knew him and was torn between finding out more and remaining in blissful ignorance.

"And does he have the luxury of choice? Or is the future of Wildewood more important?"

"Of course Wildewood is important, but yes, Miles does have a choice."

"Well, let's hope he makes the right one."

Chapter Forty Two

The weeks following the rescue were hectic with much coming and going at Wildewood. Philibutt of Mayflower returned briefly and after discussion with Hugh, his silence was handsomely bought. After discussion with Miles, the pony was also secured as a reward for Linus' role in the rescue. Mayflower returned to Durham a richer man.

Hugh came and went at will, though his knights remained only until after Miles' initial meeting with Gerard which was a strained affair to say the least. Neither man entirely happy with the compromise, but Hugh was a masterful negotiator and as a result of his skill a truce was finally brokered, which allowed all at Wildewood to go about their business unhindered by those at Ahlborett.

There was no mention of Guy who was reported to have fled the castle following the Horde's successful rescue and it was assumed by all that he'd returned to Lincoln to lick his wounds. Hugh initiated an investigation, for his knights were based nearby at Temple Breuer and he was confident they would locate him...eventually.

Miles accompanied John to Gerard's quarry to collect the first load of stone for the renovations and although Miles was no expert on stone he was an expert on surveillance.

Despite any evidence to the contrary he was unconvinced at Gerard's compliance with the truce, nor of Guy's retreat from Northumberland. Regardless he was in high spirits. Wildewood was a hive of activity and throughout the estate there were signs of new life and regeneration. Berryman had reported the safe arrival of the first spring lambs and in the fields the oxen could be seen ploughing and preparing the soil. The weather was surprisingly mild and Grace and the children had been busy in the walled garden. She had nagged Miles for seed and plants but he was unwilling to allow anyone from Wildewood to frequent the market in Ahlborett. The truce was still wet ink on parchment and he did not wish to run the risk of it smudging. Perhaps a trip to Alnwick was called for. He suspected Grace would enjoy the change of scene and it would give them some time alone. There was no better time, he judged, whilst Hugh was still able to provide a watchful eye at Wildewood.

"Perhaps you should use this opportunity to speak to the priest," suggested Hugh when Miles mentioned the trip.

"The priest?"

Hugh shook his head and his expression settled into one which revealed his patience was wearing thin. "Do you not think it time you cemented your relationship with Grace? It does not look good in the eyes of the church to have her here in your bed unwed."

Miles shrugged, "The church does not care what we do here at Wildewood."

"No, Miles, you are wrong. You may not care what they think, but the church cares very much for what goes on here at Wildewood, and don't forget that. It does not pay to get on the wrong side of the church. Remember as a knight, even a reluctant one, you serve God as well as the king and either could take everything away from you if they chose to do so. Arrogance is not one of your better qualities, Miles."

Miles was quite happy with their arrangement, and wondered why, suddenly Hugh was not.

"And what of Grace?" continued Hugh "Does she not wonder at your commitment to her?"

Miles shrugged again he doubted she was concerned with propriety, she did as she pleased not what society dictated. Nevertheless he did wonder at her commitment to him. Nothing more had been said about being taken home and she appeared to him, happy and content. Neither had grown tired of each other, however there were still things unsaid between them.

"You want her to stay do you not?" prompted Hugh.

"Of course."

"Then ask her before it is too late and your heirs are baseborn."

Miles glanced at him. "What are you saying?"

"I'm saying she has been here with you for some months and I doubt you have resisted her. If she is not already with child then she soon will be and you need to secure the future of Wildewood."

Miles looked away, Hugh was correct they could not continue their current arrangement, but he did not want her to marry him simply to safeguard any future offspring.

He wanted her to marry him because she loved him as he loved her.

* * *

"Marry me, Grace." he said simply.

"Marry you?" she repeated vaguely as her mind crowded with reasons why this could not, should not be possible.

"Yes..." answered Miles, he stepped away cocked his head and looked at her. "I confess I expected a more rapturous response. You are happy here? We are happy together, Why not?"

Grace returned his look of confusion. How could she marry him and stay here forever? Surely that would change the course of the future? Would it matter if it did? Was it even possible? Despite attempting several times to explain her situation, her remarkable secret still remained between them. "I think perhaps we need more than just happiness, there'll be times when we may be unhappy."

"Do you love me, Grace?"

She reached out her hand and gently caressed his cheek. She knew every contour, each scar and felt her belly tickle with anticipation at the feel of his stubble against her skin.

"You know I do, Miles."

"So, marry me." He pulled her closer, turned against her hand and pressed a kiss into her open palm, before closing her fingers gently to contain the kiss. "For you, Mademoiselle," he added with a smile.

Grace shivered inwardly. All he had to do was smile. This was madness. "But you don't know anything about me, Miles. Why would you want to tie yourself to some odd little thing you found in a woodland bog? I have no lands or dowry, I will never fit in at court, everyone will think you've gone mad. Just look at my hair," she smiled and pulled at the lengthening strands. "You could do so much better."

Miles returned her smile and placed her hand against his chest. She could feel the steady beat of his heart as it pounded almost as fast as her own. "Do you feel that?" he murmured, "That's the way you make me feel. I know all I need to know. You are the love of my life, Grace. We were fated to meet, there is no one better for me and I will have no other."

"I'm sure there are plenty of young ladies who would jump at the chance to marry you, Miles." And heaven help any of them who came anywhere near him, she added silently. "Just think of all those ladies with breeding and connections, ladies who will also do as they're told."

Miles smiled his crooked smile "Well, I won't argue with that. I think we've already established how irresistible I am." He kissed the tip of her nose, "But it is you and you alone who I love and want and I have grown to accept you will never do as you're told. Marry me, Grace?"

"And if I say no?"

"Then I'll keep asking until you say yes."

Grace smiled, "That could become quite tiresome."

"Very,"

"And I don't think I could put you through that."

"Are we in accord?"

"On one condition,"

He raised a brow. "Conditions already...go on,"

"That we marry at the chapel at Kirk Knowe."

"Not Alnwick?"

"No, Kirk Knowe, it's a special place for both of us."

"Kirk Knowe it is then. So, is it a yes?"

"Most definitely."

Miles held her so tightly she thought he would squeeze the life out of her.

"And can we still go to Alnwick first, and share a room and cause all the good Christian folk of the town to cross themselves and pray for our souls," laughed Grace. She could not begin to describe how happy she was. Whether what she'd just agreed was wise or even possible, she no longer cared.

"I think there is still some scope for us to cause mischief before we are tied," replied Miles.

* * *

The trip to Alnwick was transformed into rather more than the dirty weekend Grace imagined, when Martha suggested whilst there, she should use the opportunity to obtain material for her wedding gown, spices and other essentials for the wedding feast. Grace had no idea what was required for a wedding feast, but Martha dictated a list and Miles agreed all the required provisions would be ordered and sent back with a carter so they could travel more quickly on horseback. He was still cautious about travelling the county while there was no word on the location of Guy. Grace ignored his underlying apprehension and his meticulous planning of the journey. She was like a child with excitement.

Her enthusiasm however was short lived with the arrival of a messenger who came the evening before their departure to relay the king's desire to be attended on by Miles and his betrothed while they were in Alnwick. Still temporarily resident at the Castle, he wished to have his portrait painted by Grace, and a king's wish must naturally be translated as a demand.

Grace watched Miles as he read the alarm on her face as clearly as if she had announced it. Her stomach knotted with fear. It was time for him to understand but she had no idea where to begin.

"I don't want to go," she announced quietly. It was all clear to her now, the identical brush work, the faultless copy. She hadn't forged the work of a medieval artist she had merely copied her own work. She couldn't paint the kings portrait. If she did she was compounding her own future guilt. If she didn't paint the portrait she couldn't be accused of forgery, because the original would never exist. She was being given an opportunity to rewrite history and reclaim her career, but what did her career matter if she chose to stay here with Miles at Wildewood? It mattered to her, she decided, supposing she never went back, at least she would know her reputation had not been tarnished and her integrity was intact.

"You cannot refuse the king, Grace," replied Miles evenly "Why would you want to? Why are you afraid? I shall be there with you; I would not allow harm to come to you."

"I know you'll protect me, I'm not afraid of the king. I just don't want to paint. I can't explain why."

"Well, I would try very hard to think of an explanation if I were you, for the king will surely demand one. He is not used to having his wishes denied." He took her hand gently, laced his fingers with hers. "Would it be so bad to paint one portrait? You do it so easily. You enjoy it so much here at Wildewood, think about it, Grace. It would not hurt for you...for us both...to be in the king's favour."

He was correct, it was such a small thing for her to do, and so important for Wildewood. What the king had given, the king could take away. All the same she shook inside at the thought she was being offered an opportunity to wipe the slate clean, but was forced by necessity to turn it down.

"I won't let you down, Miles," she said quietly. "I know what I need to do."

Grace wandered into the walled garden to think. The work they had done over the last few weeks had transformed the area and the beds were dug and ready to be planted. She imagined what a difference a few cheery daffodils would make. Deep in thought she did not notice Hugh until he spoke and she realised he was propped up against the garden wall.

"You have things on your mind?" he asked.

"One or two,"

He joined her on the path that wound round the garden and placed her hand on his arm. "Is it not just a case of over complication?"

Grace looked up at him. "I don't think there's a way to simplify this decision any further. I either paint the portrait or I don't."

"And for some reason you do not wish to choose either?"

"There are consequences to either choice."

Hugh studied her as they walked. "There is a simple answer to your dilemma, Grace," he suggested as they reached the gate and he unloosed her hand.

"And what would that be, Hugh?" she asked with a wry smile, Hugh seemed to think he had answers to everything, yet had unresolved dilemma's of his own, which Grace considered to be of far more importance than her own.

"Ask him to remove his crown."

"Sorry?"

"Think about it, Grace, it's quite simple."

Chapter Forty Three

The king loved his children and often allowed them to travel with him and his queen, which was unusual but showed the measure of the man. So Grace's suggestion that he might be depicted as a loving father rather than a royal personage sat upon his throne, did not receive the ridicule or outrage, she might have expected. Her portrait of King Edward with his growing brood, the babe on his knee and the little ones at his feet was certainly unique and she had Hugh to thank for it.

She gained the admiration and gratitude of the royal family and more importantly sensed Miles' relief, although it was obvious he'd no idea of the significance of the painting. As she finished off her final session, almost dwarfed by the giant easel she knew she'd made the right decision and felt liberated by the knowledge.

"How has life treated you since your return, Miles?" King Edward asked with an easy smile. It was obvious to Grace that Miles was held in some regard by the king and she was curious as to the reason.

She watched discreetly, awaiting Miles' reply, concerned he might reveal the truth about Gerard despite the agreement brokered by Hugh. The truce was tenuous and Miles distrust of any agreement involving Gerard continued to overshadow his respect for Hugh's bargaining prowess.

"Life is good, Sire," he replied evenly. "I am grateful to be back at Wildewood where I belong. Work is progressing I expect we shall have a good harvest." His quick glance at Grace was not lost on the king. Grace coloured delicately. Yes, it was highly likely that Miles would reap what he had sown.

The king nodded.

"Good. And, what of your neighbours?"

"My neighbours are...accommodating, Sire," replied Miles carefully.

"Indeed." The king raised a brow. Rising to his feet, he dismissed the many attendants from the room. When they were gone he reclaimed his seat and returned a thoughtful gaze to Miles. "Are you referring to the Scots or the Baron's?"

"Both. Sire."

"Good. Both have their uses and it's important that you recognise your role."

"My role, Sire?"

"Yes, Miles. Did you imagine that I rattled the cage of my Northumbrian Baron, de Frouville', simply for the pleasure of doing so?

I gave you title to Wildewood for a very good reason."

Grace shifted her gaze from Edward to Miles and noted the tightening in his jaw as he held his tongue.

"You have proven yourself in battle, Miles, and along with Hugh have assisted me before in matters of some delicacy where a knight with less courage and more conscience may have faltered. I may have need of you again. It's important that you maintain your position at Wildewood."

Miles nodded slowly. "Wildewood is my home, I would defend it and the border with the same intensity as I have defended the crown, Sire, but I fear I am no longer the man you recall from our days on crusade."

"Sir Hugh tells me you are fully recovered now."

"Yes...Sire."

"Then you are the same man, Miles, whether it pleases you or not. We are all the product of our deeds, the glorious and the inglorious. You may wish to put the past behind you...and I may choose to allow it. However it would serve you well to remember we have all done things in the heat of battle which we may later regret. Men may critique our actions, but only God can judge our souls."

He turned and Grace coloured guiltily as it became obvious by his sardonic smile that he was aware she'd been eavesdropping. "Mademoiselle, you have a fine knight here before you, but I fear you have unwittingly grasped a tiger by the tail. I would suggest you hang on tightly if you wish to avoid his claws."

He turned back to Miles with a smile. "I hear a wedding is afoot. You have my approval. Make haste, Miles. Enjoy your delightful lady. Fill Wildewood with your sons..." He leaned forward, dropped his voice and lost the smile. "But there may come a time soon when you are obliged to revisit your past and I expect you to be ready."

* * *

"What did he mean?" Grace asked when they were free of the castle. She was desperate to know what Miles had done to deserve a reputation that even the king alluded to in hushed tones.

"Edward talks in riddles. Ignore him," Miles replied shortly. He marched ahead, dodging this way and that avoiding the crowds milling the narrow streets enroute to the market place. She was forced to run to keep up.

Grasping his arm she pulled him to a halt. "What have you done that's so bad you don't want to remember?"

Miles shrugged her off impatiently. "Nothing that should interest you."

Grace ignored the dark look he sent her way, the red flag that flashed in his eyes and ploughed on regardless. "You want me to marry you, but you don't want to tell me the truth?"

"Truth..." He pulled her off the main thoroughfare and down an alley adjacent to an overflowing hostelry. The noise of the street vendors and the clatter of hooves on cobbles were dampened by the closeness of the walls but the smell of effluent and decay was overpowering. Grace's eyes watered as she struggled against the odour.

"You ask me about truth? When you have woven a delicate tapestry of deceit and maintained it diligently to this day."

"I...." she sought for an answer, but had none. He was correct, what right did she have to demand that he relinquish his secrets when she was loathed to part with her own? She pressed herself against the grimy wall, kicked at the dirt with the toe of her shoe. "The king implied that you were dangerous," she muttered.

"Perhaps I am," he sighed. "Perhaps you would do well to run as far away from me as you can." He too dropped his gaze and Grace was overwhelmed by the sudden sense of despair that appeared to cloak him, and of her need to dispel it.

"I could never do that...I love you...whatever you've done."

"Whatever I've done?" he caught her gaze and held it.

"Yes," she replied determinedly.

"Do you still believe I would hurt you?"

She stepped toward him and slipped her hand in his, "Of course not."

"Then for now, trust me when I say there are things I've done of which I'm not proud. However, be assured they will never be repeated, despite what the king may think."

"Secrets..." she said softly as she laid her head against him and felt his embrace, "...they will be the death of us."

* * *

Early morning sunshine crept through the irregular glass windowpane creating prisms of coloured light on the chamber wall. Grace watched Miles through lowered lashes, maintaining the illusion of sleep, stretched out beneath the covers in the best room at the grandest inn Miles could afford. Offered separate rooms at the castle, it had not been difficult to decline. Grace had assumed Miles preference for the inn had been motivated by their need to stay close. They'd been through too much to be kept apart now. After the final meeting with the king she was glad his choice had kept them well away from the castle. The closer Miles got to the king the further he seemed to drift from her grasp. Her hand slid to her abdomen, she had the perfect means by which to anchor him, but sensed his need to reach a decision without her interference.

She felt the mattress depress as he leaned across and kissed her gently.

"We must make a move."

Smiling, she opened her eyes wide, casting off her subterfuge. "Feel free to make any move you like." She reached out a hand and gently caressed his cheek, knew in her heart that no matter what he had done she could never leave him.

He shook his head and flashed his crooked smile. "Enough, temptress, or we shall never leave this chamber." He slid his hand beneath the covers, caressed her silken skin and held her gaze enquiringly as he rested his palm against her belly. She lowered her lashes and he removed his hand.

"It's late the sun is well up. We should have left at first light. If we want to reach Wildewood before dark we need to leave soon."

They'd overslept having spent the night making up deliciously after the altercation in the alley and the last thing either of them wanted was to spend the day on horseback, but they needed to get back. They'd spent three days in Alnwick, longer than intended due mainly to the necessity to complete the painting before the king's return to London. The carter had returned to Wildewood the day before with all of their supplies and Miles' concern at the state of the truce was ever present. The king's words had put a damper on their trip, rekindling doubt and suspicion. Grace knew the time for secrets was almost at an end. Soon all would be revealed but first they needed to go home.

Home...Grace rolled the word around in her mind and smiled.

.

Chapter Forty Four

The journey back took best part of a day and by the time they reached the welcoming safety of Wildewood, Grace knew something was amiss. Convinced the pain in her abdomen and the rise in temperature were merely the result of the long ride she shrugged both off, confident that a good night's sleep would set her to rights.

During the night her fever worsened and she woke bathed in sweat and beset with nausea. Miles roused as she vomited wretchedly. He held a damp cloth to her forehead and cursed the humours that invaded her.

"I'm fine," she whispered weakly. "I must have eaten something tainted while we were in Alnwick." Although the food at the castle and the inn had been beyond reproach, the same could not be said for the food offered on the stalls and she recalled they had stopped to eat following their argument the previous day.

Miles rose and pulled on his clothes, "I'll fetch Martha. She'll have something to give you." He pulled the covers more snugly around her despite her need to be free of them and slipped quickly from the room.

When he returned he had both Martha and Hugh in tow and the man wore a concerned expression as he placed a cool palm against her brow.

"She'll be needin' bled no doubt," announced Martha as she heaved her bulk between Grace and Hugh causing him to take a step back.

Grace looked up in alarm, catching Miles' eye. "No I don't. I just need to be left alone. I'll be fine." She winced at the pain, and tried unsuccessfully to hide it. "Just go away everyone," she whimpered.

Hugh pulled Miles to one side and spoke quietly to him gesturing to both her and Martha. Grace tensed, if she were about to be subjected to some form of medieval doctoring then she would have to resist. Miles approached the bed and crouched beside it taking her hand in his.

"Hugh wishes to examine you, he is skilled in these matters as you know, but if you do not wish it I shall, against my better judgement, send for Gerard's physician and have Martha make up a potion in the meantime."

Grace looked from one to the other she wanted neither choice but figured Hugh to be the lesser of two evils.

"Hugh may help if he thinks he can," she muttered and Hugh nodded as Miles stepped back.

"Martha, away and make your potion, Miles go with her. Grace will be safe with me till you return."

Miles shot him a glance, seemed to hesitate then think better of it as he followed Martha from the room.

Left alone, Hugh sat on the edge of the bed and gently pulled back the covers. They were damp with her sweat. "Please don't be alarmed, Grace, I'm only going to place my hands gently against you. You must tell me when you feel pain."

He revealed her bare abdomen and pressed gently, eliciting a howl of pain. Drawing back he considered her for a moment.

"Grace, not so long ago I suggested there may come a time when it might be necessary to uncomplicate matters." He replaced the covers and smiled kindly at her. "I think that time has come."

"I don't know what you mean?" muttered Grace warily. Despite the pain she was not so befuddled that she'd forgotten her initial distrust of Hugh.

"You may well be suffering simply from food poisoning," he began, "In which case, Martha's potion will set you to rights. But as you are also very obviously with child, I could be mistaken and the pain may be a consequence of complications with your pregnancy." He ignored the look of shock on her face. "Either way we do not have the skill or facilities here to treat such a condition successfully and prevent a tragedy. It is time you went home."

"What do you mean, how do you know these things, you're a knight not a doctor...and I am home," she added firmly.

Hugh cocked his head and smiled. "Come, Grace, you know that I am more than a knight. Have you not suspected that since our first meeting?"

"My suspicion regards your relationship with Miles and your reluctance to tell him you're his father. What other secrets are you keeping?"

Hugh narrowed his eyes at her sharp tone. "We share more than an interest in Miles, Grace, and I think deep down you know that. You have simply been reluctant to face the truth."

"And just what truth do you allude to now, Hugh?" she clutched the covers to her, suddenly unwilling to confront what she'd suspected for some time.

Hugh glanced at the door. "We have little time, Miles will soon return and I fancy you are reluctant to share your account, so we must make haste. Listen well, Grace and I shall tell you my story."

The candle light flickered as he drew up a stool by the side of the bed. He gazed for a moment distracted by the patterns it created as he pulled his thoughts together and began his tale.

"I did not begin this life as a knight, Grace. My life began much as yours, many years, and many miles from here. I trained as a surgeon at a London hospital. At the height of the Great War I volunteered my skills to the defence of the country and was sent to France an idealistic young man."

"The Great War?" Grace's eyes grew wide. It was one thing to suspect, quite another to accept another's unbelievable tale. She shivered with excitement and apprehension.

Hugh continued. "If you think life here is brutal, that there is poor regard for the life of the common man, I would ask that you consider the trenches and the massacre of men within them. Cannon fodder is an oft used expression and unfortunately all too accurate. I did what I could to patch up men horribly injured. I amputated limbs that could have been saved under other circumstances, and grew a shield of indifference to the horror." He glanced quickly at her as if suddenly realising his need to be succinct, that time was of the essence. "I don't recall the exact moment the shell hit the trench all I do remember is waking some time later on a battle field just as bloody, and being carried to safety by strong and capable hands. Those hands belonged to Gerard de Frouville the Elder and the year was 1245."

Grace gasped, pain forgotten, all attention now on Hugh and his gripping tale. Hugh took her hand and smiled.

"I'm sure you can imagine how I felt, to suddenly find myself in the midst of a raging medieval battle field. In truth it was not so very different from the one I'd left behind. The noise and the fear of men are timeless. I thought at first it was a dream, that perhaps I was suffering shellshock or some form of madness, but that was not the case. By some fluke I had travelled and found myself marooned far from home with no hope of return."

He rose from the stool, crossing to the fire where he cast a log into the flames amid a shower of sparks. Resting his arm against the mantle he turned and considered her.

"We are alike you and I. I realised it the moment we met and that is why I must step in now whether you want me to or not. I do not wish the torment of my life upon anyone, particularly you."

"But I'm not tormented. I'm happier than I've ever been."

"And if I told you that your life is in danger and that you hold Miles' safety in the palm of your hand, what then?"

Grace's hand strayed to her hair. "I don't understand."

"Grace, you may be seriously ill, at the very least your unborn child might be at risk. Despite my skill, I cannot undertake an operation or treat a difficult pregnancy. The mortality rate is high and there are no modern drugs. You risk your own life and that of your unborn baby by staying. You must save yourself, Grace, go home and your baby will also be saved."

"Women have been having babies since time began. Katherine delivered Miles without complication why should I encounter problems. You're just trying to scare me."

Hugh's face darkened. "Grace, Katherine had no choice and she was lucky. You are a mere slip of a girl not used to the reality of medieval life. You cry with pain now, imagine the pain as your belly is slit open to save the child at the expense of your life. Believe me, Grace. That is what will happen if a choice has to be made."

Her hand strayed protectively to her abdomen. "I can't go home - not without, Miles." She cast about worriedly. This was madness. "I'll explain everything to him. Miles will know what to do."

"Miles must not be told."

"What do you mean?"

Hugh paced the room sweeping his gaze across her many paintings. "Did you paint the king without his crown?"

"No. I painted exactly as I had the copy. I had no need to change the past, to save my career. If it weren't for the forgery business I would never have come home to Kirk Knowe, nor walked that day in the wood. I would never have found my way here to Miles."

Hugh smiled. "I did wonder whether you would work it out for yourself."

"How did you even know about the painting in the first place?"

Hugh tapped his nose conspiratorially.

"I have a way of finding out things, which are of importance."

"You're a witch?"

He smiled.

"No, I had an interesting conversation with Edmund. He recalled a nightmare of yours that he witnessed, in which you'd recounted a strange tale of portraits.

"But you advised me to change the painting, why would you do that?"

"If you had, the circumstances that brought you here would have been irrevocably changed and I hoped that you would be returned to your former life unharmed. When you returned from Alnwick with Miles I knew that you'd not taken my advice and history was set."

"I don't want to return - not now."

"Grace, let me finish my tale and then you must make your decision." He settled himself back on the stool and took her hand again.

"I spent some months with Gerard senior, keeping my own council. I tried to come to terms with what had occurred and used my skills to assist his men. At the end of the campaign he brought me back here to

Northumberland. I witnessed his marriage to Maud, the birth of his son Gerard the younger and I met Katherine, Gerard's niece. She was a wonderful young woman, beautiful sweet-natured and of course I was attracted. It was mutual and, yes, you are correct, Miles is my son, but I did not know of him until after Katherine's death. I unwittingly left her shamed and with child while I spent the next ten years scouring every battlefield in Normandy in a vain attempt to find the way home."

"Why would you want to go home when you had found love here?"

Hugh sighed.

"Because my dear, Grace, I had left a wife and child behind in London and I was beset with longing for them and grief at their loss. I am ashamed to say for a short while Katherine assuaged my grief, but at the heart of me I still believed that I could return and my darling wife and daughter would be waiting."

Grace reached out her hand and laid it gently on his arm.

"Did you find your way?"

Hugh shook his head. "No. When I realised the futility, I accepted the loss and turned my attention to my life here." He gave a sad smile. "There are advantages to having knowledge of the future and as an avid historian I have been advantageous to those around me. I have developed a reputation as a tactician. The king is benevolent to those who are useful to him. I settled in France and although I have travelled extensively on behalf of more than one king, I know now that I will never find my way home. I've been here almost thirty years. It's too late for me, but it's not too late for you."

"When did you realise that Miles was your son?"

"The first time I laid eyes on him, the day he landed in France, fleeing from Gerard the younger. The opportunity to spend time with him, to help mould him into the man he is, was a precious gift. I began to believe that my life once again had purpose. When he suffered Guy's attack I thanked God I had the skills to save him." He gave a bewildered shrug. "Do you not see the irony, Grace, if it were not for the fact that I have twentieth century skills he would have died. And yet if I had not travelled he would not have been born." He ran a hand through his hair and refocused. "It is a subtle balance, Grace, even after all my time here I have no real answer. I can only act upon the facts that are known to me and my own conscience. If my actions have influenced the future, then I justify it with the belief that they are not changes, but are meant to be."

"And yet you've not revealed your relationship. Miles thinks he is the bastard child of a family he despises, why would you have him believe a lie when he holds you in such high regard?"

"For that very reason. His regard for me would cease to exist if he knew I had abandoned him and his mother for no good reason."

"Tell him the truth, he would understand."

"I cannot tell him the truth, and neither can you, Grace. Remember where we are, when we are, this is a time of great suspicion, you yourself have been accused of witchcraft. Miles would not understand, no one would understand. We exist in this life simply because we do not reveal the truth. I know you are tormented with the intrigue, how you dance around the deceit, how close you are to revealing your origin, but I would caution you against it."

"Why?"

"Because unlike me, you are able to return, your gateway is marked. And as I have already said it is imperative that you do so to safeguard you and your baby."

"But that doesn't explain why I can't tell Miles, he is not like the Gerard's of this world. He wouldn't bay for my blood or demand the building of a stake. He's not stupid, Hugh, he is your son. Surely you can see that he shares your reasoning and intellect. He would understand."

"Perhaps you're right but we shall never know because he must never be told. If he knew the truth he would certainly accept the reason why you cannot stay. He holds you above his own life. He would rather die himself than endanger you or his child, and he would not be parted from you. He would not let you go alone.

I have no knowledge of how this strange phenomenon works. You are the first of our kind that I have come across and have no idea whether one may pass freely between times if a doorway remains open. If Miles was able to travel with you he may be unable to return. The future of Wildewood depends upon him being here. If he is not here to lead against what is to come then unspeakable hurt will befall all who reside here. You must understand, Grace, as I tried to explain to Miles many months ago. He has a role to play which is vital and far greater than any individual need. I know this because of my knowledge of the future. It may not be what you want to hear, but it is the truth, Grace."

"How do I know you're telling me the truth? That you're not some madman in league with Gerard plotting to get rid of both me and Miles?"

Hugh cocked his head, there were footsteps approaching, he dropped his voice to a harsh whisper. "Grace, think about it. In your time did you know of Wildewood? Had you heard of this estate?"

"No."

"Yet you had heard of the de Frouville's and the castle at Ahlborett?"

"Yes."

"Don't you see, simply by being here you have changed the course of history. When you go back everyone will have heard of Wildewood. That will be your legacy, your gift to Miles. Because of you the legend of the Wildewood Horde was created. They will soon be as much a part of local history and lore as the dragon that rests upon the great stone or the creature in the lake."

"But what will Miles think if I suddenly disappear? He'll think I don't love him, that I've taken his child from him."

"Does he know of the child?"

She thought of the way he held her, his tenderness, his patience in waiting for her to admit what she was sure he already knew. "He suspects."

"If you remain there will be no child or no mother..."

"If I do as you say and go back, could I return later after the child is born?" Perhaps there was a way to salvage this terrible situation.

"I have no experience of this, Grace. But to have any chance at all, the doorway must remain intact. My own was destroyed when the WW1 trenches were filled. Yours may still remain open simply because of the ancient woodland in which it lies. If tree felling were to infringe upon the wood where you fell then we must assume that the portal would close forever."

Grace's heart sank. If she were to wait until nearer the birth of her child, then she may lose the only way back to the greed of the timber merchants.

"What choice do I have?" she asked desperately as she heard the low timbre of Miles' voice outside the door.

"If you go back you may well break Miles' heart but you ensure his safety along with yours, your child's and the future of Wildewood. If you stay I cannot guarantee the outcome.

"What do you really know about Miles' role? How do you know that his future here is so important? The king hinted that Miles was important to his plans, but Miles was adamant that he didn't want to be drawn back into a life he'd turned his back on."

Hugh smiled. "And that is exactly why he needs to stay. The king intends for something that must not be allowed to happen. Only Miles can stop it and he needs to be here to do so. I am not a soothsayer I cannot look at the leaves and predict the future. I know only key events and my knowledge of those alongside the fact that I have the Kings ear, has served me unerringly. Trust me, Grace, you must go back. If you stay and perish in childbirth you will deliver a far crueller blow to Miles than if you disappear from his life now."

Chapter Forty Five

A dose of Martha's potion was enough to sort her out and by morning the pain had gone and her temperature returned to normal. Grace convinced herself that food poisoning rather than anything suggested by Hugh was responsible. But the seed had been sown and she could think of nothing but his revelations. She avoided Hugh to the point where she began to wonder if his confession had merely been a figment of her imagination, a hallucination brought on by her illness, but she could not avoid the simple truth. Any medieval childbirth was fraught with danger. She knew that her own mother had required a caesarean delivery due partly to her diminutive stature and it was highly likely that she would require the same. Hugh had already made it clear he was not skilled enough to assist and unwilling to take a risk.

A decision would have to be made and she swung between leaving it as late as possible so that she could postpone her parting from Miles, to the very real need to act before the baby was due. At the back of her mind was the thought that her angst could all be in vain, if in her absence the tree fellers had levelled the wood.

The preparations for the wedding went ahead regardless and she was swept along as Martha and Belle created a beautiful gown, a feast was prepared and Linus talked excitedly of nothing else. On a glorious morning toward the end of May, as the sun kissed the treetops and marked their way east, the folk from Wildewood made the long journey through woods resplendent with bluebells and birdsong to Ahlborett and gathered at the tiny Kirk Knowe chapel to support their lord and his bride. Grace waited in the priest's room at the rear of the chapel as Martha and Belle put the final touches to her gown and fixed Mayflowers in her hair.

"Ye look perfect, mistress," said Martha as she stood back in admiration. "Sir Miles will reckon he's died an' been taken by angels."

Belle, cracked the door, and peeked through the gap. "They be waitin', my lady."

Grace took a breath and tried to calm her nerves. She clasped her shaking hands around the small posy of bluebell and hawthorn that Linus had gathered for her. The thought of leaving Miles was just too difficult to contemplate; leaving Linus was enough to bring tears to her eyes. She couldn't avoid the decision much longer, she knew that. Soon her pregnancy would be obvious to all and she would be unable to make the journey by horseback across the moor and back to the wood where

Miles had found her.

"Mistress don't ye be weepin' now," said Martha as she dabbed at Grace's face with the corner of her apron. "Saints above, tis the happiest day of any woman's life and here ye are blubbering like ye wer goin' to yon gallows. Ye'r weddin' the catch of Northumberland, mistress," She gave a sly grin. "I know I'd have a smile on me face if I were in yer position. That old bugger of mine gave up tryin' to keep me happy years ago."

Belle giggled which set Martha off and Grace could not resist a smile. The two were incorrigible. "Of course I'm happy, Martha. I'm just overwhelmed by it all. You've all been so kind to me. It truly is a perfect day." It was true, she was overcome with the kindness she'd been shown. The tears were solely for Miles and what she was planning to do to him.

"Are you ready, my lady?" Hugh stepped from the shadows and took her small hand in his. "You look beautiful, Grace. Miles is indeed a lucky man."

"Is he?" Grace struggled to contain her emotion. Was she not compounding her deceit with this charade? Taking vows to be his forever when she knew that was impossible.

Hugh dipped his head to press a gentle chaste kiss on her pale cheek. "He will remember this day always, with happiness; leave him with that memory at least."

* * *

Miles stood at the altar with John at his side. The big man grinned broadly. All at Wildewood shared his delight at the wedding of their lord. Grace had stolen their hearts. Miles swung his gaze around, nodding his acknowledgement at the many members of the household who squeezed into the tiny chapel. Edward and Linus stood proudly together. Tom Pandy poised with his pipes. At the rear of the gathering Thomas of Blackmore, who had arrived to represent Hugh's Templar's, favoured Miles with a broad smile and Miles was heartened by his effort in attending. He knew the men had been busy in Lincoln, he'd heard there was trouble brewing and that even Hugh would be leaving soon.

He sensed there was change afoot, that the king was orchestrating something and had been unsettled by it for some days. There was a gathering of momentum as if something critical to his future was about to happen and he was powerless to intercede. He could not forget Edward's last conversation and the promise he'd made to Grace. He would not venture down that path again. His conscience would not allow it. He flicked his gaze between Thomas and Linus and shook off unwelcome memories. His unease remained however and he knew his distraction at recent events had affected Grace.

He'd noticed the change in her behaviour, since their return from Alnwick. The hand straying to her hair, the distant worried looks when she thought he wasn't looking and her reluctance to confide in him about her most precious secret. The one she carried in her womb. He had waited patiently, his joy at the knowledge that he was to be a father tempered by her reluctance to trust him. He'd put it down to wedding nerves. Perhaps with a ring on her finger she would finally realise they were meant to be and he could announce to the household that an heir would be born. Today all the insecurity and secrets would end and they could enjoy the rest of their life together.

He nodded to Tom Pandy who took up the pipes and he turned as the chapel door opened and Hugh emerged with Grace on his arm. His throat tightened with emotion as he watched her approach. She was beautiful. As she looked at him he saw the tears in her eyes and fought back his own.

He cleared his throat, took her hand from Hugh and they turned to make their vows.

Chapter Forty Six

The celebrations continued into the early hours, though at midnight, to roars of approval from those gathered in the great hall, Miles carried his bride to his chamber.

"Bloody hell, Miles, who on earth invented spiral stairs?" said Grace, as he narrowly avoided taking her head off as he rounded yet another curve. She was putting on a brave face determined not to let what was to come, spoil their wedding night. "I'll be unconscious before you get me where you want me at this rate."

"Don't worry, I'll be fit for naught by the time I've climbed all these stairs." He struggled to open the chamber door with one hand and with a measure of relief deposited her on his bed. Collapsing next to her he drew in a much needed breath and allowed a slow smile. "I'd mention about the additional weight, but as we are all now aware, there's a very good reason for that." He reached across and pressed gentle lips against the swell of her abdomen.

Grace felt her heart constrict, bereft at what was to come. Miles had announced the forthcoming birth with such pride and the household had been jubilant at the thought of an heir. She'd accepted their good wishes graciously and studiously avoided eye contact with Hugh. Any control she may have had over the situation seemed to have been taken from her. Now Miles knew for certain that she carried his child, she knew he would covet her, protect and attend to her with utmost devotion, which would make it all the more impossible for her to leave him.

"You're very quiet," remarked Miles as he watched her in the candlelight.

She cast aside her anguished thoughts and sought a mischievous smile to cloak her sadness, "Just wondering if you're going to be a good husband."

Miles reached across and began to remove the flowers from her hair. "And how do you think a good husband should behave?" As each flower was cast to the floor he pressed a kiss to her cheek, her nose, her downcast eyelids.

"Oh, pandering to my every whim, getting up through the night with the baby..." she struggled to continue, her words catching in her throat as she realised that he would never get the chance to hold his child.

"I imagine I could do that, if I had to. Are you going to be a good wife I wonder?" He began to unfasten the many tiny laces that adorned the front of her gown, muttering impatiently at the complexity. "Are you going to obey me as a good wife should, and submit to my every demand?"

"Never," she replied and with a smile she reached up framing his face with gentle hands. She gazed at him taking her fill, storing up memories for the time when that was all she would have. His hair was now short and she much preferred it. He'd been clean shaven too at the start of the day, but now a dark shadow cloaked his jaw and she felt it prickle her skin. He watched her through half closed eyes, and the desire in them matched the sadness in her own. How could she do it, how could she walk away from this man? Hugh had said she would not survive if she stayed, but how could she survive if she left without him. She pulled him down to her and sought solace and oblivion.

* * *

If she had thought she would have difficulty in slipping away, her fears were proved unfounded by the news delivered the following day. Thomas of Blackmore, who had shared the joy and celebration of their wedding, revealed his true purpose in making the long journey from Lincoln to Wildewood. He had come on the king's orders to fetch Hugh and Miles to join the other knights in support of his campaign in Gwynedd against Llywellyn Gruffud.

"No..." protested Grace. This was too cruel, she had imagined she would have days, weeks even, to acclimatise herself to the notion of leaving Miles. She'd never imagined that he would be taken from her first.

"I must go, Grace. The king demands it and as we have discussed before, what the king has given, he might also take away. I cannot refuse him."

Grace sobbed wretchedly. "But you said you wouldn't get drawn back into anything; that you would resist."

"I'm going to support the king, alongside men I trust. I do not intend to deviate from an honourable course. It's a skirmish that has the king worrying unnecessarily, we shall have the upstart Gruffud defeated by the summer's end." He turned to include Hugh. "Isn't that right, Hugh, we shall run off these usurpers and I shall be home in plenty time to greet my child."

Hugh nodded slowly. "Grace, I shall ensure Miles returns safely to Wildewood. The venture is perhaps ill-timed but the sooner we leave, the sooner Wildewood will have its lord returned...," he patted her arm kindly, "...and the easier it will be for you."

She knew what he meant; the easier it would be for her to slip away while Miles' back was turned. "When do you leave?"

Miles took her hand "Thomas awaits us now, Edmund is preparing the horses."

"You're not taking Edmund surely?" They were all leaving her, she couldn't bear it. She felt tears hot against her cheeks and Miles pulled her to him with a sigh.

"Edmund will stay, as will John, together they will watch over you. I trust them both."

"But, what if Gerard reneges on the truce in your absence?"

Miles gave a sour smile, "You need not worry about Gerard, he too has been summoned at the king's command and accompanies us; reluctantly albeit." He took her chin gently, forcing her to look at him. "Grace, all will be well, I will return in time for the birth. I would never abandon you. You know that."

Grace clung to him, inhaling his scent as if her very life depended on it. "I love you..." she whispered as he pulled gently away.

"I know you do."

"No, I really love you...more than you'll ever know."

She watched them as they rode away, Miles, Hugh and Thomas. Three brave knights off to fight for the king. She'd not had time even to say her goodbyes to Hugh, though the look he cast her way as they cantered through the gateway was enough to reassure her that he would keep Miles safe, and that thought alone would sustain her through the coming months.

Edmund hovered nearby, his face downcast as he kicked at the dirt beneath his feet. Grace could tell he was disappointed he'd not been allowed to go with the men and reckoned she wasn't the only one holding back tears.

"Edmund, I'm sorry you weren't able to accompany the men," she said as she hooked her arm in his and encouraged him away from the gate. "But without you here for my protection, Miles would have been unable to accept the king's orders. He's very grateful, Edmund, and so am I."

Edmund gave a reluctant smile which extended into a broad beam when she smiled back at him. "We shall manage, Edmund and when Miles returns he'll be so proud of you." She felt a twist in her gut at yet another deceit. When Miles returned to find her gone, who would suffer his wrath?"

* * *

258

Her small bag was packed and hidden and she had one more task to complete before she could leave. Seeking Linus and Edmund she led them to a south facing wall within the garden and knelt by the side of a freshly dug border. From her pocket she produced the packet of sunflower seeds that had remained hidden since she'd arrived.

Tipping the seeds carefully into the boys outstretched hands she made a shallow drill against the heat of the wall.

"Plant the seeds today and when the flowers bloom you'll know the baby has been born."

Edmund glanced at her curiously. "We shall know by the sound of its cries surely."

"Of course you will, Edmund. Of course you will." Grace turned away anxious he would not see her tears. "Linus, push the seeds in as far as you can and come the autumn the flowers will be taller than you and Edmund, taller even than Sir Miles."

Linus giggled as he dug his small fingers into the rich soil and planted them deep.

Kneeling between the boys, Grace wrapped her arms tightly around their shoulders and hugged them close. "You are both so special. Remember that."

* * *

The following morning as dew cloaked the grass and the household busied themselves with their tasks, Grace led the filly quietly through the small door at the rear of the garden and out into the park. Stopping by a fallen tree she gave a final long look at the place she had come to know as home, before mounting the pony and setting off for Kirk Knowe.

She had the map from Miles' room in her pocket to help guide the way. In her pack she had her paintings of those she'd left behind. She couldn't bear the thought of the boys left to wonder at her abandonment. She had left them Fly, a small consolation balanced against the web of lies she had spun. She fretted over Edmund and his inevitable despair when he discovered he had failed Miles, in his task to protect her. She worried over Linus, the mysterious child that the Templar's seemed sworn to protect. But mostly she grieved over Miles and the life they could have shared.

With an eye to the rising sun she guided the pony and set off across the moor, trusting to God to keep her safe and well clear of any hidden dangers. The moor in May was a different place indeed from the winter bleakness she remembered but despite the flowering plants and cheerful birdsong, it was with a heavy heart and eyes blurred with tears that she headed east.

Someway behind, a rider paused and watched her progress from the cover of an ancient cairn. When the filly dipped out of sight amongst the heather and bracken, the rider lowered the visor on his helmet, rearranged his sword to a more comfortable position and proceeded to follow.

Chapter Forty Seven

It took best part of the day to navigate the safe trails, avoiding the treacherous moorland bogs. Grace guided the filly with a gentle hand encouraging her on across the high ground, where despite the mild spring weather, the wind still teased and buffeted at the pony's mane. On occasion the pony's ears would flick as if fearful of something in the emptiness behind them and she would give an anxious whinny. Grace patted her neck and reassured her as Miles would have done, but nevertheless she cast an occasional eye over her shoulder, she'd not forgotten the tales of ghostly Roman centurions who marched on the moor.

Evening was drawing in as she dropped down off the moor and into the forest. She paused to get her bearings. The ancient wood had a strange stillness about it, as if fine gauze had been draped between the trees. The air was heavy with the scent of wild garlic, insects flitted and there was a faint hum of bees as they made the most of the hawthorn blossom before darkness drove them back to their hive.

Grace slipped from the pony's back, her eyes drawn to a pool that shimmered in the fading light. The wood was no longer flooded as in the depths of winter and yet the pool remained, a beacon drawing her in. This was the spot, there was no mistaking it. She allowed the pony to drink, and knelt to run a hand idly through the water. The water was cool and clear and as she gazed into its depths, drawn by the gently moving green fronds, an image appeared - An image of a knight, with his sword raised above his head.

Taking fright she withdrew her hand and spun round, clinging tightly to the pony's reins as the beast pulled back in alarm.

The knight stood before her dressed in black. A quilted leather doublet adorned his torso, studded with metal that glinted in the dying rays of the sun. On his head a lightweight helmet, not suitable for heavy combat, but its faceguard sufficient to disguise his appearance. The shield attached to the side of his horse bore the head of a fiendish beast and as Grace's startled gaze swung between the man and his insignia, he cocked his head and spoke.

"Mademoiselle, we have unfinished business, do we not?"

Grace stared in speechless shock as Guy lowered his sword and raised his visor.

"And where are you going on such a fine day, my lady?" He cast a disparaging glance over her. "I hear you have happy news. You carry

Miles' child, and yet you seek to leave him as soon as his back is turned. Perhaps the news is not as welcome as it should be?"

Grace took a step back. Her heart raced, desperation warred with fear. She was so close. The doorway was almost within reach, yet she dare not step further and risk him following her through. Terrible though it was to leave Miles, she had at least consoled herself with the image of a life devoted to his child. Was she to be denied even that? Was she to end her days on the bed of a woodland pool after all? Had the last four months meant nothing?

"You don't scare me, Guy," she replied bravely, her voice little more than a whisper.

Guy removed his helmet, dropped it to the moss covered ground, and pushing back his damp hair he offered a smirk. "Then you are a misguided fool, though that does not surprise me. Anyone who chooses to lie with the fallen knight, Miles of Wildewood, despite what he has done, deserves pity from all."

"He has done nothing," cried Grace. "He is twice the man you are, brave and honourable. I am proud to be his wife, to carry his child. You know nothing, Guy."

"I know you sneak away furtively as soon as you are able. Why do you run from him if you do not fear his hand?"

"I'm not running from him, I'm merely out riding, exercising the filly. You're the one who should fear him."

"I am not the one who carries a child in my belly," replied Guy. He took a step closer and Grace retreated further into the growing gloom between the trees, taking the skittish pony with her.

"What do you mean?" Her hand strayed protectively to her abdomen.

"Ah, so he has yet to confess his secrets - his sins." He reached out a hand and she flinched away from it. "Ask him to tell you about the cleansing of Lincoln and his work for the king when he was merely a prince in waiting. Asks him about the child he covets and the Templar oath that ties him to his past. Ask him if you dare…"

Grace paled, confusion clouding her eyes.

"You talk in riddles, Guy, I'm not such a fool that I don't recognise evil and I see it when I look at you."

Guy shrugged and secured his sword with a thrust into the soft moss covered ground. "Mademoiselle, you expect evil from me and I shall not disappoint you." He began to unfasten his belt. "As I said we have unfinished business, and this time there will be no timely rescue from your lover. He is well on his way to Wales to meet the king, and soon you will be on the way to meet your maker. Miles' child will never take a breath on this earth and Miles will end his days in full understanding of what revenge and retribution really means."

"Why do you hate Miles? He's done nothing to you, that was not deserved."

Guy's lip curled and he advanced with a snarl. "He stole that which belonged to me."

"No, you stole from him and you were discovered and thwarted, are you such a bad loser that you can't accept defeat?"

"You really are a little fool and despite the allure of violating a wench in such a delicate condition, I suddenly have no stomach for fools." He reached for his sword and yanking it free of the earth, swung it above his head "This is not about treasure or murdered knights - this is about the boy he took. It has always been about the child."

* * *

At that, the boy who had followed diligently and had remained hidden beneath the lichen tendrils and sweet smelling blossoms, rose silently to his feet. He brought up his bow and set the arrow carefully against the string. He neither hurried nor dawdled, but did as he had been taught by his lord. He raised the bow and took aim, exhaling gently as he steadied his arm. Then, as the sword began its downward descent he sent a silent prayer to the guardians of the forest, to God in his heaven and released the arrow.

It flew straight and true, whipping its way between branch and leaf on a course finely chosen by one with a true and honest heart, toward one who's only joy in life had been to propagate evil. And as the arrow struck Guy between the eyes, he fell like a stricken beast and the pony leapt back in fright dragging Grace with it into the dark void between the trees.

Edmund dropped his arm to his side and dragged in a breath. His heart banged in his chest, his hands trembled and he felt that he might drop to his knees at any moment. He took a second breath, called silently upon all the charms he had learned at the breast and stepped forward into the clearing.

The body lay where it had fallen, half submerged in the woodland pool, the arrow standing tall and proud. The perfect shot. There was no sign of Grace or the filly. The clearing was empty but for the dead knight and the boy with his bow.

"My lady..." he called hesitantly. He had not seen the moment of her disappearance but knew that something strange and other-worldly had occurred and was suddenly fearful. "Grace..." he called again more urgently, but there was no response and although he had not the means to explain it, he knew in his heart no matter how long or how loud he called she would not hear him.

He glanced again at the body which had begun to slide of its own volition beneath the water's surface. Dropping to his knees he reached out and using what strength he had left, he dragged Guy's body free of the water.

Avoiding the dead staring eyes, Edmund crossed himself and slipped his small hands over the body. He relieved Guy of his knife, his scabbard and the chain from around his neck. He stood then and drawing himself up to his full height he used his booted foot to roll Guy's body fully into the water. He slid to the bottom. The green fronds entwined his limbs and his long, black hair intermingled with the ebb and flow of the gently moving water. Finally, the water stilled and the body remained, only the feathery flight of the arrow visible above the water to mark the spot. Edmund shuddered. There were no words that could express his revulsion of the man or the deed, but he knew regardless of his honourable motive, his life was changed forever.

Slipping his hand beneath his jerkin, he pulled out the fleece cap that had once been Grace's and now was his. Pressing his lips gently to it, he stepped as near as he dare to the darkness beyond the clearing and reaching as high as he could, he fastened it securely to a branch.

Turning to Guy's horse, he stripped off the identifying livery, disguised the shield with mud from the side of the pool and then as he had seen Miles do so many times, he reached up and muttered softly against the beast's velvet nose.

"Horse, yer have a new master, one who will treat yer well, with dignity an' respect. In return I ask that yer carry me far and faster than yer have ever galloped, for we're on a quest ye and me. We must go, in search of our lord and bring him back to this spot so he may save his love."

The horse whickered gently and stood placidly as Edmund secured his own pony's reins to the larger beast's saddle He fastened Guy's scabbard around his own thin waist, sliding the large sword home, then placed Guy's discarded helmet upon his head. Mounting the horse, Edmund gave a final sweep of the clearing.

And finally, the boy, who was now a man, turned his mount and headed south for Wales.

264

To be continued...

Coming soon...

Wildewood *Redemption*

Part 2 of 'The Wildewood Chronicles'

Northumberland 1277
A Fallen Knight
A Secret Pact
A Love Everlasting

Miles of Wildewood battles to redeem himself in his quest to secure the future of a foundling boy with a secret and dangerous past. But dark forces are gathering. Unlikely allies join forces and horrors best forgotten are unleashed. Can Grace summon the power of the Horde once more? Can love really conquer all?

Crime Fiction by the same author ...

Meet Tommy Connell a New York detective with a crooked smile, an eye for the ladies and a past that haunts him. Connell knows what the rule book says he just chooses to ignore it.

Assisted by his long-suffering buddy Marty, Connell rattles cages wherever he goes. If you like a fast-paced adventure with a touch of humour and romance, you'll love Tommy Connell.

Follow his adventures in:

Mrs Jones

Runner up in the 2011 Yeovil Literary Prize

Arriving in New York to deliver a package, Lizzie Jones witnesses a murder and finds herself on the run from the mob and the Feds.

It's up to maverick cop, Connell, to unravel the truth surrounding the mysterious young Brit.

As they run for their lives, he is inexplicably drawn back to his checkered past and an unsolved murder.

Connell's an honest cop, usually, but when the depth of deception is revealed and the prize outweighs the sweetest revenge, he discovers the true meaning of temptation.

Coming soon...

Molly Brown

Connell is dabbling in things that he shouldn't, and it's not the first time.

When a weird little kid disappears into the night and no one gives a damn, including the cops, Connell figures someone should take another look.

The good cops are busy hunting down a serial killer - good.

The bad cops are busy hunting down Connell - not so good.

The serial killer - well, he's looking for victim number twelve, which is definitely not good.

And little Molly Brown is about to throw an almighty spanner in the works.